The Dance of The Scorpions

SAL MIRABAL

WORKBOOK PRESS LLC
187 E Warm Springs Rd,
Suite B285, Las Vegas, NV 89119, USA

Website: https://workbookpress.com/
Hotline: 1-888-818-4856
Email: admin@workbookpress.com

Ordering Information:
Quantity sales. Special discounts are available on quantity purchases by corporations, associations, and others. For details, contact the publisher at the address above.

Library of Congress Control Number: 2023920418

ISBN-13:   978-1-961845-60-2 (Paperback Version)

             978-1-961845-59-6 (Digital Version)

REV. DATE: 06/27/2023

The Dance of the Scorpions

SAL MIRABAL

For My Son
Joseph Mirabal

CHAPTER 1

The night was cold, and not many stars could be seen in the cloudy sky. A slight breeze created distant sounds in the peaceful, moonless night. An adobe house, no different from the others scattered here and there, was nestled in the rural calm. The house sat five yards off the dirt road. A white picket fence, not more than five feet above the ground, encircled the house. The fence, with snagged and peeling stakes minus a gate, enclosed the old house like rotten teeth embedded in a decayed skull.

There was movement inside the house. Silhouettes of two men and a woman appeared against a white bedsheet covering the window that faced the road. Loud music and laughter echoed through the ancient wooden door and window of the house. The little party of three seemed to enjoy such a great time that they neglected the sounds out in the dark country night and allowed the serenity to soothe them into smug complacency.

A short distance from the house, three men waited inside a parked black car. The car had been chopped low, close to the ground, and had the look of a giant stingray—dark, sleek, and ominous in an ocean of night. The men inside the car studied the house with great interest and patience. A man in the back seat leaned forward and said something in a low voice to the two men who sat in the front seat of the car. The two doors of the car opened slowly. The men emerged, silent and determined.

Dressed in black, the men left the doors open with indifferent abandon. The leader of the group walked in front and supported a double-barreled shotgun in one arm, the barrels pointed to the ground. His eyes locked on the front door and window of the house. Nothing human or animal would run by him tonight. No escape and no mercy. Death to all dopers flashed through his mind like wildfire.

They approached the house like good neighbors dropping in for a cup of coffee and a friendly chat. One man circled around to the back of the house and kept a close watch on a door that opened into the backyard.

The picket fence was in better condition, and that made it a little more difficult to get closer to the door. He was careful not to get too close and trigger an alarm for the dopers inside the house. He had a bottle of gasoline and prepared to light the soaked, limp rag that hung out of the bottle. He waited for the fireworks to start in the front of the house.

The man with the shotgun rested the barrels of the gun on the top rail of the brittle fence and pointed the barrels at the front door. The third man strolled toward the front window. He held a bottle of gasoline in his right hand and a cigarette lighter in his left. A Colt Python .357 magnum revolver protruded from the pocket of his black leather jacket. A nod from the leader, and with one quick move, he lit the cocktail and pitched it through the window with remarkable accuracy. The bottle exploded, and fire and smoke erupted inside the house with ferocious intensity.

The woman screamed, and one of the men yelled at her to shut up. The front door flew open with such force that the hinges blew off. A shirtless man with long hair held a rifle in one hand and staggered out the front door. One barrel of the .410 buckshot ripped him almost in half. The impact forced his disjointed torso back toward the door. The second blast took away what was left of his knees and lower legs. The other man started firing the .357 magnum at the front door of the burning house and discouraged anyone else from running out.

As soon as he heard the explosion, the man watching the back of the house lit his bottle and tossed it at the door. The bottle hit the frame of the door and bounced off into a large plastic container full of rainwater. It didn't really matter because the house was already in flames. But to ensure that the people inside wouldn't even think of taking a shortcut out the back door, he reached in his jacket pocket, pulled out a .45 automatic, and emptied a ten-round clip at the door. The fire and smoke prevented him from seeing a naked man and a woman crawling on their stomachs out the door. He heard a sharp whistle and withdrew to the car to join his comrades.

He entered the car and sat in the front seat as before. The driver started the car, and they glanced at the house in flames for the last time before the car pulled away. They drove in silence. No high fives for these troopers.

CHAPTER 2

The mayor's office was on the seventh floor of the new building and had wall-to-wall windows. Mike Montes, the temporary mayor of Las Flores, sat in his leather chair with his reptile-skin dress boots propped up on his desk. He sipped his morning coffee and admired the panoramic view of the majestic Turquoise Mountains, a few miles to the northeast. It was a bright, clear, and warm mid-autumn morning.

As Mike sipped his coffee, he noticed the wispy swirl of grayish clouds dancing above the mountains. They seemed to be choreographed by the natural forces on the massive stage of the sky. Only a few days ago, he recalled, the droplets of rain that danced through the spears of sunlight and drifting clouds had crystallized like tears from heaven and given the mountains a golden hue. Then as quickly as they appeared, the clouds had floated south and left the fragrance of wet soil and the sun to shine unencumbered. He welcomed the clear view and bright sunlight after many years of hazy, smoggy mornings in the Los Angeles area. He was back. And this time to stay…unless—nothing. He refused to think about it. Not now anyway.

The mountains continued to seduce Mike into leaving his office for a short hike on those rocky crevices of his youth. He did it yesterday, but today he had some important appointments he didn't want to cancel. The job of mayor was not as simple as he had imagined when he was honored with the office. It was only for a couple of years or less until the general election. He was sure the politicos and their business interests would call for a special election before his two years were up to get him out and elect one of their own. The job of mayor did come with a few perks, he had to admit. He had reserved parking on the first tier of the building and all the free coffee he could drink. But the best one was a vote on all city council resolutions. Since there were only four city council members, he was the determining factor on all tie votes. It was a fact of life that could make him fast friends or treacherous adversaries, depending on where the cards fell. Mike was not easily intimidated by childish games, but he was vulnerable to honesty and good manners.

Las Flores was a growing little city, and the population demanded services that an expanding municipality was not always able to provide. The move to add two or even three city council members was on the books, but the squawkers were still squawking, and nothing was accomplished. The lobbyists representing diverse interest groups came knocking, and Mike offered them an olive branch because that was all he had to offer. It was not up to him, he declared. It had to go through the city council and then appear on the ballot for people to vote on it. But the city council had to decide from what part of the city the new council members were going to be elected. The Eastside wanted another member and believed they merited one because some felt their interests were being neglected. The Westside and the downtown area also demanded one, as did the Northeast, where the population was expanding. The only ones who were not crying were the citizens of Chiva Town. They were OK with their one and only…even if he was useless. They were realistic and understood there was nothing they could do about it.

Las Flores—Mike recalled his native history—was a busy place way before the Spanish or the Mexicans set foot in the area. From the Rio Grande on the west to the Eastside barrio, everything in between was a paradise of gentle streams, lush trees, wildflowers, verdant meadows, and plenty of game. The early Native Americans called it the Valley of the Lost Children. Raiders from various tribes captured young children in raids and skirmishes, brought them to the valley, and bargained for their release or sold them as slaves. Some ran away, but most had no place to run to. The children slept in a cave, and food was never a problem. Some remained in the valley for years because the warriors who brought them were killed or disappeared. When a few became adults, they left to claim their tribe. But some natives persisted and claimed that the children never reached adulthood; they remained children in the valley and never left. Another version Mike also read affirmed that the medicine man who cared for the children enchanted them and promised them that they would remain children and live in the valley forever. The raiders stopped taking children to the valley because they feared the power of the shaman and were troubled because the valley had become a home to spirit children. The children of the valley were never seen again during the light of day.

But there was plenty of evidence to suggest that the children frolicked at night, returning to their cave before dawn. No one ever saw the cave, and its location remained unknown.

Mike sipped the last of his cold morning coffee and placed the empty cup on the expensive mahogany desk. What a waste of taxpayers' money, he thought. Then he recalled a historian who had written that Coronado and his dogs, in search of the cities of gold, spent a couple of days in the valley on their way north. The historian also wrote that one of Coronado's soldiers on guard duty saw the lost children as they played in a stream, naked as the day they were born. As dawn advanced, the soldier followed the children to a cave between two hills. He observed only young children and no adults, with the oldest not past ten or eleven years and the youngest three or four years old. He didn't follow them into the cave. He claimed he was exhausted, having been up all night. The truth, assumed the historian, was that the soldier was not altogether that brave. In the morning, he disclosed to the captain of the guard what he had witnessed, and they searched for the cave but never found it. The captain accused the soldier of being drunk on duty or falling asleep and dreaming of naked children. But the native guides and the slaves Coronado had collected became restless and wanted to leave the valley as soon as possible. They comprehended they were treading on sacred ground, and the spirits could prove challenging. Eventually, settlers from Mexico, weary from trudging across the desert on their way to Santa Fe and parts north, settled in the fertile area close to the river.

Mike got off his comfortable chair, walked to the large windows in his office, and faced east. He studied the pattern of development as it spread east–northeast toward the mountains and southeast instead of west toward the river, as many speculated, even though there was growth in that area also. He could see numerous housing tracts. He saw parks, schools, and a new hospital. An extension college and new roads were coming and going. He could see construction at a busy pace. Some people were making money, he thought, bundles of it.

Rafael Candelaria strutted into Mike's office. He ignored Mike's secretary. He wore a double-breasted, light-blue, Italian-cut, tailor-made silk suit with a black tie and a white linen shirt. The white shirt accentuated the stocky man's singed complexion. His hair was thick, long, and graying but styled down, slick, and sassy.

Mr. Mayor, my friend. Rafa held out a manicured hand to Mike. I apologize because I am early. I have a busy, busy day ahead of me. I received your message yesterday as I was unpacking from my trip abroad. Now tell me, what is this urgency that cannot wait that you must see me about?

Mike shook hands with the older man and offered him a chair. He walked back to his own chair and fixed his eyes on Rafael Candelaria, or Rafa, as he was called by his intimate friends and others. Mike studied Rafa's thin purplish lips, which often parted in an amicable smile and revealed tobacco-stained teeth. But he knew that Rafa was quick of mind and ruthless in his articulation and delivery of insults as well as praise. And that Rafa represented the Eastside barrio as a council member, which didn't help matters any.

Welcome back, Rafa, Mike finally said. You had a good trip. I can see. About the message—I don't recall setting a specific day. I apologize for any inconvenience, but you're here, bright and early.

Don't apologize, my friend—no need. I have done the same on many occasions. I did visit Capri and Sorrento when I was in Italy. You were right, Mike; they are both beautiful places. I want to go back and spend some more time in that paradise.

Don't we all, thought Mike. I'm glad you had a great time, Rafa, but the reason I wanted to talk to you is this. And he placed half a dozen color photographs of a dwelling in need of serious repairs on the desk in front of Rafa.

Rafa picked up the photos in vibrant color, and his smile disappeared as his charcoal, deep-set eyes scrutinized the photos as if they were photos of his wife with a young lover. But he kept his cool, at least on the surface. The house in the photos showed a leaky roof and a dirt floor. The open ceiling exposed water-stained beams and no plaster on the walls. Unprotected electrical wiring crisscrossed the house. There was no evidence of running water…but plenty of evidence that people occupied the slum dwelling.

That house belongs to you, right, Rafa? Mike asked, in as moderate a tone as possible. You rent it out, and it's in the Eastside barrio on—let me guess—Mesquite Street, not far from the tracks, right?

Rafa continued studying the photos. He didn't say a word. And then he placed the photos on the desk and attempted a smile. He cleared his throat, as he did when addressing the council members, out of necessity or habit; it was difficult to say with Mr. Candelaria. Where did you get these photos, Mike, and how old are they? Looks like a house I gave my son orders to repair sometime last year. I'll check on it. That doesn't look right.

I agree with you there, Rafa, Mike said. He was relieved that Rafa had at least admitted it was his property. It looks like third-world housing. Community Impact brought me the photos when you were on vacation in Europe. They threatened to take them to the newspaper if you don't make some repairs, and real pronto. Now, as you know, Rafa, it ain't gonna look very appealing for the citizens of Las Flores to suspect that the city councilman from the Eastside is a slumlord. The more damaging photos of young children inside the house and out, they kept. They are willing to meet with you in private and discuss the complaint. If you refuse, they will engage an attorney and let a judge decide if you are indeed in violation of code—

I know the code, Rafa interrupted. His mood turned sour. I have always supported CI, always. Every time their grant comes up, they have my vote, but if they think they are going to play slop-barrel politics with me…they are out of their league. I will not stand by and let a—

Before Rafa completed his sentence, the Cotton brothers, Mike and his younger brother, Billy Bob Cotton, also known as Porky, interrupted. They just walked in as Rafa had. They also ignored Estrella Gallo, Mike's young and inexperienced secretary. They had no respect for Mike or his office, especially Mike Cotton. Billy Bob just followed. In the old mayor's office downtown, the former mayor, Eddie "Can Do" Moreno, had a private concealed door in his office that led to the basement. If he didn't want to see certain people, he just disappeared down the stairs to the basement and crossed the street to Fat Henry's, where he sipped coffee with the customers while the visitors waited and waited for him in the office. Even though Buda Henry was too fat to play that trick, no one just walked into his office. Eddie Moreno had been in office as mayor only a couple of years after Buda Henry retired. Eddie was soon offered a political position in the governor's office in Santa Fe. He jumped at the chance, and Mike Montes, having recently arrived from California with a law degree on his résumé and money in the bank, was offered the mayor's gig. Neither party wanted to risk a rival to cast the tie-breaking vote when it came to city business. So Mike Montes, at age thirty, was favored—they all figured he would be easy to manipulate, naive and young as he was, until a more seasoned political animal could be sworn in.

When the Cotton brothers barged in, Rafa fished up the photos, placed them in the inside pocket of his suit, and smiled. His pencil-thin mustache plastered to his upper lip was barely evident.

Oh, the brothers with the original names, Rafa announced. Come on in, why don't you? It's open-door hours at the mayor's office. And he chuckled.

Mike Cotton, the taller of the Cotton brothers, an orange baseball cap on his head with black block letters that read, Pray to Jesus or Go to Hell, looked at Rafa with clear, steel-blue eyes and ignored him. He turned his square jaw to Mike, who sat behind his desk.

Look, Mike, Mike Cotton uttered before anyone else said a word. I got a beef with you. I told you several times that the city is taxing us on every load we pull out of the rock pit, along with the county tax. That's a double tax, and that's not fair. Before, we only paid the county. Now the city wants a cut, and you didn't bring it up for a vote before the full council. I was there.

And as I told you before, Mike said—he was a little pissed at the intrusion but maintained a civil tone—the city owns a couple of acres of the rock pit, and the city needs the money. The county was the sole collector of the tax, but not anymore. To change it back to the way it was, you need a unanimous vote. How am I supposed to get a consensus and a clear majority when the money is earmarked, most of it, to finance our public schools?

The Cotton brothers were the latest to join the race to make cement into concrete and fill the needs of the growing construction boom. Rafa had been in the business for years and had even built his own cement plant. Construction continued unabated, and concrete was in demand. Even though the Cotton brothers were home builders, they wanted some of the action in the booming concrete market.

Mike Cotton was fully aware he couldn't muster up the votes in the city council without Mike and Rafa. He turned his attention to Rafa. He pointed at Rafa with a meaty hand. And then, scarcely moving his thin lips, he said. Next time one of your drivers pulls in front of one of my trucks at the pit, there's gonna be hell to pay.

Rafa stood up and moved behind his chair. These were fighting words, but he kept his cool.

You sure use hell a lot. Oh, I forgot. Your pastor preaches the religion of hate, he wanted to say but changed his mind and said instead. Your pastor preaches hell and damnation.

Fuck you know about my religion?

Oh. Me! You know that word. And Rafa used his hands to cover his mouth, mocking the upset Mike Cotton. Your pastor, Rafa continued. He dropped his hands from his mouth. He is gonna whip you on the butt with his big belt, but you probably like it.

Mike Cotton looked down at the shorter Rafa. His eyes were blazing, and his face flushed red. He said in a hateful voice, You're nothing but a floor scrubber, Rafa, and that's all you'll ever be.

That's what your mother screamed when I nailed her in her stinking ass, Rafa blurted out in a loud, clear voice and did not back away from the larger man.

Mike Cotton's face twisted, and his wire lips trembled as he made a move toward Rafa but was held firmly from behind by his brother, Billy Bob.

Billy Bob wrapped his arms around Mike Cotton in a clinch and restricted his arm movement.

A big mistake, thought Rafa. Lightweight amateurs. You do not cut off the only weapons the man has, his arms and hands, especially if there is a chance he might be poked in the gut by a shank. When Rafa saw the look that Mike Cotton gave him for the remark he made about his mother, his right hand slid into the right pocket of his trousers. He slipped his hand around the pearl handle of the six-inch Italian stiletto switchblade he had brought back from Italy. His thumb caressed the button gently. If the beast attacked, he would use the chair to tame him like a tiger gone berserk. If the fool placed his grubby hands on the chair and pulled on it, Rafa would slice him with the blade, just above the belly button, like he sliced a premium watermelon on a hot summer day. His blood and guts would spill out like melting crimson Jell-O, and Mike Cotton would taste the Italian import in all its grandeur. Rafa was not worried about the brother, Porky. Porky had coward tattooed on his forehead like a blinking neon lamp advertising boob night at a topless joint. The only thing that bothered Rafa was that his new suit was going to get bloody, but what the fuck, he thought. He had a closet full.

Mike Cotton was forever grateful that his brother held on to him. He could have put him down with an elbow to his big gut, but he hadn't. He had seen Rafa's right hand go into the pocket of his trousers. He had been around greasers all his life, and he was aware that a blade in the hand was bad news. Even though Rafa was older, and he was built close to the ground, he was stocky and heavy in the chest and shoulders. He was sure he could put Rafa down and maybe out, but with the chair between them and a blade, it could be a struggle. And he might have to pay a high price for the honor. Besides, Mike Montes was from the Eastside barrio, as was Rafa, and he didn't know Mike well enough to depend on him staying neutral. As for his brother, his brother was just his brother and unpredictable as rain clouds in the desert.

Mike finally stood up and said, That's enough. Stop the crap. Have some respect for the office, if not for me. This is not a cantina where you can throw blows at will, for Chrissake.

Rafa almost burst out laughing. Mike Montes had the fight in him when he was younger, Rafa recalled. He was a tough little ass-kicker and could punch it out with the best of them. Now Mike, with his jet-black, thick mustache merging with his goatee, perfectly trimmed, and not a hair on his ruddy lips entering his mouth, was not the same, thought Rafa. He looked more like an underwear model. Tall, slim, and fit. He could display bikini briefs in a glossy magazine for the in crowd. Mike, in his opinion, Rafa pondered, was a paper tiger, declawed by the mistress of the mansion so as not to scratch the expensive furniture. He was spoiled by the years in the mild climate of Southern California and the soft living. Rafa figured that Mayor Mike wouldn't do shit. All he would do was to pick up the phone and call for an ambulance to come and collect the gutted moose before the guts and gore stained his otherwise tidy office and splatter on his tailor-made suit and expensive urban-dude boots.

After the Cotton brothers had left in a huff, faster than they had barged in, convinced that they had lost this time, Rafa remained standing. Mike sat in his chair again, attempting to relax. This was ridiculous, he thought. Grown men acting like boys on booze. It wouldn't look good if Rafa cut Mike Cotton in his office. And even though he didn't see a blade, he was certain Rafa had one and would not hesitate to use it because Rafa was a product of the Eastside barrio and still carried that dare-me attitude. What a mess, he thought, close to an all-out fight, and what was he supposed to do? He was not going to get between a raging bull and a maniac with a blade. Hell no. He wasn't born yesterday. He tried to calm down, at least as calm as Rafa was. The man didn't seem to be bothered at all, Mike thought.

So, Rafa, you gonna take care of that business with the house? Mike finally asked, after Rafa just kept staring at him with a silly grin on his dark-chocolate face. What's your message to CI?

Rafa was all smiles once more. He was happy he'd held his own against the white dogs. He was not intimidated by the white dogs or any dogs. He knew most of them would never fight—just talk the talk. The big Rottweiler might be different, have a little more bite than snarl, but he doubted it. The dog wanted to impress Mike, but he had to get through him to do it. And Rafa would never bend the knee to any asshole, dead or alive.

Tell 'em I'll take care of it. OK, Mike? I'll talk to Max. He's always been a reasonable chap. Rafa glanced at his Cartier watch and said, Gotta go, Mike. As he walked out of Mike's office, he said to himself, Fuck Max and CI. In a voice dripping with honey and a grin showing teeth, he said to the secretary, Estrella Gallo, See you later, pretty woman.

CHAPTER 3

The young students marched like soldiers in cadence, going south on Santa Fe Street to the corner house on Calle Catolica, which ran east and west. They all had blue baseball caps on with lightweight matching jackets. In front of the cap-s was stenciled the letters, CI, and on the back of the jackets, an image of a tree growing in the palm of an open hand with the words above it in large black letters, COMMUNITY IMPACT. They marched in pairs to the beat of an invisible drum, led by William Moreno, nicknamed Red Dog.

When the students arrived at the house, they stopped and broke formation. Max Luna, the director of Community Impact, addressed them informally and thanked them for showing up on a Saturday morning to help. He gave William a list of jobs and advised the students to put their jackets in the front seat of the CI truck parked in front of the house. Other men from the Eastside, all volunteers, unloaded a cement mixer and bags of cement from the bed of the truck. The students spread out around the small house and talked and laughed as William gave them their assignments. Some students started mixing paint, while others, cleaning utensils in hand, entered the house to tidy up. A few with large plastic bags and rakes disappeared to the backyard, while the men mixed the cement and adjusted the new window facing the street. The old one lay on the ground to the side in charred pieces, broken and useless.

Max, after seeing that everyone was on task, continued his conversation with Rodolfo Acosta, a reporter for the Daily News of Las Flores.

See the pieces of the old window, Rudy? The cocktail hit the wood and exploded on impact. The wood on the outside took most of the hit. If it had crashed through the glass into the house and landed on the wooden floor—forget it, man—the whole inside of the house would have gone up in flames.

Was the widow in the house, and is she OK? Rudy asked, adjusting his glasses as they slipped down the bridge of his nose.

Fortunately, she was visiting her sister, who lives in the smaller house in the back. It wasn't that late when they threw it, but late enough for her to be in bed, which she wasn't. It was a loud crash, and the smoke and flames would scare the crap out of anyone. I don't care how old or young one is.

Cops have any leads yet?

Ha! The cops, Max responded. Oh yeah, they were here and put up their famous yellow tape. We couldn't get in the house to assess the damage until yesterday. Of course, they have no leads—do they ever?

Rudy pushed up his glasses again. He licked his lips and studied the men fitting in the new window. They had removed the old frame and patched up the ancient adobe around the window so the new one would fit in snugly. He felt the frustration in Max, along with the anger, but he had to get some answers to his questions if Max expected a write-up. Bad-mouthing the Las Flores PD was not going to get anything published. Max had given him a tour inside the house, and the damage inside was not bad. The question remained, why would anyone want to firebomb a widow in her late seventies?

So, Max, Rudy said. His hands were in his pockets. He didn't want to take notes because it might seem insensitive. Who do you think pulled this off? Some young punks acting crazy or...

Not on my watch, Max wanted to say. Instead he said, They hit the wrong house, Rudy. You can see it from here. And Max pointed. See the third house on the same side of the street? See it? That house was occupied by some lowlifes selling drugs. We complained to the police on several occasions. They finally stopped by. After the visit by the cops, the scum moved out to the countryside, not far from Las Flores. And they continued to do what they were doing here. The people who threw the gas bomb didn't know for sure which house they wanted to hit, but they knew who they wanted to send a message to. And they went for the first house on the corner, the widow's house. They had to be people from out of town or not from the barrio to make that kind of miscalculation. That's what I think,

Rudy. I don't think the paper will print that because it's something I can't prove. But it has to do with drugs. And about that, I'm positive.

Both men remained silent for a couple of minutes. Finally, Max put out his hand to Rudy and said, Thanks for coming by, Rudy. Write something up if you can. The more people are aware, the better for the community. The Las Flores Sun will never do it.

Did they at least come out, Max?

Are you kidding? They're still trying to compete with the El Paso Herald or the Albuquerque Tribunal. What a joke, huh? Anyway, I better get to work. I need to help. The men see me yapping so much, they're gonna think I'm trying to take over your job, Rudy. And both men laughed.

Max put on his work gloves and joined the men to help with the window. Is it going in, Frank? Frank Campos had an old wooden level in his hands. As he placed the level on the window frame, he said, They always go in, Max. You just have to work with it a little.

Was Francisco Montes here yesterday? asked Max. He helped the other two men hold the metal frame of the window in place.

Oh yeah! He was here yesterday. He was here the day after the cowards threw the firebomb. But the men in blue had the tape up, and we couldn't do anything but wait. Until we put up a fuss, they even refused Alma's request to take some food to the sisters at the house in the back. You know Francisco and Alma—they are always the first ones to help out. What about their son, the mayor, Mike? Frank asked, a big smile on his face. Has he been out here to assess the damage and get the city to help fix up the place?

Yeah, right. And Max laughed. It's Saturday. Maybe after he plays a couple of rounds of golf he might take the time to get over here. I doubt it. Who knows, Frank? He might be in Santa Fe visiting his girlfriend.

You know, that new golf course they opened in the Lomas—it is something. Eighteen holes of pure beauty. We did some work up there before it was completed. Man, what a place. You play, Max?

I will when I retire, Max said without hesitation.

They closed the old country club golf course, said Frank as he worked the level. What do you think they'll do with all that property?

Homes, answered Max, holding on to the side of the window. Homes and more homes. And as long as the snowbirds continue to freeze in the northern states, they will retire here and buy homes in the sun.

That's more work for us, Max. And there she is. She's in perfect. Hold the baby right there while I anchor her ass, Frank told the man who was holding the window from inside the house. The other man used a shovel to fill up the foundation with concrete around the window, and Frank leveled the concrete with a spatula on the sides of the window frame.

You know, Frank continued, Francisco did most of the work yesterday. He's the expert on old adobe buildings. See, with the double adobe, we had to scrape out a lot of the damaged wood and crushed adobe from the sides and top. Francisco used special filler and advised us to set the window in the center and leave a ledge on the inside and outside. I was thinking of leaving a larger ledge on the outside. I wasn't sure if we could center the baby in the middle. Now the widow can have a ledge for her potted hierbas inside and outside.

Wow, Max said, impressed. I never gave it that much thought. The man touched it up with concrete.

You don't have to hold on to it anymore, Max. It's in. See the top of the window? That's the most difficult part. In the new houses, it's just wood, sheetrock, and stucco. On an old adobe, the frame has to be set in perfect with no spaces to hold air, or the concrete might buckle when dried. The rain will eventually soak through the plaster and create problems in the future. The old-timers were pretty good builders with the tools they had to work with. We have to give them credit, and many times we don't. That's what Francisco does, and that's why we always have work. Every house you work on is different. Just like women. And Frank looked around to see if the kids were in hearing range.

Max, William Moreno called out from the side of the house. Do you have a minute? We're here in the backyard.

Max peeled off his work gloves and walked to the backyard. Large plastic bags full of weeds and junk were piled in a corner of the good-sized yard.

Hey, guys, you all doing a great job out here, Max told the students, and he meant it.

Bobby, a boy of fourteen, looked at his shoes, then looked at Max and said, I thought we were here to do some work, Max. I saw Grace doing her nails.

You're jealous because she didn't do yours, you little—

Brenda! William interrupted, before she completed her sentence.

Bobby grabbed his crotch with his right hand.

You wish, Brenda mouthed with a whisper.

Bobby smiled and asked Max, Hey, Max, are we gonna go to class after? I feel like kicking some ass.

Does the sun shine in Las Flores during summer? Of course, we are, my friend.

Where's Jerry? He said class was after we finished here. I don't see him or hear him.

That's because he's not here. He took the other truck to pick up some stuff we need and get you hardworking guys some food.

Sounds good, chimed in the other students.

Max. William got close and said, It's Grace, you know? I'll take care of things out here.

Max walked into the half-painted kitchen and asked the kids for Grace. The kids were painting the kitchen walls and pointed to the living room, half-done in blue paint. Grace, age fifteen, was sitting on a metal stool with her hands covering her eyes and her long black hair over her hands, sobbing.

Max gave a long sigh and entered the living room and sat on the floor next to her. He said nothing. He wished that William's wife, Ruth, had come along.

Why? Why? Grace sobbed. Why her, Max? She's my abuelita's friend. I call her abuelita also. She is gentle and kind, Max. She is old; she never hurt anybody, never. What if she dies? She's still scared. Who can be so wicked and so mean? Find them, Max; you…and Jerry can find them. I know you can, and…and hurt them please, Max. You can do it. I know you can.

If it was only that easy, Max thought, but he said, Grace, the police will find them. That is their job. Your abuelita is OK. You saw her. She's gonna be fine. And you know why she's gonna be fine? Because you're here. Because your friends are here. Because we are all here to help her and to show her that we care and that we love her. The bad guys—don't give them a thought; love is stronger than hate. You proved your love today and every day you give her a big hug, and that means more to her than anything else in the world. You don't want her to see you crying, Grace. She won't understand, especially around your friends. Now go wash your face and go to the back house. Then give her a hug with the biggest smile on your face that shows you are here for her and will always be.

Yeah, Max. Yeah? Grace asked, as she wiped the tears from her face with her hands.

Sure. Do it, Max assured her as he helped her stand up.

Grace gave Max a shy smile, walked to the kitchen sink, washed her face, and ran out to the house in the back.

William walked in as Grace ran out. She OK? he asked Max.

Hope so. That's a tough one. Max sighed.

Hey, Max, I was thinking. Since we are painting the living room, maybe we can peel off the old linoleum. We can strip the wood, stain it, polish it, and seal it. What do you think?

That's a great idea, William. Let's do it, man.

Do you think the widow would mind?

I doubt it. She told me to do whatever needs to be done. Just make it livable.

Jerry, Jerry, Jerry's here! the kids yelled. They were all excited as Jerry Rivera, Max's assistant drove up in the other CI truck. The other students rushed out of the house and from the backyard. He brought us food! they yelled. What did you get us, Jerry? the kids asked as if starving.

I got you guys burgers and burritos, Jerry answered, as he got out of the truck with two large paper bags, one stuffed with burgers and the other one with burritos. He was wearing a black tank top, and his tattooed biceps bulged as he carried the bags to the kids. Jerry Rivera was a big man, almost six feet, and lean—one hundred eighty pounds of solid muscle.

Did you get us some Cokes? asked a skinny kid with glasses.

No, sir, Jerry said, exposing white teeth with a big smile on his pecan-colored face. You can drink water from the tap. I'm not going to add to your parents' dental bills. You drink that junk all the time anyway. You can go without it for one meal. Sure you can.

Uh, moaned some of the students.

Do the burritos have meat or—

No! Jerry shot back before the student completed his sentence. Last time some of you picked out the meat and chucked the rest. This time I got you bean and cheese. Take it or leave it.

As the students were helping themselves to the burgers and burritos, Bobby yelled out, Hey, Jerry, are we going to practice today? I feel like kicking butt.

Before taking a bite of her burger, Mercy said, Yeah, like the last time. You had tears in your eyes when you sparred with Brenda.

Bobby made a face and said, They were not tears, you…you…I had something in my eyes.

Yeah, Brenda's gloves. And Mercy laughed out loud.

The students giggled between bites, all standing around Jerry. It was obvious they liked him and wanted to be close to him.

Grace came running from inside the house. Jerry! Jerry! What took you so long? she asked in a loud and excited voice. Before he answered, she asked, Can I take a burrito to my abuelita and one for her sister?

Sure, of course you can, and take some to Max and William and the men over there by the window.

Thank you, Jerry, she said, a cheerful smile on her face. She walked away with the food to where Max and William were sitting close to the new window and talking with Frank and his men.

I'm going to check out your work, Jerry said and walked into the house. The students followed him, eating their burritos and hamburgers, as if he were the Pied Piper of Hamlin.

Jerry came out of the house and into the backyard. You guys have done a fantastic job, and look at all those bags of trash. Wow, I'm impressed.

The kids beamed with pride; there was nothing that they liked better than impressing Jerry Rivera.

Can you beat up Max? asked Nelson Sola, the skinny kid with glasses.

Shut up, stupid, said one of the kids, his mouth full of beans and cheese.

Jerry looked at Nelson. Skin and bones. Nelson was the smallest kid in the group for his age, but he was smart and always needy for attention.

No. And Jerry smiled. No one can beat up Max—at least no one that I know of.

He looks older than you, Nelson added. He loved the attention he was getting.

Oh my God! Brenda exclaimed. Ya pendejo. And her eyes were daggers aimed at the wimpy Nelson.

No, Jerry answered with the patience of one who has been bullied for years. We're the same age. Maybe because Max has long hair and I have short hair, and he has on dark shades and I don't. Age is only a number, anyway. So don't get hung up on it, because it can mess up your life.

But you can take him? insisted Nelson, with a half-eaten burger in one hand and a burrito on the other.

Listen, Nelson, and the rest of you, asserted Jerry. No one can beat Max because Max uses reverse psychology to win his fights instead of his hands and feet. Let me give you an example. Say a guy walks up to Max all mad and blurts out, You are acting stupid, Max. Max, instead of hitting him, would ask in a calm voice, What is your definition of stupid? Tell me so that I know what stupid is and make sure you are not acting the same way. Then we will both be the better for it. The guy is confused and thinks, see what I mean?

What if the guy said something about Max's mother? continued Nelson, knowing Jerry wouldn't shut him up.

Shut up, fool, several students said aloud.

No, it's OK. And Jerry raised his muscular arms to quiet them down. If the guy said something bad about Max's mother, Max would ask him if he knew his mother on first-name basis. If not, perhaps he was angry at his own mother for slapping him when he ate his younger brother's candy. That is reverse psychology.

You guys should try it. And it works, I'd say, in most cases.

What if the guy slapped Max in the face? asked Nelson, still on a roll.

UUUOOO! came the taunt from the kids. You gonna get it now, idiot.

Well then, Max would ask the guy if he felt better. If that was going to make the rest of his day a happy one. If the guy said no, then Max would put out his lights. And Jerry laughed out loud and couldn't stop. Finally, he said between laughs, I'm only kidding, guys. Only then did the students get the joke. They broke out laughing and poked Nelson on the shoulder, but not hard. If I could only tell them the truth about Max, Jerry reflected, rubbing his eyes with his hands, they would have nightmares.

Stop it, Nelson whined as the students continued to poke him on the back and shoulders. They laughed and jumped up and down like jumping jacks.

Can you lead us back to the center? Nelson asked, still confused about Jerry's reply. William is mean; he put me in the back of the formation.

That's because he doesn't know his left foot from his right, Brenda said, laughing. He kicks people in front of him.

I do not, responded Nelson and gave Brenda a dirty look, twisting his mouth.

William is not mean. He is strict, but he is not mean, Jerry clarified. Learn to use your words, my friend. Words can be dangerous. Anyway, I'll practice with you before we go back. You'll do fine, Nelson; practice is all you need.

And coordination, yelled out one of the students, and the others giggled while placing their trash in the plastic bags.

Check out my kick, Jerry, Bobby shouted as he attempted a right-leg roundhouse kick and almost fell on his ass.

Don't go so high on the leg. Try to keep the hands high, and you'll get it, Jerry said.

While Jerry was in the back with the young soldiers, Max and William were sitting around the almost-finished window, talking with the men.

Max, sitting on an overturned metal bucket, was eating the last of his bean-and-cheese burrito. He said to Frank Campos and his compadres, who were also eating and drinking coffee from the thermos they had brought along, William thinks it's a good idea to redo the floor in the living room, Frank, what do you think?

Taking a sip of coffee and putting the burger wrapper in his pocket, Frank said, It can be done. I checked the wood under the old linoleum, and it seems to be solid. The problem would be peeling off the old, thin linoleum. I wouldn't use chemicals. It might damage the wood, and the cleanup is difficult. The chemical stuff is OK to use on concrete, like on the kitchen floor. On wood, I don't know, but that's just me talking. I've been with Francisco Montes too long. He took another sip of coffee.

I was thinking, William said, a little too excited with the idea. We could peel off the old linoleum, strip the wood, and put some stain on it.

Frank looked at William and then at his two compadres, who remained silent, and he worked hard not to smile.

That's a good plan, William, but if you don't mind me saying, I would attack it this way. I would carefully remove all the linoleum from the wood, and I mean every bit. Do not use any of the chemical solutions sold, as I mentioned. They make a mess if you're not careful and can leave chunks of melted linoleum on the wood. This is an all-the-way, on-your-knees scrape job, with no shortcuts. After that, I would remove the shoe molding around the floor and wall, and again, very carefully. You might be able to reuse them, but if you crack them or break them, you will need to buy some new ones. Then you have to nail down any loose boards and sand the wood with a vibrating sander. Use sixty-grit sandpaper if you can get it. After you have cleaned the floor, use a clean cloth to coat it with the stain. Allow the stain to penetrate the wood, and let it dry. When the wood is dry, you can apply a thin coat of polyurethane on the floor or any other sealer you choose. And here is the trick, William; many don't do it because of the time and to save some money, especially on a large floor. But on a small floor like this one, I would go over the floor with fine steel wool after the poly is dry. The steel wool fills in the open pores left on the wood and leaves it smooth. You can do another coat of poly, if you care to. Place a nice rug in the center, and you got yourself a floor, my man.

Wow, I never considered all that, William admitted. I never even thought about removing the molding around the walls.

You don't have to, but you'll eventually stain the molding, and the job would look half-finished.

Maybe you can come and give us a hand, Frank, if you're not too busy.

Maybe, Frank replied. He was ready to change the subject. Work is a little slow right now. If we all dig in, we can knock it off in a couple of days. Hey, Max. Frank turned to Max. Does the widow have any family nearby?

Max was awakened from a deep thought he seemed to get lost in. She has a son in Colorado. He comes once a year to visit her, I hear. He stays a couple of days and leaves. She also has a daughter somewhere. But I don't know if she ever visits.

That is sad, Frank said. Did the widow tell them about this...this incident?

The widow told me that she didn't want to worry them. That she was all right because God didn't want her yet, and her children knowing about it wasn't going to change anything. Her words.

I wonder if they'll come to her funeral when God does want her, Frank said, and he scratched the stubble on his sunburned face.

Oh, they'll come. Rush in. Bury the widow, sell the old house, and split. What else is new, Frank?

The kids had piled up the bags of trash from the backyard on Jerry's truck. The tools and cement mixer were cleaned up. The men were having a hard time pushing up the cement mixer on the bed of Max's truck. The boards they had used to unload it were wobbly. Jerry lifted the mixer with both hands and placed it on the bed of the truck without breaking a sweat.

¡Hombre fuerte! exclaimed Frank Campos.

It's a small one, Jerry said, a little embarrassed and not wanting to call attention to himself. OK, boys and girls, let's go back to the center and have some fun, he called out to the kids and escaped the looks from the men.

The students were all giddy. They pushed and shoved until William walked up to them and shouted, Formation!

Nelson yelled out, Uh, Jerry. You said you were gonna lead us back. C'mon, you said.

Get your jackets. Put them on. Straighten your hats, and get ready to march, soldiers, William ordered, ignoring the whiny Nelson.

A couple of the students were already handing out the blue jackets. They had their names stitched on the front, so there was no confusion on what belonged to who. They put their jackets on and were in formation in a matter of minutes. Frank and his compadres were impressed.

Formation! William shouted out again. Nelson Sola, to the back of the formation.

CHAPTER 4

*I*t was Monday morning between ten and eleven, and the director of Community Impact, Max Luna, and his staff were having their weekly staff meeting in his office. Outside, the sky was clear blue, and puffy white clouds floated by like large luxury cruise ships taking the lucky few to the end of the world. It was the middle of October, and the sun had already outgunned the morning chill. The morning sun brought the older folks, the retirees, and the housebound out to sit with neighbors and friends in their favorite spot and take in the rays of the sun. It was called la solanera, a sunny spot where they could relax and expose their aching bones to the sun. But very few would do it in the summer. Here in these heavenly sunny spots they gossiped, smoked, and joked. They commented on the silly and the serious. They enjoyed the sun for an hour or two, until the conversations became redundant or the sun burned too hot. Then they shuffled back to their jacales until the following day. It was a ritual exercised by the native New Mexicans for centuries during the winter months.

Inside Max Luna's office, the three men sat drinking coffee and joking around. Max Luna and Jerry Rivera were playing the show-me-what-you-know game. Movies were their favorite subject. One would name a film, and the other would give the name of the director, year, and actor or actress who played the part. If they knew. The older the movie, the more challenging the game became. William Moreno didn't participate because he couldn't hang with Max and Jerry. He knew only the latest movies. And that wasn't much fun.

White Heat, Jerry called out to Max.

Let me see, Max said, and he pulled on his lower lip with his fingers. Let me see. White Heat, OK. And his eyes lit up. It was directed by Raoul Walsh in1949, and the actor was my man James Cagney.

Very good. And Jerry smiled. Hit me.

Tristana, responded Max quickly.

Oh yeah, Jerry said as he licked his lips. Tristana, 1970, by Luis Buñuel, the Spanish filmmaker, and my hard-on girl, Catherine Deneuve, when she was younger.

Excellent, my man. Max grinned, and his white teeth sparkled. Your turn.

Christopher Strong, Jerry called out.

Oh, going deep, huh, Jerry? Let me see—Christopher Strong. Give me a minute, my friend. Max said nothing, and that led Jerry to the possibility that Max had no clue. Christopher Strong, Max repeated slowly. Of course! His face lit up like a kid seeing the lights of a Christmas tree go on for the first time. Directed by Dorothy Arzner in 1933. And by the way, she was the only major female director working in Hollywood during that time. The actress was a young Katharine Hepburn. A beautiful and talented actress in anyone's bed—I mean book.

Jerry gave Max a high five as they both laughed like silly kids jumping in and out of muddy puddles. I saved that one for you for a long time, brother. And by the way, that one was a pre-code movie by all accounts.

William also chuckled. He didn't find it funny, but he didn't want to be the odd man out. What's a pre-code movie? he asked, unafraid to ask.

Those were films done in the twenties and thirties, Max added. Then the Motion Picture Production Code, also known as the Hays Code, was adopted in 1930 but not entirely enforced until 1934. Many believe that it seriously stifled the American cinema for over thirty years.

See, William, Jerry jumped in. During those years, pre-code movies had strong-willed female characters, racy plots, and snappy dialogue. Some were gangster films like The Public Enemy, done in 1931, starring James Cagney. Another one was Red Headed Woman with Jean Harlow in 1932 and others.

Arzner, in Christopher Strong, Jerry continued. She was the first one to put the young Katharine Hepburn in pants, and of course that turned her, many believe, into an icon for female independence in that movie. Anyway, by 1968, television and foreign films, which were not bound by the production code, had practically nullified the code.

Max turned serious. He didn't want to leave William out of the loop and changed the subject. Do you guys think the scumbags we hit the other night had anything to do with the firebombing of the widow's house?

William Moreno, the assistant director of CI, called Red Dog because of his red hair, also serious, said, I believe some other dopers were after the same scum, but they didn't have the balls to confront them.

What do you think, Jerry? Max asked, as he scratched his beard with his fingers.

Jerry Rivera, who was in charge of athletics and maintenance, said, The dopers knew they were on a hit list, so they moved out of town. They thought they were safe and out of reach in the countryside.

Yeah, pitched in William. But they were still buying and selling from someone and to someone close by. Maybe someone in Las Flores—maybe someone in the barrio.

And, that's the someone we have to find, Max added.

Ruth Moreno walked into the small office without knocking. Ruth was a petite woman. She was pretty but not beautiful. She had a tight little body and was evenly proportioned, and that made petite women look prettier than they usually were. She wore her blondish hair in a ponytail and no makeup. She was wearing tight jeans with high-heeled black leather boots that made her look taller than she actually was. Ruth was married to William and was not intimidated working with three strong-willed men. She had a degree in business administration and a minor in social work from UNM. She was pleasant and upbeat and had a smile that would melt steel. The kids loved her, and the parents respected her for her good nature and honesty. She was the financial officer for CI and in charge of volunteers and tutors, among other things.

Good morning, guys, Ruth said, breathing heavily as if she just completed a long-distance marathon. I'm soo excited. Guess who signed on with us as a volunteer tutor.

Tell us, the three men said in unison.

You will not believe it, Ruth continued. She placed her small hands on her face to contain her excitement. Claire, Claire de Lune, today, this morning, in my office.

Who's that? Jerry asked, not knowing why everyone seemed so pleased.

That's Clairisa Amador Cotton, Max answered. Known as Claire de Lune. The wife of Mike Cotton. The self-made million-dollar man and owner of Cotton Construction, among other enterprises.

She called my office this morning and asked if she could come in and talk to me, Ruth continued. She leaned forward in her chair as if confessing a deep secret to a panel of monks in a fifteenth-century monastery. I thought she just wanted to drop off some donations, like used clothing and other items, things, you know? But then out of the blue, she asked me if we needed volunteer tutors. I was going to say hell yes. And don't tell me you're interested. But I said, with my best smile, oh, we always need tutors. And she surprised me when she said, in her soft, calm, and educated voice, I have some spare time, and I would love to help out with the children, if it's OK. I wanted to jump up and hug her right there, but I didn't. I said, in a calm voice, even though I was busting, OK, Mrs. Cotton, I'll show you our schedule for tutoring, and you can select the time you want to come in. Claire, she said in that sweet voice. Just call me Claire, please, and you choose the time. She signed up for three days and maybe four during the summer. I'm so excited, William. Wait, there's more. She is licensed as an educational psychologist. She can do therapy with children and adults. Can you believe that, you guys? Our prayers are answered. We don't have to refer out or depend on the schools anymore. She can do in-house therapy right here. And one more thing: I know you guys are anxious to start the meeting, but hear me out. We talked, and she admired the blue jackets our students wear. Guess what. She offered to buy twenty for our guys, the winter jackets. She knows a place, and they will put the logo on, and if we like them, she'll get twenty more. If we like them, if we like them—we're gonna love them. She knows a place; you know what that means? Guys. No cut-rate hand-me-downs; that's what that means.

William leaned over and gave his lovely wife a kiss on the mouth. She sat next to him in the office, facing Max. That's big, Ruth. That's big. And he said it in the sincere and tender way that only newly married couples can express. I'm so proud of you, babe. And there's no hurry for the meeting, if you need more time. He held her hand. It was obvious that he still loved her and loved her very much.

No, Ruth, take your time, Max added. No rush. You care for some coffee?

No thanks, Max. I just got carried away. But Claire de Lune! Wow! She is so together. OK. I'll stop now.

Jerry, the new kid on the block, couldn't get why Ruth was getting all emotional about a rich socialite volunteering to help out. Isn't that what rich women did to get out of the house? he wondered. Well, anyhow, he was still learning the ins and outs. He was sure to get it in time. But for now, he didn't know what to say or do. He wanted to congratulate Ruth and give her a hug. But he was not sure if that was appropriate, with her husband and all.

OK. I'm good, Ruth said. And she patted her light-brown eyes with her open hands.

You want to start? Max asked. Or do you need a few more minutes to...

No, no. I'm good, Ruth insisted. And she took out a pen and pad from her purse. We have about twenty-five grand in the budget. That has to last us until the new year, when grant money rolls in, and the city and state match up, if they are. With Mayor Mike Montes as the tiebreaker, we stand a chance. The AC and heating were going to run twenty grand, but we negotiated and got it for ten. Ray Lara, the contractor, will take the write-off that I was sure he was going to take; he just needed a little bit of convincing. This is a very large and old building, and that's why the city leased it to us for a dollar a year. The ceiling is high, and the pipes are bad. And the roof leaks. But we needed a bigger space. And Ruth smiled. We can work with the kids the whole summer and won't freeze in the winter. I'm so excited! And she clapped her hands. Oops. Sorry, she apologized and blushed.

Any questions so far? She wanted to laugh, she was so happy, but she held it in.

What about the redevelopment money? Max asked. How much came in for the roof?

Only a fraction of what they promised, Ruth replied, all serious again. And that happened because of Mike Montes. He argued that since it was city property, the city should use redev money to properly repair and pay for the upkeep. But before it went to the full council for a vote, the committee allocated some money. Francisco Montes supervised, and Frank Moreno and his men did the heavy lifting. We paid them what we could, and it wasn't much. I'm sure it covered materials. The roof needed to be repaired before any other work got started. Three classrooms are in operation. The college kids still help out with the tutoring, and they are a godsend. Oh, before I forget. The high school wanted us to help expand their teen pregnancy program. To have the girls over here, and they would share expenses. I said thanks but no thanks. I mean, I feel for the girls. Our program at this point is not equipped to have a nurse on hand, special counseling, nutritional needs, and with time, child care.

And besides, we might have to provide some abortion counseling if we expect some funds from the proabortion organizations, William added. And that will bring the antiabortion fanatics to our front door and scare the shit out of our kids. You did good to refuse, babe.

Let me see, what else? Ruth studied the notes on her pad. Oh, the community meetings during the evenings—I've had requests for more fruit and veggies, less sugary junk, and to hold the meetings earlier, especially in the winter months, and make them shorter. Any questions? I'm all ears.

OK. William, your turn, Max said as he turned to William.

William cleared his throat as if he was prepared to give a farewell speech to his graduating class. He placed his pen and pad on Max's desk and said, First, I would like to thank my beautiful wife, Ruth, for all the hard work she has done. I believe we are all doing our best to make our project work, and it is working. Saturday was a very productive day. We did our best to help an elderly woman restore her modest home and uplift her spirits. The kids were involved, and they did a hell of a job.

Sorry I missed it, babe, Ruth stated and touched William on the arm.

No, Ruth. You don't have to apologize. You were here getting things done.

Shit. Jerry thought. Is William practicing for a Labor Day speech? Get on with the report, dude.

Our home and follow-up visits will have to increase, if we are to meet the objectives on the federal grant, William added.

You gave them too high a number, William, Max objected. We can only do so many visits with the limited staff we have.

That's why you should have never hired that lunkhead Jerry Rivera, William told himself, an ex-con pinto, to boot. Who in their right mind is going to open their door to a tattooed pinto in a tank top? And a parolee, to top that.

It's OK, Max, Ruth jumped in. Those are rolling numbers, projected with growth of the program. That's the way we wrote the grant. A rolling predictability is commonly used in writing grants to mean we will grow the program—with the growth will come more resources, and that adds to more home visits—instead of giving numbers anchored in cement that we might not achieve in the short term.

Which means what? Max asked, more for Jerry's benefit.

Which means, which means, William said, butting in, that it will keep the feds and the state away from our books for now. We have to increase our home visits and follow-ups. I didn't mean today or tomorrow but gradually…until we meet the objectives in the grant.

OK, Max conceded. How about Chiva Town? Their council member has been asking me, and not in a nice way, why we neglect Chiva Town. And we need his vote for the matching funds from the city. What are we going to do about keeping someone to represent those folks?

The last organizer was a college student, William said, a little calmer. He was run out of Chiva Town. The Snipers must accept anyone we send over there.

Excuse me, William, Ruth said, polite as always. His name was Bobby, and he was a real nice guy. We took him to Chiva and introduced him to Tiny Tim. Tiny Tim, if you believe the rumors, is not the leader of the Chiva Town Snipers any longer. He spends most of his time on a rancho outside Belen, breeding fighting roosters. The rumors are that Neto, his nephew, the crackhead from El Paso, runs the show. Anyway, one night, the Snipers put the guns on Bobby for no reason and told him to get lost, and he did. I would have done the same.

I know all that, Max said. He tried to be patient. How are we going to keep a staff member working there so as not to lose the vote for funds from the unreliable councilman?

Maybe, Jerry broke in. He scratched the scorpion tattoo on the right side of his muscular neck. Maybe, we can get one of the Snipers to be our man in Chiva Town. And then ask the councilman to beg the full council to fund the repair of their rotting community center. We can train the vato on the basics, and the Snipers will have their man. The Snipers, correct me if I'm wrong, always had a very efficient method of helping their own with food and other stuff. Lock into that, and it might solve some problems.

And how are you going to recruit a Sniper to join our staff? interrupted William, a little annoyed that Jerry had come up with the idea before he did.

Maybe one of our high school students can start a conversation with a young Sniper at school and recruit him or her into the cause, Ruth interjected, optimistic as ever.

No. They group in high school, in middle school, and even in elementary. They tend to stay among their own, William responded. They do just like they did when we were in school. Someone is going to have to go to Chiva Town, sit down with the leaders, put the plan on the table, and then ask them to pick their man. And they all looked at Max.

Well, we're gonna have to work on that, Max said, and wrote it down in his folder. Anything else, William, before we pass to Jerry?

No. Oh, one more thing. There was a proposal circulating that we open a food bank and cook food for the needy. Prepare it and serve it here five days a week like they do at the community center. But I don't think so. The cost is prohibitive. To build a kitchen and staff it…I think will be too much, I say.

What do they want, a restaurant? And Max laughed.

Maybe some entertainment like dancing girls. And Jerry chuckled. He wanted to say strippers but decided not to.

William wanted to join in and say something funny. Instead he looked at his writing pad. He was talking about a serious proposal by serious-minded people who wanted to feed the hungry. He kept quiet and didn't even glance at Ruth. An awkward moment indeed.

Anything else, William? Max asked, some giggle left in his words. We don't mean to take it light, William. But you have to have a sense of humor, or you'll go nuts in this business. Anyway, we refer the hungry to the community center.

OK, Jerry. You on, my man, and make it quick. We gotta get rolling. Duty calls.

Let me see, Jerry said. He scratched the scorpion tattoo on the left side of his neck, as if his nails would wake up the beast. He didn't have a pen or a pad. The girls' bathroom is finished; they don't have to use the boys' anymore. The bathroom at the end of the building for guests is also done, shower and all. The door outside the bathroom that leads to the alley can be opened and closed now. The fire department gave us a hard time over that door on the last inspection, you might recall. There is an exit sign on top of the door, legal size. The basketball backboard was lowered, and new netting was fitted on the hoop. We only have one, but half a court is better than no court. We got new basketballs, mats, and jump ropes, thanks to Ruth. And he gave Ruth a smile. We decided to leave the boxing ring inside the building where it stands now. I know it's an eyesore to some people, but the kids love it. Our martial art classes are coming along; we're up to fifteen kids in three levels, and again, thanks to Ruth for the college kids. They really help out. And Ruth is right; the AC is going to help during the summer. The kids can stay and work on their skills instead of being bored at home. That's it for me, folks.

Thanks, Jerry. I have one more item on the agenda. Nelson Sola. Does he stay, or does he go? Ruth, you go first.

Oh. He stays. Nelson can be a little obnoxious at times, but he is so cute and very smart. He helps the slower kids with high-end fractions and prealgebra problems. And now that we have Claire to help, she can talk to him. He needs that. No, the parents will be devastated if we kick him out. They told me that they had seen an improvement in his behavior toward his siblings. And even in school, his behavior is improving.

Jerry?

I say keep him. If I understand the concept behind this program, it's to help kids like Nelson. I agree with Ruth. He is clever and loves to rattle cages, but he's not mean. He needs our attention, and he is learning how to balance his physicality with his cognitive strength and get along with others.

William?

William was a little uncomfortable. He had given the name to Max to consider an exit for Nelson Sola. But he said, I agree with Ruth one hundred percent, and if Ruth says he stays, then he stays.

He stays. Max closed his folder and placed it inside a desk drawer. Thanks again, you guys. Ruth, William, Jerry, you guys are doing an excellent job and making me look good. I love it. We have a long week ahead of us, but the project is coming together. I was nervous about moving into this building. But now I feel comfortable here. And it was Ruth who sold me on the idea. She pleaded. She threatened, and she insisted, until I said, Let's go for it. And here we are. Thanks again, guys.

Ruth and William exited the office first, and Jerry lingered behind. Hey, Max, he said when Ruth and William were out of the office. I have an appointment with my PO in half an hour. I'll see you later, OK?

OK, Jerry. Good luck with that asshole.

CHAPTER 5

Jerry Rivera drove west on Santa Teresa Street from the CI Center to downtown to report to his parole officer. It was a task he didn't look forward to. He drove west for a couple of miles all the way to Armijo Avenue and cut a right, going north to downtown. He drove an older car Max let him use until he bought his own ride. He drove slowly. He was aware he had plenty of time and did not want to get there too early. He was amazed at the growth of Las Flores. He had been away in Santa for almost ten years; take away a month or two. The barrio seemed more congested, with more people driving around. He hadn't even considered the growth on the east and northeast. Homes all the way to the mountains, expensive homes, and not just adobe jacales. There was a lot of employment opportunity in construction, and he knew that. The decent jobs with benefits were the jobs to be had employed by the feds. The state senators had thrown a lot of pork to Las Flores. And since the feds owned a lot of property close to Las Flores, new facilities opened up. There were testing facilities for rockets and warehouses for military weapons and other stuff too secret to know about. Too bad he couldn't get one of those jobs, he reflected. He was a pinto on parole, and the feds would never offer him a job. That was a fact of life he lived with every day.

Jerry passed the Las Flores Community Center on Santa Teresa. He noticed the parking lot was almost full. Close to lunchtime, he told himself, and people are hungry. He was glad the CI Center didn't serve food. It would be a circus at all times with people hanging around while they waited for a hot meal. The church was still standing on Calle Catolica, but the church was going to stand tall even if the rest of Las Flores went to hell. And he chuckled. Maybe he should pay a visit on a Sunday, he thought. Might look good to the PO. Naw, ain't got time for church right now—maybe later? he considered. Who knew? He might get the bug.

Jerry approached the railroad tracks when he passed Mora Street. Mora Street ran north and south. He noticed the numerous warehouses, machine shops, and welding operations along Mora close to the tracks.

This used to be junkyard alley, he remembered. Numerous junkyards, or salvage yards, some small and some large, had populated the area for years. The area was now blighted with splotches of tainted, darkened oil on empty lots and empty, greasy, broken-down oil tankers dozing in the sun, gathering dust. Skeletons of abandoned trucks and cars could be seen, once with colorful scrawls, but now the graffiti was diminishing like tattoos on old, wrinkled skin. The junkyards were gone, he agreed. But, Jesus, look at what replaced them. No wonder the Eastside had such a bad reputation, he reflected. People see this, and they see the barrio. He crossed the tracks, still on Santa Teresa, and entered the Westside near downtown. This area was still a little shabby but nothing compared to what he had just seen. He reached Armijo Avenue. He got a green light and turned right, going north. The traffic here was heavy on both sides of the street. He drove slowly because he had no choice until he reached Church Street, which ran east and west. He made a left turn on Church and headed west. He drove a couple of blocks, found a parking space, and walked up to the old courthouse building on Church and Main.

Jerry waited in the PO's office, which happened to be the old office of the mayor of Las Flores. The waiting room had a dozen or so folding chairs and a few dated magazines on top of a cheap card table. The carpet had seen better days, and the prints on the walls were turning yellow with age. There was no secretary, no sign-in sheet, no instant coffee, and only a closed door that led to the office of the PO, a man who had the power to alter your life—and pronto. In this case, the creature was Ulises Fuentes. A short, bald-headed asshole with thick eyeglasses. The kind of little shit you slap around in school and take his lunch money. The kind of little shit who goes to college and takes on a job with a little power and plays at payback, forever thinking that it will make his miserable life a little happier.

Jerry turned to his left as he sat down and said, Shit, in a muted voice. Sitting a couple of chairs behind him to his left was a man his age, his size, and the color of light chocolate. John Slaughter was a black man but lighter than Jerry in skin color and, in his own eyes, better looking. He also had a tattoo of a large scorpion on both sides of his thick neck. They both wore short-sleeved, white cotton shirts with heavy dirt around the collars—the same shirts they always wore for their monthly visitations.

They wore dark-blue dress pants, but John had on dirty white running shoes, and Jerry had on black, scuffed-up dress shoes he'd borrowed from Max.

Hey, Jerry. John Slaughter finally broke the silence that lay thick between the two warriors. Ain't you gonna say hello, at least?

We ain't supposed to talk to each other, John. You know the silly rules.

Here we can talk, man. Out there. And he pointed to the door. Maybe not, but here the man is in his office. We're cool here.

I know, man, but I don't want to provoke him.

I hear you got a cushy job with CI, Jerry. How did you pull that off? Ain't you working with kids?

Jerry, quick to anger, turned to face him, and responded but kept his voice low. I ain't no Chester; I can work anywhere and with anyone if they wanna hire me.

Max got you in, huh, Jerry? Nice to have friends to pull for you. I work construction, Jerry. I'm black. They never hire me at CI.

Fuck you, John. We both black. Look at you, and look at me.

John laughed and said, You ain't black, Jerry—

But before he completed his sentence, the door opened, and the creature stuck his ugly face out and yelled, Mr. Jerry Rivera, front and center.

Jerry stood up and walked to the open door. With his left hand behind his back, he threw the finger at John. John was all smiles. The creature gave John a dirty look, then almost ran behind his desk and sat. He refused to stand next to the taller Jerry.

Sit, Mr. Rivera, Ulises Fuentes barked at Jerry, as he attempted to make his voice sound tough. He had Jerry's folder in his hands and pretended to read from it, not wanting to make eye contact. I have received a couple of letters from Community Impact. They praise you on your work there, Mr. Rivera. But don't think for a minute that a couple of letters from your friends can keep you out of the slammer.

Ulises Fuentes removed his thick eyeglasses because he believed he looked younger, even though he was blind as a bat without them. He had a thin strand of grayish hair crossing his bald head like dead seaweed on a dirty beach. He brushed the seaweed straight back, hoping that he covered something, but he was too far gone for it to do any good. The back of his head was like a slice of old baloney and dotted with brown age spots.

When are you going to finish repairing that old house you have worked on since you left the institution? I need to make a home visit to assess for the record the kind of living your parole stipulations mandate. I do not want to visit your friend's abode. I'm sure he lives in a clean and decent place, and that will put you in a positive position without you doing any of the work to merit it.

It's almost done, sir.

What's almost done? asked Ulises in a haughty manner. He resented the sir, even though he was almost fifty and hitting sixty fast.

The house, sir, my mother's house. The one I'm fixing up, sir, Jerry replied, his patience almost gone with the ridiculous game.

Oh, OK. And Ulises put his glasses back on because his eyes watered, and he couldn't stop blinking. He refused to take out his handkerchief and wipe them dry as he usually did. OK, he repeated. Let's go over some routine questions, and we are done here. You are employed? Yes, to that. And he answered his own question. You are staying away from the criminal element and from places of ill repute? You do not carry on your person or own arms of any kind? Legal or illegal? Are all the questions I asked negative or affirmative?

Yes, Jerry answered, bored.

You mean yes? You are in violation of your parole? And Ulises perked up.

No, I mean no. You know what I mean, Jerry said, frustrated.

I do not know what you mean, Mr. Rivera. Do you or do you not do drugs or carry guns?

I do not, Jerry answered, and he bit his lower lip to control his anger.

You do not what, Mr. Rivera?

I do not do drugs. I have never done drugs.

We have random testing for that, Mr. Rivera. And don't be surprised if out of the blue we ask you to pee in a little white cup, sir. That is all, Jerry. You did good. Send in Mr. Slaughter, if you don't mind.

Jerry stood up. He towered over the little shit who sat behind his desk like a four-eyed reptile.

As Jerry walked to the door without saying a word, Ulises called out with a smile on his reptilian lips, Have a good day, pinto.

Jerry had almost reached the door and heard every word. He wanted to turn back, pick up the snake by the collar with one hand, and punch him so hard in the stomach with the other hand that the snake would puke up his breakfast and last night's dinner on his scraped-up, shitty desk. But he just kept on walking. He knew that if he did something that stupid, he would be back in Santa in time for dinner. And if he ever had to go back, he was not going back for punching a shit-eating worm like Ulises Fuentes. If he had to go back to prison, he would go back for something big, real big.

John Slaughter bit his nails, which were already down to nothing.

They want you in there, my friend, Jerry said. You next, guy.

Do they have the little white cups, Jerry? John asked, sweat on his face.

Oh yeah. There's a male nurse in there ready to take a peek at your dick and squeeze out a drip. And he's gonna make you pull down your panty hose, I mean pants, and order you to grab your ankles and spread your butt cheeks.

Jerry left the building laughing, in a good mood again. He never stayed down anymore. He had been low, way down low, and visited every corner of hell and survived. A puny jackass like Ulises Fuentes was spit on the sidewalk of life as far as he was concerned. Besides, he had to take care of business with Big Bertha before he reported back to work.

Traffic was thick on Church as cars headed west, but Jerry drove east, away from downtown. It was the lunch crowd, he thought, and he was going for lunch himself. The tasty kind. He wondered if the chili burgers at Fat Henry's were still good. He would have to go check them out but not during the busy workweek. Maybe on a Saturday or Sunday. He stayed on Church. He noticed everyone in a rush to get somewhere. He, on the other hand, drove slowly—not too slowly, but leisurely. He just loved to drive. He was so proud because he had passed the driving test his first time out and received his driving license. The written part was not difficult, but the driving test was nerve-racking, and the copper gave him the eye all the time. Little by little he adjusted to the freedom he had not experienced for years. Minor stuff, like driving a car or grocery shopping and cooking; what the hell. It didn't make sense half the time. But thank God, Max was there to help out. Max had always been there and had never failed him. He even let him use his older car. And not a bad car to practice on and run around town until he could afford his own. Max insisted he needed a license to drive the trucks the city had donated to Community Impact. They were old trucks, but they came in handy.

Jerry continued east on Church Street. He passed Baca Street, and he caught a light on Calle de los Angeles, which ran north and south. He made a right on Calle de los Angeles and headed south for a couple of blocks. He kept his eyes out for Esperanza Street, which ran east and west. He continued to think. He was big on thinking. He had spent so much time in isolation that he had made it an art.

He loved his job. The only thing that embarrassed him was when the older kids asked him for help to solve algebra equations. He could help the younger kids with basic math and even some fractions, but when they brought algebra problems to him, even basic algebra, he ran for help. He learned from the college tutors, and he was learning fast. Max, William, and

Ruth all had degrees in something. And he felt there was that gap when it came to him. He could hold his own because he was well-read, but he couldn't go deep with them, except when it came to films. Max and Max's mother, Victoria, had sent him many books when he was locked up in the dungeons of misery. Books on films and the people who populated those films had made his life a little easier. Max read excellent novels, and after he read them, he would send them to him, three or four at a time. And Victoria, Max's mother, was a librarian in Chicago, and she also sent him novels by the best writers in the world. He was fortunate he did not read trash like many of the brothers and waste time. He loved good dialogue in his movies and didn't blow out his eyes and mind, watching slapstick or tacky movies that didn't challenge the urge in him to be entertained and entertained by the best. He also worked in the prison library when he was not in isolation and read many of the classics that were ignored by the majority of the inmates. And he had access to older films on reels and tapes that had been donated to the prison for years. Numerous people who had worked in the business in some capacity retired in Santa Fe and Taos and donated many excellent films to the lockup. And Max had lived in Los Angeles for years. He had visited movie studios and seen movies being made. That was Jerry's dream—to watch all the great movies from all over the world and one day go to Hollywood and visit a studio to see a movie being made, even talk to a real director. Why not? He knew they shot films in New Mexico. He just had to find the location and take a few days off and check it out.

Jerry made a left on Esperanza, going east toward the housing units where Big Bertha lived. He recalled when he was with Max in the third or fourth grade. They played tackle football in the field with the other boys without any gear on. They banged each other around rough-style during recess. Big Bertha and a couple of her friends would stack up mounds of dirt, pointed on top, and they'd lie on them and hump the mounds. The girls stared at the sweaty boys roughhousing with smiles on their lusty faces. Max and Jerry, along with the other boys, were so young and stupid, and they ignored the needy girls.

Big Bertha developed very young. By the time they paid attention, Big Bertha had been discovered by the older boys, and it was too late for them. She became conceited, and as her tits grew bigger, she ignored Max and Jerry even more. By the time she got to high school, she was the queen, the bronze queen of Las Flores High. She also stepped out with college boys, and her future looked bright. She had plans to go to college herself. Jerry was gone during their senior year of high school, but he heard from Max that the future didn't pan out as Big Bertha had envisioned it. She got pregnant that year and married a loser. And that sometimes happened to good-looking mamas who believed their shit smelled like perfume. After a year or two of hard times and a messy divorce, she was pregnant again and married another jerk off. This marriage also lasted three or four years and ended in separation and finally in divorce. By then, Big Bertha had become friendly and smiled at anyone and disregarded the notion that she was better than folks because she had large tits. She never attended college and secured a job at the Bandera Azul—the Blue Flag Bar—owned by Luis Calles, pushing drinks.

Max told him he should go check out Big Bertha at the Bandera Azul. Jerry was aware that the Blue Flag was a rowdy place and always had been. He couldn't visit that kind of place because of his delicate status. He had an appetite for a piece of culo though, and he decided to visit the bar just before they closed, but not on a weekend.

Jerry arrived on a Thursday night and ordered a beer. The bar was way out on the edge of the barrio, close to Highway 47, west from the tracks on Mesquite Street. Calles got a lot of business from the boyeros during the summer and from the folks who lived and worked west of Highway 25. The vicinity around the bar was dark; the city ignored the area because not many people lived there. Big Bertha served him with a smile, and she kept her eyes on him. The dim light in the bar and some of the customers put him off. He couldn't really see her that well, except her breasts. Nothing could hide those mountains.

She finally came over to the end of the long bar where he sat alone and said, Drink up, Big Boy. We close in ten minutes.

This was his last chance to say something, he thought. He didn't want to wait outside in the dark for her because she might think he was a pervert. Hey, Bertha, remember me? What else could he say?

Big Bertha stopped. Her hands were full of empty glasses and bottles, and she stared at him for a few seconds. Wait a minute, she said and smiled her killer smile. Jerry, Jerry Rivera, from school? I'll be a...

It's me, he said in a low voice, still not sure how to proceed. It'd been a long time since he had hit on a woman. I was in the area and stopped in to have a beer.

Sure you were, purred Big Bertha. Haven't seen you in years. Listen, Jerry, we close in ten minutes. Hang around, and you can walk me to my car. We can talk—if you have the time, that is. Jerry still remembered that night. The longest ten minutes of his life. When she finally finished doing this and that, she grabbed her purse and said, Let's go, tiger. She told the bouncer it was cool and that she was leaving with a friend. They walked outside and left Calles and the bouncer to close up.

Jerry was still nervous and silent when he walked out with Big Bertha. He thought she would say good night when they reached her car, and he would have to go home alone and beat his meat again.

When they got to her beat-up car parked in the back of the bar, he knew time was slipping away fast and said, You look good.

So do you, she answered.

And then she floored him when she said, Are we going to give each other compliments all night or find a bed somewhere and fuck like the devil was betting on it? And she laughed like she meant it. Since that night, he knew Big Bertha had a sense of humor. He followed her home, and they had sex until dawn.

Jerry kept east on Esperanza until he saw the housing units on the right side of the street. The houses were clustered together and had been painted a rust color some years ago. Now the paint was faded and peeling from time and neglect. The houses had small yards in front with larger ones in the back and some trees. He could see the dry golden leaves around the gray trees like a blanket that protected them from the night chill. Other leaves were scattered about the yard and waited for the feet of young children to crunch them into dust. He parked his car next to hers in the driveway and walked up to the screen door. He tapped on the screen door, and a voice from within the house said, Come on in, Jerry. The door is open. He walked in and closed the wooden door behind him.

Big Bertha Parra came out of the bathroom like Cleopatra of the Nile. Her long black hair was wet but not dripping. She had on a bathrobe that once had been white, the kind they provide for guests in decent hotels, but some guests brought them home. She smiled. Her thick, fleshy lower lip did not complement her thin upper one when her lips parted. But when Jerry sucked on them, he didn't mind. Because of her bronze skin, her teeth seemed whiter than they really were. Her tan was natural from head to toe, and her skin was soft, except around her lower middle belly, where she was getting thick. The stretch marks were discolored and evident. He closed his eyes when he visited the Valley of the Dolls. Her huge papayas fought gravity but still held their own.

Have no fear, my big daddy! Bertha's here. And she laughed out loud. I just got out of the tub. She hugged him and kissed him on the mouth, giving him her tongue.

Jerry put his left arm around her waist, pulled her in tight to him, and placed his right hand on her tits. He loved those huge melons, and even though they looked more at the ground these days instead of straight at you, they were still firm. And her nipples resembled large, juicy, dark-brown olives ready to harvest. He helped her out of the robe and let it slip to the floor as she struggled to unbutton his shirt and flung it on top of the couch. She pulled him tight to her and kissed the scorpion tattoos on both sides of his neck. She wanted to grab his buns of brown brick and show him why the ancient Greeks were so intelligent, in case he didn't know. But not yet—he might be a little sensitive in that area. They usually were when they first came out, she assumed.

Jerry was hard as penitentiary steel, but she didn't want to say that. Big Bertha grabbed him by the hand away from the cheap leather couch and into her bedroom. The couch was for lesser men she sometimes brought home. Men with high expectations who juiced after a couple of strokes. Then they stared at her with their limp worm between their legs, red in the face, with an angry expression. They reproached her for their inadequacies and expected her to do all the work. But Jerry was a stallion. Young, lean and mean like a nuclear submarine, and ready to spread his wings after being locked up in a dark cellar for many long years and played with his five sisters or worse. He was shy and unlearned. She would train him like a seal pup, and every time she showed him her fish, he would splash out of the water and fly to her. She knew her stock was falling and losing value; soon she'd be at the penny scale, and maybe, just maybe, she could keep this one.

Big Bertha led the Big Boy by the hand to her bed. She grabbed the top of the bedspread and pulled it straight back to the floor, along with everything else that lay on top. She unbuckled his belt, kissed him, and pulled his trousers down, drawers and all. She pushed him back steadily onto the bed, where he landed on his back, and his flagpole pointed to the heavens. She removed his shoes and the trousers already on his ankles and placed her soft lips on the iron rod that seemed to expand in her mouth. She stopped before the Big Boy juiced and moved up to stick her moist tongue in his mouth.

Jerry wanted to say, Don't stop! Don't ever stop! But he knew it was his turn. He sucked on the enlarged nipples. He moved from one to the other. He couldn't make up his mind which one tasted better. He was intoxicated with the aroma of the lavender bath gel she had bathed with. She gave him a gentle cue with her firm hands, and he knew it was time to visit downtown. She moaned and murmured sweet nothings as he maneuvered his tongue in and out of bush city. He was learning fast. One thing he learned pronto was to keep his eyes closed when his tongue reached the stretch marks and then keep them closed in bush country. She had a slight odor, but it wasn't bad. He could handle it. After he'd spent some time downtown, she pulled him on top of her. He mounted her and pounded her without mercy. The bed creaked, and they rocked and rolled to the Stones' "(I Can't Get No) Satisfaction," which she always put on when they made love. Then there was a huge explosion, and she thrust her hips up with the strength of a mule and held him tight, with her nails in his back like a wrestler until he got hard again.

After an hour or more of dancing, the young couple lay in bed and talked. Jerry sipped water, and Big Bertha drank lemonade with ice. They held hands. Jerry released her hand and turned sideways to face her.

Hey, Bertha, that bouncer who works with you—ever do him?

Big Bertha placed her glass on the nightstand and turned to face Jerry.

No. We call him Dog. He likes that. I have never seen him with a woman. He claims he has a girlfriend, but I've never seen her. He spends all his time at the bar helping Canas. He likes Canas a lot, and maybe he fucks Canas. And she laughed.

They still call Luis Calles Canas?

Oh yeah. You know the story, right?

Refresh my memory. I kinda forgot.

This is what I heard, Bertha said as she sucked on a piece of lemon. One night after Canas closed the bar, he was doing a waitress on top of a table. He claimed he saw his grandmother naked on top of the bar. She screamed her head off at him to stop screwing around and go home to his wife. The thing is, his grandmother had been dead for years. The next morning, his hair had turned white—all of it. And from then on, the name Canas stuck.

Wow, Jerry said. That's something. A little scary, if you ask me. You ever do Canas?

No. He tried. But couldn't get it to work, poor guy. He is the nicest man, Jerry. When we're real busy, he helps with the tables. And any tips he gets, he passes them on to me. And he pays me cash, so I can still get my county check and stamps. He always buys stuff for the kids during the holidays and on their birthdays. He allows those drunks to keep tabs, and most pay them off. The first of the month, they come in swaggering with cash in their pockets after cashing their checks. By the middle of the month they're begging for tabs. By the end of month, them suckers are desperate. The tabs are too high, and they hang out, suck on a beer, and wait for some fool to buy them another one. And even then, Canas has instructed Dog not to kick them out as long as they have beer in the bottle.

Does it get rowdy on weekends? Jerry asked and sipped a drink of water. Like it used to?

Not really. During the summer, we get a lot of business from the boyeros. There's a rough bunch of vatos. And locals who have been banned from the other watering holes. They know Canas is cool, and they drop in to spend money. They get it on with the Tejanos, you know—that kind of shit.

A lot of drug activity going on in the bar?

Not inside the bar. Maybe outside. Dog patrols outside. He carries a leaded baseball bat. You know, to check on the cars and shit.

Does he ever use the bat?

Oh! Let me tell you. And Big Bertha sat up with her back on the headboard of the bed. Jerry did the same, tired of being in the same position. There was this pack of thugs, Big Bertha continued. They came in from El Paso, and don't ask me why. I know there are plenty of places to booze in El Paso, not to mention Juarez. I have no idea if they came to buy or sell drugs. It was like five or six of them, and they always parked their car next to that little hill. The little hill facing the road. You seen it. They never parked close to the bar in the parking area. I mean, there's always plenty of parking. It's a huge parking lot. Anyway, they never caused any trouble, and they dropped their money not only on beer, but they mixed. Canas told me and Dog, as long as they spent money and were peaceful, to serve them. They tipped handsomely and never came on to me too aggressive like some punks do.

Big Bertha took the last sip of her lemonade and asked Jerry if he wanted another glass of water. She was curious why he never wanted ice with his water, even on hot days.

Anyway, she continued, one hot summer night last year, the hoods from El Chuco got into an argument with a local. They took the discussion outside, and it turned ugly quick. They were beating the crap out of him until Dog attempted to break up the beating with his leaded baseball bat. And you know. Big Bertha licked her lips and still tasted Jerry. The thugs turned on Dog. Dog ain't nobody to fuck around with. He swung that bat and hit the first pendejo so hard on the shoulder I heard bone crack. Honest to God. The bat splintered with the force, and they came at him like hyenas on a wounded wildebeest. He kept them at bay with what was left of the bat, but they were all around him. They kicked and jumped back when Dog turned to swing at the kicker. Then another would slug him or kick him on his blind side. They couldn't put the Dog down, but they stung him like angry wasps. Finally, a little shit face put a shoulder on Dog from behind, a flying tackle above the knees. The sonovobitch must have played football, and Dog went down like a giant oak tree. He fell on his back and lost the piece of bat when he hit the dirt because it was kicked out of his hand. Then they surged in like vultures to finish him off. Any other man would have cried uncle, but not Dog. He swung with his powerful arms and huge fists and struggled like hell to stand up. The kicks and blows from the crazy bastards rained on him nonstop. I screamed at them to back off, but they wanted blood, and they got it. As Dog came up on his knees, one of the killers flashed a razor and slashed Dog on the lower back. A long horizontal gash that cut through the leather vest he always wore, through his shirt and undershirt, and opened the skin. The blood gushed out, dark red, and soaked his lower torso.

Big Bertha wiped her brow with a tissue from a box she always kept on her nightstand. She drank the rest of Jerry's water without asking him. She breathed heavy and kept looking at Jerry to see if he was awake.

Jerry was all ears. Don't leave me hanging, he finally said. It was a good story, and he loved good stories, even if this one was fiction. Fiction was the essence that made his life livable.

Let me catch my breath, Jerry, she said. As you can see, it was quite a night, and I still get goose bumps when I recall it. All this time, Canas was in his back office, probably taking a nap, which he did on occasion when business was slow. I ran in the bar and screamed that they were killing Dog to see if Canas or the other men in the bar would come out and help him. By this time, Canas heard me screaming and came out with the double-barreled sawed-off shotgun he kept behind the bar. The blood, even though he couldn't see it, made Dog go crazy. He half crawled, half stumbled on his hands and knees toward the door of the bar because he knew in his gut that Canas was bringing the gun out to him. The punks continued to kick him and punch him as he attempted to reach the door of the bar. The slasher couldn't get a good angle on Dog because all the others did not let up. When they saw Canas with the gun at the door of the bar, pointing it at them, they froze. And they paid dear for that error. Because when they stopped beating on Dog, he made a rush for the door, grabbed the gun from Canas, blew the slasher's arm away at the shoulder, and put him on his ass. The blade fragmented. All this happened in a split second. When the jackals saw the gun in Dog's hand and that he fired to kill without hesitation or warning shots, they split. Like bats out of hell, Jerry. And she laughed again. Dog shot another one in the ass, and he went down. I know it's not funny, Jerry, but I can't help it. The others ran into the night and disappeared. Some said they ran all the way to El Paso. I never believed it. They had their car on the ready, and the car was also gone.

Big Bertha kissed Jerry on the mouth and waited for his response.

Jerry could have started another marathon, but he wanted to hear the conclusion of the story and head back to the center to get some work done. So what happened, Bertha? What happened to Dog?

Bertha, a little disappointed that Jerry didn't take the bait, said, Anyway, when Canas handed over the shotgun to Dog, he went inside the bar to the phone and called the police and an ambulance for Dog. Canas knew that Dog, with a gun in his hand, could hold off an army. When the ambulance arrived, Dog didn't want to go to the hospital and leave us alone because he believed the gangsters would return with the rest of the pack and hurt us. Canas assured him that they would only patch him up, and he would be back before the bar closed. He finally agreed and left with the second ambulance. The medics in the first ambulance taking the wounded assassins didn't trust Dog to ride with them. They feared the bleeding rats would never reach the hospital alive. The cops came, of course. They wrote their report. They looked at the gun, smiled at Canas, and followed the ambulance to the hospital.

Quite a ruckus, Jerry said. Did the pendejos come back with the rest of their gang?

No. We were worried until Canas drove up with Dog all patched up. Dog went home and brought along more guns and a couple of his dogs. When the bar closed, he left one dog inside the bar, and he went up to the roof of the building with his guns and the other dog. As you know, it's an old adobe building with a flat roof. He made himself a little shelter on the roof, spent the night, and waited for the fuckers. He spent several nights up on the roof until Canas ordered him to take his dogs and guns and go home.

Where does Dog live?

You know that dumpy trailer park near Highway 47 on Martinez Street? Not too far from the bar. See, Dog was a wonder. He was homeless and broke when he ended up at the Blue Flag. Canas got to talking to him and offered him a job as a bouncer and cleanup man. At first Dog slept inside the bar until Canas secured for him a small trailer at the park. And he has been there ever since, loyal to Canas as anyone.

That is some story, Bertha. I gotta run. Before I leave though, let me ask you—can you cook?

Oh. I can cook, Big Boy, in bed, or haven't you noticed? And she laughed out loud. Then she said when she settled down, Of course I can cook. I can boil water. And she giggled. No, seriously, I can cook. I have to. I have two kids, and they are always hungry. Junk food is OK once in a while, but it gets expensive, and it's not good for them. Bertha smiled. She believed the Big Boy was thinking about moving in. She wouldn't mind having a hunk with a job to hang around the house and help out with the kids.

I thought you had three kids, Jerry said as he put on his trousers.

I do, answered Bertha. She was disappointed because Jerry was leaving. My older son is in Houston with his father, a big-time loser. His father, not my son. He's a teen and wanted stuff all the time. New and expensive stuff and not hand-me-downs. Little prick. Besides, he was a bully at school and beat up on his younger brother and sister. He stayed with my mother for a while. She takes care of my kids when I work, and she spoiled him. Grandmothers tend to do that. Anyway, I got tired of his bullshit and fighting with his father over child support. One day I told the jackass, you take him and forget the child support, which I never got anyway, and he did.

Jerry put on his shoes and looked for his shirt. He was ready to leave before Big Bertha gave him another hard-on and they spent the rest of the afternoon in bed.

Why did you ask me if I could cook? Bertha asked as she followed Jerry to the living room. She picked up her bathrobe from the floor and put it on but left it open. She exposed her large tits just in case Jerry was interested.

Oh, Jerry said as he buttoned his shirt. I just wanted to know because I'm fixing up my mom's house, and the kitchen is almost done. I wanted to know if you could teach me the basic stuff to cook. Nothing fancy. Stuff like beans, rice, chili, some chicken, you know, stuff.

Not a problem, Bertha said with her hands in the pockets of the robe. Tell me when it's ready, and I'll come over, and we can cook…food, I mean. Oh, Jerry, before you go. And she moved closer to him. Would you, and she put on an innocent face and pleaded with her big brown eyes. Would you tattoo a heart on your chest in red with a capital B in the center? Whata you say, Big Boy?

Jerry looked at her as if she was crazy. I don't do TTs anymore, Bertha. I'm trying to get rid of the ones I have. But I'll think about it, sweetheart. See you. And he walked out the door.

Big Bertha was disappointed. Not only about the tattoo, but he didn't even kiss her goodbye. He never did. Then she said out loud, Oh shit. I gotta pick up the kids from school before they call again.

CHAPTER 6

That same day, when Jerry was visiting Big Bertha and Max was elsewhere, William Moreno and his wife, Ruth, were in William's office at the Community Impact building, talking. Ruth had cleared out her own office so that Clairisa Cotton could utilize it when she needed the space to talk to a student or staff member in private. She left the desk and some chairs for Claire. Ruth decided that it was the best office for Claire because it was located on the east corner of the huge CI building. It was a distance from the newer cubicle structures that had been constructed when they moved into the building. These two offices were occupied by Max and William. They were close to the front door of the center, facing Santa Teresa Street. Ruth had moved her old Mac computer along with some files and placed them in William's office, along with other knickknacks. William's office was smaller, and it was a tight fit, but they didn't mind, as long as they were together. The closer the better.

I think that's everything, Ruth said to William as she moved his stuff around to make room for hers. Claire was surprised when I offered her my office. And she placed folders in a metal cabinet. She fought me all the way. I convinced her she needed the space more than I did. I told her you spent most of your time out in the field, and I'm in and out a lot. She finally agreed. Claire is so nice. She was happy with a small space in a corner or a classroom. I said no way. You need an office. The classrooms are always utilized. I'm so glad she's helping out.

We all are, William said. Anything else you need to be moved, babe?

No. I think that will do it, William. Thank you so much. Sit. And let's take a break before the kids show up.

William and Ruth sat in the crowded office close to each other with their chairs turned to face the door. The door was open, and they could see if anyone arrived through the front door of the building. Ruth placed the fingers of her right hand on William's lips.

Ruth, William said with his eyes half-closed. I love you, my darling, my little mamita. I love you ever so much. Let me thrust my tongue deep into your throat. And they both giggled as if they were in the back seat of a car on their first date.

It means so much to me when you call me darling. I think it's so romantic. Darling. What a beautiful word, and coming from you, William, it makes it even more special.

Remember, Ruth, the first day we moved into the building? We were in your office, and we made out on top of your desk.

Oh yeah. How can I forget? It was hot, real hot. Too bad we can't do it here, right now, but we can't, sorry to say.

Not anymore, my love. This place is too busy now. But thank God we're married, and we can go home and enjoy our lovemaking without interruptions.

Aren't you glad we're married, William? It was such a hassle. Always looking over our shoulders and sneaking a quickie here and a quickie there. And our parents are so conservative and always anticipated the worst.

Oh, I agree, sweetheart. And William kissed her on the mouth. A quick kiss so it wouldn't lead to anything more substantial.

Ruth settled back in her chair and said, William, baby, I don't want to change the subject. You said, about three months ago…you said you would tell me about Jerry.

William kissed her hand and said, I did, Ruth. And because we are man and wife now, and Jerry is part of the staff, I guess I should. But remember, Ruth, this is a very touchy subject. Not even Jerry or Max talk about it. So please, never, ever let a word of this spill out, because Max will know it came from me. I know you won't. I just want to make sure.

Don't worry, babe. Ruth was a little hurt. I won't breathe a word to anyone. I promise.

I'm sorry, Ruth. I didn't mean it like you would. It's just that Jerry and Max joke around, and you might think it's OK to mention something from that time in their past, but it's not. They never talk about it. And no one does, especially when Max and Jerry are around. I apologize if I offended you in any way. I didn't mean to, mi amor.

No. I get it, William. I mean those guys are tight. I know the story—the public version, that is. But I want to know the real story, what really happened. That's all. And I love it when you call me amor. She smiled.

OK, babe, you got it. William turned his chair to face Ruth with his back to the door, and their knees touched. This happened about nine or ten years ago, during the summer. I was a couple of years behind them, and you were a year behind me. So that made them juniors ready to go on to their senior year and me a freshman. Jerry lived with his mother and an abusive stepfather. The man got drunk and beat up on Jerry's mom. Max told me the story when they organized my bachelor's party. He had been drinking with the rest of the guys. They started early. We were in the other CI office alone, just before he drove me to his house where the party was going to be held. We sat, and Max took out a bottle of brandy and some paper cups. He wasn't drunk. Max never gets drunk; that's not his thing. He said Jerry Rivera was going to be released from prison, and since he was going to work with us, he thought it was better if I knew the truth of the tragic incident that sent Jerry to prison. I was like you, Ruth. I knew bits and pieces of the story. But never anything that came from Max or Jerry. No one did.

Are you sure you want to talk about it, William? I mean, Max told you with confidence that it wouldn't be repeated.

Like I said, Ruth, we're married. We share everything. The good with the bad and the in-between. As Jerry got older, the stepfather threatened to kick Jerry's ass many times, especially when he came to the defense of his mother. You have to realize, Ruth, that Jerry and Max were pals, even back then. Max's father was killed in a hunting accident when he was five or six years old, and his mother moved to Chicago soon after. Max was left with his maternal grandparents and later started to hang out with Jerry, whose own father had left and gone to Texas. The father wanted to take Jerry with him, but Jerry refused. Jerry wanted to take care of his mother, as most boys do. Jerry and Max practically grew up together, both without a father. When Jerry was older, and he saw more black eyes that his mother couldn't cover up, he decided that enough was enough. The stepfather beat up on Jerry for trying to help his mom. Jerry wasn't a little kid anymore. And that's when Max decided to make up a plan to stop the beast and discourage him from being so abusive.

Did they include you? Ruth asked.

Are you kidding? I was just a kid in their eyes. They're only a couple of years older. They were up and coming. You know. They had reputations. They could and would kick ass. Anyway, Jerry threatened the drunk in not very polite words that his nuts were going to be sawed off if he didn't mend his ways. Apparently, some people heard him, and that proved damaging later on. The man did not change or even try. He got worse. He ridiculed Jerry and pushed him around. One day he slapped Jerry in the face, which to a guy is more insulting than a punch. Jerry's mom intervened, and she got the worst of it. Jerry, after making sure his mom was not hurt bad, ran to Max's house trembling with anger. He shouted that the beast had to go down. Max calmed him down and reminded him of the plan. You know Max; he always has a plan.

And what was the plan? Hit-and-run?

Funny, but close. They knew his MO. Every Friday night the man got polluted at Veto's Bar, the one on San Mateo Street. It went out of business a couple of years ago. The bar was close to Jerry's house, and the drunk didn't have to drive—not that he could in his condition. They would kick him out of the bar a little before closing. But because he was a regular, they let him out the back door. Maybe they figured he was in less danger stumbling out the back and not exposed to cars and trucks. Who knows? It was a shortcut to his house through empty lots and abandoned houses. The path was well traveled except at night, and he could walk or crawl on it without much difficulty.

Please, sweetheart. I believe I can figure out the rest.

No, Ruth, wait, William pleaded. He was burning to tell the story to someone now that he had started. Stay with me—the most interesting part is yet to come.

You mean the most violent part? I'm sorry. Go on, babe. I asked for it.

See, the plan was simple and well thought out. You know Max. It was only to scare the wife beater, and that was all. Max emphasized that to Jerry. After the surprise, they were going to camp out in the mountains. Max said they left town and found a campsite, stayed until nightfall, and then drove back to town close to ambush time. They parked the car behind an abandoned house about a block away from the site and waited. They had cloth bags over their shoes, gloves on their hands, and they were ready. They had a baseball bat between them, and that was all they had. But that was all they needed, because it was easy to dispose of. It was about a quarter to two in the morning when they left the car, walked to the designated spot, and waited for the target to show up. Max said the waiting was nerve-racking, and he said he whispered to Jerry if he wanted to cancel the surprise, but Jerry shook his head and said no way. Max could see that Jerry was tensed. They had been in situations before. Max knew Jerry wasn't a runner, a rabbit, as they called the fellows who panic and run at the start of a fight. No way. To Max, Jerry was solid. The best cornerman he could count on. But this time, the man who was going to taste the bat was his stepfather. The man his mom slept with. This might be a little different, and they had talked about it. Jerry insisted on being the basher, and Max told him, Be my guest.

William paused and studied Ruth. He knew Ruth loathed violence, but she had to know that Jerry hadn't done time for a senseless killing. Sure, it was senseless to many, but not to Max and Jerry. Jerry did time for a miscalculation, he thought. Maybe that was the word. But he did it for a noble cause—to save his mother—and who could argue with that?

May I have a sip of water, babe?

Ruth passed William the water bottle. She had heard enough, but she knew she wouldn't stop William from telling it. He wanted to tell it, and that was human nature, she believed. And who better to tell it to than her, his wife? As long as he wasn't involved. But what if he was? It wouldn't change her love for him. Nothing would. Well, almost nothing, and she bit her lower lip.

So what happened? Ruth asked, knowing damn well what had happened.

William took another sip of water and passed the bottle back to her. He licked his lips and continued. By now, Max was getting a little more animated, like he had to talk about it. Then Max said that they finally heard uneven footsteps coming their way. The babbling of a drunk getting closer to their little trap was scary to Max…but exciting at the same time. And Jerry, Max said, grabbed the bat a little too quickly from his hands for his liking but said nothing. They waited as their hearts beat faster and the adrenalin raced through their veins and pumped them up. The drunk stopped to take a piss, and the waiting was like an eternity. Gallons of piss later, the drunk continued on, sluggishly. He staggered. And probably anticipated his comfortable bed and the woman who waited for him in his cozy house. He finally reached the shrubs that hid Max and Jerry. The few clouds that they had not noticed before seemed to race over and cover the moon, as if to aid them in their effort. As the drunk weaved by, Max, from his crouching position, sprang and forced his shoulder into the drunk's lower legs, and the drunk flipped backward and crashed down on top of him. Max scrambled out from under the drunk and pushed the drunk away from him. He expected Jerry to be making use of the bat. The drunk was on his back and made a feeble effort to get up. That's what Max thought the drunk seemed to be doing. Or going for a knife or worse, a gun. A loaded pistol. Max pleaded with Jerry to do it and pronto. The drunk began to sob. Max didn't know if the man cried for Jerry to spare him or cried for Jerry to help him. Somehow, he was aware that it was Jerry who held the big bat. And he hovered over him like an avenging angel of death. Then Max saw tears in Jerry's eyes. His arms seemed to be frozen, and the big stick was not moving any which way, while precious minutes ticked away. Max grabbed the bat from Jerry and swung down so hard on the drunk's head that he believed he had cracked all the bones in his hands.

A grunt was heard, and the drunk stayed down and silent. The image of Jerry's mom with black eyes and cut lips came to Max as he went crazy and swung the bat a thousand times on the drunk's head. The head was turned to mush, Max strongly believed. Jerry finally stopped him, but only after a struggle for the bloody bat that dripped with gore. Max gave up the bat. He whispered, out of breath. His heart thumped and churned in his chest so badly that talking was painful. He told Jerry to get the wallet. Jerry said he couldn't touch the dead man. Max couldn't argue and couldn't blame him, either. Max reached for the back pocket that held the soiled wallet. He took out a couple of dirty bills from the wallet and pitched the wallet on top of the crumpled body. It had to appear like a rip-off gone bad; that was part of the plan.

William paused. He took a drink from the water bottle and thought that maybe it wasn't a good idea after all to tell Ruth about what had happened that warm summer night ten years ago. But it was too late to worry about it now.

Ruth touched William on the arm and said in a tender, loving way, Please go on, babe. Don't stop now.

Are you sure, Ruth?

Yes, I'm sure.

OK, you got it. They ran back to the car, Max told me. They wrapped the bat in the sport pages and headed back up the mountain to their campsite. They prayed no one had seen them or, worse, recognized them. Max said the drive back up the mountain was no picnic. His heart and breathing had settled back to a normal pace, and there were few cars on the road. And that was a good thing. Jerry was steeped in silence and stared straight ahead. Max, on the other hand, didn't want to seem callous and respected Jerry's silence. But Max wanted him to break it soon—the sooner the better. See, Ruth, Max needed a high five. But more than that, he needed to know and had to know if what they had done was what they both wanted. That the plan had succeeded or failed—anything. He couldn't be left hanging. He needed feedback, and here is where Max got emotional. He attempted to hide it, but it was difficult. He said he had taken a life. He was sure the man was dead. No one could take that much damage to the head and live to talk about it, he rationalized. And maybe it was not a good life, but a life nevertheless. And he had to be told that it was a good thing he did, and not tomorrow or the following year. Can you imagine, Ruth, the psychological drama Max was going through at that young age when it hit him that he had taken a life?

I don't know what to say, William. And Ruth had tears in her eyes. I'm surprised and shocked. I don't know. This is something. And they were so young. Young, kids…only kids.

It is sad, Ruth. Let me tell you the rest. Finally, Max told me he broke the silence that draped them like the dark shadow of a giant vulture. He asked Jerry to say something. To give it to him straight. That he had to know. Jerry, responded in a dejected voice. He said, Sorry, Max. I let you down. I couldn't do it. My balls went dry. What can I say? I should open the door and jump out of the car. And maybe with a little luck, I'll be killed. I know that's a coward's way out, but that's what I am: a coward. Then Max assured him that it was his fault because he didn't give him enough time. That he grabbed the bat away from him too soon.

What else could Max say, Ruth? William asked her, not sure himself what Max could say or what anybody could say under those circumstances. He couldn't handle another tragedy. And he sure didn't want anything to happen to Jerry, his best buddy. Max reminded Jerry that they were almost at the campsite. Once there they could start a fire, settle in, and talk. You're not a coward, he repeated several times. I know you, c'mon now. Jerry settled down and stopped talking about jumping out of the car. Max still kept an eye on him and slowed down some. They finally reached the campsite. They started a fire. They tossed in the bloody bat, newspaper, booties, even the gloves, and opened a bottle of Sotol. They sipped their drinks slowly. They couldn't sleep anyway and were too scared to. They just kept their eyes on the fire as their future danced in the flames.

It was done, Max continued. He didn't like himself one bit at that moment. Maybe he thought, just maybe, Jerry really loved his stepfather. And he just wanted him scared a bit. Roughed up. He realized he had gone overboard with the violence. It was at that moment that he made a promise to the stars up in the sky as they sparkled like fool's gold not to indulge in any more senseless violence unless it was to defend his loved ones. He put more wood on the fire. It had to burn white. In the morning, they would scatter the ashes. They couldn't afford to leave any kind of evidence around. They kept their fingers crossed that no ranger would surprise them to check to see if they were doing drugs. The Sotol was giving him a buzz. He put the bottle away because Jerry wasn't touching it. He inched into his sleeping bag. They weren't tent campers. Their kind of camping was open sky. A potato in the fire for dinner, and that took care of the dishes. No frills, Max insisted. Only good open-air camping. A bottle and a sleeping bag; that was luxury for some. A bottle and a blanket were closer to the truth for others.

William paused. He noticed that Ruth seemed uncomfortable. You OK, honey? I can stop if you wish.

No, babe. I'm good. And Ruth attempted a weak smile. It was sad, she thought, but also disturbing. William knew so many of the exact details. She knew Max was a good storyteller, and William was good on exact reporting, but this…this was…what if William had been there all the time? What if he was not telling the whole truth? No way, she told herself. Not William. Not her William. And she tried to smile again. Please go on, baby, she said, and she put the insane thought behind her.

Are you sure you're OK with this, Ruth? I can stop. Just say the word. You know Max. Even if it grieved him to talk about it, he's a good storyteller.

He read my mind, Ruth speculated. Oh, I know. Please go on.

William cleared his throat and continued. He wanted to finish the story before Max or Jerry came in and spoiled the ending. Max wanted to talk to Jerry. He could see Jerry needed space and time to chew on it and make up his own mind on which way he was going to lean. He couldn't do it for him. Jerry was his closest friend. He still is. A true brother. A brother he never had. He knew Jerry was hurting. Max couldn't take the hurt away. He could try, but only Jerry could do that. As I mentioned before, Ruth, when his father left Jerry's mom, Jerry stayed with his mother. He could have gone with his father, but he wanted to stay and protect his mother. He never thought that in the coming years he was going to take some beatings along with his mom from that woman beater. That night Max slept on and off. He expected the cops to come and lock them up. He would doze off for ten minutes or less and then jump up when a field mouse or squirrel ran through their camp. Then he would doze off again, have a crazy dream, and then up again. He waited for the police car that never appeared. He didn't think Jerry slept a wink either, but he couldn't be sure. Morning finally came and then the afternoon and still no cops. Jerry said little. He was still sad. They packed up, scattered the ashes, and drove down the mountain to face the music. When they arrived in town, there was nothing to alert them of anything out of the ordinary happening. A typical late Saturday afternoon in the Eastside barrio. He dropped Jerry off in front of his house. Jerry's mother, all in black, came out and embraced him. Max drove off. He didn't want to see Jerry's mother. That would come later. He wanted them to mourn in private. He was sure she felt something for the deceased.

And when did they pick up the boys? Ruth asked, a little disappointed with the outcome. She couldn't explain why, and that made her feel uncomfortable.

It took the cops about a week to put two and two together, William continued. Some bozo claimed that he'd heard Jerry threaten the drunk on several occasions. And they figured Max had a hand in it since they were best friends and were together that night. Max told Jerry before they were separated not to say a word; the cops had nothing on them. On the second or third day of incarceration, while Jerry's mom and Max's grandparents were hustling to get them out of jail, the cops released Max to his grandparents. When Max asked them about Jerry, they told him not to worry about Jerry and to thank his lucky stars he wasn't going on an extended visit up north. The DA offered Jerry a plea. Jerry gave them a confession and was sentenced as an adult. The charges were reduced to voluntary manslaughter from second-degree murder. And because of his age and the physical abuse meted out by his stepfather to his mother, he would be out in five years with the max of seven years with good behavior. Jerry gave the cops the story that he and he alone did in his stepfather. And after the hit, he met Max, and they went camping. The drunk was pounded to death next to a pomegranate bush. I don't know if you remember, Ruth, but the paper called it the Pomegranate Murder. Some people got a little scared. They believed there was a killer on the loose in the Eastside. And when Jerry confessed, it was all good again. The DA ran for governor on the publicity that he had prosecuted and secured a conviction, ending the terror of the Pomegranate killer. Even though the asshole lost, it was a tight race all the way. Max was not allowed to see Jerry after the plea, and the grandparents shipped him off to California with relatives before he did something stupid. That's the story Max told me, babe. And I don't have any reason not to believe him.

Ruth had a sad look on her pretty face. She didn't like the fact that William continued to say that drunk when referring to the dead man. It was a total disregard for the deceased, but what did it matter now? What really mattered was Max, and she said she couldn't believe it was Max. All this time I believed it was Jerry. I remember when we returned to school in September. It was still a hot item. Some of the kids were in shock. Jerry became a hero in some circles. They were saying he defended his mother from that monster. And even now, some of the women at the community meetings admire Jerry for what he did to defend his mother. They say they feel safe around him because they claim their husbands talk the talk but would never lift a finger to defend them from a nut as Jerry did. And now you're telling me Max was the killer. Max, the intellectual. Mr. Cool? Wow! It floors me, William. It really does. It's kind of creepy. It—

Please, Ruth! Stop it. How do you think I felt? Everyone believed it was Jerry. Not only did he do the time, but look at Max and look at Jerry. I mean, Max is bad; don't get me wrong. But Max didn't have a problem with the drunk. Sure, the brute hit Jerry's mom, but to go off and bash in his brains with a baseball bat. I mean, how many men do you know who beat on their wives?

At this time, Nelson Sola ran into the building as if his pants were on fire. He ran straight to Ruth's old office. He hadn't even bothered to glance at William's cubicle.

Ruth! Ruth! She took it, Ruth. She took it.

Ruth rushed out of William's office and called him over to her. Nelson. What's the matter? Who took what?

Nelson, breathing hard and all sweaty from the run, said, My teacher. She took my jacket, Ruth—my teacher…

William also came out of the office and not in the best of moods. We told you, he almost yelled. We told you not to wear your jacket to school until we cleared it with the school board.

Nelson, not expecting to see William, froze behind Ruth and struggled not to shed tears.

It's OK, Nelson. It's OK, Ruth said comfortingly and put her arm around him. It's fine. I'll talk to the teacher and get it back for you. You can wear mine. Would you like that?

Really, Ruth. Can I? Can I? Nelson cried out, all smiles. Then he said, But yours has your name on it. I…I can't wear it with your name on it.

Not a problem, Nelson, see? And Ruth removed the plastic name tag on her jacket. She took off the jacket and helped Nelson put it on.

Awesome, Ruth. Thanks. Thank you. I was cold this morning. That's why I wore it to school. Honest, Ruth. I was cold.

It's OK, Nelson. Listen. I got some new math problems for Carlitos. Remember, you were going to help him with his math? Ruth, her arm around Nelson's shoulder, walked him to the classroom and left William behind, fuming.

CHAPTER 7

The following day, close to noon, Max Luna, the director of Community Impact, sat in his office behind his desk. The office was a refurbished cubicle. It was furnished with a desk, three or four chairs, and an old gray metal filing cabinet. The desk faced a large window, and through the window, Max could see the boxing ring in the middle of the building. The old building was around one hundred thousand square feet. The building had been used as a boys' club and boxing center when the city vacated it. They'd had the ring built, and it had stayed because no one had bothered to dismantle it. Ruth and William had stepped out for lunch, and the students were not expected until they were released from school. Jerry Rivera was working out with the weights in the workout area behind the ring, and Max couldn't see him.

In the office, facing Max, with his back to the window, was a man in a suit and tie, conversing with Max. He was of medium height with cropped hair and a red, pockmarked face with dried, peeling acne scars. Max was wearing a white polo shirt and khaki trousers, his usual attire. His long black hair was brushed to the back of his head and held with a rubber band. He was clean-shaven, and his olive skin was smooth, without flaws. It was obvious he took good care of himself without making a big production about it.

The man was all business, briefcase and all. I tell you, he said to Max and smiled. His thin lips parted and exposed teeth that were no strangers to tobacco. This is the deal. The mother of all deals. It's like taking candy from a baby. We can make a very handsome profit, you and me, the man continued, delighted. I can return the note to you in less than twenty-four hours with no risk to you. The deal is set at my end. Twenty-five grand, and I can double your investment.

Max looked at the man and tried to show some interest. He was familiar with this type of animal. A parasite, always looking for new blood to suck. They wore suits now, carried briefcases, and made deals in offices.

None of the hiding and sneaking around in dark corners. No, sir. Not anymore. Now they lobbied for legitimacy and demanded respect.

So what do you think, my friend? continued the man. More persistent than a snake oil salesman of old. He was annoyed that this hayseed was taking his fucking time to make up his fucking mind. This is a sweet deal, man, he said. And a nostril hair peeked out of his nose when he smiled. I just want you to make some fast green.

Max finally said, I think I get the picture. You're a smart hombre to come up with such a sophisticated plan. You have some real talent for… for planning and…thinking—yeah, for thinking and coming up with a gem of a setup such as this.

Max saw Jerry standing in front of the ring looking toward the office window. Max stood up and gestured with his hand for Jerry to join them. Jerry had been hitting the heavy bag and was still wearing his gloves. He was in a tank top and cutoffs, and he wore gym shoes without socks.

Let me introduce you to Jerry, my director of finance, Max said to the man. Jerry handles all the financial data and signs all vouchers and transfers. He has a keen eye for this type of business. Jerry, Max continued, attempting to come off as earnest, this man is a true genius. A man with a plan. And guess what, Jerry. He wants to make us some easy—what did you call it?—green stuff.

The man looked at Jerry, who was all sweaty and smelly. He said to himself, Oh man, another muscle-headed jerk off, God, give me patience. He didn't want to look at Jerry. He had seen enough. But he had to, and he attempted a weak smile. His words came out of his mouth, but his thin lips remained stiff. His red face showed telltale signs of coming under the knife too often. He had the kind of skin that bled as soon as a stiff fist made its first visit. He was not fat yet, but his destiny was obvious. He raised his paw to Jerry, who was standing next to Max's desk like an obelisk from an unknown desert kingdom with shimmering hieroglyphics from head to toe. His arms were crossed over his strapping chest, and his gloved hands held on to his large biceps, as if they might run off and create some mischief.

Jerry ignored the man's extended hand and said in a flat voice, OK, vato. Tell me your plan.

The man attempted again to smile, but nothing came of it. Anyway, he said, as I was telling your director, all you have to do is sign a voucher, check, or money transfer. Anything that you guys use to make transactions. You hand it over to me at the end of the day. I'll run it over to my moneyman at the bank. You don't need to know which bank. You understand why, right?

Go on, Jerry said. And he rubbed the tattoos on his arms with the tips of his fingers.

The man noticed the black leather gloves for the first time. They weren't standard heavy-bag-hitting gloves. They were regular leather gloves with the lining taken out and the fingers snipped at the joints. He could see the huge, bony knuckles covered by the skintight leather gloves. He swallowed hard. His throat was parched like a dry sponge.

I'll run the note over to my banker friend. He will let me have the cash as soon as I hand him the note. I'll take the cash, buy the goods, and then resell the goods. The contacts are waiting. I will return the cash to my friend and get your note back. I return your note and leave you a nice bundle of cash. You tear up the note, and the money never left your account. We can pull the same trick over and over. Who's to say?

The man looked at Max, then at Jerry. Max smiled. He wanted to laugh, but he didn't. Jerry was all serious. He studied the man's face, which reminded him of a cut of raw meat: red and lardy and ready to be sizzled on a hot grill.

OK, OK. Max finally broke the silence. What if, let's say, your banker friend, and we aren't asking who it is, cashes the note to cover his ass because you didn't make it back on time? Maybe some thug ripped you off and pistol-whipped you. He runs off with the cash, and your banker friend has no choice but to cash our note. And we get audited because an expenditure over ten grand went through without the approval of the city council, and Jerry's signature is on the note. What do we do? How do we come up with twenty-five thousand to cover our ass?

The man raised his hands as if the gesture would clear the air of any doubt. He'd thought he was getting over, but now he wasn't so sure. Perhaps the country bumpkins were fucking with him or just being cautious in a stupid way.

No, man—no way, he continued, his face blushing red and the dead acne scabs turning pink, resembling scales on a scabby creature. He wanted to grab the two clowns by their necks and knock their skulls together to show them he meant business, but of course he wouldn't dare. Nobody, no one, will rip me off, man. I have security. I pack heat—no way, no how. Believe me, folks: no way in hell. I wouldn't risk your gem of an operation here for anything. Trust me. He lowered his voice to almost a whisper and looked out the window to make sure that no one was close. Then he repeated, Trust me. They show me respect out in the streets. They wouldn't fuck with me in a million years. I guarantee you that, my friends. And with a smug look on his scaly face, he relaxed. He took out a pack of cigarettes and a lighter, and he offered one to Max.

Put that shit away, Jerry said in a stern voice. We have kids in here all the time, and smoking is prohibited.

The man put the pack and lighter back in his coat pocket, not altogether happy with Jerry's tone. But his shoes were already too deep in the shit to walk out over a little verbal slap. Besides, he was more than sure that the two donkeys were in the game. As long as he didn't piss on their hay too much, it was skin-it-back time for him. As for the steroid-guzzling, tattooed freak, he would save him for a later encounter and put some hurt on him.

Let me see what you're trying to sell us here, amigo, Jerry said. And he looked straight at the man. You buy the shit—we ain't asking what—for twenty-five thousand. You cut it, and depending on how much you dilute it, you sell it for at least a hundred thousand. You return twenty-five grand to your banker friend; no need to tell us who. You have seventy-five left. I'm working with the lowest number you gave us, five thousand dollars, and you and the banker split the seventy. Now that leaves you thirty-five each on an even split, and we end up with a measly five grand, so my take is twenty-five hundred dollars for my signature. And since we match with the state and feds, if we fuck up along the yellow brick road, we get federal time added to our behind-bars time, or maybe you don't believe embezzlement or money laundering, although white-collar crimes, are taken seriously by law enforcement.

The man at this point knew that he had to put his best foot forward to convince the two clowns that he was there for them. He was also dying for a smoke and a piss break. What are these yo-yos thinking? he asked himself. He could cut their balls off if he cared to. All this bullshit about this and that. Stop it. Or I'll really cut them off, fucking cream puffs. And he wanted to chuckle, but he didn't think it was a good idea at this point.

Look, my friends, the man continued, beads of sweat appearing on his meat-loaf forehead. The money is there. And remember, I take all the risks. I have the connections, so of course I see more money. If we do this little operation three or four more times, well then, you will see the pot multiply. We'll all see more money in the pot, and that's the name of the game. Correct me if I'm wrong.

You're right, my man, interjected Jerry to stop the man from repeating himself and sweating himself silly. I'll sign the note, and Max will initial it. And presto, we get the magic beans.

The man was left with his mouth open as he attempted a futile smile. Dried saliva had caked around the corners of his mouth and looked like dried cottage cheese. His feelings were hurt because Jerry was taking long, sloppy drinks of water from his gallon plastic jug; Max sipped cold mint tea with ice; and he was offered nothing, absolutely nothing—not even a coaster to lick.

Now, this is what'll happen, Jerry continued, before the man licked his cottage cheese–caked mouth and grossed him out. Our take will be ten thousand each. Max needs a down for a new truck, and I want to go to California on vacation and get some more tattoo work done. Follow me to my office, and I'll sign the note.

Jerry walked out of the office, and Max turned his attention to the mint leaves in the glass. The man looked at Max and then turned to look at Jerry, who was already in the middle part of the building, where the boxing ring was set up. He jumped to his feet, grabbed his briefcase, and almost ran to catch up with Jerry. Jerry was already across the huge building in front of the bathroom door and waited patiently for the man. He held the door open for the struggling man to enter. Jerry followed the man inside. Once inside, the man dropped the briefcase on the floor and went straight to one of the two urinals on the right side of the bathroom entrance. The man unzipped his fly with one hand, lit a cigarette with the other, and heaved a sigh of relief, not giving a shit about any smoking rules.

Jerry faced the mirror on the opposite side of the wall. He toyed with the faucet and studied the man's reflection in the mirror. He turned and casually walked to the man and propelled his size-12 gym shoe right into the man's buttocks with such force that the man's privates slammed into the urinal. His head hit the wall, and the cigarette smashed into his mouth, singeing his nose. He swallowed smoke, ash, and tobacco, all at the same time. Jerry pulled him around by the shoulder with his left hand and crossed with a right so hard to the man's mouth that the worn leather on his glove screeched, as if the cow was cheering him on. A cocktail of blood, tobacco, teeth, and other shit he couldn't name gushed out of the man's busted mouth like out-of-control diarrhea. The blow pinned the man between the two urinals. He was coughing and spewing blood out of his mouth, and tears filled his eyes. He attempted to clear his throat before he choked. He had one hand on his bloody mouth when Jerry gave him a soccer ball kick to the balls that seemed to lift him a couple of inches off the floor. The man emitted a moaning, animal sound that gurgled from somewhere deep within him.

You have no right to come in here and molest my students, you sick pervert, Jerry yelled at the man as he pulled his trousers all the way down to his ankles. One trouser leg went over his shoe. That made it difficult for the man to pull it back up, especially in his condition. Jerry grabbed the man by the coat collar and dragged him across the floor. He picked up the briefcase with his free hand, kicked the bathroom door open with his right foot, and dragged the man through a short hall that led to an exit that opened to the alley. He placed the briefcase on the floor, unbolted the door, and opened it. He threw the man out the door into the alley like the carcass of some worm-infested animal. And then he grabbed the briefcase and threw it out at the man, missing his head by inches.

Next time I see you lurking around here, I'm calling the cops. You hear me, motherfucker? Jerry shouted at the injured man on his back in the alley with his trousers around his ankles and bleeding profusely from the mouth and nose. Before Jerry closed the door, he said in a tempered voice, By the way, ese, I didn't get your name. Well, I guess it doesn't really matter. And he slammed the door shut and bolted it.

When Jerry locked the door, he went back inside the bathroom. He hosed down the muck on the floor and mopped the blood in the hallway. He took off his muscle shirt and put on a clean T-shirt from his locker. I hate the sight of blood, he kept repeating.

After he tidied up, Jerry joined Max in his office. Max was still contemplating the tea leaves.

Did you take care of your friend? Max asked, keeping his eyes on the tea leaves.

Yeah, Jerry answered. I gave him a booty slasher.

Ouch, Max said and made a face.

But he didn't leave me his card. Well, maybe next time.

Max studied the tea leaves in the glass. He concentrated on the leaves at the bottom of the glass. The tea leaves clung to one another like newfound relatives, all with provoking tales to tell.

What's with the leaves, Max? I know you can read them, but it's usually bad news. Is your mom feeling better?

No, man. She's been back a week, and all she does is stay home and look out the window. She refuses to see anyone or tell anyone she's back. I think she came home to die. He put his hand on his face and rubbed his cheek. She told me the doctors in Chicago weren't helping her. She has an appointment with a doctor here tomorrow. I don't know, Jerry. It's tough, real tough.

Sorry to hear it, Max. Your mom saved my life many times. The letters she sent me were full of hope, and she encouraged me to cheer up and read and study. The books she sent kept me going when times were bad for me. The care packages provided me with munchies and other items that came in handy and helped me survive. When my mother passed, you and Victoria were the only people on the outside I had contact with. Damn, why do good people always go first?

Both men were silent, thinking of Victoria Luna in different ways—Max as a mother he'd really never had and Jerry as a mother he wished he'd had. Victoria Luna was a complex woman who loved them both from a distant city but never made any effort to have them close to her. Victoria Luna was an intelligent, educated, modern woman who never let her emotions blind her against what was best for her son, her only son. The love of her life. And she loved Jerry as she did Max because she knew deep in her heart what Jerry had done to spare her and Max of the worst nightmare. Her boys were now men, and as men, they had to grasp the truth that a traditional mother she could never be. But her love for them could fill an ocean and was never diminished by her absence.

Jerry eventually broke the silence and said, You know, Max, that hamburger-face asshole didn't pack any steam, and I still need some action. What about it, big boy? Wanna take me on?

Max looked at Jerry and thought, Might as well. I need to get out of this mood. All right. And he smiled. But only if you know this one: The Seventh Seal.

He is really brooding, presumed Jerry. He said, The Seventh Seal, directed by my main man, Ingmar Bergman, in 1956, and the knight was Antonius Block, played by Max von Sydow.

I thought it was 1957, Max said with a puzzled look on his face.

No, sir. It was probably distributed worldwide in 1957. Max von Sydow was also in Hour of the Wolf with Ullmann, but that was in 1968, in case you ask.

How about that? Live and learn, Max said. OK, Jerry, let's get in the ring, but take it easy with that big wallop. You're home now. None of that kamikaze shit you did at state.

The men entered the ring. They put on the headgear and gloves and stretched on the ropes. The ring was regulation size, and some sections of the rope didn't have any tape or very little. It tended to scratch or even cut the skin if some poor soul was battered for any extent of time on that section of the ropes.

Are you sure you want the eight-ounce gloves? Jerry asked Max in a concerned voice.

Why not? Max answered. I know you like them. And you always say too much fluff in the glove when we use the fifteen-ounce gloves.

They walked to the center of the ring, tapped gloves, and moved back, ready to box. Jerry was a little worried about Max wanting to take so much punishment with the older eight-ounce gloves. Hell, he thought, Max could give as well as take. He needed this, and Max was the only one around who could take the kidney blows he inflicted. Besides, Max was solid, with thick shoulders, and deep chested. He wasn't built like Jerry, the bodybuilder, but was almost as tall at five ten or eleven. Max might have had a few pounds on Jerry, but Max never worked out. He was naturally strong. He could bench-press three fifty without a sweat and never made a face or grunted like a hog. Max wasn't into body building or working out, but he played basketball and boxed with Jerry. He was getting thick around the middle but still had a couple of years before it would embarrass him.

Jerry jabbed with his left, and Max blocked it. Both men were thinking of the best strategy to get in and out and not pay too high a price for it. Jerry jabbed hard and quick, coming in fast. Max blocked and moved left, then right. Jerry jabbed and crossed with a right. Nothing. Max came in with a left hook that connected to the kidneys. Jerry brought his glove down to deflect the blow. A big mistake, as Max crossed a powerful right to the face. Jerry was stung but countered with a left hook of his own to Max's head and missed with a right as Max danced to the side. Jerry dodged and cut him off with a double hook to the stomach and a solid right hook to the head. Instead of backing off, Max surprised Jerry by standing flat-footed and going at it with both barrels in a flurry of punches. Jerry deflected most of the blows and tied up Max against the ropes. Max couldn't push Jerry off, and the ropes were cutting into his back. Max punched Jerry on the back and sides until Jerry let up and backed off. Max came straight ahead, like a bull seeing red. He threw lefts and rights, missing the dancing Jerry with most of the blows. Jerry, with his chin almost touching his chest, switched to left-hander and moved in with straight right jabs to the head and punishing left hooks to the body. Max tied him up. The body blows were taking their toll. It was difficult to keep his arms up, and the pain was sucking up his energy.

William and Ruth had walked in while Max and Jerry hammered each other in the ring. They watched for a few minutes until Ruth couldn't take it anymore.

Can't you stop them, William? Ruth asked, concerned about the war going on in front of her.

I can't stop them, William said, amused. Nobody can. They'll stop when they've had enough. He wished he could take on one of them in the ring, but realistically, he knew there was no way. He was a lightweight compared to those heavy hitters. Ruth walked away to her office. She refused to witness any more violence.

Jerry knew Max was in pain, but he wasn't going to let up at this point. He was going in for the kill, and he would apologize afterward. He got cocky and too confident. The lion was going down, but he was still dangerous. Jerry kept jabbing his right to the head and left hooks to the body and then to the head. Jab, jab to the head, double hooks to the body. Max was confused. It was awkward, as the right jab was in his face instead of the left, and the right foot was leading. But Jerry forgot, and Max didn't, the vulnerability of the left-hander. When he jabbed right and hooked left, he left himself open for a second or two. Jerry lifted his head and exposed his chin as he smiled at Max, jabbing right and hooking left. And pop, Max came in with a rapid-fire right hook to the head and followed with a left hook to the opposite side of the face. Jerry winced with pain and shock and tied up Max with both arms, and Max did the same. Exhausted and in pain, Max started to laugh. An uncontrollable laughter seized him, and he hugged Jerry tighter. Jerry, a trickle of blood running out his nose, realized that was the end of the match. Once Max got the giggles, that was it. Then Jerry started laughing as he attempted to disengage from Max. Max held on tight because he couldn't stop laughing. Now both men were laughing and doing a little dance until they let go and dropped to the floor of the ring on their backs. They laughed until tears ran out of their eyes, and Max said, almost choking, A booty slasher, Jerry—a fucking booty slasher. I would have paid money to see the look on that son of a dog. And he laughed even harder.

Jerry was the first one up. He ignored his bleeding nose and helped Max up. Max was in pain. Every left hook to the body was like a jackhammer piercing his skull as his lungs screamed for oxygen. But he still had a burst of the giggles as he tried to take off his gloves. He noticed William smiling at them and said, Hey, William, let me tell you what happened when you went out to lunch.

CHAPTER 8

Mike Cotton had his big feet on top of his desk. He was drinking coffee and looked out the window at the homes being built. It was the middle of October, and the morning sky had a deep-blue tinge with a few puffy clouds to the northeast. He was in his portable office before sunrise when the desert sky was deep blue. People who were not familiar with the desert sky expected to see that color all the time. But the greatest depth of deep blue could be seen only in the morning before sunrise. Then it changed color to a dark blue, almost purple. Mike Cotton knew about the desert sky almost as much as he knew about building homes. At noon, the sky changed tones. By then it was a pale blue or yellowish, even rosy. Most people noticed only when it changed to pink and gold or orange in the late afternoon.

Mike Cotton was always the first to arrive at the construction site in work clothes and ready to work. Even though he owned Cotton Construction, he never came in with suit and tie. He was a hands-on kind of guy. He spent his time with the men and was not afraid to get his big hands dirty. He liked to work with the Mexicans. They were his best workers. He could only hire so many because the paper thing was a big nuisance. His second-best workers were the natives. They were the Chicanos born in Las Flores and the surrounding areas. They called themselves paisanos or primos. Most were third-, fourth-, and up to seventh-generation hombres. Some were overly macho and had bad habits. The majority were decent and solid workers. He sometimes hired bad apples and let them go as fast as he hired them. They couldn't keep up with the Mexicans from Mexico and called them frijoles and worse. They smoked dope on the site, and that pissed him off more than anything—except profanity, because many times they used the Lord's name in vain. Mike paid his men better-than-average wages, and that discouraged union activists.

Mike Cotton came in early to observe the sky and think without any interruptions. This morning his father came to Mike's mind because he'd had a dream about him before his alarm went off at 4:30 a.m. The dream hadn't stayed with him. He concluded that it was probably the same as the others. His father had come to the state from a sleepy little town outside Tulsa, Oklahoma, when Mike and his brother, Billy Bob, were young children. He couldn't find work in Oklahoma, so he did what others had done before him: he migrated out of the state. He settled in Albuquerque because that was as far as the old car got them before it fell apart. The man was a farmer without a high school education or marketable skills, but he had a mouth that would never stop. He tried different jobs in Albuquerque. He saved as much money as he could to continue to California, the land of milk and honey—the dream of the southern migrant and many others. He started selling used cars. He discovered he had the knack for it and called himself Earl the Pearl, for reasons that were obvious only to him.

Earl Cotton was an ambitious man, recalled Mike. He figured out right soon that he could make decent money in New Mexico, and the standard of living was not as high. He worked long hours seven days a week until he owned the used car lot and purchased others. He visited Las Flores on business on several occasions. He liked it because it reminded him of his rural Oklahoma. He sold his main business in Albuquerque, relocated to the Westside of Las Flores, and opened a used car lot with a decent inventory. He never made as much money as in Albuquerque, but he didn't need as much to live a good life. He noticed there was a lot of vacant land for sale, and few were buying it. Earl the Pearl was a visionary of sorts and recognized the future potential in that desert land. He reasoned that even if he could never do anything with the land in his lifetime, there was no reason his sons couldn't. Earl was content that he owned a piece of the rock. He always dreamed of being a land baron, and even if his land was undeveloped arid land, he couldn't care less. He bought parcels of ten to one hundred acres at a time on the cheap. Over the years, that added up to a vast holding.

Mike Cotton placed his hands behind his head and relaxed. This was his time, and he made the most of it. The men arrived at work later, and the phones didn't ring until eight or nine. He studied the sky and then the half-completed homes that were going up in an area that had been sagebrush and cactus for hundreds of years, if not more. His father would have been proud of him, but his father had suffered a fatal heart attack at age fifty-three. He never saw the fruits of his son's labor. Earl never saw how successful his favorite older son had become. He never had the chance to brag about Mike and the beautiful wife he had married and the big house he had built for her. His father, Earl, was an Oklahoma Baptist and attended services on Sunday—more to hustle car sales than anything else, or to brag about Mike's athletic prowess. The man wasn't a fanatic on religion and was known to visit the Catholics or other denominations if he could score a sale. The pastor always got a small check from his father. And his father ended up selling the pastor a discounted used car. His father always insisted on sending the two boys back to Oklahoma for at least two weeks during the summer, so they wouldn't forget their roots, as he put it. His father was always happy and in a good mood, a trait Mike Cotton did not inherit. He was a loner and happy only when at work and making money, an obsession that many times kept him up at night.

Mike Cotton scratched his head with both hands and felt the need for a haircut. He took a sip of cold coffee and looked at his watch. He still had some time left to enjoy the quiet before the site came alive with men, equipment, and noise. His mother came to his mind and with her the sadness and always the grief. He could never leave her out when he thought about his father. He wanted to, but he couldn't. His mother was a tall woman with dishwater-blond hair and pale blue eyes that seemed to turn yellow in the sunlight. She was an unhappy woman who never wanted to stay in Albuquerque or, worse, Las Flores. She had dreamed of California for most of her life, and Earl had promised her he was the ticket to get her there. Earl the Pearl promised a lot of things to a lot of people. That was his way. His mother was from the poor area of Tulsa, not from the sticks like Earl. They met at a country-western dance when Earl was looking for work in Tulsa. They were married within a month, against her parents' wishes. They struggled in that city. They lived hand to mouth with two little boys and one in the grave. They eventually hit the road when Earl couldn't borrow any more money and the creditors were closing in on them.

They were poor and lost in Albuquerque until Earl started selling used cars. His mother had a taste for bourbon. Bourbon put a smile on her face and allowed her to forget California, at least for a time. When they had a little extra money and the bourbon worked its magic, she would grab him by the hand and drop his little brother off with a neighbor. They'd hop on a city bus and head downtown. She would take him to an ice-cream shop. They sat at the counter, and she would buy him a strawberry milkshake with real milk and ice cream. She would watch him suck on the straw and take out chunks of ice cream with a long spoon. He was in heaven, as any kid his age would be. He had never tasted this treat back in Tulsa. He hadn't even known it existed. But the best part was that they were alone together. He loved his dad, but he never shut up, and they just listened to him yap nonstop about everything and nothing. With his mom, it was a different story. She listened to him and hugged and kissed him. And not only once, but a lot. It was something she would never do at home, because then she would also have to hug and kiss Billy Bob. After, she would take him to different toy stores. Only to look. She would make him promise and not buy. He would handle the toys and dream. He never asked for any or made a fuss when they left the store empty-handed.

He remembered he had tried that with his own kids. They'd created such a ruckus that they had to leave the store. Then his wife, Claire, got on his case because he hadn't bought the children what they wanted—the lesson lost on her also. The only thing he didn't like about their little escapades was that after his treat and the toy stores, she would take him to a bar. They sat on barstools just like at the ice-cream shop, and she ordered a double bourbon with ice. Men approached her and joked around, and some even put their arms around her shoulder, and he hated that. She would finish her drink but never paid for it, as drinks appeared on the bar in front of her without her ordering any. She eventually noticed that he was right there, sitting next to her. She apologized and smiled. She said goodbye to her friends, and they exited the bar. She left a little unsteady but still coherent. There was never any rush to get home. His father was never home in time for dinner, and picking up Billy Bob was never a priority. His mother left him with a neighbor who had so many children that one more didn't make any difference.

Mike Cotton placed his feet on the floor and put on his large work boots. He felt sorry for Billy Bob, but what could he do? He always heard that the first child was the favorite. He knew it wasn't true. Not with his own children, anyway. When they moved from Albuquerque to Las Flores, the Cotton family lived in luxury compared to all the other dumps they had occupied. It was a nice house in an older neighborhood. A real home. It was clean and freshly painted with newer furniture. He was in the third or fourth grade, and his little brother was a couple of years behind him. The solo trips with his mom ended, and so did the strawberry milkshakes at the ice-cream shop. She made them at home now, and it wasn't the same for him. His mom had her own car, and the adventure of taking the bus also ended. His father was still as busy as ever. He sold cars and trucks. He bought vacant land and got to know the movers and shakers of Las Flores. His mother was also busy in her own way. She dropped them off at school and did her own thing. She now had reliable transportation and more money in her purse. She hit the bottle early and more frequently. She hated Las Flores more than she had Albuquerque, even though she was living in nicer digs and drove a year-old car. She soon enough discovered the watering places that were compatible with her personality. She met Rafa Candelaria in one of those places, and they hit it off. Rafa was her main man for a while, and there were rumors of divorce. Rafa could drown her in bourbon, and he did—the expensive kind, not the cheap brand she was used to drinking. That's why he hated Rafa: although he couldn't blame him for all her indulgences, he blamed Rafa for many of them.

In a couple of years, his mother, a tall, large-boned woman, started to fill out those bones with flesh—a nice way to say she was getting fat, and the whiskey wasn't helping, expensive or not. Rafa dumped her, as men usually do when younger, more attractive, sober women enter the picture. She took it hard. She didn't want to be rejected by the flashy, big-money-spending Rafa. But it wasn't up to her. She had become a wrecked train and an embarrassment to Rafa and his party friends. Even his father avoided her. He spent more time in Albuquerque than he had to. She began to hit the seedy areas and bars where white trash and knife-carrying greasers made their homes, venturing from the stylish lounges of the downtown and country club locales, where businessmen and politicians sucked on their whiskies and cocktails, to the less reputable watering holes on Mora Street, next to the tracks where the poor folk fought over pool tables and the music depended on who had the most coin to feed the jukebox. And here is where she met the crazy ex-con from Oklahoma by the name of

Wayne the Pain Cruthers. They became regular drinking buddies right away. She felt comfortable speaking in their Oklahoma jargon that not even Earl used anymore.

The tall, long-legged Wayne lied to her. He told her what she wanted to hear. He kissed her frequently on the mouth and told her she was beautiful. And as long as she bought him drinks and provided lunch money and money for other bad habits he happened to have, the man was happy. Who wouldn't be? But things turned ugly quickly enough when Wayne insisted she leave Earl and the children and run away with him to Dallas, Texas. She refused, and that was the end of her. Some hunters found her after she'd been missing for a couple of weeks. They found her half-buried in the high mesa across the river, beaten to death with a shovel. Wayne was arrested later in Albuquerque when he ran a red light in her car at high speed and crashed into an elderly couple, killing them instantly. Eventually, they linked Wayne to her murder in the mesa. A jury found him guilty and gave him a life sentence in the prison in Santa Fe.

Mike Cotton wiped away the tears from his eyes before anyone saw him. After his mother's death, his life had changed. He seldom smiled, and he became determined that one day he was going to make big money and avenge his mother's savage murder. His father, Earl, although sad, seemed relieved at the same time. No more having to search for his polluted wife. No more calls from school reminding him to pick up the kids because they were still at school, waiting in the main office. No more excuses at church because she was too hungover to attend and no more jokes behind his back at the country club about horns. His little brother, Billy Bob, was difficult to read. They were in their early teens, and he had been ignored so much by both parents that he learned to mask his feelings pretty good. But the killer was still alive in the Santa Fe prison, and his revenge would never be forgotten until the man was dead, and he had a hand in it.

It made him so angry that he wasn't there to help his mother in her hour of need. She might have had a drinking problem, but he still loved her and missed her more than ever when she was gone. She was so kind and loving with him, and she tried so hard to stop drinking for his sake, but she was ill, and he knew it. She needed to drink to make her life more tolerable. She was going to stop. She promised him a million times. He still remembered how he would take her clothes off and put her in the tub before Earl came home. He made her drink black coffee and even brushed her teeth to sober her up and cleanse the smell of tobacco, cheap whiskey, and other filth he didn't care to know about. He would gather her dirty, smelly clothes and throw them in the washing machine, not bothering to separate whites from colors.

The only time he got angry at her was when she appeared at a ninth-grade school dance drunk with Wayne by her side. The dance was held at the school gym, and all the boys were in suits and ties. The girls were in formal dresses. It wasn't a sock hop. His mother waltzed in wearing old, faded jeans with a long-sleeve man's shirt that hung to her knees. She held the hillbilly Wayne by the hand. He was also in dirty, faded jeans and a soiled T-shirt. His mother, drunk and loud, shouted at the band to play country-western music, while Wayne the Pain encouraged her. Billy Bob, his brother, made a run to the bathroom when the students pointed to his mother and her bronco-busting, drunk sidekick. He, on the other hand, rushed to them and insisted on taking his mother home and was ready to swing at Wayne. His mother persisted in dancing with her son in that obnoxious way that drunks have. Wayne laughed at him and taunted him to throw the first blow. He promised it would be his last. Finally, the principal came along with security and showed his mother the chaperone list. He repeated that her name was not on it. Security escorted the drunks out. He found his brother, and they left the dance through a side door of the gym. They did not care to face the students inside the gym. The following day, his mother didn't remember a thing. And there was no point at staying mad at her. He blamed Wayne Cruthers, as he usually did.

Mike Cotton jumped out of his chair. He was so angry that he wanted to punch the wall of his portable office. At that moment, he saw his foreman, Juan Vela, drive up in his old Ford pickup. Juan Vela drove in from Valencia where he stayed with relatives during the workweek. On the weekend, he returned to Ciudad Juarez, where he lived. Juan Vela arrived at the work site by seven in the morning or earlier on the hot summer days. He got off his truck with a level and measuring tape in his hands and went straight to the half-finished homes to double-check the previous day's work.

Juan Vela was a short, wiry man with jet-black hair, combed and gelled straight back, sides and top. In his work boots and jeans, Juan seemed taller than he was. He sported a thick mustache that covered his upper lip. He always smiled and flashed almost perfect white teeth. He never talked trash about anybody. His dark good looks reminded Mike of the Mexican singers and movie stars he saw on the tube when he flipped channels. Juan Vela was a perfectionist when it came to work, and he could get work out of the men as no one else could. The Mexicans didn't need much prodding; it was the natives who were the challenge. But they all liked him because he didn't kiss butt; he didn't have to. And he didn't act all puto around Iron Mike, as the men called Mike. The natives saw him as another wetback who scratched out a living and stayed in an adobe jacal in Old Juarez, like the other workers from Juarez. Mike knew better. He had visited Juan Vela in Juarez on several occasions and had seen his mini-mansion in a gated community and several foreign cars parked in his five-car garage. He had a beautiful stay-at-home wife who took care of his kids and a mistress here and there. Juan never talked about his private life. He ate his tacos and bean burritos, heated on top of a metal screen over a fire pit at lunch, with the other workers and with no pretentions.

Mike Cotton smiled when he saw Juan Vela. They were always the first ones at the site. Mike liked and trusted Juan Vela more than anyone, even more than his own brother, Billy Bob, called Porky by some. He had been waiting for Juan because Juan got him out of the ugly mood he was in when he thought of his mother and what she had gone through in her short life. He was also glad to see Juan because the stone-wall masons were coming in from Juarez to start on a couple of projects. The trenches were ready, and the trucks that delivered the quarried stone were due anytime. He liked to use mortar on his walls because to him they took a better finish, and he could go higher with the stone. Many of the buyers loved the stone walls, and the best masons, in his opinion, were the men from Juarez. He didn't like the dry stack method, or dry walling as some called it, because it lacked the professional look he preferred to complement the beautiful homes he built.

Mike saw Juan Vela making his way to the potable office and went out to greet him. Buenos, hermano, que tal? he said, all smiles. The last smile anyone would see on his face for the rest of the day.

Buenos, Mike, answered Juan. Everything looks OK. Everything ready for the wall people? How high they going, Mike?

Two going six feet and two going four. Pasa, let's have some coffee.

The two men entered the portable office, a routine they followed every morning when they were on the site. Mike poured Juan a huge mug of black coffee from a pot that was on all day. Both men took their coffee black, so there was never any sugar or cream around to bother with.

That's a lot of piedra, Mike, Juan said, as he took a sip of his coffee.

Yep, mucha, going around the three thousand square feet of backyard, but that's what the buyer asked for; guess they want privacy. The others are lower though. You think the men will make it up here in time?

Oh yeah. They want the work, and they know you pay good wages. I talked to their boss last night and reminded him to bring on a couple of extra boys, just in case. Have they cleared up that other property you want to start building on next? We should be done here in about three weeks, a month max.

Yep, last I checked. I'll have Billy shoot on down there and check it out again.

Talking about Billy, here he comes. And Juan took one more drink of coffee. I'll let you gents alone, he said, and he walked out of the office.

Mike was disappointed. He enjoyed talking to Juan Vela in the morning when no one else was around. The rest of the day was nonstop, and Juan didn't say much when the others were around. His brother, Billyhe never used the Bob after Billy. It came off as if Billy was a hick, an Okie. And they weren't. They were from Las Flores and not from Oklahoma. It was his paternal grandfather's name, and Earl felt the name had to stay with one of the boys to honor his father. He never called his brother Porky either; that was the name he'd been baptized with at school. And later the beer-and-taco crowd he liked to hang out with had resurrected the name.

Morning, Mike, Billy Bob said, and he went straight to the coffee pot. He was dressed in a suit and tie. He didn't like to get his hands dirty working next to his brother. He had done a lot of that work when they started out. They'd struggled to complete projects and had been broke most of the time. Now they didn't have to help the help, and he didn't. Most of his time was spent securing loans. And meeting with the attorneys and bookkeepers they carried on the payroll. He also kept an eye on their other business interests. He didn't understand why his brother, Mike, would dress in work clothes and slave in the hot sun, as if he was one of the workers, when he didn't have to. He had the money to socialize at the country club with his beautiful wife, Claire. Sip champagne and nibble on tasty munchies. Oh, he forgot: Mike was a Christian, and he never touched the devil's poison.

How did it go with the bankers yesterday? Mike asked Billy, hiding his disappointment as best as he could.

Billy Bob took a sip of coffee and grimaced. He needed something stronger than black coffee to clear the mush from his brain. But he knew there was nothing in the tiny office stronger than coffee—his brother would have a heart attack if he ever brought in a bottle or two of strong spirits. Oh, you know, Mike. It's the same bull. He was going to say shit, but he didn't want to get Mike riled up so early in the morning. The guidelines are getting ridiculous. They keep coming back to the debt-to-income ratio and higher credit score. They demand documentation proving we have six to eighteen months of cash reserves, including taxes and insurance, or a big balloon.

So we're going to have to go back to our old bank and pay higher interest?

Yeah, it looks that way. But we really need more financing if we want those five hundred acres northeast of Santa Maria that Mike Montes also wants.

Did you talk to his partner?

Sure did. But it's the same story. Mike has controlling interest. Without Mike giving the OK, nothing gives. Besides, Mike knows the landowner, a woman by the name of Vivien Madrid. She lives in California, but she's from Las Flores.

What about the old man, Juan Jose?

You mean the invisible man? I'm not sure if the old hermit is even alive. I've never seen him. I've gone up to Santa Maria on several occasions, and if he's alive, he does a good job of hiding.

Mike Cotton studied his coffee mug and then put it on the table. He was disappointed on not getting closer to the five hundred acres. He needed that property for his pet project. He could use his own cash, but he didn't want to deplete his own reserves until he added to the pile. He planned to do that soon. He was aware that Mike Montes was clever and an attorney to boot. He hated lawyers. He had a couple on his payroll. Billy Bob dealt with them. Mike Montes with his Rayos de la Luna development company and slick ads had taken many wealthy clients not only from him but from others as well. His low-maintenance, native-landscaping, custom estates sold as soon as he could build them. The older, wealthier snowbirds loved the one-level, large homes with open vistas of beautiful sunrises and sunsets. No more struggling up and down stairs on old knees and hips ready to collapse. And that's what Mike gave them without hinting they were old. Age was a tricky number. The rich didn't want to hear it. Now he had to build more one-level homes, and it took up more property. Mike Montes could afford to do it because he had the land. Mike Montes could put the large homes on four to ten acres as he was doing on the Dos Cerros and La Luna Negra developments. He couldn't figure out how Montes, who had been in California for the last ten years, owned so much undeveloped land along with his silent partner, an attorney from Albuquerque who was somehow connected to Las Flores.

Billy Bob broke the silence and asked Mike, How's the new boy working out?

John Slaughter? Mike responded. He's doing good.

No, Billy Bob said, a little on edge because of his headache. The other boy.

Oh, him. I haven't had a chance to talk to him since he's been out. I will soon.

Let me know when you plan to talk to him, so I can make myself scarce. Billy Bob had a bad taste in his mouth. Before Mike responded, the phone rang, and Billy Bob answered it. Yeah, he said. Oh hi, Claire. And a huge grin appeared on his fat face. He went all soft when he talked to Claire de Lune, like most men did…or all hard. That depended on how close they were to her. Oh, I'm fine, and how are you? That's good to hear. Yes, here he is.

Billy Bob handed the phone over to Mike, sort of disheartened because he hadn't had a chance to converse with Claire.

Mike made a face. He grabbed the phone and said, Yeah. And not in the most loving voice. OK. If that's what you want. Bye. He hung up the phone and said to Billy Bob, so he'd know that Claire wasn't checking up on him, Claire is gonna do some volunteer hours at the CI Center.

That's nice of her. Billy Bob wanted to tell Mike not to be so mean to Claire. But that wasn't his place. Besides, Mike was his older brother and unpredictable. One punch and his fat ass would hit the floor and stay there. Instead he said, I gotta go to Albuquerque to meet with another banker, then meet with our attorney about the leases on the cement trucks. See you tomorrow.

All right, then. And Mike looked outside and saw the men arriving, ready to start work. He also saw Billy Bob as he left in his blue Caddie. Mike felt good inside. He knew Billy Bob was dying for a drink. He also knew Billy Bob would meet with the bankers, which would take half an hour, meet with the attorney, and then hit the watering holes in Albuquerque and maybe even take a ride up to Santa Fe. It wasn't that far from Albuquerque. He was happy for his brother. He'd had a rough life growing up, and if he could find a little happiness doing what he was doing, more power to him.

They could afford it. He also thought about Claire volunteering at the CI Center. He didn't take to the idea at first. He couldn't let Billy Bob know what he was thinking though. But now, he believed it wasn't such a bad idea after all. He would have an excuse to have a conversation with Mr. Jerry Rivera since Jerry worked there. And it wouldn't be so awkward. He wanted to hire Jerry along with John Slaughter. Max Luna got him a job at CI before Jerry was out of prison. Mike put on his work gloves when he saw the rock-wall masons working on the walls. He loved to see those guys work on the walls. And he even offered to help, so he could be up close. To him every wall was a piece of art—a masterpiece in his eyes— and the rokeros, as they were called, were the artists who stitched the quilt together, stone by stone. And that's why he preferred mortar. It gave the walls a cleaner mosaic look and not just a bunch of stones placed one on top of another.

CHAPTER 9

Max Luna and his mother, Victoria Luna, sat in between the large roots of an old alamo tree, next to the riverbank. The Rio Grande, at this time of the year, in this part of the state, was all but dry, except for a few pools of water here and there. It was the middle of October. The ancient tree had already lost most of its leaves. The giant tree with its exposed ashen roots was right on the edge of the riverbank and resembled the snarled foot of a giant who attempted to touch the water with his toe. The knotted roots, stripped of soil when the river ran high and fast on its way south, now provided a perfect location for people to sit and talk or study the hills to the west across the river. Doves and other birds made their nests in the trees on both sides of the river. It was a quiet place, especially this time of the year. The sky was pale blue with white wispy clouds that moved slowly in the midday silence. The sun was out, but the day was cool enough for Victoria to wear a scarf to cover her head and a sweater.

Max and Victoria sat on the sand, hidden from the dirt road off Highway 47. They conversed in a leisurely fashion. Victoria Luna had returned to Las Flores. She had lived and worked more than twenty years in Chicago, and she was uncomfortable sitting on the sand—she was not used to being outdoors, exposed to the sun and the breeze. She didn't complain. She knew Max liked this place, and so had she, when she was younger and full of life; it seemed a hundred years ago. She pushed the wool scarf back over her shoulders and adjusted her dark shades.

Did I ever come into your thoughts? Max asked her. Did you ever wonder how I was getting along, all those years?

I did. Always, answered Victoria. And what about you? Did you ever wonder how I was getting on, alone in that cold and distant city? All those times that your grandmother fed you those baked apples with cinnamon right out of the oven in that kitchen full of love. Did you ever stop before you took the first bite of the apple and think of me? You had the love of my parents, your grandparents. I gave up their love and yours and set upon a journey and struggle that altered my life. I left you behind because here you had a stability and a mature significance that I could not guarantee. I was sinking fast after your father's tragic accident in a world that held many restraints, cultural and social—you name it. I needed a new direction, another way of seeing and doing things in a new place. I refused to be the lonely young widow and mother you to death on false dreams and future expectations that could never be realized. I ran when I could. Not away from you, Max, but from the conditions that were going to strangle me. As time passed, you were all my parents had, and I had…memories and dreams of one day reuniting. They remained only that: dreams that got me through the long days and longer nights. Fortunately, Tia Lorena helped me out in Chicago until I got on my feet. I saved us both, Max. Look at it that way.

I've looked at it every which way, Max said. His eyes were hidden behind dark shades, and a black wool beret was on his head. Once there was anger and bitterness and all the ramifications they involve. I was only five when you left. Eventually, I slowly struggled out of that self-centered skin. You could say I shed it and began to see life in a more sensible and agreeable form. With time, I saw you as a unique mother. A mother and a proud woman, alert to the traps of her gender.

Please, Max, Victoria interrupted. You make me seem like a soldier. Let's stop this. There's no point in it.

Max touched Victoria's bony, pale hand with his large, strong, healthy one and could feel how cold it was.

Victoria pulled her hand away and used it to point to a large pool of water in the middle of the river, not comfortable being touched, not even by her son. See, Max. And she gestured to the pool of water. We used to bring you out here, and you would run through the pools chasing fish. And your father and I would run after you laughing. You loved to run naked through the pools of water, and it wasn't that warm, either. We had so much fun here, Max, just the three of us.

I only remember coming here with my grandfather and Nana. And Max felt hurt because his mother had pulled her hand away.

That stung. Victoria comprehended that losing one parent was a disaster, and losing both was unforgiveable, especially at that age. Victoria turned her head. She pretended to be looking at something across the river. Maybe she was selfish, she reflected, to come back after twenty-plus years to claim a place in her son's heart after leaving him behind at a tender age. She still remembered, and it still hurt when her relatives, especially the women, condemned her for deserting Max, something that was not done in their culture, they claimed. They refused to see what life was going to be like for a young widow in a small town. She had no plans to marry again and live under the restrictions of a husband, a culture, and a religion she found suffocating. She had the opportunity to do what many women could only dream of, and she wasn't going to blow it by waiting around for a husband or riding on the coattails of a man. She wanted only the freedom to do what men had always done. The freedom to explore life and define her own existence. She already had a son, so the maternal need to give birth was already satisfied, and she refused to be a martyr when her son could live a safer life in the solid world of her parents. They loved little Max as only grandparents can and wished her well. They knew they couldn't stop her. So now she refused to see any of her relatives, and not because she was better than them. She knew she wasn't. The circumstances, the time, and space had created a chasm between them. They were like the trees on the riverbank. The trees on the opposite side of the river had different features from the ones on this side. But they were still trees and still family.

So what happened to my father? Max asked.

Victoria bit her lower lip. She then said, in a breaking voice, It was all so…so unnecessary, Max. Your father insisted on going hunting. I begged him not to go. But he was a macho man and had to go with his drunken friends. His friends were going to Colorado to hunt elk in the winter. Your father didn't have the right gear for that kind of mountain cold. He went along anyway. Only a week. He kept saying, I'll be back in a week, Vicky baby, as he used to call me. I never knew what really happened. I do know they were drunk in camp in freezing weather when a shot was fired, and it hit your father in the chest. Then, because of the cold, they stripped him and placed him in the belly of a gutted elk. That's how they brought him down the mountain. He didn't freeze. He bled to death. There were conflicting accounts on what happened among his friends. Some claimed he was cleaning his gun, others that he was mistaken for an elk. It wasn't clear what really happened. It was declared a fatal accident by the investigating officials. I was left a widow, and you were fatherless, just like that. And Victoria snapped her fingers.

There was a long silence between mother and son as they sat on the riverbank. They contemplated the sands of time as many before them had done, seeking answers to the insurmountable questions of life. They were contented and discontented at the unpredictable churn of events that shaped the rhythm of their otherwise tranquil existence. Young Max, wise beyond his years, was burdened with the intractable resolution to free himself of the past and embrace the woman with all his heart. This woman, his mother, who had risked so much to give him life and then abandoned him at age five to swim in the sea of adversity. For Victoria, the sands of time were only blinding sandstorms that could not obliterate the truth that cut like a sharp sword and left a bloody corpse to remind her of her ride with destiny. She was blessed with a healthy son, yet left to challenge the shackles of tradition and see with her own eyes if she was alone in doing what her heart entreated her to do. She had returned, bleeding and helpless. And yet not certain if it was to end it all or for the love of her son. A love that was at times a burning flame that turned cool like water in a brook, high in a mountain meadow.

Max finally broke the silence. Let me ask you. And he was going to say Mother, and he wanted to, but it still felt awkward. Let me ask you, Vicky. Who made the decision to send me to California?

Victoria Luna studied the purple veins in her slender hands that carried blood throughout her ailing body. Reluctantly, she said, It was my decision, Max. I sent my parents the money to get you to California. They told me how you wanted to talk to the DA and confess your part in the… the killing of that woman beater. Jerry, your best friend, had confessed and taken a plea for whatever reason, Max. Jerry saved your life and threw away his. Don't think I am not grateful. I love Jerry like a son. He wanted to do the time, and you didn't have to. And before things got hot, I made the call. Remember, that man had family. You were putting yourself and your grandparents in danger if you stayed in the barrio. I called top criminal attorneys in Albuquerque to take your case. I wasn't going to stand by and watch my babies swing, no way. But with Jerry's confession, I dropped it; what was the point? Do you understand why I did it, Max? I would do it again if I had to. It wasn't that I wanted to separate you from Jerry. Jerry made that decision, not me.

Victoria rubbed her hands together as if she had a chill. She looked at Max. She couldn't see his eyes behind his dark shades, as he couldn't see hers. Always hiding, she thought. Perhaps they were the concealed emotions and feelings locked up in secret compartments of the heart and mind. She wanted to hug him and hold him tight. She knew it was too late for her. Max had given the best, the sweetest hugs to his nana and had all the right in the world to do that. It was his nana, her mother, who had been there for him, when Max, in the most delicate awakening of his young life, needed those hugs. In the long, lonely winter nights when he struggled in a world of confusion, Nana had been there to soothe his pain and calm his fears, as she had calmed hers and her brother's and sister's. Now she couldn't expect anything, or very little, from her only son. A grown man, who had lost the only mother he knew when his nana passed. They studied a hawk in silence as the hawk soared and danced in the blue sky. The majestic predator, king of the sky, was in search of food to feed its young. That concern of the hawk for its young gave her a hint of guilt.

Victoria turned to Max and asked, Did Grandma Luna ever come to visit you, Max?

Max, still admiring the hawk, said, Yes and no. She came once with my uncles and told my grandfather and Nana that she was moving to Denver and was going to take me with her. My uncles seemed uncomfortable. They stayed in the car the whole time. They were reluctant and refused to approach and discuss it. I panicked. I did not want to go to Denver with Grandma Luna, or anyone else, for that matter. I was seven or eight and had seen the woman maybe once or twice in my life. She had a strict and mean look about her. I ran and held on to my grandfather tight. Nana came over and dried my tears with a handkerchief. But my grandfather in a calm voice told Grandma Luna that you had signed papers with an attorney leaving me in their custody until the age of eighteen. And if she wanted to see the papers, there was a notarized copy in the courthouse for any relative to see, if they cared to. Grandma Luna made a face and said she would do just that and left as abruptly as she had arrived. Needless to say, that was the last I saw or heard of Grandma Luna. Did you really have a document written up by an attorney? Max asked with a grin on his face.

Of course not. And Victoria chuckled. Your grandfather was a smart man. Parents have been leaving the oldest sibling with grandparents since who knows when. Your grandma Luna was a difficult woman to get along with. But she knew she had no right to take you. It was arranged that you were to stay with my parents. I made that clear before I left to her and all the Lunas. And that was the reason I was never her favorite daughter-in-law. I wasn't intimidated by her like the others were.

Max heard a truck drive up a short distance from where he'd parked his car. He took a peek from their sitting place and saw a pickup truck with four cowboys crowded in the cab like sardines.

Oh shit, he thought. He knew what they wanted. Stay here, Vicky. Whatever happens, stay here unless I say different.

Whatever you say, Max, Victoria responded. She had her eyes on some birds flying in and out of the trees and shrubs across the river. She trusted Max to do what he had to do.

Max left his comfortable hiding place and walked slowly to his car, not far from the old tree. He went straight to the trunk of his 1950 Mercury. It was a chopped two-door custom, dark-purple, almost black, attention-getting car. He opened the trunk and thought about what he was going to need. He picked up a tire rod and then put it back. Too messy, he thought. He didn't feel like tussling with the cowboys. His side still hurt from the runaround with Jerry, and his mother might freak out. He opened a gym bag and pulled out a stick of dynamite with a short fuse. He wasn't even sure if the candle was any good. He'd had it for a long time and was going to use it against the dopers that night. He decided to use gasoline bottles instead. Shit, he said, and checked in his pocket for a lighter. He always carried a lighter, even though he didn't smoke. It was a habit from his youth. He also picked up a staple gun and secured it in his back pocket. If the dynamite bluff failed, a one-inch, rusty roofer's staple in the eye might discourage the cowboys from getting too chummy. He left the trunk of the car open so that his mother would be shielded from any ugliness that might occur.

Max sat on the custom hood, careful not to scratch the chrome grill and bumper of the sleek-looking car. He held the candle in his right hand and the lighter in his left. He flicked it on and off. He studied the cowboys. Three stood in front of the old pickup, and one was inside the cab, behind the steering wheel. They could be out-of-state students, and some of them tended to be racist. Some attended college in Las Flores, and some came to visit friends from the cowboy college in the southern part of the state. The local cowboys weren't as racist. They had been around the primos for years. He hated to fight with the cowboys. They always chewed that shit they loved so much. When he smacked them hard on the face, the brown shit, mixed with blood and teeth, splattered out of their mouth and soiled his clothes. Some could fight; most ran after the first hit. They were strong and wrestled their opponents to the ground. That was their style of fighting. He, on the other hand, punched hard and kicked to the balls when they left themselves open. His style. He noticed that one of the cowboys was taller than he was. The cowboy was lanky and older than the others. A mean-looking asshole. One was skinny, and Max figured he would be the first to haul ass after a good punch to his acne-inflated face. If only Jerry were here. Jerry could take the tall one and the skinny one easy, and he could take the driver and the heavyset one. The driver didn't seem too interested in starting anything. When he saw Max with the candle, he started the truck, ready to take off.

Hey, that car for sale? blurted out the tall, lanky one. He spat tobacco juice out of his twisted mouth. Max was sure now they weren't packing because they'd parked too far out, away from his car. If they had guns, they would have come in closer to block his escape. The confidence that guns give was just not there.

You see a for-sale sign anywhere close to the car? Max didn't even attempt to temper the sarcasm.

We just…we just wanna see the car, the cowboy insisted.

You seen the car. Now it's time for you girls to get back in your hot rod and disappear, 'cause my hand is getting itchy, holding this hot stick.

The cowboys noticed the short fuse on the stick of dynamite, and even if they could rush him, it was still dangerous. They were all bunched together, not spread out to make an attack more practical.

The driver of the truck pulled out in reverse slowly. The three cowboys turned their heads a little to see the truck as it backed up. The skinny cowboy with the sparkling pimples turned and headed for the truck. He didn't see any other alternative. He had no plans to die or end up a cripple over a car, even if it was a classic.

The tall, gangly cowboy, his left cheek puffed up with a full wad of chewing tobacco, said, Well then. I guess we'll leave, since the car ain't for sale. And they walked backward to the truck. They kept their eyes on Max the whole time. The truck was on the dirt road, and it moved slowly to Highway 47.

Max waited until they were out of sight before he placed the stick of dynamite back in its plastic wrapper inside the gym bag and made a mental note to take it out of the trunk when he returned home. He also put the staple gun back in the trunk. He was sure the cowboys wouldn't return. He worried more about his mom. She was known to carry a loaded, ladies' 9 mm handgun in her purse. He was afraid that if any shit went down, and the cowboys were pounding on him, she would come out shooting, and he'd get shot in the confusion. Max closed the trunk carefully and chuckled. What a bunch of idiots, he thought. They probably planned to beat on him until he ran away or leave him useless on the dirt. Then they would get their way with his girl. They were sure there was a girl. And take the car. He thought he recognized the driver of the truck. A local cowboy, maybe. He wasn't sure and walked back to rejoin his mother.

As the cowboys drove back to town in the crowded cab of the old truck, the driver, who had lived in the area longer than the others, said, I told you guys that was Max Luna. Loco Max or Mad Max, as some call him. He's a crazy motherfucker, and he ain't gonna let anybody take his car without a fucking fight. Jesus Christ. That was real dynamite. Didn't you guys see it?

Let me use your cup, Chip. And the lanky cowboy spat some juice in the cup. Nope, that wasn't for real dynamite, he said through blackened teeth. He was jest bull riding us. And I don't much care what they call that there chili eater. Next time I happen to cross paths with 'em, I'm gonna teach 'em what his momma done forgot: manners. Bet money on it. The other two were still too shaken up to say anything but chew on their tobacco in silence. They were glad they were getting farther away from that Max, or whatever the hell his name was.

Max sat next to Victoria between the roots. The same place he was before the cowboys interrupted.

Everything all right, Max? Victoria asked, her arms crossed with her hands warm under her arms.

Yeah. Everything's cool. They just wanted to know if the car was for sale. I get asked that all the time.

I love to ride in that car, Max. And Victoria smiled, even though she was uncomfortable and in pain. It makes me feel like a teenager again. I don't know why. It just does. You brought the car from California. Right, Max?

I did, Max answered. The cowboys were still on his mind. I wasn't a lowrider, or anything. I just bought the car off a friend about a year before I returned. He needed the money, and he gave me a good deal. I didn't drive it out here because the custom V8 flat head is heavy on the gas, and the custom wheels and rims would take a beating. I rented a truck and hauled it out here myself, along with my other stuff.

Did you like California, Max?

I didn't at first. East Los Angeles was crowded and dirty, to me. My uncle's house was small—not to them, though. You know. Here I had my own bedroom and my own bathroom, and over there I had to learn not to take forever in the bathroom. Here, I could go out anytime of the day or night. Over there we couldn't go out after certain hours because of the gang thing. But I got used to it. My cousins were cool, and that helped. The gang vatos didn't mess with us because they knew we weren't interested, and as long as you don't mess with them, they pretty much leave you alone. My primos were into sports, and I hit the books big-time. When my transcripts were finally sent from Las Flores High, the college counselor was impressed and told me I had a chance at a full scholarship at UCLA. Affirmative action was on its last legs, and they needed minorities to fill up some slots, so I got in.

I'm sure you were more than qualified, Max, said Victoria. She didn't want him to think it was an insignificant thing.

Oh, I had the grades. It was just that when we were taking classes and working our butts off, some assholes always hinted that it was because of affirmative action that we were there. And I used to tell those pigs that all the affirmative action programs in the world could never compensate the people of color for the institutional racism that had gone unchecked for hundreds of years.

Good for you, Max. Victoria was proud of her son for being so aware of what was going on and of his educational accomplishments. Max, she continued, when the decision was made that you were to go to California to live with your uncle, you didn't give your grandfather a hard time, did you?

Max became sad. He didn't want to show it. Never, Victoria. My grandfather had the first and last word. Let me tell you a little story about my grandfather and me. I was about eight or nine years old, and I was going through that silly, selfish stage. You remember when grandfather had goats, right? I picked this pure white goat and claimed him as my own pet. I loved that little goat more than anything else. I had other goats before this one, but I felt this one was special. It followed me around everywhere. My grandfather always warned me about getting too attached to goats.

One morning I woke up early. I was anxious to feed and play with my goat. I saw my little goat roasting over an open pit, and I freaked. I was so angry. I ran up to my grandfather with tears in my eyes, barely able to speak, and asked why. Why him? My nana was busy cooking all kinds of food in the kitchen, and I ran to her crying. She held me and comforted me. I stayed in my room. I was sad, and I cried. I missed my little playmate. Around noon, my grandfather called out, Max, let's go. All the food that my nana had cooked, along with the meat of the goat, was in the car. We drove to Chiva Town to a rundown house that my grandparents were familiar with. As soon as my grandfather parked the car, these skinny, starving-looking kids my age and older came running out of the house. They were so happy to see us. We all helped in taking the food inside the house. The parents or grandparents of the kids were also happy to see us. We all had a great meal. The parents were so grateful; they couldn't stop thanking my grandparents. I went outside after eating. I tasted the goat meat, but only a bite. I played with the kids for hours, and that took my mind off my little pal, the goat. We had dinner with the leftovers, and there was some left for them not to go hungry for a couple of days. It was late evening when we finally left. I sat in the front seat of the car with my grandfather. He said to me, See, Max. That little goat was here for a purpose, and that purpose was not to be your plaything. That purpose was to feed those hungry children and their parents. Did you see how happy they were? It wasn't so much about the food, Max. It was the idea that we prepared it especially for them and sat down and ate it with them. And then he said. We have plenty of food, Max. Thanks be to God. We share with the less fortunate, and that makes us better human beings, Max. Don't ever forget that, son.

Max pulled on his lower lip with his thumb and the index finger of his left hand. He studied the plateau to the west, beyond the river. It resembled a citadel. Or a gigantic fist forced out from beneath the earth. He had been up there during summer nights when the only sound came from the breathing river below as it rushed south. It was an isolated place called La Mesa de la Luz Roja, the Table of the Red Light. Many stories had been told about the place. Some claimed to have witnessed a reddish light radiating beams from the center of the mesa to the heavens above— thus the name. That brought treasure seekers who had heard the stories of gold buried in haste by Spanish soldiers when attacked by indigenous natives. The story was told that a cross that measured six feet made of pure gold was also buried there. The most infamous was the murder of Mike Cotton's mother. She had been beaten to death with a shovel and left half-buried in a shallow grave. She was found weeks later and unrecognizable. Max's skin reddened as he thought of his own mother being murdered like that. That would be reason enough to make anyone, son or daughter, go insane, he thought. And the killer was still alive and well, fighting the system to get out of prison and probably kill again, Max assumed.

Max, Max. Victoria touched him gently on the arm to bring him back. You OK?

Yes, he said. He never wanted to leave his mother's side. Yes. I'm good.

Why did my parents move to California, Max?

My uncle in East Los Angeles thought my grandparents were too old to live alone in Las Flores, and he had this idea that if they came to California, I would stay and finish college. They came. And they weren't happy. I stayed in the dorms on campus and visited on the weekends, or tried. I was too busy and into college life to notice the freedom they had in Las Flores was swallowed up by concrete and traffic. And even though my uncle purchased the house in the back for them, it still wasn't the same. They had a little garden. It was city living and city gardening. After three years, my grandfather wasn't the same man. He was often ill, until I brought them home. My uncle Chema, your older brother, stayed in the house when they left for California. My grandfather died as soon as he returned to Las Flores, and my nana followed him four months later. The funerals were a disaster. My uncle Chema was angry because my grandparents left the house to me. He complained the whole time about how he did this and that to improve the property and how my grandfather had promised the house to the oldest son, blab, blab, blab. I almost put my hands on him. I didn't out of respect for the rest of the family. You were there. You remember how embarrassing it was.

Oh, I remember. Events like that are not forgotten that easily. And it was strange because everyone knew the house was going to be yours at the end. Your uncle Chema, just because he was the oldest, thought he was the boss. And his wife was worse. She was the one who accused me of abandoning you. She called me all kinds of names, not to my face, but behind my back, like that was going to convince me to stay. Too bad we didn't have a real conversation back then, Max.

I know. Max was still frustrated because so many things had gone wrong during that time. But with the grief and all the infighting, he continued, it was difficult for you and me to take off somewhere and talk. Besides, I had just started working for the city of Los Angeles as an urban planner, and two funerals in Las Flores and all the bullshit my uncle Chema put me through left me exhausted. I told him before I left that he could live in the house while I was in Los Angeles. If I ever returned, he would have to move out.

And you stayed in Los Angeles?

I stayed for another five years. I had a decent job. I completed my master's. I loved the weather and the life. You know how it goes. After almost ten years away from Las Flores, I missed the great open space and the deep silence. I got tired of the busy and crowded city. I like to sit, like we are right now, and be able to see and feel the distance between things, think deep thoughts, and attempt to comprehend what it all means. Why we are born and for what purpose. A divine calling, or do we carve out our own destiny with a carving knife? The more I read, the less I knew about life, and I couldn't get that. I needed clarity. The noise and all that makes a city a city, I thought, muddled my perception. I believed I needed the great open space to come to some conclusion and grasp at something that was real. The definition of real escaped me. You know what I mean, right?

I know exactly what you mean, Max. My real was the opposite. I loved the concrete jungle with all its pitfalls. I didn't miss the sun or the stars and adapted to an almost exclusively studious existence. It took me some time to complete my degree in library science. Once I started working, though, I dedicated my life to that work. I fed my mind from the best food the world of literature had to offer. My soul burned in the deserts of Paul Bowles's novel The Sheltering Sky, and I felt sorrow and the pain of death in Kazantzakis's The Fratricides and Lorca's Boda de Sangre. I read and traveled the romantic and murderous roads of the Russians, English, Spanish, French, and all other writers who created a sense of adventure and moved my heart to tears. You see, Max, I was in a way a coward. I didn't seek the great empty space and deep silence to find my purpose in life. I let others do the heavy lifting, and I followed their passion like a blind woman and made their life's work mine. The great suffering along with the happiness and love affairs of their characters—all mine. I lived, you can say, in a cloud, Max. A cloud of never-ending thrills and places in the world I never had to visit because I knew they existed, and they were ingrained deep in my mind, as if I had lived there all my life.

I realize it's a poor excuse for not coming to terms with reality, Max. I had enough of reality when I lived here. I had enough of the open space and clear blue sky that seemed to expose my thoughts and left me vulnerable for any clown to come into my life and take it over and shape me to his liking. I lived that life, Max. I married a man, your father, whom I thought I loved. I gave and gave, and he took and took until I was exhausted and dead inside. You were my only escape, Max. In my opinion, that's why women have children: to get away from the man who sucks you dry. The drinking, the games, the stupid friends, the bills, and the affairs, real or made up—they all hurt, Max. I brought you here to the same tree when the river was running wild with water from the northern mountains, and you don't know how many times I contemplated jumping in with you in my arms. With my luck, I would have probably survived, and you would have drowned. And knowing the people here, they for sure would have accused me of being a witch and burned me at the stake.

When your father was killed, Max, I felt the loss. I grieved; did I ever. I was in the worst predicament that I had ever been in. So I ran before I was paralyzed with fear. The great enemy. It wasn't easy in the big city, Max. Several times I packed my bags and purchased a ticket to return. But my aunt Lorena, bless her heart, she pleaded with me to reconsider. They will torment you with gossip, she told me many times. I stayed in Chicago, Max. I lived in books and the faith of better things to come. And look at me now. And tears rolled down Victoria's pale cheeks. She removed her sunglasses, and her eyes were bloodshot. I'm sorry, Max, she whispered.

Max was torn. He struggled to hold back his own tears. He had never realized it was so difficult for her here with his father. He put his arm around her and gently held her against his chest. This was his mother, he thought. A woman who had disappeared from his life when he was a child. A woman who used to come on a quick visit from a city he couldn't even pronounce. An elegant lady. Always dressed in fine threads that made the rest of them look shabby. Maybe that was why his aunts disliked her so. His mother, the woman who, with blood and tears, had brought him into this world and held him tight for the first five years of his life. And now he held her, twenty-plus years later. Now she was the child. The irony of life, he thought, and he was mystified. He could feel her heart against his, and her tears flowed as her chest and throat throbbed and released years of pent-up despair.

It's OK, Mom. He said the word. And it came out easy and natural. It's OK. I think we should leave. There's a chilly breeze coming in.

Give me a few minutes, Victoria said, as Max helped her to her feet.

Max walked alone the short distance to the car, not sure what to do with his mother. Maybe she should have stayed in Chicago, he considered. He felt bad for thinking that way. He looked up at the blue sky and saw a hawk being chased by three tiny sparrows. Two sparrows were close behind the hawk, and the third one was on his flank. Max didn't know if the sparrows and the hawk were playing catch me if you can or if the silly sparrows chased the mighty hawk away from their nests. He did know that the hawk could switch tactics in a split second and crush a sparrow in its deadly claw and snip its head off with his powerful beak. But the hawk, king of the sky, didn't do any of that. He just played along and allowed the tiny birds to have fun and believe they were bad. He saw his mother walking toward the car in her black business suit. She didn't wear jeans anymore because she had lost so much weight that she looked starved in them. The expensive black wool suit looked better on her because it was loose fitting. But she was a frail sparrow nonetheless, thin and pale. And she seemed even smaller as she walked away from the giant tree. A delicate little bird, he deemed. He wondered when the mighty hawk would swoop her up in his deadly claws. He wanted to scream out in agony and curse to the world that it wasn't fair. After all those years apart, they were together again as mother and son. And she was going to leave again. This time for good. Max kept his cool. He helped his mother into the car and said nothing.

CHAPTER 10

Rafa Candelaria, the city councilman who represented the Eastside; William Moreno, the assistant director of Community Impact; and Ruth Moreno, William's wife, financial officer for Community Impact, were all in Rafa's office in the downtown courthouse building. Rafa was in a single-breasted charcoal, pin-striped wool suit. He sat behind his desk. William and Ruth sat in two chairs. They faced the angry Rafa, who acted like an agitated high school principal lecturing two students who had been caught making out under the stairwell. He waved a folded newspaper around in his right hand and finally laid it on his desk as if it were too hot to handle.

Did you see that? He pointed to a dilapidated-looking house on the front page. You promised to give me time so that I could do something about that property. But you didn't, did you? Rafa placed his hand on the newspaper. He wished it would disappear altogether. Where's Max anyway? He's the one who should be here. This is serious business.

William looked straight at Rafa. He was not intimidated by the older man's position and wealth. He said, Listen, Rafa, Max is the director, and I'm assistant director, and we're all on the same page on this. He knows we're here, and we represent Community Impact and not any one individual who works there. We gave you ample time to get things done. The mayor even gave you more time, and you didn't move on it. We took the photos to the mayor and not to the press. We believed he could convince you to make some changes to the property. You said to him that you would. Nothing was done, and the building is still in a sorry condition.

Think of the family who lives there, Ruth jumped in, feisty as William. The kids who have to live in substandard conditions, and all because of what? Think of the parents who have to draw water from the outside pump to simply keep clean. And then you attempt to evict them, as if it was going to be kept a secret. Of course they told us. They were almost in tears because they had no money to find another place. It's a hard time for people, Rafa. Ruth had come out punching. And even though Rafa's vote was vital for matching funds, it was too late to compromise.

And even Mike Montes assured the family, William interrupted, that it was illegal to evict them without probable cause. That you had to provide six months' rent and find them a suitable place to live. Come on, Rafa. This ain't like the old times.

Oh, so you had to run to Mike Montes with the problem, Rafa said. He was not very happy with the direction the conversation was taking. Listen, guys. Rafa softened his face and even attempted a smile. I've known you kids since you were way little. You're my Tommy's age. I have also known your parents. All good people. I don't want this to become, let's say, too personal. We get along in the Eastside, always have. I'm just saying you come to me on this. I've got a big business to run, as you know. Besides, my city council obligations demand time. I deal with a lot. A lot of comings and goings. I left this little problem for my property manager to handle. It got away from him somehow, as far as I can see. But I'll put it right. All I want from you is a retraction in the Daily. And he pointed to the paper to make sure they saw the paper on his desk. My property manager somehow screwed up. Call up your pal Rudy and explain to him that it was a mistake. A mistake, that's all. As you know, the Sun didn't touch the story. I don't know what they're smoking at the Daily, but I'll get to the bottom of it.

The Sun is a political-and business-orientated paper, and it caters to business interests and to politicians and their political whims, Ruth articulated, calm and collected. The Daily is more of a people's paper and reflects more of what happens in the lives of average people. They print the truth, and if the shoes fit, wear them. That's all I have to say. And Ruth leaned back in her chair.

Rafa caressed his clean-shaven chin with his right hand. He began to dislike the two little monkeys. He didn't want to get heavy-handed. Not yet, anyway.

You sound like a socialist, Ruth, Rafa said. I'm sure you're not. You're too young and bright and were raised solid to fit in that camp—

Socialism is not a bad concept, William interrupted and smiled. If it is run the correct way. But that is neither here nor there. We cannot retract anything, Rafa. It's too late. And even if we wanted to, which we don't, Rudy would never print anything even close to that. We have shown him the property, and he took his own photos. He might expand on the story. That's up to his editor, not up to us. We did what we had to do. Really the only decent thing to do. Whether you approve of it or not, that's out of our hands. It's up to you now to do the right thing, Rafa. Fix up the house, lower the rent for the folks who live there, and Rudy might paint a more positive picture of your image. Do nothing, and you will definitely hear from our attorney—and soon. Enjoy the rest of your day, Rafa. We gotta go. We have a center to run. And don't bother to show us out. We know the way.

When William and Ruth left Rafa's office, Rafa was left scratching his head. Little shits…how dare they? And he almost shouted. He made a face, and he mimicked Ruth. If the shoes fit. I'd like to fuck her in the ass—that's what I'd like to do to her. He still couldn't believe they went to the paper. He picked up the paper and flung it to the far corner of his office. Who the fuck they think they are? he asked himself several times. And what pissed him off more was that he had supported all their programs from the inception. He had voted for matching funds for CI on every occasion, and for what? Look at how they honored his staunch support. They plastered his picture next to a house in the Eastside that looked worse than many a house in old Mejico. That bastard, Rudy, he avowed. He's the one who put legs on the story. He'd remember Rudy. Rudy would be put on his shit list. And he said out loud, Fuck, yeah. I will show them they can't fuck with Rafa Candelaria and get away with it. He took out his switchblade and made cutting jabs and sounds at imaginary individuals. He finally folded it up and placed it back in his pocket. He picked up the phone and told his secretary, Laura, to call Vincent Duran and tell him to get to his office ASAP.

About ten minutes later, Vincent the Sloth Duran was in his office. Vincent Duran was a professional committeeman. He was always appointed to some committee, regardless of who was in office. This time around, Vincent was chairman of the Las Flores Redevelopment Agency and allocated funds to city agencies that the city council favored. He was also one of Rafa's lounge lizard pals. Vincent believed in the siesta with his whole heart and told anyone who would listen that it was one of man's best inventions. He would not be seen or heard from between noon and two o'clock. He was an easygoing man in his middle years and so tall he hunched. He would sit if there was a chair close as not to make an insecure short man feel bad. He would laugh at a bad joke when no one else did because he knew it would get him a drink or a meal. He agreed on most things people said—even if they were asinine—as not to appear knowledgeable. He knew that most in his circle of acquaintances disliked taller men. They disliked tall, clever men most of all. Most people assumed that because he was so tall, almost six five in shoes, he had been a good basketball player in his younger days. But the truth of the matter was that Vincent couldn't even play cards without screwing up. He wanted to be a police officer like his father was, but he never passed the physical. He was top-heavy and bottom weak—in other words, a klutz. He loved to hang out with cops because he didn't have to put on a masquerade with cops and be a yes-man.

Vincent Duran walked into Rafa's office close to noon. He deliberated on a place to take his lunch and siesta. He wore a coat and tie. The coat was extra-large, and the tie hung almost to his fly. The tie was wide and flapped with every step. His arms were so long that his bony, hairy wrists poked out of the coat sleeves.

Hey, boss, what's up? Vincent asked in the same calm voice he always used. He went straight to the chair Ruth had warmed up for him.

Sit, by all means, Rafa said. The sarcasm was difficult to hide. You've seen the Daily, by now, I gather? Rafa asked, rather embarrassed.

No. I haven't, Vincent lied. Everyone who could read and wasn't blind had. He didn't want to venture into unknown territory. That wasn't his style. He was a yes-man, and a yes-man never volunteered anything unless compelled. It was an art in itself.

Well, perhaps you should take time from your fucking siesta and read the fucking paper now and then, Vincent, Rafa cried out. He knew

Vincent was slow to react, unless he was buying him a drink. Then he could bend the elbow with the best of them. They, and I mean Community Impact, is attempting to paint a picture of me as a slumlord, Vincent. Whatcha think of them apples?

Vincent loved apples. He ate one every day, two at the most. He was going to have a green apple after his siesta. He wasn't going to mention it to Rafa. Rafa was edgy today. Who wouldn't be, he figured. Slumlord was not a kind word to say about anyone, especially a city councilman. And a wealthy one to boot.

Vincent put his long arms out with his large hands on his knees. He always sat that way because he never knew what to do with his arms. He wanted to cross them over his chest. He believed he looked odd when he did that. So he played it safe. He placed them on his knees, and there he felt they were OK. I guess, he finally said. He wasn't sure what Rafa wanted to hear. The CI people are barking up the wrong tree.

The wrong tree, Rafa repeated to himself. Fucking moron—useless thick-skulled motherfucker. No wonder they call him the Sloth. Wrong tree—what the fuck does that mean?

Listen, Vincent, Rafa stated, losing his patience. I don't know anything about any fucking trees. Here's what I called you in for: Hear me out before you make any more of your brilliant remarks? OK. When CI wrote the proposal to lease the old city warehouse, they sent it to your committee to review it. You and your people approved it and sent it to the city council for a full vote. Follow me, Vincent? I know you do. We in the city council lobbied for it. It passed on a unanimous vote. And CI got the building for a dollar a year for, what, five years? Now here is what I want done, Vincent. I want to undo the lease agreement. I want it null and void, now. The sooner the better. Can it be done, my friend?

Vincent Duran was hit between the eyes with a hammer. He didn't want to be in the same office with Rafa at that moment. He needed his siesta more than anything. He needed his beauty sleep to make him forget what this crazy man was trying to do. Forget it, he wanted to tell Rafa. He understood Rafa Candelaria was an important player in Las Flores.

He could make or break any man or woman who crossed him. Besides, he wanted an invite to Rafa's kid's birthday party this coming Saturday at his million-dollar hill home. Rafa always put out the best of everything when he entertained. The liquor flowed, and food kept coming and never stopped. Rumors circulated that the governor or the lieutenant governor, one of the parasites, was attending. And Rafa was big on invitations. If you didn't show one at the door, unless you happened to be his mother-in-law, he would set the dogs on you. And real maulers, those dogs were. Vincent had to give him a good answer or forget about the fiesta.

Vincent was going to place his large hands on the desk. He changed his mind. He might knock something down or off the desk. Not good, he thought. Rafa, he said slowly. Too slow to please Rafa. I'm not a…a lawyer, Rafa. You gonna have to get his opinion on this. I mean, breaking a lease… you know, Rafa…CI put in some repairs, cost money.

You know, Rafa, you know, Rafa mimicked Vincent in a whiny voice. I know, fuckhead. That's the reason I asked you here, man. C'mon, Vince. You go through those fucking leases all the time. Think of a clause, something that most pendejos never read. C'mon…help me out. I'm dying here, Vince.

Vincent reflected. It was difficult to put the party out of his mind and all the expensive booze and food. And the music. The music. Top bands, always. This time Rafa was going to allow the birthday boy, who had his own band, to play a couple of riffs. Just for the hell of it. He knew he had to throw Rafa a bone and not step out of his mold. Rafa could spread the word that he was a little clever, and others might think he played them for drinks. And he did. They didn't mind, unless someone brought it to their attention.

Rafa, I was just thinking, Vincent said almost in a whisper. There is a…a contingency clause in the contract for the CI lease. That's all I have.

Rafa studied Vincent's big horseface and admitted that the man wasn't as stupid as he looked. Then he changed his mind: then again, maybe he was. Contingency. Rafa considered. He didn't have a formal education beyond high school. He was a big fan of Mr. Webster and always had a dictionary around. He even gave them out as Christmas gifts. He wasn't going to discuss the contingency clause with Vincent. Rafa doubted that Vincent understood the term. And maybe with an uncertainty of occurrence, which could mean anything, he could get his attorneys to find something rotten in Denmark. He could get the contract for the lease revoked and kick CI out of the building. Oh, he was so clever, he told himself. OK, Vince. Thanks for your time.

Vincent knew he was dismissed without a word about the party. He also knew the CI lease was solid as steel. And it would take a big to-do for the city to break it and not lose its shirt in a lawsuit. Vincent Duran got out of his chair slowly, as was his way. Going to the club later, Rafa? he asked when he approached the door of Rafa's office.

I'll call you, answered Rafa, already on the phone. Richard, where the hell are you? Rafa barked into the phone.

I'm out here talking to Laura.

Get your ass in here now. And he slammed the phone down on the receiver.

Richard, Rafa's younger son, entered the office. He was of medium height and on the thin side, and his hatchet face was almost as dark as his father's. He had a high green Mohawk haircut, wore diamond studs in his ears and nose, and wore a mustard-yellow leather vest with no shirt. He also had on burgundy leather trousers and black leather open-toed sandals.

Now tell me, Richard, if I may ask, uttered Rafa. He talked to his son as he did to everyone else. What happened to the work you were gonna do on that house on Mesquite Street?

Richard sat in a chair without being asked. He crossed his legs and put his right elbow on top of his knee. His leather pants crinkled. He put his right hand on his chin and stroked his peach fuzz. His left hand was on his crotch. He fondled the leather with his thumb. It was more of a habit than anything else. Let me see, he repeated, to his father's agitation. Oh, I remember. I gave that house to Anthony Juarez, my drummer.

Who the fuck is Anthony Juarez?

Oh my, Pops. You're in a cussing mood today. What happened? That shit in the paper get to you?

That shit in the paper is not what bothers me, Richard. What bothers me is the fact that you're my property manager and you pass on the responsibility to some…some drummer?

It's cool, Dad, chill. Anthony's OK. He lived in California for years. Now he stays here with relatives. He's a badass drummer. We like him.

What! snapped Rafa, frustrated because he couldn't go crazy on his son. You like him because he's from California? And I'm sure he does drugs, right?

No, Dad. Richard made a face. He twisted his feminine lips a certain way. You think all my friends are druggies. You paranoid, man. We rock; that's all. Don't need no drugs for that.

OK, OK. Now tell me, what happened when you paid a visit to the house that needed work?

Well, like I said, me and Anthony, we pay them a visit and told the old man we wanted to fix the house up. That they had to move out. The old man started talking shit in Spanish about he got no money, no place, and many kids. Said he go to CI, go to CI, he kept repeating in half-assed English. Then Anthony said to me, we gonna have to evict the old fucker along with his poor-looking family. But Anthony was only kidding, Dad. Only kidding. I told Anthony, We don't talk to tenants like that; be nice. The old guy picked up on eviction and asked if that was our intention. He was obviously coached by the people from CI.

Shit, then what happened? Rafa asked. He knew this mierda was going to cost him, in votes and cash.

We left and forgot about it. At least I did. I left it to Anthony to follow up. Guess he didn't. It's no biggie, Pops. Call *la Migra*. I'm sure they're wet. Make them disappear. We fix the dump and rent it out again.

Rafa jumped out of his chair like an electric puppet. His face was distorted with rage. He pointed his finger at his son and growled, Don't you ever, ever talk like that again in my presence. Do you hear me, young man? In our family, we don't ever do that—never. We do not mention or threaten anyone with *la Migra*, not even in jest.

I bet if Tommy said it, you wouldn't be so upset, right?

Tommy, Tommy. You always bring up Tommy when things don't go your way, Richard. Tommy is studying in Italy, where he wanted to study, and he is your older brother. Show some respect, please.

He's not dead, Pops. Respect, my ass. The only reason he's in Italy, studying in Bologna—Mother calls it baloney—is because you wanted him away from that girl. You know, the girl you paid to get rid of Tommy's child.

Look, son. Rafa sat again and attempted to reason with his younger son in a calmer voice. Look, Richard, try to understand. Tommy was too young and immature to get tangled up in a marriage with a family. He made a mistake. We all make mistakes, Richard, when growing up. Some mistakes are too costly and can't be rectified. Some you can. And as parents, we do our best to…to help out.

Both men studied each other in silence. Richard had always been aware that Tommy had been Rafa's favorite, and he would be untruthful if he claimed that it didn't bother him. It had always been a thorn deep up his ass. It had been worse and more obvious when he was younger, and he had worked so hard to please his father. Everything he tried ended in failure, letdowns, and more pain. Eventually, he gave up and discovered drugs, sex, and music. Now he didn't give a shit. He was known as a rich, spoiled kid, which he was. He had never had to struggle for anything in his life. He took everything for granted, except when it came to Tommy and his dad. That still burned, even though he would deny it all the way to his grave, if he had to.

Rafa also studied his younger son, Richard—an unexpected surprise that his wife had hit him with one fine morning. She had claimed for years that she was beyond her childbearing years. He was about to leave her and do with his life what he wanted to do. He had stayed because she begged him and promised him the space he always had desired. Besides, she argued, the newborn shouldn't grow up without a father figure to guide him. And Richard came into the world. He was tiny, dark, and colicky. He cried constantly. Rafa, by that time, believed he had a complete family with two older, useless daughters. He believed they were good only to bring children into the world. And their husbands worked only when he hired them. But then there was Tommy. He was tall and light-skinned like his mother and a handsome devil in anyone's eyes. Tommy was intelligent and resourceful and loved the girls. Tommy would run the business one day, and Rafa would retire with a young chick to keep him warm during the cold nights. But then along came little dark-skinned Richard. A picture of himself at that age. He remembered how cruel the kids had been when he was growing up. They had called him the Chunky Monkey all through school. He didn't wish that on Richard, but there was nothing he could do about it. He concentrated on his business, politics, and Tommy and neglected Richard. A big mistake.

And by the way. Richard finally broke the silence. Why didn't you take Mom to Europe with you? She wanted to see Tommy as much as you did.

I asked her, Richard, more than once. Which was a lie. She wanted to go to Hawaii again. Christ Jesus. She always wants to go to Hawaii. We've been there so many times, and she still wants to go. What's so adventurous about staying on an island full of obnoxious tourists? Rafa didn't vacation in the States anymore because many times at the high-end resorts where he preferred to stay, some asshole mistook him for a waiter or kitchen help. And I also invited you, he continued. I always do, and you didn't show the courtesy to say yes or no.

Europe is good for one time; we saw it all. The fucking French with their little cups of coffee, repeating merci, merci—fuck that. I mean how many times can you see the Tower Eiffel? And the Louvre, uuuo, mustn't forget the Louvre. Don't let me get started on Europe. And besides, Richard resumed with a smirk on his weasel face, I didn't want to go to Bologna and visit Tommy. I got the word Tommy, your golden boy, denies he's a Chicano from New Mexico and tells his girls over there that he's a third-generation Italian American from California. And knowing Tommy, he's probably not even studying. He's passing his time with hookers and partying, as he did here. All expenses paid by you, Pops. International business. Ha, what a joke. He smiled and exposed uneven cannabis-stained teeth.

Rafa stared at his son. He bit his tongue because he couldn't open up with both barrels on him, and it wouldn't do any good if he did. He couldn't lay his hands on him because he was too big for slaps and such. And to cut off his allowance was pointless. His mother would give him any money he needed. What he said about Tommy really hurt though, and that was his intention. So Rafa said, That's not true, Richard. What you said about Tommy. I talked to his professors in Bologna. They all said he was doing good work, learning the language, and working hard. A degree in international business is not a joke, Richard. It can come in handy if one day he decides to take over the business. And another thing, son, any kid around here would give up his left nut to tour Europe. As you have done, on several occasions, if I recall.

I'm not any kid around here, Richard jumped back. I happen to be your son. I didn't ask you or anybody else to bring me into this lousy world. You did that on your own. My guess is that you couldn't control your animal appetite. Am I right, Rafa, or am I wrong?

Rafa hated it when his son Richard called him Rafa and talked about not asking to be born. But again, there was nothing he could do about it. The kid had him in the corner, and he couldn't slug his way out.

OK, Richard, Rafa stated and attempted to be tough. You know your mother doesn't appreciate it when you bring up that subject. It hurts her to hear you talk like that.

Richard turned and looked around the large office with a juvenile smile on his ferret face. He loved to whack his dad around. Hello! Anybody home? I don't see Mom in the office, unless you have her scrunched up in one of your desk drawers or under the desk with your big feet on her back.

Rafa squeezed his hands tight on his legs. He knew that Richard couldn't see them. Man, he thought. The hello shit was another expression he hated. More so when it came from adults who wanted to sound cool and mimicked the kids.

Let's change the subject, Richard. This conversation is getting us nowhere. About your party Saturday…don't invite too many kids, only your closest amigos. I'm gonna have some people over, and I don't want many crazy kids spoiling the fun. You can play two or three songs with your band, but that's it. I have a great band coming in from El Paso and a DJ for the younger set later. The ones who care to dance until the sun comes up.

I doubt many of your Ben-Gay crowd will be on their feet by then, Richard said. He was a little pissed off because he couldn't really call it his party. And another thing, Rafa, don't tell people I'm an accomplished musician, OK? Some might come up with the idea that I'm a classical pianist or something. That I can read music. It might be news to you, Dad. I can't read music because I never learned because I never cared for the piano that much. I found the piano boring, as were those clowns you paid to teach me. The way you exaggerate, some might walk away with the impression that any day I will debut solo at Carnegie Hall, playing Rachmaninoff's Rach 3. I play lead guitar in a punk-rock band, Dad. That's it. That's all I want to do. Richard was enjoying messing with his dad until Rafa interrupted, as he usually did.

No, Richard, you have it all wrong. The only reason I pushed the piano lessons on you was because one of your teachers advised us that playing the piano would improve your math scores. Your math was pretty bad, Richard. And it improved, and you know it. It improved a hell of a lot.

Yeah, sure it did. Why did you make such a big deal and pretend the party was for me?

It is for you, Richard. It's your birthday. It just happened to fall on a date I had circled on my calendar for months. You know, one of those events I give every year to pump up my supporters. The invites went out months ago, Richard. I couldn't cancel; that would be political suicide.

We can pull off both events. And who knows, you might receive more expensive gifts. Oh, and tell your friends not to do that cheap, hippie blow they do. It stinks up the house and scares my guests. Tell them if they want to get high to use pills or other substances that people can't smell while they're enjoying their booze.

So you're encouraging drug use, Dad? I thought you were always a fanatic against drugs.

No, no, don't misunderstand me, Richard. I don't want you to do drugs. But your friends…I can't stop them. I won't even try. It would be like talking to fish. Rafa giggled. I just don't want the smelly shit around when I'm entertaining guests; that's all.

I heard rumors you invited the governor. That true?

Rafa scratched his head and looked at his watch. I always invite the governor and lieutenant governor. It's more of a courtesy invitation than anything else; many do it. The governor and his people are very busy people, Richard. And unless I was to give a huge donation, which, believe me, I will never do, they won't bother. The invites go out nevertheless. You never know how desperate any one of those assholes may get. But listen, Richard, don't feel bad. You can have another party at the river levee and invite all the people you care to invite. You can rock out for days, and your friends can indulge in the substance of their choice. I'll provide you with one of the large generators for your electrical equipment or hire a DJ— whatever you want, son. I'll even hire private security, so the cops won't have an excuse to pay you a surprise visit. Whatcha say, Richard? Deal?

I'll think about it, Richard replied, and he left Rafa's office with his battle half-won and half-lost, as was always the case with Rafa.

Rafa looked at his watch again and thought about giving it to Richard for his birthday, but he changed his mind. Richard would probably give it away, he thought, just to charge him up. Richard was a high-maintenance kind of kid, but he loved him—always had. It was only that when Richard came along, he'd been done playing daddy. His other kids were much older, and they didn't require much attention. He had a business and a political career that took up most of his time. And the perks that came along down the road were too tempting to ignore. His wife had raised Richard practically on her own, and now he was paying for it. The boy was difficult to please, and his jealousy of his brother Tommy was a major concern.

Rafa had given Richard the job as property manager because his wife had insisted. She had argued that Richard, who had no employable skills, should learn something about something. Rafa couldn't put him out with the cement crews or driving cement trucks because the way he dressed and carried himself would be a distraction, to say the least. Property manager was the easiest job he could offer him, and he already had mucked that up. Goddamn, he said out loud. Fucking kids. Now he had to clean up the mess. He still blamed CI more than his stupid son. Slumlord Councilman read the headline on the front page of the Daily. He could see it from where the paper lay on the floor in a corner of his office. He could sue the paper for slander, but they had photos. It would be a waste of resources. Fuckface Rudy, the four-eyed reporter who had taken up the case, was also to blame, Rafa believed. Now he was in a fight with CI, and he couldn't back off. He had other rentals that needed repairs. He held off because the renters practically destroyed the place and then moved on. The house on Mesquite Street had been a mess when he bought it. Field workers had lived in it for years, and the owner had done nothing, absolutely nothing, to improve the property. The renters never complained because they were seasonal. He should have gone out there to check it out, but he had bought it unseen. What the hell—that's why he had a property manager in the first place, he resolved.

Rafa picked up the phone and said to Laura, Laura sweetheart, give Andy a call, and tell him to meet me in my business office in thirty minutes, OK? Rafa hung up the phone and placed his short legs and expensive shoes on top of his desk. He'd decided he was going to let his attorney look into the CI lease. If Andy could find something, then he would wash his hands of the matter and let Andy take care of it. That's why he paid him the big bucks. And if any concerned citizens questioned him on the scrutiny on the CI lease, he would remind them that it was his duty to look out for the interest of the city and the Eastside in particular. Then he thought of Max Luna. Shit. If it came down ugly, he would have to face him eventually. Not that he was afraid of Max; well, he was a little. They didn't call him Max el Loco for nothing. He got along with Max. It was his friend, Jerry Rivera, that crazy-looking pinto that worried him more.

Rafa was on his feet. He put some papers in his briefcase, ready to leave. He then recalled that Victoria Luna, Max's mother, had returned to Las Flores. He remembered Victoria Luna as a fox in their younger days. She had perfect alabaster-white skin and long black, wavy hair with light-hazel eyes, flecked with gray. She wore tight skirts above the knees, which amplified her well-proportioned body. She wasn't tall, or short either. A doll. Eye candy in all aspects. He could never score with a girl like Victoria. Few could. And even though they had been almost neighbors, he might as well have lived on the moon, as far as Victoria was concerned. She was always with her brothers and sisters and seemed aloof and bookish. And then to everyone's surprise, she married one of the Luna brothers, Manuel Luna. And the pendejo had to go and get himself shot, hunting. Rafa shook his head and thought, Some people push their luck.

So many of the guys in the barrio, himself included, were getting a hard-on just thinking about being the first to get into the young widow's pants. But again, she had surprised them all by splitting town. She left little Max with her parents and never returned until now. He was sure she was still good-looking. That type of woman always took care of herself and stayed fit and attractive far longer than most. And now that he had money, maybe, just maybe, that would advance his cause a little. He could call and ask her out to dinner and reminisce over old times. By now he was sure she was aware of how well he was doing financially. Shit, he considered. There was Max and this thing with CI. He would have to wait and see before making his move on Victoria Luna, the woman of his dreams. At least she never called him Chunky Monkey—not to his face, anyway. He would remember that because he had loved her since, since he was a chunky monkey. And he laughed out loud. Mi amor secreto, my secret love, he used to whisper when he spied on her from his hiding place. He beat his meat while she hung clothes on the outside clotheslines, in her short shorts.

Rafa closed his briefcase and looked at the calendar, the only thing on his desk other than the phone. Now. And he chuckled. I can get all the Victorias I want. 'Cause money buys love, plenty of love, and he did a little dance. Then his mood changed. He still recalled the Chunky Monkey jokes, and it still hurt, and hurt deep, in a place he didn't like to visit. The taunting had become worse in the third and fourth grades when the kids called out, Peanuts for the Chunky Monkey. Then the Mexican kids learning English would mimic and repeat, Penis foor monki. And the older bullies would call him a chora eater, and that was the lowest form of punishment because a cocksucker he was not. He had to use his fists because that was the only thing left for him to do. He got his ass kicked almost daily. The name-calling. The hurtful jokes. And all the crap he had to put up with gave him an edge.

He didn't get into drugs or booze or other crazy shit kids his age were doing. He attacked his rage with hard, physical work. His father told him that work was the only thing, second to women, that could cleanse the soul. He worked construction with his father, one of the best cement finishers in Las Flores. He also became a cement finisher at seventeen. Cement finishers were some of the highest paid in the construction industry. But he was smart enough to realize that he couldn't do that job for too long. That the arthritis and other health issues would cripple him at a young age as it did his father and many of his uncles because of the long hours on the wet cement. Rafa, instead of spending his money and his time foolishly like many of his friends, saved his money. He learned everything he could about the cement business. Little by little he bought used trucks, any kind of truck, big and small. With trucks, he could make extra money charging people a fee to move stuff around. Eventually, he learned about credit and borrowing. The banks ignored him in the beginning. He had no collateral, and his father couldn't help him. His father was on medical disability and financially in bad shape. He borrowed from the finance companies and paid out the ass in high interest rates. He had no choice. He learned fast and made friends and money. He learned early on that owning the cement trucks would make him more money because the demand for concrete was high. He bought a used one and added to that one until he owned a fleet because the drive to be rich kept him up nights. He was going to show them all that the Chunky Monkey was not a chora eater. He paid the back taxes on old abandoned homes, made some repairs, and rented them out. In case his cement business went south, he had his rentals as a cushion.

He soon learned that you didn't have to be a genius to be successful. He looked at men like Earl Cotton and others. Not very bright people, who had the drive and learned how to make money without having any to start. The first thing he did when he moved into his plush new business office in the Arroyo Seco division was to blow up a print of a chunky monkey feeding peanuts to a starving honey badger locked up in cage. The print, in full color, forty by forty inches, in a nice frame, was hung up high behind his desk. The print was for the bullies who kicked his ass and called him a chora eater during his school years. The ones who worked in construction. When they came in for an interview in need of a job, they couldn't help but look at the huge print as they sat with their hats in their hands. They showed him photos of their ugly, smiling children with bad teeth. Rafa said nothing as he listened to their stories of hard times, messy divorces, and child support payments. Then dismissed them with a promise to call them if something came up, which he never did. He hired only younger, hardworking men who had no knowledge of his youth. He hired men from Chiva Town. And even a Sniper or two who wanted to work and not mess around all day bragging about how many women they had.

Shit, Rafa said. He looked at his watch. I best get out of here. The city business is done for the day. He closed the door to his office, stopped at Laura's desk all smiles, and told her he was leaving.

Laura studied him with a silly grin on her round face.

What? Rafa asked her.

Oh, nothing. It's only that your son Richard is so crazy.

Tell me something new. And Rafa still smiled.

No, it's nothing. It's just that he keeps insisting you're having an affair with my sister, Blanca. But I keep telling him you're too old for her.

Rafa's smile vanished like the first falling snowflakes on the hard rocks. He wanted to say, I'm rich, bitch. And if it wasn't for me, your sister would be pushing burgers in some grease joint or worse. He couldn't make up his mind if Laura was naive or stupid, and he didn't have the time or inclination to speculate on which.

Don't listen to Richard, Laura, Rafa finally said. You know him by now. Gotta go—time is money. Rafa took the stairs instead of the elevator in case he met any of his constituents coming to see him about some inconsequential bullshit he didn't have the time or patience to go into. He was getting hard thinking about Victoria Luna, and after talking to the attorney, he was going to visit his Casa Chica and practice some dance steps with his amorsito, Blanca, Laura's big sister. As Rafa started his new jet-black BMW 740Li, he said to himself, My old man had a Casa Chica. Maybe that's why we were so poor. Huh, I never thought about it that way. And he chuckled as he peeled out of the underground parking.

CHAPTER 11

Jerry Rivera walked back to his group of kids in the CI building. He saw Ruth talking to Clairisa Cotton outside her office. When Ruth noticed Jerry, she said, Hi, Jerry, have a minute?

Hey, Ruth, Jerry answered. Sure, what's up?

Have you met Claire yet?

Jerry got closer and said, No, I haven't.

Claire, this is Jerry Rivera. He's in charge of the athletic program. Jerry, this is Clairisa Cotton. She's our tutoring volunteer and psychologist.

Oh! I've heard Jerry's name mentioned many times by the students. And Claire smiled with a smile that could melt diamonds. May I call you Jerry?

Please do, replied Jerry. He tried hard not to go all silly over Clairisa Cotton. Damn, he thought, she must be the most beautiful woman he had ever seen in the flesh. His heart thumped hard in his muscular chest, and he was sure the women could hear it. He feared he would say something stupid. He felt as if he had swallowed his tongue, and it went down his throat all tied up in knots. He didn't dare talk. He stuck out his huge hand to her, if only to be sure she was made of flesh and bone. Clairisa Cotton took his big, brown hand in her small, soft, manicured hand without hesitation. She was steeped in the superior confidence beautiful women can get away with. And she even gave him a little squeeze. A good grip, just to show him that she wasn't as soft as she seemed. Jerry wondered if his imagination played tricks on him, or was the goddess holding his hand tight longer than usual? Ruth seemed to be looking at them with a smile on her face. And the smile implied, Down, dog. Or please let go of her hand, and get back to work. Jerry didn't care. Ruth and everything else disappeared, and only Clairisa Cotton remained. She was radiant in the amber light that the late afternoon cast through the large windows on top of the old building. He didn't want to release her hand and held on to it as long as he could. Clairisa was the woman he had seen in his dreams in the dark dungeons of despair and saved him from going mad.

Finally, Ruth said, I'll leave you guys to talk, and walked off to her own office.

Jerry released Claire's hand, and they both giggled like children sharing an ice-cream cone.

Jerry. And she looked at him straight in the eyes. You have a minute? I wanted to ask you a few questions about a student.

OK. Sure, Jerry said. He did not want to wake up from his dream. He refused to admit what was happening to him.

They walked into her office, and she closed the door behind her. Ruth's old office was windowless and larger than all the newer cubicles in the old building. Claire had brought in a small couch and an extra table with chairs for her group therapy sessions. Ruth had left her old desk and a metal filing cabinet for Claire to use. Claire sat on the couch, and Jerry pulled out a chair from the table and sat as far away from her as he could possibly get. She wore a turquoise workout suit made out of a pricey material and a white silk or cashmere top under the jacket of her suit. On her feet were soft, black leather moccasins with tiny turquoise stones embedded on the top and side, sold in the trendy, expensive boutiques of Santa Fe. Her hair, the color of teak wood, was thick, with more deep brown than yellow, as were her gorgeous eyes. Her skin was olive but tanned, and Jerry didn't know if by lamp or sun. Either one, he believed, had done a great job. She wore no makeup whatsoever or jewelry of any kind. Not even a wedding ring, and that puzzled him a little. He couldn't really size her chest because of the workout jacket. He was positive a woman of this caliber had nice, ample tetas. Whether her own or implanted, it didn't matter. Now he comprehended why Max, William, and Ruth called her Claire de Lune, which represented everything beautiful associated with the name. He had expected Claire to be some rich bitch with diamond earrings that dangled from her big ears and a patchy face caked with makeup. He'd thought he was going to meet, eventually, a swanky skank with plastic hair, who demanded to be treated like royalty, even though Ruth claimed she was nice.

Jerry had some experience talking with counselors, therapists, and the like, in the pen. He was rough, tough, and well-read. He could go back and forth with the people assigned to get into his head. He could exchange mind blows with the best, he'd always believed. But with this precious stone, he took a powerful left hook to the kidneys and couldn't recover. He didn't have the familiarity or vocabulary to express or comprehend what he felt. He felt something magical and scary at the same time.

Jerry crossed his muscular arms across his massive chest in a feeble attempt to cover the animal tattoos on his biceps with his hands. The scorpions on his neck were the ones that people seemed to notice more. He couldn't hide those because he was wearing a tank top. It didn't seem to matter much. Claire was focused on his eyes and nothing else. He had read somewhere that some people could read the soul by looking into a person's eyes. If anyone ever read the deep corners of his soul, they would need deep psychiatric therapy for years, he thought. And he wanted to laugh. He decided not to. At this point he attempted to relax. He had no other choice. He recalled some of his favorite actors from the forties and fifties, and some weren't that great looking, but they had been excellent actors. He was taller and had a better built on him than many of them, and in his dark and rugged way, he was considered handsome by some. So he thought, Hell with it. He was going to try to act as he always did. This was just another acting role, and he played them all the time. Never with butterflies jumping in his stomach though. That and falling for the leading actress were the only differences. It was huge, he realized. A huge part to play. He wanted to smile. He didn't dare. Instead he slouched a little in his chair. He placed his muscular leg on his opposite knee. He was not concerned if Claire was turned off by his shabby gym shoes.

I'm listening, he finally said. And he caressed her with his dark eyes.

You know, Jerry, Claire said, addressing him in a soft voice as if she had known him all her life, Nelson Sola really admires you, and I wanted to get your feedback on his behavior around you and the rest of the kids. Some of his teachers are pushing for a full assessment. They are well aware that if his scores are marginal, he will qualify for an IEP and will go to special classes. But his math scores are too high, and I refused to assess him. Those same teachers had convinced the mother to sign the consent form for testing. I talked to the mother before she signed the paperwork, and she agreed with me that special classes will not help Nelson in any way. The mother signed the consent form for me to talk to Nelson, but here, at the center. I want any information you can provide that might help me get a better reading of Nelson and his behavior.

Jerry was disappointed. That was all she wanted: a chitchat about Nelson Sola. Then he snapped out of it. What did he expect? For crying out loud, he reasoned. Did he really believe she wanted a date with him or a tumble on the couch? Calm down, he kept telling himself. Calm down. This is a sophisticated, educated, cultured woman who had done it all and more. Mike Cotton, in his younger days, was not a kick-sand-in-my-eyes kind of guy. He was a jock, as Max called him. A big, ass-kicking fullback for the Las Flores High Bulldogs. An all-American fucker who tossed the shot put a hundred miles' distance in track. So she wasn't impressed by any tattooed body-building, macho male. She had two kids, and they hadn't been conceived by an angel, although he wanted to think so. She was a woman who knew and got what she wanted. What she didn't want, she crunched up in the garbage disposal. But she was so beautiful he wanted to scream at his practical side to shut up.

Instead of playing the disappointment card, Jerry Rivera, who was in the greatest role of his young life, prepared for act 1. He had talked to many therapists at the state pen. He had learned the vocabulary and facial expressions to get what he wanted most of the time. He put his dark, hairy, brawny leg down and leaned toward her.

Is it Clairisa or Claire? he asked with the smoothness of an insurance salesman at his slimy best.

Claire, she replied. And she placed her arms around her knees and pulled them toward her, like the kids did.

Stop. You're killing me, Jerry wanted to cry out, and then it hit him. It was her. His babe. The image he took with him when he was beaten and put in the hole for days. The image of a young Vivien Leigh, and not from Gone with the Wind or Caesar and Cleopatra, but from That Hamilton

Woman, done in 1941. That's why he was struck with her. Damn. He admitted Claire resembled Vivien Leigh. And he had been so in love with her for years, until he saw her in A Streetcar Named Desire. She'd played Blanche DuBois. She had disgraced herself all over Brando as he abused her. He should have never seen the movie. After reading the play, by one of his favorites, Tennessee Williams, he thought he could handle the movie. It had killed him. He'd cried for a month.

Jerry cleared his throat. He attempted to control his feelings, not sure he could. You know, Claire, I'm Horatio Nelson, he was going to blurt out, but he bit his tongue. Nelson has come a long way, he said instead. When I first started to work with him, he was so active. He couldn't stop jumping around for a minute. He messed with the girls all the time and whined when they slugged him. One day I really gave him some time. I listened to him tell me about his day at school and here. Once he was confident I wasn't going to make fun of him, he slowed down some. I taught him some breathing exercises to help relax him, along with some physical stuff to learn how to take care of himself. He liked that. I also noticed that when he focused in on something he really liked, he gave it all his attention, for long periods of time. You know, like kids who have that…that mild autism?

Asperger's, Claire clarified, taking in every word Jerry said.

Yes, that. He engages and interacts. He makes eye contact, so I don't think it's Asperger's, but what do I know? Anyway, we found out he was good in math, and we asked him if he wanted to help the kids who needed help with math. He jumped at the idea. And he's not bossy. Well, he is a little, but he's working on it. With your help, Claire, and Jerry wanted to touch her perfect face, I believe Nelson Sola will be a stronger, more considerate, confident student and learn to get along with his peers way better.

I'm so glad you feel that way, Jerry. And Claire beamed with a sincerity that was difficult to fake. Nelson always talks about you. Jerry's my man, he tells me. Jerry can go deep. He taught me how to fly. You know, things of that sort.

Claire placed her feet on the floor and was about to say adios, amigo, when Jerry put on his concerned face. He lowered his big black eyes. He furrowed his forehead and strained his voice to a heartrending pitch.

Claire. He did not want to let go, not yet. I don't know if this is appropriate. I need to ask you for a favor, a big favor. I don't know if you are aware…if you know that…that I've done time. And to satisfy my parole, I need to get in some hours of counseling. I don't know if you work with the staff. I want to do my hours with you. If it's OK, I mean. And your schedule is not too tight, that is.

The whole world knows, Jerry, my dear boy. One look at you is enough, Claire told herself. She didn't want to say anything to hurt this big hunk of steel. She kind of liked him. He was different from most men she knew, way different. She said, delighted he had asked, Of course, Jerry— not a problem. Let's set something up. I don't know if Ruth told you, but I'm always here for the kids, the parents, and the staff when they need me.

Terrific, Claire. And Jerry breathed a sigh of relief. You have saved my life. And he wanted to hug her, but it was too soon for that.

Not only that, Jerry—I saved you the hassle of driving to the Westside in search of a psychologist. They both giggled. She has a sense of humor, thought Jerry, and he liked that.

Jerry left Claire's office in a wonderful mood, and he wanted to skip as he had when his pocket had jingled with coins after he had cleaned out all the other kids at the corner crapshoot. He then noticed his group waiting for him to start them on their meditation exercises. He felt so alive and strange all over, body and mind. He wanted to laugh for no reason, no reason at all. What did that woman do to me? he kept asking himself over and over.

While Jerry was having his little heart-bouncing get-together with Claire de Lune in her office, Max, Ruth, and William entertained Mrs. Wilma Harrison. She was the deputy to the state's chief auditor of all nonprofits of matching or nonmatching funds or grant money of any kind. She was a middle-aged woman dressed in middle-aged attire who loved to travel the state and see for herself how the taxpayers' money was being utilized. She wasn't a hard-ass. She left that nonsense for her minions who did the follow-up visits later, if she noticed any discrepancies. She was all smiles and always insisted on meeting everyone on the staff and knowing what their positions were. She liked Ruth and William and admired their youthful passion to help the needy in the community, something she herself never enjoyed. She particularly liked Ruth. She admired her energy and her meticulous style of writing grants, squeezing every penny she could out of the state. She had offered Ruth a job in her office on several occasions, but the young woman was determined to stay on her idealistic path and help the poor. A waste of talent, she thought, but to each his own was her favorite saying. Maybe one day Ruth would open her eyes and change her mind about helping the poor and take her up on her offer, as Mrs. Harrison strongly believed others as dedicated as Ruth had done. Mrs. Harrison didn't care that much for Max Luna, the director of Community Impact. He was too clever for his own good, and it bothered her to say so. He had a sense of humor that didn't go well with her. It just rubbed her the wrong way, and she was always puzzled because she could never understand why. She liked William though. William, with his freckled face and carrot hair, was short but well-built. She would give a month's salary to see Ruth hump him, both naked in front of a blazing fire. Her tight little body locked in his, screaming with pleasure. Passionate little fuckers, she thought. The only passion her husband exhibited at his age was when he gulped down a slice of pecan pie along with a warm glass of milk and had a rigorous Bible study before going to bed early.

Oh, Mrs. Harrison, Max interrupted her naughty thoughts. Let me go and get the newest member of our team. Be right back.

Max walked over to the far corner of the building, beyond the boxing ring. Jerry sat cross-legged on top of a padded black leather mat. Six students sat in front of him in the same position. They had just completed their meditation exercises and were looking at Jerry in a calm but detached manner as if they had just arrived from a distant journey. Jerry waited for them to land and grasp the realities of their present-day world. This time he had used deep-breathing concentration to regress them back to when they were little children, their favorite trip. Some of them made baby noises and sucked their thumbs. After the exercise, he would have them write a poem about their experience, and the stuff they wrote, he thought, was amazing. He would have to share the writings with Claire one day. Now they wanted to spar and kick ass, as they called it. His only regret was that they weren't old enough for him to show them body and mind separation and the art of soul travel he had learned in prison to escape the hole.

Some of the students were still in the lethargic stage. They studied their hands and feet with a sad look on their youthful faces. Others were stretching, and Nelson Sola was already by Jerry's side talking up a storm. I was flying, Jerry. I was floating away from everything. I love it. When can we do it again? Please.

Remember, Nelson, Jerry said. He still had Claire on his mind. Don't fly away too far because you might not find your way back, and your parents will be very sad.

Yeah, right. Nelson grinned. Hey, Jerry, Jerry, he cried out, all excited as if he had never relaxed at all. I have one for you. You ready?

OK, buddy. Hit me.

What can you hold without touching it?

Let me see. And Jerry scratched his ear. I give up. I don't know; tell me.

Your breath. Nelson laughed and jumped around like a wild colt.

Jerry also laughed at seeing him so happy. That's a good one, Nelson.

Jerry, Max called out from a short distance.

OK, guys, Jerry announced. He saw Max was calling him. Stretch out good, choose a partner, and I shall return.

Jerry walked over to Max and said, I saw an angel, Max, a real angel.

Big Bertha come over for a visit? Max replied, and they both laughed out loud.

Jerry gave him a playful jab to the stomach. No, man, seriously. You didn't warn me Claire was so fucking gorgeous.

Why do you think they call her Clair de Lune? 'Cause she looks like Frankenstein's wife?

I know. Damn. I thought you guys were playing with me. She's a beauty, a really good-looking, out-of-this-world beauty. She's like a movie star. She could be in movies if she wanted to, I bet.

Get it together, Jerry, Max responded, a little exasperated. She wouldn't get a second look in Hollywood. Not by the people who count, maybe by the perverts and pimps. Besides, she's the wife of that snake, Mike Cotton, don't forget. Anyway, I want you to meet a big cheese, deputy director of compliance or auditor for the state, some shit like that. She wants to meet all the staff for reasons that only she knows. So put on your hiking boots, my dear boy, and get ready to climb the mountain. And they both cracked up again.

They walked unhurried and still laughing toward the visitor, Mrs. Wilma Harrison, who was still yapping and smiling with Ruth and William. Jerry was still in his black tank top and black, baggy shorts that fell to a little above the knees. He wouldn't be caught dead wearing tight, skimpy shorts.

Mrs. Harrison, meet my good friend and assistant, Mr. Jerry Rivera.

The good woman almost lunged at Jerry. She stuck out her paw. What she really hoped for was a tight, tit-crunching hug from the tattooed savage.

Jerry smiled the smug smile of a man who can sense perfectly clear what the client really wants but has too many hang-ups to ask for.

Jerry Rivera, at your service, he said, as he grabbed her sweaty paw and gave it a tiny squeeze, just enough to hint at the young, hard cock game she was missing out on.

To Mrs. Harrison, Jerry's hand felt like a hot biscuit at the county fair, and a large biscuit at that. All it lacked was honey, and she would have had it inside her mouth. She could melt on that dark-brown skin like butter on hot toast, but she dropped the image. That kind of dreaming was a little below her upbringing. And with a huge smile, she said, I'm impressed with your class, Mr. Rivera, or may I call you Jerry?

As you please, ma'am.

The ma'am part was a turnoff, but she reconciled with the fact that the boy was polite as well as sexy.

And if I may ask, your class with the students was what?

You may. It is part of our martial-arts training. The emphasis is to develop mental strength to direct physical action toward positive results.

Very impressive, if I may say so. And were you at State also, Jerry?

Yes, I was.

May I ask what you studied at State?

You may. I majored in Russian literature with a minor on the erotic literature of the Aztecs.

Ruth, who was a little behind Wilma Harrison, turned fire-engine red. Max and William had to bite their tongues to keep from busting out laughing. Jerry kept his cool as if he were being interviewed for a position with the chamber of commerce.

My, my, what a fascinating career you are going to have, Jerry. And Mrs. Harrison inched closer to him. She wanted to smell his sweaty, musky, well-built body. I wish they had more interesting classes when I attended college, but they didn't, sad to say. Well, everything seems to be in order, Max. I went over the books with sweet Ruth, and your program seems to be going the right direction. I will send an official correspondence for your records that you are in compliance. Keep up the good work, and I will see you in six months, God willing. Wilma Harrison still had to drive south to the heathen city of the crosses, where she would spend the night at the boring Holiday Inn. But maybe tonight she would meet a young Latin lover at the bar. She would buy him a couple of drinks to get him interested and take him to her room, where he would turn back her clock and make her forget about work and other things she'd rather not think about. If it was only that easy. She cursed as she started her state-owned car and drove out of the parking lot.

As soon as Wilma Harrison stepped out the door, the three men busted out laughing like little boys comparing their little cocks. Ruth couldn't believe it at first. With one nod of her double chin, Wilma Harrison could flush down the toilet months' worth of work. She was all smiles in person, but when she had her minions write and send her reports, she was a ball-breaker. Ruth studied Max, who laughed the loudest. After what William had told her about the intellectual Max Luna, she saw him in a different light. At first it was Jerry she pondered on. Jerry, with all his swagger and macho gestures in his tank tops, and it wasn't even summer, was a bit of a worry. Jerry, recently released from prison, had given her the creeps, especially the first week he'd reported to work. But then she got to know him, and he turned out to be the nicest guy. And he did time for a good reason, for defending his mom, and that made it much easier to warm up to him. But Max, hiding his eyes behind his frameless wired granny glasses, even inside the building, was another matter. But then she thought she was getting paranoid over nothing. William said they were OK, and she trusted him 100 percent. They were her boys, and William assured her that Max and Jerry were the best guys to have in your corner. She loved to see them laugh and banter like children, but they could get serious, even vicious, at the drop of a hat.

CHAPTER 12

ike Montes was in his office. He examined his face in a small mirror he kept in his desk. He had shaved off the mustache and goatee the day before. He felt naked. He also looked younger. The mustache and growth on his chin were OK in Los Angeles, but here people were a little more conservative, and in his position as mayor, he had to appear less of a vato and more of a representative of all the people. Besides, it was time-consuming and a hassle because he had to visit Flora's Beauty Salon and have Flora trim it every other day. She opened early for him, and she kept every hair in place. She also did his hair and kept it in presentable shape, not too long or too short. He still styled it combed to the back, never with a part to the side; that wasn't him. Flora was a nice woman, and she did exactly what he asked for and kept his face as pretty as possible. He tipped her generously, and she loved to fuss over him. She would probably be disappointed because he had shaved at home and hadn't let her do it. She wouldn't say a word. She wasn't that type of woman. She still had the hair on his head for her soft hands to play with, so he didn't feel bad shaving the hair off his face on his own. Now he had to apply higher UV sunscreen protection to his face because the climate here was harsher than in Los Angeles, especially during the summer. Flora would see to his needs in that department also. He could depend on her for his face not to turn leathery, like his uncle Arturo's. His father still had decent facial skin because he always wore a hat and never worked in the hot sun for many days straight. His mother had beautiful skin. She spent most of her days inside the house when the sun was strongest. She got some sun when she worked in her garden and when she walked to church. And she loved the hot summer days. And that was because she came from the cooler Mimbres Valley climate.

Mike put the mirror back in the desk drawer, leaned back in his chair, and placed his feet on top of his desk. He didn't wear his boots anymore. Even though they weren't pointed cowboy boots—they were handcrafted—he didn't want people to get the idea that he was into cowboy boots. Real vatos, in his opinion, never wore cowboy boots. Never. Not in Las Flores, anyway. Maybe in California it was a fashion statement, but here it could be seen as a political statement. Guys like Max Luna or even Rafa would never be seen in public wearing ugly, pointed-toe cowboy boots. He felt better wearing his J&M's, and they were very comfortable shoes. Shoes made for presidents. How could I go wrong? he thought. He pushed a button under his desk drawer, and the Native American flute music of John Rainer Jr. filled the office. His office was electronically wired, so he could listen to his favorite sounds at a push of a button. He recalled when he had purchased Songs of the Indian Flute in Taos Pueblo. John Rainer Jr. had been in the shop. He'd autographed the CD and then had given him a flute carved out of pine as a gift. That had made his day—not only did he meet the great John Rainer Jr. in person, but he got a gift from him as well.

The flute music filled his office like a cool, gentle breeze in a golden meadow, high in the mountains. And the cool breeze swayed the yellow wildflowers to dance their dance. The flute music soothed his busy mind and brought back the time he'd spent in his mother's arms being rocked to sleep in the old rocking chair. A time of peace and calm when being held by his mother, Alma, was the center of his young world. The flute music went high and low. And it captured within him a euphoric crescendo that John made you feel with the power of his flute and with all the feeling of love he expressed through his music. Then the chants came in deep, and the human voices with their rich pitches traversed the soul like a magical, musical wind with drums. The mesmerizing and enchanted vocals that awakened the deepest emotions veiled in his active life. He drifted in a lake of natural sound out of his physical body. His body was discarded on the lake's shore like a useless entity. His heart and soul connected to the natural elements—the sound of the flute and the chants in a language not his own. A big part of him, in a spiritual way, knew no language barriers. He never wanted to leave this feeling of pure pleasure. This ecstasy of a nonmaterial existence he only dreamed of, but lacked the courage to follow in its path. Maybe one day, he reflected. When, he couldn't say.

Mike turned the music off, afraid to go deeper into his thoughts. The spirit of the flute did funny things to his head. Alexis Cordova Riley, his girlfriend and maybe future wife, was going to spend the night with him on her way to El Paso, and he had things to do. They had met in law school at USC. She was from Oakland, California. Her father was a retired professor of romance languages who had taught at UC–Berkley for over thirty years. Her mother, also a professor, was from Spain, where she'd met Alexis's father when he was in Europe studying. They fell in love and married. Mike liked the old professor. He always insisted he was a distant relative of the Irishman John Riley, who had led the Saint Patrick Battalion during the Mexican-American War of 1846. He had almost come to blows on several occasions when some of his colleagues called John Riley a deserter and mercenary interested more in the land grants and financial incentives the Mexican government promised him than the motivation to fight for the Catholic cause against an imperialist nation. He recalled when he first had met the professor and asked him, with tongue in cheek, if he wasn't a little uneasy about his daughter dating a Chicano from New Mexico. The professor, with a little chuckle, stated that he trusted his daughter's intelligence and upbringing to date anyone she fancied. Besides, at his age, he worried more about having a good bowel movement than whom his daughter dated.

When Mike had made the decision to return to Las Flores, Alexis had secured a transfer from the Diocese of Oakland to the Diocese of Santa Fe. She was an attorney for Catholic Charities. Even the professor, her father, relocated to Santa Fe and shared a house with Alexis. Alexis's mother wanted to work more years. She remained in Oakland. It worked out perfectly for Mike because he didn't have to fly to California, and Alexis didn't have to fly to Albuquerque to meet up. When Mike completed law school and passed the bar, he was offered a job by the law firm of Gutierrez, Sanchez, and Sanchez. The same law firm that kept his trust and dispensed his allowance until he reached the age agreed upon. He was hired on as a tax adviser and property consultant. He had worked in that department part-time when in law school. His main task was to find ways to reconfigure tax assessments—a euphemism for finding means to lower property taxes for the wealthy. After he worked for the law firm for a couple of years, his money transferred to his name, and he decided to go out on his own. By then he had a lot of contacts, and he could keep up to 50 percent of any money he saved his clients on property taxes. But after three or four years of pushing hard and making money, he decided it was time to make his move. Younger attorneys just out of law school were getting into the game and did whatever it took to get a piece of the action. They donated time and money to elect a county assessor who would provide them in return the names of the commercial property owners and tony zip code homeowners. Then the sharks would promise the owners they would find a way to reduce the value of the property and split the refund down the middle. Mike knew the bubble was going to burst, and he didn't want to be around when it did. Besides, he already had his company, Rayos de la Luna, here in Las Flores and enough money to make a go of it.

Oh shit! Mike cried out loud. He remembered he was to meet Vivien Madrid at the Azteca Restaurant—the one on the Eastside—at eleven this morning. Vivien Madrid was in New Mexico with her husband, a director in pursuit of a movie project. He was sure she wanted to sell the second five hundred acres he needed to connect them to his Dos Cerros and Luna Negra projects. He needed to talk to her before Mike Cotton came in with his offer. He believed Vivien Madrid also wanted to contact her godfather, Juan Jose, to find out if the old man held on to any more land or cash. Vivien had to be handled with silk gloves, he acknowledged. The last time he saw her was in California, and it almost had turned out to be a disaster. He had invited her over to his pad to make an offer for the five hundred acres given to her by her godfather. He made an offer. She accepted, and they ended up in bed. She just lay there on the bed and didn't even pretend to enjoy it, but he'd gotten the first five hundred acres and at a great price. He was sure this time it was going to be different. She was more mature and undoubtedly savvier of the housing explosion in Las Flores, considered Mike, as he pulled out a file.

The phone rang, and Mike didn't want to pick it up. He was sure it was Vivien Madrid, canceling their meeting. Shit, he said. And he picked up the phone by the fourth ring.

Mike. There's a…a woman here to see you, Estrella Gallo, Mike's secretary, almost whispered into the phone in her timid voice. She calls herself Shonofa, and she…she insists in seeing you.

What! Mike said to himself. Then he said into the phone, Estrella, give me five minutes and then send her in. He had no choice but to see the woman in black. He still remembered her exact words: If I ever need any favors, I will come calling. He put his hands on his face. He was worried that this could be the beginning of the end. Everything was going so great for him, he thought. Why did he ever trust her? Ramon was out of the picture for good. This woman knew too much of his past. He tried to calm down and relax.

The door to his office opened, and Shonofa, the woman in black, walked in with a huge smile on her face. She was still in black but not rags. She was in a long black dress of quality material. Her hair was still long, black as night, but professionally coiffured. Her face was round. A little fuller. Still tanned, and still wrinkle-free, with no makeup. She smiled with the confidence that success can bring, and she was not at all like someone in need of a handout.

Mike also attempted his best smile. He remained standing behind his desk. He did not approach her because he didn't trust himself to either hug her or strangle her.

Miguel, my son! Shonofa exclaimed. She was happy to see Mike and not doing anything to hide it. You look healthy. And I can see you have done well for yourself. And your parents—how are they?

Great. Thanks for asking, Mike responded. A little more relaxed. You look as if you've done OK yourself.

I have. Thanks to Her. She was holding a thirty-by-thirty-inch canvas without a frame, covered by a black silk cloth, and she set it on the edge of his desk. My artwork is selling, and not only here, but in Europe as well. She removed the silk cover from the canvas and said, I brought you a little gift. I pray you like it.

It was a painting of the Turquoise Mountains with a full moon that seemed to be rising in a brilliant, golden splendor behind the summit known as the Eagle's Peak. The silhouette of the Eagle's Peak against the luminous tone of the full golden moon spread out mauve and red-orange to the rest of the lower mountain. The lesser peaks on the left and right of the Eagle's Peak resembled the huge wings of a mighty eagle in flight, with the main peak as the head of the massive predator. The eyes of the great bird were turquoise embedded in molten lava, and they peered out in defiance. To Mike, they seemed to say, I am the beginning, as I am the end. And on the floor of the mountain were the vividly glowing, tiny lights of the city of Las Flores, like inverse stars, fallen from the heavens and scattered all over the floor of the valley.

Mike was speechless. He couldn't get over the painting. Thank you, Shonofa. Thank you so much. I love it, he finally said. He picked up the painting and walked it over to the floor-to-ceiling window, and the colors on the painting seemed to change with the direct sunlight. Wow! he said. I have a perfect place where this beautiful painting is going to go in my house.

I didn't frame it, Miguel. I was not sure if you were going to like it and, if you did like it, where you might hang it.

Mike placed the painting very carefully on his desk. He sat and offered Shonofa a chair. She sat and stared at Mike with the same huge smile on her calm face.

Oh, oh, here it comes, Mike thought. First the gift to butter me up and then the bad news. So you continued with your painting? he asked. He wanted to delay the bad news as long as possible.

Yes, I did. About a year after you went to California, a woman from Santa Fe was driving close to Snake Town when she stopped to ask for directions and noticed my paintings. She asked me if I would go to Santa Fe and show my art at an art gathering. She was a connoisseur and a collector and was always looking for new talent to display their work. I promised her I would have something ready for her in a couple of months. I didn't see her again until a year later when she appeared in Santa Maria. She apologized. She said she came down to Las Flores but couldn't find me. She had a friend with her, an artist who worked out of Santa Fe. I gave them permission to take my paintings, the ones I felt were OK. I couldn't go with them because my man, Santiago, was not well, and I could not leave him alone. To make a long story short, they apparently liked what

I captured on canvas, and it sold fast. The woman returned and placed a bundle of cash in my hands. Santiago, my man, reminded me in a gentle way to keep only what we needed for our simple needs and give the rest to the Las Flores Community Center, which I did. After all, Miguel, they did feed us many times throughout the years. The woman left me her card and invited me to go paint in a studio in Taos—at no cost and all supplies were free—whenever I wished to.

That is a very interesting story. And Mike pondered on the questions he really wanted to ask her. Is your man, Santiago, with you? he asked instead.

No, dear, no. And Shonofa's smile spread on her deeply bronzed face. He passed about a month or two after the woman's last visit. I was sad, of course, but joyful at the same time. His spirit was finally liberated from his frail body, and he was free to fly as he was born to do. Juan Jose—you remember Juan Jose, right, Miguel? Of course you do. Juan Jose assisted me in putting Santiago in the ground in an unmarked grave outside Santa Maria, just as he wished. Juan Jose also convinced me to go to Taos and work on my painting. But I still see Santiago every night in my dreams. We still communicate. He gives me advice on how to live my life and talks to me about his travels in that world of light and shadows that will eventually be my home also.

Yes, Mike said. He did not want to continue that conversation for too long. And you left Las Flores, went to Taos, and did your thing?

I grieved for a couple of months. Not exactly the grieving people normally do. My grieving was dancing on Santiago's grave to assist him to reach the heaven he always wished for. Juan Jose would beat on his drum or play his wooden flute, and I danced around the small fire and sang his favorite songs. After we were sure Santiago had reached his destination, and he did leave me plenty of messages, I left. I loved the place the women worked at. It was outside Taos, next to the mountains, and had this tremendous energy, and I couldn't stop painting. The brushes and canvas were of higher quality, and I still used my plant-made paint. I learned to mix store-bought tubes, and the results were to my satisfaction.

Damn, Mike said to himself. That's the dream I kept having. He wanted to know if she made any money or came to visit to hit him up for some. I can see by the gift you gave me that your paintings have a certain quality.

Of course they sold, Miguel. Do not worry. I did not come to ask you for any assistance. My paintings today sell for thirty or forty thousand apiece. I have exhibited in Paris, London, Berlin, and Madrid. The French, who are known to be selective, loved them. I sold out in a week in Paris and have returned five or six times, all with the same success. Then Shonofa placed two fingers on her lips and got a sad look in her big brown doe eyes. I apologize, Miguel. Santiago never wants me to talk about my work in that way. Boasting is for the weak-minded, he always used to say. He is content now because I opened a school of art for children with few resources, and I channel all my earnings to the school. Rich children can apply, but I charge their parents a high tuition to discourage them. Some still enroll. You know, Miguel, I didn't know anything about paying taxes. I never held a job. I learned soon enough, and that was another reason I opened the school.

A smart move, Shonofa. Mike felt shitty for being so suspicious of Shonofa. If you ever need help with the taxman, you give me a call.

Thank you, Miguel. I definitely will. Now I must run. I have a plane to catch, and my driver is waiting in the parking lot. I have a showing in Dallas and one in Chicago after that. Listen to me; I am boasting again. And she laughed. I was so afraid of flying until my man, Santiago, advised me to close my eyes and hold his hand. And when I did that, well, now I fly anywhere I desire. Give my regards to your parents, Miguel, and continue having a wonderful life. See you.

Mike rushed from behind his desk and gave her a quick hug before she walked out the door, and then breathed a huge sigh of relief. Happy days are here again, he sang out. And he studied the gift from Shonofa. He knew exactly where he was going to hang it in his new condo. He suddenly stopped singing and sat in his chair. Ramon came to his mind. The painting reminded him of Ramon—talented Ramon, who could have gone a long way with his art. He recalled he had stopped at the hospital to visit Ramon when he was in Albuquerque, catching a bus to Los Angeles. They told him at the hospital that Ramon was on suicide watch and was not permitted visitors. Ramon, his good friend, never had recovered his mental facilities. He had attempted suicide when he was close to recovery and had to be medicated for his own good. The heavy sedation put him in a vegetative state, almost a coma-like existence where he endured in a tomb of silence that lasted months at a time. Mike hadn't attempted any more visits, and he felt terrible about it. He realized Ramon would never recover his memory, even though the doctors had attempted many known and experimental therapies on him. He never found out what happened to Estela, Ramon's mother. He had asked around because he wanted to help any way he could. No one could tell him where she was or if she was still alive. Sad, he thought, as he studied the painting.

Mike glanced at his watch for a second, and he recalled the dream as if his watch had some kind of power over his dreams. The last time he remembered having the dream was a couple of months before he left Los Angeles. It was the same recurring dream, and it was always in Snake Town or Santa Maria. Shonofa danced in the light of the moon around a small fire. The Flying Man, Santiago, played on a wooden flute, and Juan Jose beat on an elk-skin drum. Shonofa, the woman in black, her coal-black hair loose to the waist, moved to the beat of the drum and flute with a rhythmic grace. Shonofa smiled with her eyes half-closed, and the magical sound from the flute and drum seemed to make her glide on her bare feet, whirling and leaving the ground at will. Then in a slow, deliberate motion, she stopped and pulled out a little cloth pouch of tiny dolls bearing the names of Mike's family members and pitched them in the fire. There was a puff sound, and flames of different colors flew skyward like a fireworks display, and Shonofa laughed with glee. Then Mike saw Hector. Hector sat next to the fire with a large sack full of dry cornhusks, and he threw them in the fire one at a time and smiled. Before he woke up from the crazy dream, or maybe it was another dream, he saw Ramon in a wheelchair. Ramon was close to the same fire. He was legless with a huge snake around his neck and stared at the fire with dead eyes. When Mike had woken up, trembling and frightened, he'd considered canceling his return to Las Flores. Thank God he hadn't—everything had worked out so perfectly for him on his return.

Mike glanced at his watch again and said, Time to go and make a deal with Vivien Madrid. Mike stopped at Estrella Gallo's desk; looked at his young, shy, beautiful secretary; and said, I'll be at the Azteca, Estrella. No calls unless it's an emergency. Estrella blushed red like a ripe tomato, as she always did when Mike addressed her.

Everything OK, Estrella? Mike asked. He knew damn well the young woman was in love with him. In his younger days, Estrella Gallo would have been his for the taking. Now he was a mature man, the mayor of the town, and almost engaged to be married. Your classes going OK, Estrella?

Yes, she answered. She did not look at him and pretended to be working on some papers. Her heart pounded in her full chest.

OK, then. See you later. Oh, Estrella, I'll be at the Azteca, he repeated, in case Estrella had failed to catch it the first time. No calls. Unless it's my parents.

Mike Montes sat in his usual place inside the Azteca Restaurant. The restaurant was located on Calle de los Angeles, which ran north and south. It was in between Calle Catolica, which ran east and west, and Calle de las Golondrinas, which also ran east and west. The Azteca was positioned in a perfect location, close to Our Lady of Guadalupe Church. The Azteca was owned by Santos Romero, a Tejano who had arrived in Las Flores when he was very young and never returned to Tejas. He sold burritos from the back of his pickup truck to construction workers. Then he utilized other trucks to sell his famous burritos all over town until he had enough cash to open the Azteca. He eventually bought the building and decorated it with Aztec motifs and whatnots. The food was authentic and tasty enough to attract some tourists who yearned for good, reasonable New Mexican food. Santos was so successful that years later he had opened another larger Azteca on Sierra Street in the Westside for people who were too finicky to venture to the Eastside but wanted delicious food at a good price.

The Azteca was not a large place, per say. It was long in front, and it stretched out from south to north, like an old-fashioned dinner. Santos had enlarged the building to create more practical floor space in front and back. He had added a dance floor. It wasn't very large but was adequate for dancing or for adding more tables when needed. He placed tables in the back for the folks who wanted to see but not be seen. They had a view of the street and the patio in front. Santos accomplished this by putting in large windows all along the front of the building, which allowed more natural light to filter into the building. The natural light accentuated the spectacular reds, oranges, greens, and many other colors of the pre-Columbian culture that was displayed on murals throughout the restaurant. The macramé wrapped around colorful hanging pots was not overdone, and the place in general was very clean.

Mike Montes sat in his usual place, a secluded table in the back part of the Azteca. He studied the colorful murals of the well-built indigenous men and women in skimpy dress. In his younger days, he would get a hard-on just looking at the beautiful women exposing all that bronze cleavage and perfectly shaped legs. He wanted to laugh now. Instead he took a sip of his iced tea and glanced at his watch. He wondered if the movie star Vivien Madrid was going to show. When Santos had enlarged the Azteca, he'd raised the back part a couple of feet so it would be higher than the main floor but still be part of the main floor. So even though he sat in the back, Mike could see anyone coming in or leaving through the front door. He glanced at his watch again. He didn't want to lose his patience; he couldn't afford to. Vivien Madrid had what he wanted, and he had to be on his best behavior, even if he had to eat a little shit to get it.

He finally saw Vivien asking the waitress for his table as she entered the Azteca. She wore a not too tightly fitted patterned dress. It was expensively cut and not above the knee, as was usually the case with Vivien. It was of a beige and darker-brown color, in soft suede. Her shoes, flats, matched her dress and purse. Her long, thick hair, streaked with gray more for fashion than age, was brushed to the side and held by a jade brooch. Her makeup was minimal, and her skin was still the shade of Japanese pearls.

The waitress ushered her over to Mike's table. Mike stood up and pulled out a chair for her. The waitress returned with the menus and a glass of water for Vivien and left them alone.

Traffic bad, Vivien? asked Mike, not wanting to sound too sarcastic.

You wouldn't believe it, Mike—worse than Los Angeles.

Mike observed Vivien without making it look too obvious. She was as beautiful as ever. With her sea-green eyes, refined skin, and a body like a Greek goddess…if only she had talent, he thought.

Did you invite me here to what, Mike, stare at me…or are we going to talk business?

Vivien, I'm delighted you still have a sense of humor. I thought you would like to order something before we…we get into the business end.

All right. Let's do. She turned to the waitress, who stood ready to take their order. I'll have a large glass of freshly squeezed orange juice, toast with spelt bread, a side of goat cheese, and another side of orange marmalade.

Spelt bread? asked the waitress, attempting a smile.

Yes, Vivien said. She rolled her eyes. You want me to spell it out for you?

Santos Romero, the owner of the Azteca, walked out of the kitchen and asked the waitress for the order she was writing up.

I'll take it, Janet, he said in a calm voice. He had the experience to deal with picky customers. Well, look who's here, he said in a cheerful voice. Vivien Madrid and our handsome mayor, the flower of Las Flores. Welcome to our humble cocina, folks. Anything for you, Mr. Mayor? Our special for today will be our famous shrimp enchiladas with rice, salad, and refried or whole beans—your choice. It's early, but I can tell my chef to prepare it for you if you wish.

No thanks, Santos, Mike replied. He wanted to laugh because that was the way he bantered with Santos, but he was worried Vivien might think they were laughing at her.

Vivien Madrid never had liked Santos and seldom frequented his restaurant when she lived in Las Flores. That was nothing new. She never liked many people in town, and she wasn't going to start pretending she did now.

No. Just get me my order. We're in a hurry, she said as curt as she could cut it.

As you wish, Santos said, and he returned to the kitchen. He smiled as he always did, even when the customers were rude with a capital R. He demanded that of all his staff. There was a large sign in colorful letters on the wall behind the cash register that read for all to see, Service with a Smile.

So, Vivien, Mike said. He wanted to get the conversation started. You divorced your first husband after our brief get-together in Los Angeles? Don't get me wrong; I'm not suggesting it was because of me.

Please, Mike. Don't be silly. I still remember when I sold you that property. You took advantage of me in more ways than one.

Wait. Hold on, Vivien, Mike interjected, a little ruffled at the accusation. You must also remember that was five or six years ago. The property values were lower back then because of the recession. Nothing was happening around here back then, or very little. Construction was sluggish, and homes weren't selling. I gave you a fair price, and you told me your husband had a project, and you were going to be cast as the lead character and needed the cash.

Vivien took a sip of her orange juice. She did not touch the water. Perhaps she'd forgotten she was in New Mexico, her birthplace, and not in Old Mexico. She studied Mike and felt like slapping his clean-shaven, handsome face. The son of a bitch was still a good-looking man. Attractive as ever, she thought. He was clean-cut, rich, and mayor of Las Flores. How the hell did he manage that? she asked herself. Where did he get all his money from? They would have made a picture-perfect couple, especially in Hollywood, where people were judged on looks and how much they had in the bank. They could never be a couple though; their mind-sets were like night and day.

It was a vanity project, Mike, Vivien continued. She did not want to fall again for his smooth bull. My ex, who was a total idiot when it came to picking projects, cast me in an old remake of some fucking dud movie. He promised it was going to make us money. And I sold you the land cheap.

And now you have another project?

And now I have another five hundred acres, and you're not the only one who's interested.

You remarried? asked Mike. He did not appreciate the fact that she had mentioned another buyer.

Yes, I did, she answered, not wanting to talk about it.

Is he also a director?

Yes, he is that.

Is he…is he old? I mean older, like the first one?

Preceramic. Is that old enough for you, Mike? Christ Jesus. I gravitate toward mature men. Is that a crime in your book?

No, no, of course not, Vivien. I've seen it all before. It's a Hollywood thing. I get it.

Well, if you get it, let's go back to the second five hundred acres my godfather, Juan Jose, bless his soul, left me. And how much you're offering per acre. The first of the five hundred acres he left me, you took me for thirty-five thousand an acre. And you gave me only half down and the rest later.

Vivien, please. Let's be civil about this. We're still friends, after all. Lifelong friends, if I recall. I didn't take advantage, Vivien. I offered you a fair price; you accepted it. I gave you half down. That's standard procedure in the business.

I don't know about standard procedures in the business, Mike, but you're right. That's in the past, and you did pay all of it eventually.

Mike didn't like the way the conversation was going. He was worried Mike Cotton had made her an offer higher than he was willing to make, and she was toying with him to make a killing. He was biting his lower lip, a bad sign that he believed made him appear weak, worried, or both. If Vivien hired an attorney to negotiate for her, he was screwed. He had the investors all lined up, and he refused to use his own money or his partner's money. He was betting that Vivien didn't want to waste her time on attorneys and that her husband was pressuring her to come up with the cash and not knowing or caring about the skyrocketing prices of the once valueless land. That was the advantage he had. He had to move fast before Vivien and her hubby were advised on the valuable acreage in their hands. To Mike, they didn't seem like the kind of people who would take advice. He still had to make an offer and negotiate. First, he had to stop biting his lip like a kid about to get his first piece of ass.

I'll give you forty per acre, Mike said with a straight face.

Please, Mike. You disappoint me. And Vivien smiled. She showed her even, white, perfect teeth. You gave me thirty-five thousand per acre the last time, and that was what? Five, six years ago? I hear the acres are going for eighty max these days.

No way, no how, Vivien. Maybe a select few by the river, bottomland, maybe. We're talking about semidesert land in the East Mesa area with little water and less greenery.

And yet the snowbirds are willing to pay top money to live there, right, Mike? And your development company is building million-dollar-plus homes in that hostile, dry moonscape, or is that another no way, no how, Vivien?

Mike stared at Vivien and wanted to laugh out loud and bang his hands on the table with glee. She had done her homework and was playing with him. But the bottom line was that she needed the money and soon.

OK, Vivien. You're a ballbuster—always were. I'll give you forty-two per acre, and that's me being generous.

Give me forty-seven; be a darling. And I'll pick up the tab.

Mike knew he was in because she didn't ask for anything above fifty.

I'll give you forty-five thousand per acre, and I'll throw in a goat for your goat cheese.

Funny boy. And Vivien smiled her killer smile again. I'll take it. And only because we're almost family, and I want those other assholes to stop pestering me. I don't know how the hell they ever find me.

Mike stuck out his hand to her across the table. He really wanted to jump over the table and give her a deep, wet, tongue-in-the-mouth kiss. But that would only create a scene in the restaurant, and after all, he was the mayor. Hell, he was so happy he got the deal he wanted. And he had planned to go up to fifty thousand per acre. He would never say it out loud, and now he didn't have to. Hey, I'm good, he kept telling himself.

OK, Mike. Stop congratulating yourself. Vivien busted his soap bubble. You're going to get a hard-on, and I'm sure not going to put my hands under the table on your dirty thing. Maybe the waitress will. I'm sure you tip her good.

The waitress was behind Vivien with the food they ordered and heard every word. She was hesitant to approach because of Vivien. The waitress blushed but forced a smile until Mike gestured with his hand to put the food on the table. She carefully placed Vivien's order on the table. She didn't want any trouble with the crazy woman, because from the way Santos carried on, she had to be a high-priced call girl from California or Las Vegas. She gave Mike his small salad and asked him if they needed anything else. She didn't even bother to look at Vivien, who was already picking at her food.

Mike ate his salad with green goddess dressing that he loved so much. He didn't want to eat anything heavy, especially beans. He expected Alexis that evening, and he was going to prepare a light dinner for her. After dinner, they'd probably go on a hayride, and he didn't want to release any gas. At a young age, it could have been amusing. To him now, it was gross. For a couple to be farting while having sex was something to be avoided at all cost, in his opinion. He took a shower before having sex and after, unless he was exhausted. And that was rare, and again that was him. He didn't mind when Alexis followed his lead. If she didn't, it was fine because she didn't have that particular odor that some guys love. She was big on the Brazilian, which turned him on big-time. He didn't like the bush—once he'd been doing this girl and her bush had been so matted with filth that he couldn't get it in. Mike pushed his salad to the side. He had lost his appetite. And not only because of the bad memory, but because he was so excited he had succeeded in his quest for the Holy Grail. He noticed Vivien putting a dab of goat cheese on one side of the toast and the orange marmalade on the other half and then cutting the toast into quarters. She took tiny bites. She ignored Mike and focused only on the squares of spelt toast. What a meticulous bitch, he thought. She probably never expected Santos to come up with her order, but Santos kept up with the latest food trends because he could never tell when a superstar like Vivien Madrid might walk in.

Mike continued to wait for Vivien to finish up or complain about the goat cheese or something. She inspected every bite before putting it in her gorgeous mouth. Mike wondered if she adopted the same caution when she put her old husband's cock in her mouth, if she ever did. He could not comprehend how a righteous-looking mama-sota could settle for an older caballero with saddle sores. He knew Vivien had a clean, beautiful body, and he knew for a fact there were many cow-burros who would be delighted to take her out on a midnight stroll. When he'd had her, years ago, the one and only time, he had almost rolled over when he saw her naked for the first time. Once he was on her, he performed what he believed were his best magic tricks. And she just lay there like a dead fish, minus the smell. It was like she was waiting to clock out of a boring job, run home, and turn on the evening news. And he recalled what old Hector had told him once: beautiful women were high-maintenance, and you had to have the time and patience to cultivate their love.

Vivien finally finished eating her squares of toast and touched her mouth with a napkin. It was only out of habit, because there was nothing on her lips to suggest she had just eaten. She took a sip of orange juice and looked at Mike like a woman who was content with her life.

Not bad, she said. I'm impressed. I'll have to bring my husband, and he can try the shrimp enchiladas.

If she goes to the bathroom and barfs, I'll shoot myself, Mike thought.

She didn't. Vivien Madrid was ready to talk and be heard. Here is the deal, Mike. And she placed the cloth napkin back on her lap. She handed him two business cards she had slipped out of her purse. This card has the number for a joint account we have set up, and this other card is my private account number I have also set up for this money. Put the first eleven million in our joint account, and I expect to see the second eleven million in my private account in, let's say, a month or so. I trust you. There's no reason not to, right?

Aren't you going to put all the cash in your joint account to beef up your movie project?

Fuck no, Vivien said, shaking her head and smiling. I'm putting five million of my own money into the project. The other players can come up with the rest. They'll have to. Or I'll pull out of the deal. The first time I trusted that shithead I married, I was about to lose every penny. I didn't, and let me tell you the reason, Mike. When I left Las Flores, I stayed in some shit corner of East Los Angeles. I stayed with my aunt, her husband, and her three daughters, my cousins. My aunt would tell me every fucking day that I would find a job, a husband, and maybe, if I could manage the time, enroll in a community college. I would roll my eyes and say, Yes, ma'am. But every day I would jump on the bus out to Hollywood, Santa Monica, the Sunset Strip, and walk around. I just walked around and dreamed. I searched for the perfect gig, or to be discovered, or something. I talked to people here and there. I also got a lot of doors shut on my face before I even said hello. I finally made friends with some girls, and we rented an apartment in West Hollywood. I said goodbye to my aunt, all my cousins, and told them I was moving to Frisco.

I started out as numerous others have, Vivien continued. She took a sip of her juice, and her eyes lost the assertiveness they always seemed to have. I did auditions, odd jobs, commercials, and extras on movies— anything. I was poor, Mike. And I wanted...things, lots of nice things. My mother cut off the measly allowance she used to send me when I left my aunt's home, and I'm positive she prevented my godfather from sending me any money. Then I met my first husband at a party. He was older, but so what? I was impressed because he was a director. Small potatoes maybe, but still a director. He was working on a project, he claimed. I was so naive and so new to the whole movie thing. I didn't know what was what. Then you came along and offered me more money than I had ever dreamed of. For some property I didn't even know was mine and, of course, a tumble in bed. I was so paralyzed, Mike, with the idea of having money in a town where money is God that I couldn't react to your heat, your passion. You already had money. And it seemed to me you were doing damn good. I felt bad, Mike. I really did. I know you thought I was a cold fish that night. I just wanted to go home and tell my husband how lucky he was and start the project that was finally going to advance my career. When you dropped me off at the house later that night, I started to think and asked myself why was I going to give all my money to a man with a poor track record or no record at all? What if the film bombed? Very common in the industry, as you know. So that night I decided to give him some—not too much—and I banked the rest in my name. I didn't want to be poor, not in Hollywood, not anywhere. Well, the movie bombed, and we divorced a couple of months later. I had my stash and bought myself a decent pad in the hills, an expensive car, and lots of clothes and jewelry.

There you have it, Mike. The story of my life. And Vivien's eyes took on the brightness again as if it had never left. And you, what's this I hear that you're the mayor now? You just returned, and they make you mayor—I don't get it. How much did it cost you, Mike? Are you even at liberty to discuss it?

Mike chuckled and said, It didn't cost me nothing but my time, Vivien. It's only temporary until the general elections.

And I suppose you're going to run and stay in office the rest of your life like Fat Henry.

No, of course not. I'm not a politician; I've got better things to do.

I bet you have, Mike. But tell me, where did you get the money to pay me for the first property? I mean, you were just out of college and—

No, Mike interrupted Vivien before she expanded her question or dug into an area that was of no concern to her. I had been out of college for five or six years, and I was working as a tax adviser and property tax consultant. I ran my own business. I worked for wealthy clients with their property taxes, and the money was great. I also had a company and investors I could depend on for money, so buying you out was not that much of a problem.

I see, said Vivien, aware that Mike didn't want to discuss his money sources. So, Mike. And she changed the subject, as clever women do to keep men at ease and talking. You still going out with that…that woman, the nun?

You mean Alexis?

If that's her name.

She's not a nun, Vivien. She works for Catholic Charities.

Why do you think she works for Catholic Charities? Maybe she doesn't wear the habit. Don't fool yourself, Mike. She's a nun or wants to be one. Let's put it that way.

Well I don't know about that. And Mike almost laughed. I'm still going out with her, and now that she lives in Santa Fe, I might even ask her to marry me.

My goodness, Mike. That's good to hear. In need of some children, huh?

Yes. Children are a possibility. Maybe two or three. Who knows? How about you, Vivien? Any children in your future?

Me? Naw. Vivien gestured. Her face told a different story of a topic she had struggled with and debated among herself, on many occasions. I would probably be a terrible mother. And she attempted a weak smile. I'm not like those women who have children because they have nothing else to do and then treat them like shit when they realize how much work it takes to be a good mother. Children are not like dogs or cats you dump at a shelter when you get tired of them. It's a lifelong responsibility, and if your life is not together, how can you expect to have the wisdom to nourish an infant to adulthood? Anyway, that's what I got from my mother. She was a woman with a broken heart that never mended, and my brother and I paid a very high price for her weakness.

Vivien remained quiet. She contemplated the memories that strangled her whenever she thought about her mother and brother, Danny. That's why she wanted to complete the property sale and cut her ties with Las Flores for good. Even if she lost money on the transaction, she was done with it, unless her godfather had left her more property she was not aware of.

And the funeral was painful, Vivien? asked Mike. He didn't know what else to ask. He saw that Vivien was a little upset about wanting and not wanting children.

Yes. Yes, it was, she said. She looked at Mike, and her eyes lost the brightness again. After the funeral, I went to the old house alone. Your parents had some food and people over at their house. I stayed for a little while. I gave them my thanks for all their help and left to the old house. It was dark and gloomy in the old house. Even the dog was gone. It must have died or something. I was ready to leave—I couldn't stay another minute in that house full of bad memories. As I grabbed my bag, my godfather, Juan Jose, walked out of my mother's bedroom. He scared the shit out of me. He was dressed in black from head to toe. At first, I didn't recognize him. His hair was long and gray to his shoulders, and he was thicker and shorter than I remembered him. I could tell he had been crying. He kept his grief private. He wasn't at the church service or at the funeral. He just kept away and grieved on his own. That was his way of doing things. I felt so bad for him, Mike. I wanted to apologize for all the crap my mother and I put him through. I was almost in tears when he walked over to me and handed me a large, thick envelope. He grabbed my brother's guitar that hung on the wall. It belonged to my father. My godfather exited the house without saying a word.

Vivien paused. She put her hand around the glass of juice but didn't drink any. She looked at the half-empty glass and then at Mike. I left, she continued, right after he did. I drove on Piñon Street all the way to

Highway 25, then north to Albuquerque. It seemed so dark and sad driving through Las Flores, Mike. I just couldn't wait until daylight. I couldn't. I had to catch a flight out of Albuquerque back to Los Angeles as soon as I could. I caught the last flight going out just in time. When I got back home to Los Angeles, I opened the envelope and saw the deed to the property I just sold you. All the paperwork was in order. The taxes were paid. The property was transferred to my name, everything. What broke my heart, more than anything, Mike, was that my godfather had purchased US saving bonds in various denominations throughout the years, lots of them. When I added them up, it was like forty or fifty thousand dollars, with interest. Then I saw a note written by him that stated that he bought the first one the day I was born. That really brought the tears to my eyes. I mean, what can you really say to a man like that?

Mike and Vivien were silent, considering all that was revealed. Vivien felt a little silly talking about her feelings, but she was certain this was the last time she would ever see Mike in person. And Mike was thinking that he'd never had a chance to thank Juan Jose for saving his life.

Mike finally broke the silence and said, I owe Juan Jose big-time.

Vivien, being Vivien, again responded in her direct manner. I don't want to hear about it.

OK, Mike said, relieved that he didn't have to go into any details. So what about the old house?

What about it?

What are your plans for it?

Vivien drank the last of her juice. She wiped her lips with the cloth napkin and said, I have no idea. There's this man, Rafael something. He offered to buy it. I guess I'll sell it to him—can't be worth much.

Don't sell it to Rafa, Vivien, Mike interjected. He'll build tacky apartments on the property. I know him. Sell it to me, Vivien. My mother has been asking me to build low-cost housing for seniors, but she wants them built in the Eastside. I have a plan to build one-and two-bedroom apartments with room for a small garden in front and back and a small park in the center. The property is a little over an acre, Vivien. It can be done.

Well then, Vivien said with a cool smile and not really interested. Maybe this Rafa person will make it worth my time.

No. Listen, Vivien, Mike said. He was a little concerned. Rafa will hee and haw, and before you know it, the price is way below what he offered you early on. They're all the same, Vivien—everyone cut from the same cloth.

And you're not?

Vivien. Vivien, my dear friend. You're as sharp as ever…

Cut the bull, Mike. Give me one good reason why I shouldn't put it on the market.

All right, Vivien. And Mike tried to keep his composure. This is no bull. As you know, the property is off San Albino, not on San Albino. It goes off San Albino into a weird cul-de-sac of its own with no outlet to Piñon Street on the north. It's boxed in all around, and it'll be an extra expense to open it up and give it any value for commercial purposes. Rafa will build tenement apartments up to six floors and put as many families as he can in them. He will not care if they have a proper exit or not.

OK, Vivien replied. She didn't want to trouble herself with the old property. I'll sell it to you on the condition you will do what your mother proposed. Now how much do you think the property is worth?

The old house is in sad condition, and it's not worth restoring. My father did some minor repairs throughout the years, mainly to keep the rain out, he told me. And Juan Jose did his best to keep the squatters in check, but that baby's time has come.

I know your father did his best. He's so kind and such a good man. Is he really your father? Ha ha, only kidding, Mike. And Vivien smiled her golden smile.

I'll give you forty grand, Mike countered, more than glad Vivien was in a good mood. That's the best I can do, Vivien, under the circumstances.

Sold to Mr. Mike, the moneyman from Las Flores, Vivien declared, not even giving it a second thought.

Please, Vivien. Lower your voice, Mike almost whispered to Vivien. This is Las Flores, and the lunch crowd is arriving.

Ask me if I care. And Vivien chuckled. Send the money to my private account, and you take care of the paperwork. I'll send you the deed and the rest of the paperwork that relates to the house. Do it as quickly as you can, Mike, please. I need to let go of everything that brings back any kind of…of memories, of this place.

Remember, Vivien, when we were kids and your mother took you and Danny to visit us? Mike asked. He wanted to remind Vivien of some happy times, so she wouldn't leave with such a bad taste in her mouth. We played hide-and-seek, and I would rush to find you and sit close to you. My heart beat like crazy as we waited for Danny to find us. Remember how much fun we had at that age?

Vivien's smile returned to her beautiful mouth, and she said, Yes, I remember. And later, in the evening, your parents would put on some music, and they would dance. And we would jump around, laughing and mimicking your parents. We pretended we were great dancers. Your mom would cook a marvelous dinner, and we sat at the table together and talked. I loved those times, Mike.

I believed you were the most beautiful girl in the whole world, Vivien. And I had the biggest crush on you; did I ever.

I was, wasn't I? Only teasing, Mike. Vivien then got the serious look again. But after, when your parents drove us home and we were alone, my mother made us kneel in front of her little altar to pray. We prayed and prayed as if she wanted to exorcise the good time we had at your house from our souls with prayer. That's what I didn't like about my mother. She didn't like for anyone to have a good time.

Well, admitted Mike, he'd tried. Vivien kept coming back to the same old thing, her poisoned past. He asked instead, Do you want to eat anything more substantial before the lunch crowd arrives?

No, Vivien answered, and she glanced at her watch. We have an early dinner in Albuquerque with some people from the New Mexico film industry. We're going to go over some tax incentives and other goodies they're willing to give us for filming in the state.

Do you have a project ready to go?

Almost, I hope. We're making a movie from the old play Night over Taos, by Maxwell Anderson.

Wasn't that done before?

There was a TV drama in the fifties, but not a movie.

Do you have the rights?

We're meeting tomorrow in Santa Fe with members of the family, and so far, our attorney informs us that they are very receptive. I don't think they're going to be too particular over a play that's been dead for years.

Do you have any actors in mind?

We're negotiating with Olmos and Smits, plus others.

Are you going to play Diana?

Funny man, Mike. You should open a comedy club in the barrio and make people laugh. No, I'm not going to play Diana. I'm not taking any acting roles; I know that breaks your heart. I'll be the executive producer, if anything. Perhaps you can instruct me on how to procure money from people without compromising my core values. You seem to make a go of it.

I can teach you more than that, countered Mike with a smile, ignoring the dig.

Don't be silly, Mike. You're practically engaged to your nun girlfriend. Those days are over for you, my friend.

Vivien stood up and put on her trendy sunglasses, ready to leave.

Mike almost ran around the table, hugged her, and was going to kiss her on the lips. Vivien turned her face and offered him her cheek.

So long, Mike. And she disengaged and walked out of the Azteca. She turned heads as she walked out to her rented car.

Mike wanted to punch himself in the face. He was more than disappointed at himself for even thinking Vivien would want a tumble in bed. He didn't do that anymore. Vivien was right—those days were over for him. He rushed out of the Azteca when he was sure Vivien was gone. He realized he had a lot of work to do. He smiled when he thought of the look on Mike Cotton's face when he got the news that he had purchased the property from Vivien Madrid.

CHAPTER 13

While Mike Montes and Vivien Madrid were sharing bonbons at the Azteca, Max Luna and Jerry Rivera had just consumed a couple of hot chili burgers at Fat Henry's in downtown Las Flores. They left the diner just as the noon crowd arrived. Max had on his black beret and dark granny shades. Jerry was in his usual tank top and joggers. They joked and laughed as they usually did. They walked at a leisurely pace to the truck parked on Church Street and Main behind Fat Henry's.

Those are still the best chili burgers in town, Jerry remarked. He had a toothpick in his mouth. I didn't see Fat Henry though.

Oh, Fat Henry comes in only once in a while, Max said. And he scratched the new outcrop of thick, black facial hair thriving on his face like spring grass. They have to wheel him in. He's a pretty big fellow and not in the best of health these days. Then Max saw the lanky cowboy approaching them. He seemed to walk in a daze. He wore old scuffed-up cowboy boots and a faded, tattered baseball hat on his big head. He was headed to the place they had just left or Jimmy's Pool Hall, a short distance from Fat Henry's.

That's the cowboy I told you about, Jerry. He claimed he wanted to see my car when I was at the river with my mother.

Jerry gave the cowboy a tap with his shoulder, pretending to bump him by accident.

What the fuck! cried out the cowboy. He was thrown a little off-balance. He also had a big wad of chewing tobacco in his left cheek. Can't you all see where you walk? Thick scar tissue almost covered his dark-brown eyes, and his lips were thin and twisted when he talked.

You still wanna see Max's car? Jerry asked, almost on top of him.

The cowboy blinked several times before he recognized Max, who was standing to the side but close. He ignored Jerry and addressed himself to Max. You two greasers are too tall to be Meskins. I believe you all arr ni—

Before he completed another racial slur, Jerry flashed a right fist to the puffy side of the cowboy's face, and a tsunami of brownish tobacco juice and blood exited his filthy mouth. His left leg crossed behind his right leg like he was attempting some crazy dance step. Then he fell back down hard on his ass and stayed down, as his head crashed on the concrete lot. The cowboy didn't move a muscle. He hardly breathed and pretended to be out cold. He knew damn well Max and Jerry would stomp him into an early grave if he tried to run.

When Max heard the splat of fist on flesh, he stepped back. He checked his clothes to see if any slime from the zapped cowboy had stained them. When the cowboy was on his side and bleeding from the mouth, Max told the wounded man, You're disgusting, and he walked away.

Jerry flicked the toothpick at the injured man and joined Max. As they approached the truck, Max turned to Jerry and said, That cowboy flaunted signs of an educated man, wouldn't you say so, brother Jerry? And they both laughed out loud, happy as a pair of skunks stinking up a garage.

Jerry and Max drove in the CI truck east on Church Street and made a left on Baca Street going north. Church was a short street and ended after crossing Baca. That was something the city planners could never explain. They drove north on Baca until they reached Piñon Street. They made a right and drove east toward Chiva Town, hoping to see Tiny Tim. It was a beautiful, sunny autumn day. Not too cold or too hot. The leaves were turning golden and the grass brown. The Turquoise Mountains sparkled as if encrusted with gems of varying colors. Fiery opals, light-yellow-green peridot, golden topaz, and green emeralds illuminated the summit. The day was almost perfect with a slight breeze keeping the temperature comfortable enough for Max and Jerry to drive with the windows down and their elbows sticking out. They enjoyed the drive. They had already forgotten about the man with busted chops bleeding in the gutter back downtown. They were in a good mood. They joked about the Chiva Town Snipers. Max and Jerry were not intimidated by the Snipers—or anyone else, for that matter. They respected the Snipers, as most did. They did not fear them, and that was the difference. They would never pick a fight with the Snipers; there was no reason to. And the Snipers would not mess with them either; again, there was no reason to.

Max made a stop on San Albino Street, which ran north and south. He crossed San Albino and made a left on Santa Fe, driving north. As Max made a left on Santa Fe, Jerry asked Max, Hey, whatever happened to La Conga?

Max turned to Jerry all serious and said, Why? You want a blow job? And he laughed.

Fuck you, Jerry replied and laughed.

I think she retired, Max said. I'm sure she'll remember you and won't mind giving you her special…at a discount, of course.

Us—remember us, Jerry reminded Max, and they both giggled in a childlike manner.

She was good at what she did, and no one can say different. She made a lot of vatos sing with joy or cry in shame, added Max.

That she had the power to do, Jerry said. I wonder if she did women.

Of course she did women, Jerry. With that tongue of hers and those delightful fingers, I'd say not many women would resist. But that is something she'll take to her grave. We'll never know for sure.

Before Max and Jerry reached San Miguel Street, which ran east and west, they turned their eyes to the right to check out La Conga's house. The house was a couple of houses in from the street, but all seemed quiet. When they reached San Miguel, they spotted the wall that separated Chiva Town from the Eastside barrio. Max stopped at a stop sign on San Miguel and then drove into Chiva Town.

Wow! exclaimed Jerry. This place has grown. Look at all those pads. And the fucking wall is still there. And the dump in the shadow of the wall where the kids used to play.

Cheap housing, Max said.

Santa Fe Street crossed into Chiva Town and ended in Chiva Town. Some homeowners wanted to push it through and beyond Chiva Town up north into the desert, where some new homes were being built. Max kept on Santa Fe. Once in Chiva Town, he cut a left on Oveja Street, which ran east and west.

Oveja Street. And Jerry smiled. How appropriate. These people are original. Why not Chiva Street? Isn't it why Chiva Town was named, after all?

Don't worry about it. Chiva, Oveja—they're all related. It doesn't make any difference. Max's eyes were behind his dark shades, and a quick smile was on his lips. Here we are, bro, and he parked in front of a house with no number anywhere in sight. Max and Jerry got out of the truck and walked to the side of the house, which led to the backyard. A young Sniper came up to challenge them, recognized Max, and said nothing.

The backyard of the house was large. It was shared with the backyard of the house in back. A couple of tables were placed together to make one long one in the middle of the yard. Several men sat at the tables ragging one another. Watermelon seeds and rinds were scattered all over the table and on the brown grass. Tiny Tim sat in the middle of the group, splitting seeds with a huge sharp bowie knife whose blade sparkled in the midday sun like polished chrome on the bumper of a lowrider car. Neto, his nephew, would at times place his long index finger on top of a seed, and Tiny Tim brought down the knife in a chopping motion full force on top of the finger and seed. Neto moved his finger out of the way quick as a cat, and the knife came crashing down and smashed into the watermelon seed, slicing it in half. It sent each piece to the ends of the table and beyond. Then all the Snipers laughed and banged their hands on the tables as if it was the funniest event ever. But no one risked a finger except the stupid Neto.

Max! Max! cried out Tiny Tim when he saw Max and Jerry enter the backyard. Come on in, brother. He appeared happy, all three hundred pounds of him. His hair was long and grayish. It fell all over his face and shoulders as he attempted to push it back with the same right hand in which he held the knife that he laid on the table when he saw Max and Jerry. His beard was also gray with strands of black here and there. And wild as his hair. It came down all the way to his huge gut. He had on large, round-framed, prescription sunglasses. They covered his eyes and the fat under them. He had watermelon seeds and dried red juice all over his mouth and beard, and he didn't seem to care.

How the hell are you, Max? Long time no see, bro, he bellowed, genuinely happy to see Max.

I'm good, Tiny. How's your old ass getting along?

It still comes out, brother. It still comes out. I'm sorry I can't offer you any melon, Max. They're gone, Max. Last of the summer melons. Ain't that a shame? This must be little Jerry. Ain't seen Jerry in a long time either. Momo kept an eye out for you at the big house in Santa, I hear. That right, Jerry?

Jerry wanted to say that Momo was nothing but an overweight punk chora eater. And everyone knew it except Tiny Tim. He kept silent. He had his hands in his pockets. He did not want to disrespect Tiny Tim and the Snipers on their own turf. He couldn't believe Tiny Tim had gone south that bad. Tiny Tim reminded him of the scene from the Last Supper, minus a Judas, but perhaps Neto was his Judas. It was difficult to say. Tiny Tim was wearing an old shirt with cut-off sleeves, and the muscles on his huge arms had turned to Jell-O and hung loose on his flabby arms. The numerous tattoos all but disappeared in the rolls of fat. Man, Jerry admitted. Max had not prepared him for this. Fucking Max, always being funny. He didn't know whether to laugh or cry.

Neto, on the other hand, sat to the right of Tiny Tim. His bald head didn't call for shaving anymore. He was bone bald and seemed uncomfortable. He had deep wrinkles from his eyebrows all the way to his scalp, and his fair-skinned face was also wrinkled. And he wasn't that old. He sported ink teardrops on the lower corners of his pale eyes. He had a cross tattooed between his eyes, among other tattoos on his bony arms. They were all done with a sewing needle and India ink, and all done badly. His long, scrawny neck was scabbed and reddish and bore tattoos of different names and animals in front and back. He stared at Max, and his thin lips on the sallow face didn't move. He wasn't happy with the idea that Max could just walk in uninvited, as if he were a member of the organization, which he wasn't. If he were in charge, and that could be soon, he believed, things would be different. He turned from Max to Jerry. Jerry stood there like a dark, graffiti granite slab, like the ones he had seen at the City of Rocks some years past. And said to himself, Maybe not.

And what brings you out to our lovely part of the world, Max? asked Tiny Tim. He picked watermelon seeds out of his outrageous beard, like a dog biting off ticks on a hot afternoon.

I need you to select a vato, Max answered. He knew firsthand Tiny would never choose a female. Someone to represent Chiva Town for Community Impact. He will work out of the center here and be the organizer for Chiva Town. But he will be under me and report for meetings and training at the CI Center in the Eastside.

The rest of the lounge lizards, stuffed with watermelon and drenched by the sun, opened their sleepy eyes and looked at Max as if for the first time.

Only Tiny Tim smiled and asked, And what will this organizer do for Chiva that has not been done already?

Max also smiled. He kept his eyes on Tiny Tim. He'll visit the homes in need of repairs and help get some grants to do the repairs through low-cost housing loans or at zero cost to the homeowners. Fix up your crumbling community center and get some activities going for the kids. After-school tutoring, games, sports, you name it. Extend the food service that you already have going and make it all-inclusive, not just for old Snipers but for anyone who qualifies. Help the people get services like food stamps, Social Security benefits, and health screening. I can go on and on.

The lizards almost unleashed when Max mentioned the old Snipers. Some thought, this hombre comes here uninvited and talks about aged Snipers as if they were old dogs. Nerve of the fucker. But they couldn't do or say shit because Tiny Tim was all eyes and ears.

This organizer…uh, person, jumped in Neto. He gonna be like a…a census taker, asking people all kind of personal questions?

No, not at all, responded Max, quickly. The questions are not all that intrusive, and the people here will know the organizer. It won't be a stranger pulling up to the door.

I like it, Max. Tiny Tim smiled before Neto asked another stupid question. I really like the idea. We will select a young man and send him up to you at CI. Is that fair? Anything else, Max?

Yes, replied Max. One more thing. Get your councilman to ask the full city council to fund the repairs for the center. Or better yet, get him to ask for a new building. Mike Montes will probably vote for the funds, and with Rafa, that will make three votes and a majority.

I will do that, my friend, avowed Tiny Tim. And I like that Mike Montes returned. After getting his education and all in Califa, he came back to help his community. And you did the same, Max. I'm proud of you guys. You didn't forget your roots and turn all puto, like some do.

Max didn't say anything. He wasn't sure if Tiny was talking out his ass or being serious. He said adios. He didn't expect the big man to stand up and give him an abrazo, like the old times. He didn't want to embarrass Tiny any more than he had to. He had come to say what needed saying, and Tiny had behaved like the gentleman he was.

As Jerry and Max were leaving through the side of the house to get back to the truck, a young Sniper approached Jerry and said, Hey, Jerry, my older brother in Santa said you were bad, a bad fucker—his words. Jerry turned to face him. The young Sniper noticed the black scorpion tattoos on Jerry's neck. He shut up and walked away.

When Max and Jerry were driving back to the CI Center, Jerry asked Max. What's up with Tiny Tim? Put on a little weight, huh?

Max turned to Jerry and said, Maybe he should ease off the cock breeding, and they both busted up laughing.

CHAPTER 14

Max and Jerry walked into the CI Center after returning from Chiva Town. Ruth was about to leave to do some home visits. William was out also. Hi, Ruth, they said. Ruth returned their greeting and told Max his mother had called and asked for him to call her back.

Oh, Ruth, Max said before going to his office to make the call, Tiny Tim is going to send a prospect for an interview.

Great. Ruth beamed. Then it hit her. What if he's a…

Sniper, Max said, completing her sentence. Don't worry about it. We'll decide if he's a good candidate. And if he's not, we have the last word.

Max walked away to his office, and as Jerry was going to the bathroom, Ruth said, Hey, Jerry, I have a message for you.

Jerry stopped. He turned to Ruth and waited.

Claire told me to tell you if I saw you that you can start the sessions today, before the kids arrive.

Jerry fought to suppress the smile on his face. He wasn't successful. He couldn't help himself. He had been dying to see and talk to Claire for days. He had thought about her day and night, and being with her was what he wanted most in life. At the same time, he knew he was chasing the elusive butterfly of love, as sung about in love songs.

Ruth also smiled—it was obvious Jerry was madly in love, and he couldn't hide it, not from her anyway. He could act tough and be all macho with the guys. With her, he let his sensitive side take over. She worried about him because he was blind to the fact that he was stepping on a minefield that could harm, or even destroy, lives. But she believed it was not her place to warn or lecture him about the unpredictable feelings of the heart.

Claire is helping me fulfill my hours for counseling, Jerry stated. He wanted to make sure Ruth understood the reason he was seeing Claire and knew it was the only reason. His body language and facial expressions were not easy to conceal, and he was positive that an intuitive woman like Ruth could read him like an open book.

I know, Jerry, responded Ruth. Claire is so nice. She's waiting for you in her office. See you later.

Jerry almost ran to the bathroom. He took some things out of his locker. He peeled off his tank top. He washed his face and under his arms with soap, and he brushed his teeth. He put on a clean white T-shirt and shorts and put the musky clothes back in his locker. He walked rapidly to Claire's office and prayed she was alone. His heart thumped fast with excitement, and he couldn't slow it down. God, he didn't want to love her. He repeated it over and over. He was quite sure it was too late, however.

Claire opened the door to her office, and a breath of fresh air hit Jerry. His knees almost buckled.

Oh, hi, Jerry. Come in, please. And Claire was all smiles. She flashed white teeth like polished pearls on an expensive necklace. She closed the door after Jerry entered. Jerry entered like a little boy going into the principal's office for patting his female teacher on the ass. She wore a matching outfit of a different color. And her feet were in brown suede boots with a low heel. Her jacket was on a coatrack behind her desk, and her red cashmere sweater, a little tight, showed off her prominent chest. Her hair was made up with a large, thick braid in the middle of her head that fell to her lower neck.

Sit, Jerry, she said, and still smiling, Jerry sat in the same place he'd sat the last time. Claire sat on the couch, facing him. Jerry noticed a poster Claire had enlarged and tacked up on the wall close to one corner of the office. The poster, in large block letters, read, Understanding others is wisdom. Understanding yourself is enlightenment. La Tsu. Then Jerry turned to his right, and on the opposite wall, he saw another large poster, also in large block letters. That one read, Educating the mind without educating the heart is no education at all. Aristotle. Very appropriate and profound, Jerry thought of the two posters. He also noticed that Claire had done a little work in the office—minor things, but they made the room more homey. A colorful rug in front of the couch, for example. And lamps and candles on tiny tables and other knickknacks, all in good taste. It made the office more conducive to opening your heart and soul and expressing your true feelings with confidence.

Claire kept her eyes on Jerry, and seeing him nervous puzzled her. She liked Jerry; to her, Jerry represented the opposite of every man she had ever known and liked. She wanted to share his pain and make him aware she could be his friend, a real friend. In her world, real friends were few and most just users and takers. And that included her husband. In Jerry, she saw possibilities. In Jerry, she saw honesty and a sincerity that could never be equaled by the phony set of people who called themselves her friends. She also comprehended that Jerry was a man, a passionate man, whose needs might be so deep and complicated that she could be of no help to him. And maybe she would help only in confusing him more. She didn't know, but she had already opened her door, and to close it now might be a terrible mistake. She would not only hurt Jerry, but some damage might come her way because she was as lonely as Jerry seemed to be.

So, Jerry, how are you?

I'm good, Jerry answered. He relaxed in the subdued light of the lamps and candles. And he was certain he could hide his nervousness, if not his feelings. Then he became aware of the end of Lucia Mendez's heart-crushing song "Corazón de Piedra"—"Heart of Stone," in Spanish. Claire walked over to her desk and clicked the off button to her portable CD player.

I love that song, Jerry cried out. I didn't know…you listened to Lucia Mendez…to that kind of romantic music, in Spanish.

Oh yeah, said Claire. She was happy that Jerry also liked the heart-wrenching lyrics and sound of the legendary singers. My mother used to play her music, along with others, when I was in my middle teens and impressionable. She would gather us girls in her bedroom and play the most romantic, heartfelt music that brought tears to our eyes. She listened only to female singers, and I could never understand why until much later.

Anyway, I was the only one of the girls who embraced the music. You can say it stayed with me. My sisters forgot it and turned to the younger singers, all in English. I did too. I also continued to listen to the torch songs in Spanish and still do. How about you, Jerry? How do you know this music?

My mother also listened to the torch songs when I was young. She cried, and I cried with her. I had no idea why until later. I also turned to the rock groups, but those emotional songs of the heart stayed with me. And when I heard Lucia's voice coming from your box, I didn't know what to think.

Why, Jerry? Claire responded, a little defensively. Because I'm too white and married to Mike Cotton?

Jerry could feel Claire was hurt, and he felt bad. No, Claire. No, not that at all. And he attempted to clarify, but he felt he had stuck his big foot in his big mouth. It's just that this music is…is…you know…

It's OK, Jerry. Claire didn't want to start off on the wrong foot over cultural differences on their first session. Let me explain something in case you're not aware of it. My parents and their parents, and other Hispanic people from Santa Fe and Taos, always had this thing about being Spanish, descendants of Spanish blood from Spain. Now you know, Jerry, as well as I do, that was all for appearances. It was more for public appearances to impress Anglos, I guess. The ones who had a little money were worse, like my parents and grandparents. Behind closed doors we were just Mexicans, like the rest of the Mexicans. We ate Mexican food and listened to Mexican music, the works. My maiden name is Amador, Jerry. I guess that tells you everything. We can discuss this again later, if you care to. For now, we better get our session going before our little friends arrive.

Wow. What a woman, Jerry told himself. How could he not fall in love with her? I don't know where to start, Claire, Jerry finally said. And that was the truth. He had so much on his plate.

Just relax, Jerry. Say what you feel, but feel what you say. You're just talking to a friend you can trust. A friend who will never repeat what was expressed in confidence. OK.

OK. Claire, I keep having this dream. I'm on this black horse, a stallion. I'm holding on with my arms around his neck and no saddle. The horse is galloping in this huge, dark cave; going deeper into the cave; and gaining speed. The horse suddenly stops and goes up on its hind legs and kicks wildly with its front legs. I hold on, trembling with fear. Then I see a huge fire in front of us, and that was the reason the horse stopped. But then he rushes through the flames into a silver lagoon of liquid metal, and the black horse and I disintegrate into a million pieces. I wake up drenched in sweat.

Claire studied Jerry for a short time and then asked, What do you think it means, Jerry?

Jerry, with his big hands on his knees, said, I have no idea. I used to think it had something to do with…with my death.

No, Jerry. It's just a dream. Dreams are just fragments of reality. Let's say you like cowboy movies and particularly horses. OK. A certain movie with horses impressed you—you really liked it. When you dream, parts of that event, along with other events, are released by the subconscious, and a mosaic is created that interacts in ways that cannot be controlled by the dreamer. The dream takes you, depending on your life experience, in a direction you may not want to go or like. The most vivid dreams are the ones we remember when we wake up. The worst dreams are the ones that stay with us longer.

But what does it mean, Claire? Jerry asked with a concerned look on his face.

Well, there is no exact science for dream interpretation. There are of course many theories, and people come to their own conclusions on the subject, but it's not clear-cut. In your case, I would say that the powerful stallion is your power or energy. The fact that you have no saddle on the horse, the horse is taking you to an unknown place, and you cannot stop the rushing motion of the horse, could mean that you, in your everyday life, are or feel powerless. That the more you understand life and live it, the more you slide backward instead of forward. The more you embrace it with all your heart, the more your mind rejects it because you feel the odds are against you.

What about the fire, Claire, and the lagoon with melted metal? And me and the horse spilling into it and splintering into a million pieces?

Again, Jerry…and Claire wanted to change the subject. This is a symbolic profile of the dream and not necessarily what is happening in your life. The fire is the wall that keeps you on one side, away from your desires or aspirations. You break through with your strength and character, the stallion, but end up in the lagoon, and you split to pieces. And this is the most difficult part because I see you reaching out and searching despite the challenges, and you will not be satisfied until you find what will make your life complete. But we all go through that aspect of life, Jerry; that's normal. If you had the same dream every single night, then I would be worried. It's just a dream, Jerry. And some dreams are nice, and some are not.

No. I don't have that same dream that often. Maybe once or twice a month now.

You had it more often when you were in prison, right?

Oh yeah. A lot more often. She's good, Jerry told himself. He had disclosed that same dream with different variations with various shrinks when at the Big House. The bullshit they'd told him had been hilarious. Claire was right. Everyone wanted to be the expert to satisfy his or her own ego. Claire pulled up her legs and wrapped her arms around her knees as she had the last time. She looks so lovely doing that, Jerry thought. He estimated she was maybe five or six years older than he. She looked younger than a lot of younger women. He wanted to cuddle up with her on the couch. He knew it wasn't the right moment, and he refused to make a fool of himself.

Claire studied Jerry and resolved that his images, if they were truly his, were very creative. But she doubted that his dreams were of that nature. His dreams, she concluded, would be more sexually explicit and a lot wetter, having spent many very productive years locked up. He could be a reliable connection if guided the right way. As for now, he was an expert in hiding his insecurities. And that huge hole in his heart was getting larger and larger by the minute. She could perhaps help the firestorm from spreading, but like any wildfire, she could put herself in danger of being consumed by it.

You OK, Jerry? Claire finally asked. She flashed her smile. And he wanted to pick her up in his arms and kiss her seductive lips and never stop.

I'm good, Claire. He didn't know what to do with his hands. I know we're running out of time. And I have something that bothers me. Can we…can we talk about it?

Of course, Jerry, anything you want to discuss.

When I was in the lockup, he said, and his left hand was wrapped around his right wrist, I got into a lot of trouble, especially in the first years. The reason—there were a lot of reasons—but the main one was that I felt I was missing out on a lot of stuff back home, here in Las Flores. You know, things like holidays, parties, and hanging out with my friends. The dances and the girls. You name it. I was seventeen years old, and I was angry. So right before the big holidays, I would get into a fight. I would hit a guard or do anything to get thrown into the hole and isolation. The hole was bad news. It did something to your mind. Then one day Max sent me a novel by Jack London called The Star Rover. It was Jack London's eighth and last novel. Are you familiar with the novel, Claire?

No, I'm not. I've read some of his other novels, but not that one.

Anyway, Max and his mother, Victoria, send me books all the time. And although I was never a fan of Jack London, this novel was different, Claire. Jack London's friend spent five years in solitary confinement in San Quentin. I guess the efforts to get him out inspired him to write the novel and illustrate the horrors and inhumane conditions of prison life. But what caught my interest in the novel was the time travel and the adventures the convict experienced while secured in a straitjacket when in the hole. I read up on soul travel and other methods of the mind leaving the body and venturing to past lives or future events. I experienced some out-of-body travel myself to escape the confines of the hole. After I was released back into the population of inmates, I wasn't myself, Claire. I felt I was floating, and my spatial awareness was awkward. I would bump into objects that I could see, but I couldn't judge the distance. I was sapped of energy and felt agitated for at least a week. I couldn't tell if I was drugged when they put me in the hole, or it was self-hypnosis, soul travel, or just plain sleep and heavy dreaming I used to escape. I learned how to survive the hole and deal with the isolation. One day, during that first horrible year, the warden and a shrink talked to me and told me that I could be released in four years, but with my disruptive behavior, they couldn't guarantee anything. They also informed my mother about my behavior. They believed she might convince me to think about my actions. Christian Charities took my mother to visit me and were assisting to get me released.

That's my husband's group, Claire was going to say. She decided against it. Go on, she said instead. She saw Jerry being himself and didn't want to put him off by mentioning her husband.

Jerry took a sip of water from the water bottle Claire had put on the table for him. I thought I was going crazy, Claire, he continued. And to be crazy among the crazies in that place was almost normal. Not to me though. To me it was a big deal. I decided to clean up my act because I really wanted out. I didn't wanna be a lifer—anything but a lifer. I got a job in the library and began to educate myself by reading and learning. And I also took any class offered. Then my mother passed, and I had a relapse. Back to the hole, back to the degrading punishment, and back to the out-of-body travel. I just wanted to die. My mother was the only living relative who truly cared if I lived or died. And I asked myself, why go on?

Claire listened to Jerry, and she was almost in tears. She wanted to hold him close to her and perhaps soothe his pain. She couldn't. She had to stay professional and not permit her emotions to cross any ethical guidelines. And even though she couldn't control the circumstances that set limits to a more tender approach, she was certain she had her man. The right man, at the right time.

Where was your father all this time? Claire tried hard to hold in her feelings. She kept her eyes dry and presented herself as the professional she was trained to be.

My father, my father? And Jerry had a lost look on his face, as if the image of his father was long lost and erased from his mind for good.

Oh! He was in Texas, is in Texas, he said, with his big dark-brown eyes on Claire. See, Claire, when I was little, my father moved to South Texas alone. He wanted me to go with him, but I refused. My parents were going through a divorce, and I just couldn't leave my mother. I visited a couple of times, but I got some bad vibes from his new wife, and I never returned. When I was in prison, his new wife made it known she didn't want my father and her children around me. And he submitted to her wish, so that was the end of my relationship with my father. When my mother passed, I was in shock. The pain was numbing. I had no way of dealing with it, so I was back in the hole, and my anger was out of control. I wasn't permitted to attend her funeral because of my behavior, and that hurt. The warden and the shrink had another talk with me and told me they were extending my sentence two or more years. Instead of five, I was going to do seven for sure, and even more, if I didn't change my ways. All that upset me in more ways than I can tell you, Claire. I begged to get back my job at the prison library, and when I did, I hit the books big-time. And even though I didn't visit the hole as often, I was still in and out from time to time. The light-headedness, the awkward and destabilizing spatial loss of equilibrium still persist. Maybe not as often, but it comes, without warning. You think I'm losing it, Claire?

No, Jerry, Claire answered, as calmly as she could. You went through a very traumatic time in your young life. But now you're in a more stable environment, and things will get better for you. The nightmares will become less intense. And the spatial incongruity will stabilize because you function in a wide-open space, not in a dark closet. Your perceptions will alter in a positive direction, but it takes time. So be patient, Jerry, and I'll help you as much as you allow me to. She was going to ask him about the scorpion tattoos on his neck. She hadn't because she was aware that the young man had enough recalls for one session.

Claire stood up and Jerry did the same. Don't worry, she said. Everything is going to be OK. She held his big hands with her small ones and said, Promise me you'll visit again, and soon.

Jerry was speechless. He wanted to hug her, but he was afraid he might crush her in his emotional state of being. He took in the fragrance of her hair and her clothes, and asked himself, Damn, how can a woman smell this good?

Jerry, she said. She still held his hands. She threw all caution to the wind. It is very difficult to meet here. I have a private office at my home, and we can hold the sessions there, if you care to. We will have more privacy and more time, but it's up to you.

Jerry was confused, more than ever. The most beautiful woman in the world, his world, held his hands and had just invited him to her home—was he dreaming or what? Was this for therapy or something else? He knew this happened in movies but not in real life, and to him? No way.

What about your husband, Claire? he asked, just to get a feeling of where this was going or could go.

Oh, don't worry about him. He comes and goes. Most of the time he doesn't even notice. He's always too busy. He even goes away on some weekends, and alone. She almost said, And I don't even ask where because it doesn't matter, and besides that, we sleep in different bedrooms. She held back on that because she didn't want Jerry to think that she belonged on the couch instead of him. It's his business, Jerry, you know. It keeps the man busy.

Jerry got a little closer to Claire. He still held on to her hands. He was hard but not crazy. He asked her just to see if it changed anything, What about your children, Claire? You have a couple of kids, right?

Yes, and they are dolls. They stay in Santa Fe with my parents. They attend a private Catholic school in Santa Fe, and my parents are really close to them. Besides, my father owns a small horse ranch outside Santa Fe, and the kids have their own horses that they ride almost every day. I drive up there on some weekends and sometimes stay with them a week or so.

Jerry couldn't believe why Claire told him she was practically on her own and could do what she wanted to do with her time. He wanted to pinch himself to see if this was for real or another one of his fantasies he had about her. If he cared to, she had asked. Damn right he cared to. He was out of his mind for her; of course he was going to her house, and God help any pendejo who attempted to stop him.

OK, Jerry, Claire said. She was still sweet and tender. I'll give you my number to my home office, and we'll set up a time to meet. She released his warm hands and gave him her business card. I hear our little friends arriving. We best get ready for them.

Jerry didn't want to let go of her soft hands. He knew he had to. He put her card in his pocket and made sure it was in there securely; that was a number he couldn't afford to lose. He opened the door in slow motion, facing her all the time, and finally said, I'll call you, and walked out of the office. He walked straight to the bathroom without seeing anyone or anything except Claire's lovely face in front of him. He entered the bathroom. He locked the door, stripped, and jumped into the shower. He showered with cold water for what seemed hours. He thought about Claire until he was raw and red. When he realized the water was cold and his composure was almost back to normal, he turned the water off and searched for a towel.

Claire, on the other hand, walked up and down in her office when Jerry left. She was a little nervous and a little worried about how she came across to Jerry. She couldn't deny that she felt warm when she held his hands and the closeness of his body almost touching hers. She smiled, and a warm blushing sensation seemed to possess her body. She was like an overheated teenager, she thought, and laughed out loud. It had been so long since she'd felt like this. She was excited and at the same time uneasy about Jerry exaggerating and telling his friends more than what happened. She reminded herself that Jerry came from a place where being a big mouth could lead to a lot of trouble. Besides, he was too smart to spoil a good thing, if a good thing was where this was going. She was sure Jerry could hold in his emotions as well as she could, maybe even better. She put her hands on her face to feel how warm it was, and that was what she had to watch out for. Ruth would be the first to notice what she felt. She figured Ruth was young and cool to the changes in another woman's makeup. She didn't have to worry about her husband. He was oblivious to her feelings or any changes in her temperament. And if he happened to notice anything, he would just stare at her and walk away. She blew out the candles, turned off the lamps, and turned on the big ceiling light. And was still smiling when she heard a knock on the door. She took a quick glance on the mirror and walked casually to open the door. She was sure it was Nelson Sola because he was always the first one to stop by with a little something special to give her. He brought her an apple; a dry, colorful leaf; or a little smooth stone—anything he found on the way from school. Claire opened the door, and sure enough, there he was with a small pumpkin in his hands. It was Nelson with the huge smile he always had on his face when he saw her.

CHAPTER 15

The evening was cool. It was in early November, and the sun had been down for half an hour. There was a slight breeze, and the odor of dead vegetation mixed with old adobe attacked Jerry's nostrils. He couldn't stop thinking about Claire. He was anxious to see her again. He didn't discuss Claire with Max or anyone else because he still couldn't believe it was for real. He had never been in love before. And if love was what this was, the emotional balancing act was disorientating, to say the least. For now, he had to put Claire out of his mind and concentrate on the business at hand.

Jerry waited patiently for the mark to appear. He was told the mark usually walked on this street, Santos Street, on the way to the park in front of the church to meet his customers. Jerry leaned on an old cedar tree. His right foot rested behind him on the trunk of the gnarled tree, ready to push off, if needed. He was confident there would be no need for that; he was familiar with the area, and it would be difficult for anyone to surprise him. Across the narrow sidewalk was an old abandoned house. The windows were boarded up. It was a well-known crash pad for people without resources. He kept his eyes on the house. The crumbled plaster dropped from the ancient adobe walls and left gaps, big and small, like lesions on a decayed body. It was a house not much different from the others in the neighborhood or the one he lived in, except for the neglect. He wondered how many women had been screwed inside those ancient walls and how many children conceived. He wondered how many fiestas and drunken fights, and children sent to school on cold mornings. He wondered how many grandfathers and grandmothers had lived and died and how many meals were consumed. And if a murder or two had ever occurred in that timeworn house of ghosts and midnight visitors. This house, like many others, had been a home throughout the years for so many people. Happy or unhappy, it had been a home, he thought.

Jerry could see from his resting place clearly to his left and right and to the front at the old house. He could turn to the street behind him, where he'd parked the truck, and would notice anyone approaching from all angles. The moon was in between a sliver of clouds, and the stars glistened like nuggets of polished gold. For years, he had dreamed of evenings such as these. To look at the sky and breathe the fresh air, with no time limits, no bars, and no smell of urine or stinky feet. Out of the dank, dark hole and free to move or not at any given time. And best of all was to fall in love with a lovely angel. It was difficult for him to contain his happiness. Then he heard the footsteps on the sidewalk of the person he waited for, and he cracked his huge knuckles, more out of habit than anything else. Time to get down to business and leave the love scene for later, he told himself. A little disappointed.

Anthony Juarez whistled an old Elvis tune. His hands were in his pockets, and he walked like a man on top of the world. He was of average height, on the thin side with long arms, and not an altogether a bad-looking young man. His long black hair was slicked down toward the back of his head, and the peach fuzz on his upper lip seemed to give him confidence in acting as he did, with little concern for consequences. As he got closer, Jerry called out as not to startle him. Anthony Juarez didn't startle easily; in his business, he was always approached from different angles and at various times by numerous people. Not that he was cocky, not at all, not Anthony. He just came off that way. He was well dressed and always smiled. He could even fool the fools.

Anthony Juarez walked up to Jerry without hesitation and asked, What can I do you for, brother? He knew exactly what the tattooed night creature wanted. Anthony's eyes were almost shut, and his smile stretched almost to his big ears. He asked it with the poise of an experienced doper and none of the paranoia of a weekend warrior.

Jerry hadn't moved an inch. He studied Anthony Juarez for a few seconds and made up his mind this was going to be easy. So, Anthony… that's your name, right? Jerry asked in a friendly demeanor.

Yes, sir, Anthony Juarez is who I am, he answered in a singsong voice and smiled. Don't be shy, he continued. Tell me what you need, and I'll get it or try hard; there's nothing to lose and lots to gain. That's the name of the game, but you know that, or why be here, looking to dull the pain?

Jerry disliked him right away. He didn't like people who believed they were clever. The real clever ones he didn't mind because they were few and far between. The cute ones, like this clown, irritated him. He had no tolerance for dopey fools, no patience whatsoever.

Say, Anthony, Jerry continued. He stayed in the same position as before. Only a little more serious. You still roam around the middle and high school soliciting and picking up young chicks? I hear you even graze in elementary turf. That true?

Man, if they bleed, they is ready; business is business, he responded with a chuckle.

Jerry's expression didn't change. He just looked at Anthony as he had all along. A real scumbag, a real piece of work, Jerry told himself. So, Anthony, Jerry said. He changed the subject. I want you to take a ride with me. Some friends want to meet you. It won't take long. OK?

Wait un momento, amigo, Anthony bleated out like a goat, and he attempted to keep his smile. As a rule, I don't take rides—no exceptions. I walk or take my own car. It's not that I don't trust you—

Before Anthony Juarez uttered another word, Jerry pushed off the tree trunk and hit him openhanded on the face. Anthony was on his back before he knew what hit him. The smile was erased from his smart mouth, and even his bloodshot eyes opened wide with surprise and fear. Jerry held back his blow; he didn't want to break Anthony's face and bloody him with a solid hit. He needed him in one piece.

Jerry yanked Anthony up by the shirt collar and half dragged, half carried him all the way to the truck. He opened the door and shoved him into the passenger side. Before he shut the door, Jerry grabbed Anthony by the neck with his left hand, his forehead furrowed, and he attempted not to lose it. He blurted out, You little, skinny motherfucker! Next time I tell you to move, you don't give me any fucking lame excuses about anything. And don't say a fucking thing unless I give you permission, or I'll beat you so bad your own mother won't recognize you. Do I make myself clear? You can nod or raise your hand. I believe you'll enjoy the ride. He said, in a calmer voice, And I'll bring you back in no time.

Jerry drove south on Santos Street toward Martinez Street, which ran east and west. He didn't say a word. His mind was on beautiful Claire, and he wanted to be with her. He drove slowly as not to attract attention. Anthony Juarez, on the other hand, was afraid, as well as confused, because he didn't understand what was happening. He didn't owe anybody any money, and he felt deeply that he didn't deserve this kind of treatment. He thought he could jump out of the truck and make a run for it. The crazy fucker would probably run him over or chase him down and beat him to death, as he had promised to do. Anthony couldn't think straight. He couldn't decide on what action to take. He always had options for this kind of emergency. And they all seemed silly and useless now. Sure. He had sold stuff in the rough and tough streets of Compton, but this was different. Over there, they just shoot you and forget it. Here, in this hick town…what is this about? he asked himself over and over. And the worst thing was that he couldn't even talk to plead his case, whatever it was.

Jerry made a stop on Martinez Street and turned right. He headed west, still not saying a word. Martinez Street led toward the edge of town, and the traffic was lighter, so he drove faster. When he crossed the tracks and continued to drive west, Anthony Juarez said, Shit, to himself. Now that Jerry drove faster, Anthony's chances to jump out of the truck were riskier. He'd probably break his back or neck instead of a leg or an ankle. He didn't even dare to look to the side or at the big gorilla, who seemed to be in a blissful mood. The houses were now fewer and farther apart. When Martinez Street turned into Highway 47 and Jerry kept driving west, Anthony Juarez knew he was in serious trouble. When they crossed the river and Jerry kept driving on a dirt road to the dry hills and mesas beyond the river, he panicked. Unless, unless, he told himself, in an effort to keep one last ray of optimism alive. Perhaps someone is having a private party out here, and they needed a drummer, he considered. But wouldn't they ask him, instead of dragging him out here like a criminal? And imposing all kinds of restrictions and physical rough stuff on him? That didn't wash, and the panic returned.

Jerry drove up into the parched hills on a winding dirt road in a cloud of dust. He apparently knew where he was going, but Anthony Juarez was in the dark in more ways than one. Anthony had never visited this isolated, forbidding hideaway. The only light came from the headlights of the truck, which bounced up and down, creating devilish images in the rising dust. They finally reached what Anthony thought could be their destination. There was another truck with a camping lamp on the hood parked next to a huge dried up tree. As they got closer, he noticed another big man dressed all in black. The man was digging for something in the bed of the truck. Jerry parked close to the other truck and ordered Anthony to get out. He walked Anthony a short distance from the tree and told him to sit on the dirt. Then he walked over to the other man and started a conversation as if nothing out of the ordinary was happening.

Anthony Juarez studied the two men from the short distance that separated them as they stood in the dim light of the lamp next to the truck. He couldn't recognize them. They could be narcs, but he didn't think so. He was afraid of the big tattooed freak who had forced him out here—against his will, as he was going to tell the cops when they rescued him. Kidnapping, he thought, was a serious felony. Oh shit! he almost cried out. The big gorilla was coming to talk to him. He prayed it was only talk.

Stand up, Jerry ordered, like a military boot-camp sergeant. Where you get that shit you peddling?

Anthony Juarez smiled a nervous smile and said, I didn't ask for names.

Jerry let out with a quick left hook to the side of the nose. Only to wake Anthony up, and not to hurt him too bad. Anthony made a quick sit-down, and blood gushed out of his nose, and tears rolled from his eyes. Get up, motherfucker, Jerry barked, like a mad dog. He reached over and pulled Anthony to his feet by the already ripped shirt. I'm gonna ask you again, asshole. And if I hear smart one more time, I'm gonna bust you with my right fist. I guarantee you won't get up as easy, and maybe you'll never get up.

Anthony Juarez had never been so humiliated and defeated in his life. He was from Compton, after all. He couldn't stop the tears. And now the blood from his nose ran into his mouth. Jo…hn, John, he said through trembling lips.

Describe him, Jerry screamed at him.

Light…light…color guy…ta…tall…

John Slaughter? Jerry asked, and he pulled on his black leather, fingerless gloves to make them fit tighter on his fists.

Yeth, said Anthony. Blood ran out of his nose and spilled out of his mouth, and he quivered like a hare in the grip of a hound.

Jerry threw a soiled rag at Anthony's face and said, Clean up, you disgusting pig. Then he walked back to Max, who was still searching for something in the back of his truck. Yeah, it's Johnny boy.

Motherfucker, said Max, almost humorously. We gonna have to talk to that good old boy.

Anthony Juarez saw the bobbing and weaving lights from the approaching car in the distance. The lights disappeared as they went around a bend in the hills and then blazed again like the flashing eyes of a demon from hell, as the car snaked through the blackness of the night. The dust clouds the tires raised floated in the air like hazy, yellowish particles of gold in the bright headlights of the oncoming car. Anthony's hopes elevated to a certain degree. He prayed it was the cops come to rescue him. He didn't want to get too excited, because the big guy had hit too hard for him to start jumping up and down for something that might not be. Instead he waited. He held the soiled cloth soaked with blood to his nose and spat blood from his mouth. He was scared and frustrated at not knowing why he had been abducted and brought to this dreadful place. He didn't have any real money for a shakedown, and he only had a little bit of weed left. Maybe it was John Slaughter come to help him, he presumed. And these guys, whoever they were, might listen to Big John. But down deep he doubted it. These guys were crazy, and crazy never listens, as he knew so well.

The car arrived in a dust storm. The driver and the passenger waited in the car for the dust to settle. Then the passenger door opened, and a tallish young female in tight jeans and pointed cowgirl boots exited the car and slammed the door behind her. She walked without hesitation straight to Max and Jerry. Ruth stayed in the car. She did not want to participate any more than she had to.

Grace had a killer look on her otherwise adorable face. Where is he? she asked, furious as hell.

Max had not seen Grace for some time. She seemed taller than he remembered. Taller than Ruth, for sure. And she filled out in the places only a woman can. Her long black hair was held down behind her head with a clasp or something, and she had no makeup on.

Come here, motherfucker! Jerry yelled to Anthony Juarez, who was close by and not deaf.

Anthony Juarez walked slowly toward them. He almost had a heart attack when he recognized Grace. Shit, he said to himself. I'm cooked. He was in deep mierda, and it had nothing to do with a little weed he had sold to high school kids. He'd been warned about these fuckers, now that he recalled, and he had ignored the warning. Now it didn't matter because he was deep in the vipers' den, and his chance to get away in one piece was not good, not good at all. Fuck, he said, almost in a whisper. His nose still hurt. The bleeding had stopped, and he dropped the filthy, blood-soaked rag in the dirt.

This him, Grace? Max asked. He put on his gloves. Get closer, motherfucker! Max yelled at Anthony. The camp lamp on the hood of the truck gave off a dim light, and Anthony could see Max meant business. His face was a menace of growling teeth. Anthony credited the tattooed gorilla for being scary. Now this fucker, he thought, had killer dancing in his eyes and mouth like a dizzy nightmare. Rasputin came to his brutalized mind. And even though he wasn't a student of history, that Russian character had always stayed in his imagination. Maybe it was the beard, he tried to rationalize in his tormented mind. He wasn't sure of anything anymore, only the compulsion to stay alive, and that kept him going.

That's him. And Grace spit in Anthony's face. That's the son of a bitch who took my…my— She was so enraged she couldn't complete her thought. He lied to me, she continued after catching her breath. He told me we were going only for a ride. He forced himself on me like a filthy hog.

OK, Grace, Max said. He wanted to calm her down. He realized it wasn't the same gentle Grace, and he couldn't blame her for feeling the way she did. Take the first shot, Grace.

God, no! Anthony cried out, and he soiled himself. He believed they were going to put a gun in her hands, and she was going to shoot him in the nuts. Anthony Juarez was too naive to comprehend the imagination of these folks. To shoot him was way too easy.

Please, Anthony begged. It…wasn't me…pleez…

Then Grace kicked Anthony right in the balls with such force that Anthony closed his eyes in pain and released what sounded like an animal sound. His hands moved instinctively to cover his privates, but it was too late. The damage was done. He gave another little cry. He tried hard to suppress it and show he was still a man, but it came out just the same. The tears flowed again, and his feet turned inward to face each other. His knees touched as he struggled to breathe.

OK, Grace, Max said, as gently as he could. He walked her to the car where Ruth waited. Max opened the car door and told Ruth to drive her back to town. Ruth didn't say a word. She started the car, made a turn, and drove out of the scary place as fast as she could.

Anthony Juarez bit his lower lip. He was still in pain. He saw William Moreno materialize out of the darkness like a goblin in a low-price movie. William pitched the shovel he held in his hand into the bed of the truck. He slipped off the work gloves and also flung them on top of the shovel. With his hands, he dusted the dust off his clothes and hair. He wasn't as big as the other two freaks but no doubt was just as brutal, calculated Anthony. He looked around at the disturbing blackness that boxed him in the frightening death trap. The light from the moon was no help because the wispy clouds seemed to follow and cover the moon at will. And when he turned to look at the dim lamp on the hood of the truck, his vision became even more distorted when he focused to either side away from the light and attempt to figure out the best area to run to, if running was what he was going to do.

Did you finish up there? Max asked William, as William continued to battle with the dust on his hair and clothes.

It's ready, William answered.

Do you know that fuck? And Max pointed to Anthony Juarez. Anthony stood alone in the dark a short distance away, like a lost soul who waited for some reliable companionship.

I know of him. I don't know him personally, answered William, as he pulled on his fingerless, black leather gloves. He used to work for Rafa Candelaria until Rafa fired his ass for incompetence. Then the pervert got pissed at Richard, Rafa's son, and told him his band sucked and that they knew nothing about playing real music. Richard kicked him out of his band and made sure no other band in the area would take him on.

Who does he stay with? Do you know?

That's a mystery. He stayed with his aunt and uncle in the Eastside, but when Rafa told them the boy was a doper, they gave him some money and advised him to return to California. I guess the boy don't grasp useful advice.

Perfect, said Max.

While Max and William were conversing, Jerry walked over to Anthony Juarez and said in a casual voice, Run if you like, pervert. And I'll hunt you down in the night like the rabid dog you are. I'll use a bow and arrows with poison tips and a machete. And when you go down, and you will, I'll chop you up like blood sausage, motherfucker.

Anthony was going to promise not to run when Max and William approached. They were dressed in black and had the silly black gloves on.

OK, amigo, Max said as the three men surrounded Anthony. The victim has identified you as the perpetrator. We are the prosecutor, judge, and jury, and we find you guilty of the rape and kidnapping of a minor. You are also guilty of selling drugs to underage students, another unpardonable crime that will not be tolerated in the Eastside. Your punishment will be what we call the Piñata Initiation. If you survive the Initiation, you will be free to go, but you have to promise to leave Las Flores and never return.

Anthony Juarez was in shock, even more now than before. How could anybody just grab him off the street and force him out here to this unpleasant place? The thought raced through his mind like a burning fever. He wanted to scream out to them that this was America, not some third-world country or banana republic where abductions were a common happening. How could they get away with this? He wanted to shout at the crazy fuckers. Fear paralyzed his mind, and instead he lowered his head and said nothing. Words wouldn't help him at this point. Maybe he wanted to believe they were just having fun at his expense and only wanted to scare him and make him leave town.

OK then! Max barked. Let's do it.

Jerry grabbed Anthony Juarez from behind and held him while Max and William returned to the bed of the truck with the lamp on the hood.

Bring him over, Jerry, Max ordered. He took a long canvas bag used to pick cotton from the bed of the truck. William took out a long rope from the same truck and threw one end over a thick branch of the old tree about seven or eight feet above the ground. As the rope came down, William grabbed it and held on to both ends. Jerry pushed on Anthony. He forced him to move to where Max was holding the bag and William the rope under the solid branch of the tree.

No. Please don't...do this, pleez, I'll...I'll get you some money, pleez, Anthony Juarez pleaded, tears in his eyes, and his lips trembled.

Attempting to bribe officials of the court? Max asked. Ain't you in enough trouble already?

Stop your whining, you pervert, Jerry shouted at Anthony. The coyotes around here will think you're a bitch and come looking for your ass after we're done with you. They all giggled, except Anthony Juarez. Jerry took off one of Anthony's shoes, pulled off the dirty sock, and stuffed it in Anthony's mouth. Then he picked Anthony up with one arm under his legs and the other on his back and carried him over to Max. Max held the mouth of the large canvas bag open as Jerry placed Anthony Juarez, feetfirst, inside the bag.

Raise his hands, ordered Max.

Jerry held Anthony's hands above his head, and William tied them firmly around the wrist with one end of the rope. Then Max closed the mouth of the bag over Anthony's secured hands and looped the rope around the bag and hands. Max then made a knot around the bag and hands and lifted the bag off the ground with both arms while William pulled the free end of the rope downward. The bag hung like a big canvas piñata, about three or four feet above the ground.

Anthony Juarez had never been in so much pain in his young life. The canvas bag was old, it had a sickening smell to it, and he could hardly breathe with the sock in his mouth. He couldn't move because it hurt his arms, shoulders, and hands. He wanted to know when this insane game was going to be over, so he could go home.

Max took over the rope from William and said, You won the toss, big guy. Swing that bat.

William was all smiles. He ran to the truck and returned with a heavy bat made of solid wood. As William came close to the bag with the bat, Jerry gave it a push, and the bag swung back and forth. Fuck. That's not fair, Jerry. And he circled the bag, looking for the head to crunch. Finally, he came in with the bat on a leveled swing and crashed it full power at the bag, crushing Anthony's right elbow.

A smothered sound came from inside the bag when Jerry took the bat from William. He was about to swing when William gave the bag a shove with both hands. Jerry waited for a second or two, and when the bag came toward him, he took one step back. When the bag swayed back, he came forward and chopped down with the bat hard, catching Anthony Juarez with a blow on the back of the skull, between his raised arms. The hit from Jerry was so powerful that the canvas bag almost ripped with the blow. All they heard was a dull thud, and there was no doubt that Anthony Juarez was history. William took the rope from Max, and Jerry handed Max the bat. Max circled the bag and cracked it with the bat on the area where he believed Anthony's face was, just to make sure the boy wouldn't come back to haunt them. William let go of the rope, and the body bag dropped with little noise to the dirt. The rope slipped down with ease. Max grabbed one end of the blood-stained canvas bag and Jerry the other, and they lobbed it onto the bed of the truck like a side of old beef, rope and all. William picked up the bloody rag and Anthony's shoe. He pitched them next to the bag, as if they were contaminated with deadly plutonium. Max put the remainder of the loose rope in the truck on top of the bag. He switched off the lamp and placed it carefully in one corner of the bed of the truck and told William to jump in.

You follow us, Jerry, Max told Jerry. William gave Max directions on how to get to the area where he had dug the hole. They drove on a dirt road up a parched hill, then over the hill into an isolated dry wash. They stopped the trucks but left the lights on. They found where William had dug the hole, next to some scrub. Max and Jerry took the body bag from the truck. They carried it over to the hole and dumped it in. William brought down a five-gallon can of lye and poured it on top of the canvas bag. Then he threw in the shoe and bloody rag. Jerry mixed some ready-mix concrete with water he had brought in his truck. He used a plastic container and then emptied half of the concrete into the hole on top of the lime and bag. Max tossed some large pieces of broken, cement-crusted bricks from his truck into the hole. Jerry dumped the rest of the ready-mix concrete into the hole, while Max lobbed in some more pieces of brick. Then they all grabbed shovels from the truck and filled the rest of the hole with dirt, not saying a word. Jerry gave William a ride back to the center for his car, and Max drove back to town alone after they had completed the gruesome task.

Ruth dropped Grace off at a friend's house. She was too worried about William to trouble herself with Grace. She loved Grace and all, and she was sad about the events that had put a huge dent in her life. But William was her husband, and what she had witnessed up in the remote mesa did not sit right with her. After Grace told her she was moving out of the state to complete her high school education, Ruth said goodbye and good luck.

Ruth rushed home to wait for William. When she got home, she couldn't stop thinking about the mesa and the boy they held up there. She had stayed in the car when she drove Ruth up to the scary mesa. William and Max had talked her into driving Ruth up there at night. And even though it wasn't that late, it was the same place where the decomposed body of Mike Cotton's mother had been found. It gave her the creeps just to think about it. And when she saw Grace give the boy a kick to the balls, she had almost screamed. She didn't see William there. She wasn't sure if he'd hidden when she drove up. What was this dangerous game they were playing? She wanted to know. She paced up and down and around the kitchen table and imagined the worst. She opened a bottle of wine and couldn't even finish a glass. She put the bottle back in the fridge and continued to walk toward the kitchen window to see if William had arrived.

Ruth sat on the living room couch, and their little cat Pluma jumped up to her, meowing. Pluma was a smallish, black-and-gray, longhair cat. She was light as a feather and cute as could be. She was meowing for William. She went to Ruth only when William wasn't around. She wanted Ruth to bring William home to her now and not tomorrow. I know, I know, Ruth said, attempting to soothe her. He'll be back soon. I miss him too. And she scratched Pluma's neck and head. Feo, the tomcat, sauntered in from the kitchen after he'd stuffed his face with his favorite dry kibble. Feo was a sixteen-pound shorthair, brown-and-yellow alley cat who had dropped in for a visit one day and decided to stay. Ruth and William had named him Feo, and not because he was ugly; he wasn't. It was that when he finally returned home after pursuing the female cats in heat around the neighborhood, he appeared as if he had been in battle. He returned home skinny and chewed up. One of his ears was almost gone, and he had deep scars on his head and face. Ruth and William nursed him back to health, but after a couple of weeks, he was at it again. Sometimes Feo came back in one piece and stayed strong and healthy for longer periods of time, but that didn't last for long.

Ruth finally saw the headlights of William's car pull into the driveway. Pluma jumped off her lap and ran meowing to the kitchen door. She knew it was her daddy. Ruth wanted to remain on the couch and act all cool when William walked in, but she couldn't do it. She ran after Pluma to the kitchen door. She was anxious to see William and put her arms around him. As soon as William opened the kitchen door, Ruth almost jumped into his arms. Pluma rubbed against his legs and sniffed his dusty shoes. Then Ruth stepped back and gave him space to step into the kitchen, and she closed the door behind him. She scrutinized his clothes. And she did not want to be obvious about it.

There's no blood, sweetheart, William finally said. And he smiled. It wasn't a lynching or a bloodbath.

Oh, William. And Ruth broke into a defensive grin. I was so worried and scared. That place is awful. I don't know how I ever found it. Grace knew the way though, and she guided me.

You did a great job, babe. And Max and Jerry send their thanks.

It was spooky, William. And that lamp on the truck and the old dead tree in the middle of nowhere. My God, William, that gave me the creeps. And Jerry and Max with those…those gloves. What's up with the gloves, William? You don't own a pair, do you?

William was going to lie and say no. He decided to tell the truth. Yes, I do, sweetheart. They're just old leather gloves that we cut the fingers off and take out the lining. We use them to hit the heavy bag at the center.

And Max, continued Ruth. Max seemed to be in a rage and all dressed in black. He…he looked like he was…

William cut her off and said, Listen, Ruth, Max would give his life to save yours or mine. With Max and Jerry on our side, we don't need anyone else. I would seek Max's help before I went to the cops for help, and you should also. Don't be suspicious of Max, Ruth. He would never, in a million years, hurt you. He doesn't hurt innocent people, only people who hurt others for no reason.

I know, William. And Ruth kissed him on the mouth. I'm just being silly. Even Grace said she would tell only Max about what had happened.

Do you think she talked to Claire about what that creep did to her?

I doubt it. Grace stopped coming to the center after that, and the other kids said she missed a lot of school days. The only reason I found out about the rape was because one day I ran into Grace at the grocery store. I practically had to force her into my car. She finally broke into tears and told me what that pervert did to her. After we hugged and cried, she was adamant about not going to the police. I begged her to go, William. She insisted that if I reported it, she would deny it. She said she didn't trust the cops, and the only person she would talk to would be Max, and not at the center. I sneaked Max out of the center one day and drove him close to the park, where Grace waited. Before Grace said anything, she warned Max that the police would not be involved. At the end, Max asked her if she would ID the pervert, and she agreed. Max told her where the meeting would take place and asked her if she wanted me to drive her there when the time came. She said yes.

And you did a great job, babe. I'm proud of you, William said. And he gave Ruth a peck on the cheek.

But you didn't…you didn't…

Kill him? Maim him? No, William said. He answered her question before she completed it. The pervert deserved it though. It could have been you, Ruth, that he raped…or your sister or mine. How many other kids were in danger with him around? How many other children has he molested or sold the poison he peddles?

I didn't see you there, William, and that's why I was so worried.

I guess I was buying the one-way ticket to California at the bus station when you arrived. That's why you didn't see me.

But you guys didn't…you didn't…

No, Ruth. Max and Jerry just slapped him around a little and drove him back to town. They put him on the bus and warned him that if he ever returned, anything could happen to him. That was all, Ruth; nothing dramatic happened.

I'm so glad, William. I know he deserved more than what he got for what he did. You know he'll get it eventually. He'll pay. Anyway, I have some cold cuts, cheese, and a bottle of white wine waiting, my love.

Thanks, honey. Hey, why don't you fill up the tub, and I'll put on our favorite music and have a good soak, just you and me.

That would be simply marvelous, Ruth replied. She raised her hand above her head and did a little curtsy. She was relieved that William was home safe. They both laughed. Meanwhile, Pluma still meowed for William's attention and humped her small back as she rubbed on his lower legs. William picked her up and cradled her like a baby in his arms. He scratched her head and neck and talked to her in baby talk. Pluma purred out loud. She loved the attention from William. Feo sniffed once or twice at William's shoes and then positioned himself on his side of the couch, on his back, with his hind legs spread apart. He cleaned his belly with his tongue and wondered what the commotion was all about. William walked over to Feo with Pluma still in his arms and said, What's up, lover boy? He bent down and scratched Feo on his big head and neck. Feo stretched out his legs even more and purred. William liked to have Feo around because Feo would charge like a raging lion at any tomcat that attempted to mess with Pluma when they were in the backyard. Even though Pluma was neutered, some of the tomcats didn't care. They just wanted a taste of little Pluma. Besides, Feo kept the house rodent-free. He was a ferocious hunter. William had plans to get Feo neutered also. It had become more difficult to apply the medicine on his cuts every time he returned all chewed up. But when they had the time, Feo was never around, and when he was around, they were busy.

William put Pluma down on the couch. He stripped and placed his dusty clothes in the clothes hamper. He slipped on his flip-flops and joined Ruth in the bathroom. He had a glass of wine in each hand and a piece of cheese in his mouth. Pluma was already on his heels. He placed the wine on a small table next to the bathtub where Ruth had lit some candles and returned to the kitchen to make sure the door was locked. He also flipped off the lights. Ruth was already in the full tub. She blew big, puffy bubbles to Pluma, who was perched on her own little wooden stool opposite her. As a bubble reached her, Pluma tapped it with her paw and waited for another one. That was her favorite game, and she would stay there all night if she had to. She watched them bathe and waited for bubbles.

Don't forget the music, love, Ruth reminded William, who then returned to the living room to slip in a disk.

William was in the tub with Ruth between his legs. She leaned on him as "Sweet Dreams" by Air Supply flooded into the bathroom. He held a soft sponge in his right hand and softly sponged down her neck and breasts while he kissed her gently on the back of the neck. With his left hand, he massaged the nipples of her perfect breasts. I love you, Ruth, he whispered in her ear, as the music and warm bathwater washed away the ugliness of the world outside.

You remembered our song? And she massaged his muscular legs with her hands. Oh, William, this was the first song we heard on our first real date, remember?

How can I forget, Ruth? William nibbled on her ears with his lips and felt himself get hard. And then it came back to him, and he drifted back to the mesa and the hit he'd given the boy inside the canvas bag. He was sure his hit hadn't killed him right off—he'd heard muffled sounds from inside the bag. He was more than sure that Jerry, because of his height, had cracked him on the side or the top of the head, and that did it. Then Max hit him so hard with the bat he thought the bag was going to rip open and the boy's head would fly out. That would have been a mess, he thought. Only Max could dream up a bizarre plan like the Piñata Initiation. He wanted to laugh, but he held it in because

Ruth would want him to share, and he had lied enough to her already. He said instead, Let's change places, sweetheart. Ruth took the sponge, and they exchanged places. Ruth now planted gentle kisses on his neck and, with her left hand, played with his pecs.

Oh, this is heaven, Ruth. William massaged her well-built legs with his hands. He was sure he was going to be up all night thinking about the Piñata Initiation. At least he had Ruth, and Ruth never came up with excuses when he wanted to make love to her. You know, babe, we can throw the mesquite logs in the fireplace and put on some classical music. Hey, we can open a bottle of that chardonnay your father brought us back from Sonoma. His father-in-law had taken the family up to San Francisco for some family function and driven back through the wine country and brought back a case of wine for him and Ruth. Ruth's father liked William; most people did. He even let William and Ruth live rent-free in the old house in the barrio when he purchased a newer one in the Westside. Meanwhile, Pluma waited patiently for more bubbles, but they stopped coming. William and Ruth were doing something in the tub she had no interest in. So Pluma took a nap on her stool.

CHAPTER 16

*M*ax Luna drove home as fast as he could without getting a ticket. He was concerned about his mother and her medication. It wasn't that late, but it wasn't that early either. The event at the high mesa had taken longer than he had anticipated. The pervert had to be dealt with, and he didn't know any other way but his way. Reporting him to the police was a waste of time, and even though rape of a minor was a serious offense, the criminal had too many safeguards and the victim too few. Grace was such a beautiful, honest, and sensitive young woman, and she had trusted the boy to be the same. Her world had been shattered when he'd turned out to be a fraud. Max was aware Grace's life would change, and her relationship with the opposite sex would never be the same because some scumbag believed he could abuse anyone he wanted and get away with it. It made him angry that he hadn't kept a better watch on Grace, but it was difficult to keep an eye on a teenager who was not a blood relative. Max pulled into his driveway, and he noticed the car of Vanessa Renderos parked next to the porch. Oh shit, he said. He parked the truck and ran to the house.

Max approached the open porch, and Vanessa Renderos came out to meet him. She's OK, Max, Vanessa said in a calm voice as not to alarm Max. I gave her some medication, and she went to sleep.

Max sighed with relief. Thanks, Vanessa. Thanks a million. I got held up at the center, and she won't take her meds if I don't give them to her.

Tell me about it, Max, replied Vanessa with a shy smile. She asked for you, Max. And she fought me all the way when it came to her meds.

She gets that way, Vanessa, and sometimes she fights me over her meds. She feels that the meds don't help any. It's difficult. Then she refuses to see anyone, and that doesn't help any.

I know, Max. Your mother has always been a beautiful and classy lady. Now she feels less beautiful and doesn't want people to see how she imagines she looks. That's part of the illness, Max. It's not only physical but psychological as well. It does a number on people's head, and it's not easy to deal with.

Sit with me, Vanessa. Max pointed to a couple of chairs against the wall of the house, inside the porch. They had some protection inside the porch from the breeze that blew in the cool November night.

Vanessa Renderos was the program director for outpatients at the Las Flores hospital. She and Max had been dating for a little over a year. She was from Mora, up in northern New Mexico, and she had a five-year-old son, whose father had disappeared, as often happens. She had relocated to Las Flores when the job at the hospital came through. She had blue eyes, as many people up there do, and her brownish hair was cut short in a professional style. Her skin was fair and turned red with too much sun. She had a well-proportioned body. She kept it in shape by a rigorous workout routine and healthy eating habits.

Max gave her a light kiss on the mouth before they sat down. And as Vanessa was about to embrace him for a stronger kiss, Max pulled away and held the chair for her to sit. Vanessa was disappointed, but she kept it to herself. She noticed that Max was dusty, and his hair was disheveled. That made her think; Max was always so neat and clean. She also noticed his beard was growing thick with the mustache almost over his upper lip. She loved to see Max with a beard. In her opinion, he resembled an artist or a professor.

Max realized that his black shirt was still dusty. He took it off, balled it up, and placed it on an empty chair next to him. He took his beret out of his pocket and put it on his head. He sat in the chair in his T-shirt and dusty pants. He attempted a smile and then looked straight ahead into the night without saying a word.

Vanessa dug in her purse and pulled out a small ring box and handed it to Max. Please take it, she said in an unhappy voice.

Max looked at the box, and from the light that came from the kitchen window, he recognized it right away. Vanessa. Please. Come on; it's yours. I gave it to you to keep.

Yes, you did. And once it meant something…something special. Now it's just a ring in my jewelry box, among others.

No, Vanessa. And Max was hurt because of her words. Once the ring represented the love I had for you. And now, because circumstances have changed, the love that ring represents has not necessarily changed.

I always believed, Max—and don't take offense, please—that if it's genuine love, few things can change it. Couples work together because of that love to make things better, and they don't give it up at the first sign of trouble or problems that might eventually be resolved. I don't know, Max; that's just the way I feel about it.

Max was silent. He was unable to respond. Vanessa provided a solid case, and his position was not easy to defend. He loved her, or he thought he did. He was close to her little boy, and Vanessa was the most sensitive and mature woman he had ever been with. She was a woman with zero pretentions who at times made him feel like a phony. She was generous beyond a doubt and compassionate in every sense of the word. She had helped him with his mother many times when he found himself in a state of despair, uncertain of where to turn. He had been ready for the first time in his life to commit to the relationship. And then his mother had arrived. And maybe that was an excuse, but since then, his feelings for Vanessa Renderos, the woman he was in love with, the woman he planned to wed, had changed. Now he wasn't sure anymore, not only about Vanessa but about many other things as well. So how could he make her comprehend that it wasn't just that simple to talk about love or lack of it, when other emotions demanded attention? How could he ever begin to tell her about his propensity for the violence that played havoc with his life? Or the guilt that dominated hours of his time over the years his best friend, Jerry Rivera, had spent behind bars? And how could he explain to her that even though he loved her son, he feared his useless father would show up one day and claim him? Or that after he showered the boy with love and gave him a good home, the boy would take off and search for his biological father? Max knew that would break his heart. He wanted to tell Vanessa so many things, but he was a coward and said nothing.

They both sat and stared at the quiet street in silence. It was late, and the breeze was colder. It was a clear night now, and the moon was a bright yellow. Max wanted to invite her inside the house. He was afraid he might get weak and hurt her even more with promises he couldn't keep. He wasn't the type of man who played games with women or anybody else. His life was complicated enough as it was without additional layers and schemes added to it. He wanted her to stay, and at the same time, he wanted her to leave. He wanted her as a friend, but he didn't want to involve her in his unresolved, confused, and at times violent life. She could be physically and emotionally hurt, and she had her son to consider. Why risk it? he thought.

Vanessa Renderos thought about staying. If Max was against it, there was not a thing she could do about it. She had bent over backward to please him and his mother, and it didn't seem to accomplish anything. His mother, Victoria, she could forgive because of her condition. Max, on the other hand, was a mystery and continued to be one. She knew from the moment she met him that he was different. He was a man with a deep intellect, but he shared very little of his own personal life. And Vanessa had always known to stay clear of men such as Max, but curiosity got the best of her. He was so handsome and charming that when he flirted with her, he won her over. And besides, everyone who was a native of Las Flores praised him and his family to the fullest. It started out so innocent and so simple. A date here and there. And double dates with his friends Ruth and William Moreno. They had so much fun together. And he seemed to get along so well with her son, Ricky, that people who saw them together believed he was the biological father. Even her parents, who visited from Mora, were impressed by Max with her young son, Ricky, and the love and respect he displayed toward her. Then Max's friend Jerry Rivera was released from prison, and she noticed how Max started to change. Not in a drastic way, but in ways mostly obvious to a woman. The biggest change she noticed was when Max's mother, Victoria, arrived, ill and in need of assistance. Victoria, who didn't even know her, disliked her from the first minute. And Max, for the first time since she had met him, seemed confused, and if not confused, not himself.

I have to leave, Max, Vanessa confessed in a somber voice. It wasn't the truth, but since she was not invited to stay, she had little choice.

Max stood up as if he had been reminded of something pressing. Keep the ring, sweetheart, he wanted to say, but he said instead, Keep the ring, Vanessa. Please. It belongs to you, and you should keep it.

I'll keep it, Max. It's a beautiful ring, and if what you said about it is true, I'll keep it. Oh, Max. And she tried hard not to release any tears. Visit little Ricky when you get a chance, OK? He's asked me about you, and he wants to know when you are going to take him fishing. I guess you promised to take him, and as you know, kids never forget.

Max felt worse. He attempted a fake smile and said, I will, Vanessa, as soon as I have some free time. I will. Max didn't even like to fish. He couldn't stand the smell of fish and the time wasted trying to catch one. He had promised to take the little boy puddle jumping. That was when you chased after fish in the puddles when the river was almost dry and whacked them with a stick when the fish jumped out of the water. It was a lot more fun than fishing with a pole. I apologize for my mother, Vanessa. He wanted to change the subject. I know it's been rough with her, but it's her health…she's not herself. If you only knew her when she was healthy. She was a different person, full of life, and you two would have gotten on.

I understand, Max. I hold nothing against your mother. She's going through a difficult time. I don't take it personal. It's you I worry about. I can see the effect it's having on you. My advice to you, Max, is to get some help to live in or put in some long hours to help you out.

She refuses to see or talk to any of our relatives, Vanessa. I have pleaded with her to allow them to come and at least keep her company. She retreats into her room, locks the door, and doesn't talk to me for hours when I ask her to at least consider it.

I see, Max. Perhaps it's because they're relatives. I'll provide you with the names and numbers of women who do this for a living. I utilize them for outpatients, and they work out well. They're not nurses. They are trained in this area of providing home care and are very professional in what they do. Some can stay in the home for as long as they are needed, while others put in long hours. Maybe your mother will feel comfortable with one of these women; it's worth a try. All I'm saying, Max, is that you need assistance and soon, before it's too late. I have to go, Max. I left Ricky with my neighbor.

Max gave Vanessa a hug but not a kiss when she left. When he saw the taillights of her car on the street, he asked himself out loud, How can I be so cold? Vanessa Renderos was the kindest and most giving woman he had ever known. And he had known plenty of women in his time. He hated himself at times like this and wanted to kick himself in the ass for being so selfish. One kiss and some tender words to show her that he was still human and not the monster he felt he was turning into or had become. He felt like going after her. He would apologize and ask her to marry him tomorrow or the day after. Instead, he sat back down in the chair and decided to take a shower and clean up. He knew that when he went inside the house he had to see his mother asleep in her bed. He resented her at times like this when he felt so lonely, and it was so difficult to have anyone around. He missed Vanessa and her little boy, Ricky. At times, he felt like crying. He remembered when Jerry finally had come home, and he'd stayed with him. They had so much fun every day and night. They stayed up all night and talked about people they knew in the barrio. They talked about movies and music and everything. And that was the plan—for Jerry to live with him and make up for some of the time they were separated. And it was during that time he decided that Vanessa couldn't be part of his life, which was stupid, as he now saw it. Then his mother arrived and not in the best of health, and she didn't want anybody else around. Even though she loved Jerry like a son, he had to go. Jerry went to live in his late mother's old house, which belonged to him now. Max nursed his mother alone and was miserable a lot of the time.

Max finally decided to go inside and get out of the cold. He stripped to his boxers. He grabbed a towel and was going to take a shower when he stopped at the open door of his mother's room. He saw the tiny, frail body barely breathing under a blanket. Her head was on a pillow and her face turned to the wall. His anger dissipated, and he felt like going over to her and holding her in his arms. Another torrent of emotion flooded his brain, and he felt so bad and sad about his mother and her condition. His mother would have done everything and more if the circumstances were reversed, and on that he would bet his life. She had always been there for him, even though she lived hundreds of miles away. She never refused him anything he asked her for. Now all she asked for was to die in peace in the house she had been born in, with the only person she loved close to her. What a monster I am, he told himself and walked off to take a shower and crawl into bed like the insect he had turned into. After his shower and once in bed, he was going to call Vanessa and have a serious conversation with her. The only problem was that now he had a bad taste in his mouth and wanted only to go to sleep and wake up tomorrow and pretend everything was normal. He needed to rest; he had a long day and night ahead of him. His mother might wake up in the middle of the night and call him. She would be disorientated and needing help to use the bathroom. He took a bottle of brandy from the drawer in his nightstand, took a hit, and put the bottle back. He took one last look out of his bedroom door. He kept the door open just in case he heard his mother walking around the house like she sometimes did. He didn't see her or hear anything. He turned off his night-light and hit the sack. He was not in the mood for reading, as was his habit before turning in. He closed his eyes with the satisfaction that tomorrow he would see Jerry, Ruth, William, and the kids and have some laughs. At least that's what he hoped for.

CHAPTER 17

Mike Cotton paced back and forth in his little work trailer. It was Sunday morning, and the work site was quiet. He was alone, and he was angry. He had known since Friday that Mike Montes had been successful and purchased the property from Vivien Madrid. He was sure the paperwork was in escrow, and there was not a thing he could do about it. He was glad Claire had gone to Santa Fe to see the children. He was in a sour mood, and Claire had seemed to be in a cheery mood for the last couple of weeks. He never got the chance to inquire why she was suddenly so upbeat. Perhaps it was the volunteer work she was doing at the CI Center, he assumed, working with the kids and all. Or maybe it was that she had deep conversations with Max Luna and his buddies. They were a bunch of crazies, as far as he was concerned. He wanted to laugh, but nothing came out. Mike Cotton waited for his brother, Billy Bob, to show up. He wanted Billy Bob to explain to him what the attorney had advised him about eminent domain. It took some hard talk to convince Billy Bob to show up on the site on a Sunday. He agreed after some harsh words were exchanged between them. It wasn't even that early. It was just that Billy Bob quit work on Friday afternoon and wasn't seen until late Monday and sometimes Tuesday.

Billy Bob Cotton drove slowly into the construction site. He didn't want to get his Caddy dusty. He'd had it washed and waxed the day before. He never had the time to take the car in on Sundays to have it washed. He had plans to take his woman friend out to dinner in Ciudad Juarez, and he liked to drive in a clean car. He had a slight headache from a party the night before, and he needed a strong Bloody Mary to fix him up. He still had to gas up and pack a light bag in case they got too inebriated and had to spend the night in one of the finer motels in Juarez, across the Bridge of the Americas in the Chamizal area. He never visited the old part of Juarez unless he was with the men from Juarez he employed. They danced at the clubs or looked for putas in the puta clubs on the Calle Mariscal. His favorite club was the LA Club on the Calle Mariscal. The girls in that club were young, friendly, and beautiful. He never encountered any problems in that part of Juarez because he would tell the crew from Juarez where he was going to be and at what time. Most of them would meet him there, eager to party with him because he would pay for the booze and the girls. El Gato Negro was not one of his favorite clubs. Many of the putas in the Black Cat were older and in many cases ugly. They stayed for a while, had some drinks, and left to check out the other clubs. They always ended up at the LA Club.

Billy Bob saw his brother's truck parked in front of the old, dusty office trailer. He knew his brother, Mike, was going to Sunday service, and he never even bothered to drive a decent car. He had several expensive models in the five-car garage that only Claire seemed to utilize. Billy Bob was fully aware that his brother was more than pissed because Mike Montes had purchased the property he had wanted for so long, and he wasn't even given the opportunity to make an offer. His brother was naive or stupid if he believed that he even had a chance at the property. Vivien Madrid and Mike Montes had a history. And Billy Bob had no idea how close they were now, but when he saw her that one time, he figured it had to be close—more than close. Tight. He parked the Caddy and noticed that his brother was pacing inside the shabby trailer. Jesus, said Billy Bob. Why won't he buy a new, larger trailer? They sure the hell could afford it. He was embarrassed when he brought over important players in the construction game to discuss and sign off on all the fundamentals that went into building homes.

Billy Bob walked up the three old, rickety wooden steps and opened the metal door. He walked into the small space the trailer provided. Morning, he said and went straight to the coffee pot that was cold with old coffee. Mike was in one of his bargain-basement suits and ties that he wore on Sunday when he went to praise the Lord.

Hey, Billy. And Mike Cotton faced him. His complexion was red as a steamed lobster, and the wrinkles around his eyes were more pronounced. Did you talk to the attorney?

I did, Mike. And Billy Bob attempted a smile, but he knew it was no use. I had a long conversation with him, and he did run over some points on eminent domain. And to be honest, none of them seem to be promising. He said it was rare for the government to use that power to create parks or open spaces, but it can be done. It comes down to how much influence you have or how much you can pull together. He also said the county or the city can use it to preserve open space because public access to the property could damage the natural environment, as well as the habitat for some protected critters, such as cactus and desert tortoise. And he named those as an example. But then you would have to convince the county or the city to sell or lease the property to you. And that's a tough nut to crack—his words, not mine.

So there's little hope? That's what the man meant, right? Mike made a fist, and his blue eyes blazed with anger.

Well, there is one more thing that might make it worth the effort. And Billy Bob backed away from Mike.

Which is? Mike asked. And he inched forward as Billy Bob inched back.

Don't get your hopes too high though. The government can seize private property to promote economic development. Now if you can convince the government that your project will provide jobs and taxes for the city and county, maybe then.

Mike Cotton smiled for the first time all week. His square jaw and even white teeth seemed like they were about to crack like granite, when it takes a blow from a hammer. I like that, he said. And he continued to smile, which was rare for him. So there is a possibility something can be done in my favor. My project will provide employment and taxes. I will show Mike Montes that I can be smarter and outmaneuver him at his own dirty game.

Don't get your hopes too high, brother, Billy Bob said to himself. He would rather have Mike smiling, but he had to say it. Mike Montes is no fool, and you know it. He passed the bar exam the first time he took it in California and here, in New Mexico. He's an expert in real estate law, and I'm positive he's familiar with all the facts on eminent domain. All I'm saying is don't underestimate him. Besides, his partner is also an attorney who practices law in Albuquerque. You're up against brains, Mike, not just a bunch of silly guys who talk out their asses. They also have those wealthy investors in California with deep pockets who don't seem to put a limit on their credit cards.

Mike Cotton didn't care to hear about Mike Montes and how smart he was. He disliked attorneys, all attorneys. He believed the bar exam was rigged. In his eyes, they were not any better qualified than him to practice law or build homes or anything. He had what he wanted, and he never even had to set foot in any law school. He repeated the words to himself—to promote economic development—that was the key that would open the door shut in his face. Mike dismissed Billy Bob. He glanced at his watch and gave him that certain look that he was not needed anymore.

Billy Bob knew the look, and he welcomed it. He had done his part and refused to argue or debate with his stubborn brother. That would be a waste of time and energy, and he needed all the energy he could muster in case he stayed the night with his woman friend in Juarez. He had his fingers crossed that Mike wouldn't ask him where he was going. He wasn't in the mood to hear a religious lecture on morality and faith. Mike's name for El Paso-Juarez was Sodom and Gomorra, and Billy Bob had no time or the stomach for biblical references this early in the morning. If his brother was fulfilled with the rantings of Pastor Monroe, that was his choice. He, on the other hand, was more like his late father, Earl. He attended service once in a blue moon to check out the women, and he distributed his cash to all denominations as to be covered in case Saint Peter refused to open the pearly gates and allow him entrance when his time was up.

Billy Bob said goodbye and left the construction site in his Caddy. He believed his brother was going nuts for thinking he could use eminent domain to take the property away from Mike Montes. But his brother was always doing strange things and surprising people. Billy Bob glanced at his watch and smiled. He had time to stop at Mi Casita and have a bowl of hot red chili menudo and a stack of buttered, handmade corn tortillas on the side. That was his Sunday ritual to help cure his hangover. If some of the work crew happened to be there, he would probably drink a couple of cold cervezas after the menudo before he picked up his woman friend. Life is good, he said out loud and turned up the volume on a disk of Tito Puente's Cayuco.

Mike Cotton locked up his little trailer. He jumped in his work truck and hit the road. He was going to take Piñon Street west, all the way to the Westside. He liked to drive through the Eastside barrio. The only reason he wasn't going to stop at Mi Casita on Santos Street was because he knew for sure his brother, Billy Bob, was already there, slurping up some hot red chili menudo. Some of his crew would be there also, and Billy Bob was a show-off when he chugged cold beers with the crew. He didn't even consider the Azteca for menudo because that menudo lacked taste and pico. It was more for tourists and white people, Mike believed. Even Santos, the owner, was seen at Mi Casita on occasion. He sat in the kitchen and sucked on some hot, tasty menudo.

Mike Cotton just drove on slowly. He took his time. He thought about his children and Claire. He wished he had his children with him, and they were all together on their way to service, but that was not the case. At first it was awkward to have to explain to the busybodies in the congregation that his own children lived in Santa Fe and attended a private Catholic academy. Claire had a thousand answers for the nosy women who dared to ask her about it. But then that was Claire. She saw no conflict in sending her young children to a Catholic school while she and her husband were at Sunday service with the Baptists. Mike was sure the children were taken to Sunday mass by the grandparents, who were staunch Catholics. And Claire probably never said a word about it because she didn't follow any religious doctrine. To her, all religions were the same. She spent her time on committees and helped the neediest in the congregation. She promised Mike the children would return to Las Flores once they completed elementary school—the most formative years, she claimed. But Mike knew the grandparents, and as long as they were alive and healthy, they would never allow the children to leave. And Claire always sided with her parents.

Mike continued to drive and think. He was almost on Mora Street, which ran north and south. The streets were almost empty of cars and people, and that was what he liked most about his Sunday drive. After Mora, he would pass the tracks and drive by downtown into the Westside where the Baptist Church was located. It was a bright and clear morning, and this was the time he missed the children most. He missed their chatter. Claire would answer all their funny questions. During the week, it wasn't so bad because he was so busy, but on the Sunday drive to service, it did get a little lonely, he had to admit. But he could never live in Santa Fe, close to Claire's family. They were a pretentious lot, all of them, except Claire. They were short on money and big on showing off. He recalled when they were first married and invited to family gatherings. One of them, usually one of the older siblings, would say, Move the demi lune to that corner over there. All he saw was a half-moon-shaped table, but they had to call it by some strange name to show him what was what. Or someone else would say, Oh, look at the wonderful plinth I discovered. My Greek statue can now be seen by all. Or they would start a conversation in English and switch to Spanish. Since he could understand Spanish, they would start to converse in French. Claire would attempt to translate until the conversation got heated, and then she would forget about the translation and join in. Miss Know-It-All couldn't help it. Finally, one of the kids would cry out, People. We have company. English, please. Then some of the adults would look at him and in their twisted minds blame him for killing the conversation in French. Mike took it all in stride. If it bothered him, he didn't show it. He knew what he was about. These people—and he had made up his mind, after all—lacked manners and money, and they would never admit it. He recalled how his father-in-law used to brag about his horse ranch. A ranch that was once run by his great-grandfather. A ranch that had dwindled from over two hundred acres to fewer than twenty because the old fool had to sell pieces of it just to keep the horses fed and healthy. Mike had to step in and subsidize the place so that his kids could keep their ponies fed. And Claire's answer to everything was, Well, if you can help, do it; if you can't, don't.

Mike continued the drive west on Piñon Street. He wanted to make a left on Main Street and stop at Fat Henry's for a cup of coffee, which he sometimes did, but he decided against it. He wasn't in the mood to converse with the fools who gathered there on a Sunday morning. He drove on instead and deliberated on Claire's family. He wanted to laugh, and many times he did, but not this morning. He recalled when he finally completed Claire's dream house, and they were going to throw a big party to celebrate the completion of the sixty-six-hundred-square-foot Mediterranean-style house on twenty acres of land. Claire was certain her parents would come out and stay with them for at least a couple of days. He had also built a casita, or guesthouse, behind the main house. It was a twenty-five-hundred-square-foot house, larger than many homes in the Eastside barrio, with all the modern conveniences. His father-in-law didn't make it. He made an excuse that some of the horses were ill. Mike knew the old man would never drive anywhere south of Santa Fe. He would take a plane to Mexico City or even Europe, but he refused to drive the little over a hundred miles to Las Flores, even at his daughter's request. The older brother, the one they called Chuy, drove the old hag, his mother-in-law, to Las Flores. She refused to stay in the guesthouse. She called it the servants' quarter. The only reason Chuy, Jesus, his Christian name, who liked to be called Nazareno for reasons obvious only to him, drove Claire's mother to Las Flores was that he was going to play the ponies at Sunland Park, and he wanted to hit Claire up for some cash, which he did. Claire had to drive the old woman back to Santa Fe when Chuy didn't show up after a couple of days. A week later, Chuy called Claire and begged her to wire him some money because he was stuck somewhere between Guadalajara and Mexico City and needed the money to get back home. That was the kind of con man Claire's older brother was. He never completed enough credits for a degree. He called himself a financial planner or adviser. He took people's money in Ponzi schemes until he got busted and did some time in federal prison. That was a well-kept family secret. Claire's sister's husband was an attorney. He advised the old man to transfer all his assets to his daughter's name. The court expected Chuy to pay restitution to the people he swindled, and the old man's name was somehow linked to Chuy's shenanigans. The old man, Claire's father, didn't have that much to transfer. Besides the horse ranch, he lived off some rental buildings he still owned and a small pension he collected from the state. He worked at the governor's office. He mostly sat on his ass and collected a paycheck from the taxpayers. He even got Chuy a job with the state treasurer, but Chuy had sticky fingers and was fired soon after for misappropriation of funds. And the only reason he wasn't prosecuted was that his father was on first-name basis with the governor.

Mike Cotton loosened his tie and the top button on his shirt to give his thick neck a breather. He recalled after that incident with his mother-in-law that he'd told Claire the casita would never be offered again to anyone while his property manager, Alfredo Palomares, and his wife, Sofia, stayed there. And Claire agreed because she enjoyed having Sofia around. Sofia cooked and kept house for the Cottons and even went along with Claire to Santa Fe to visit the children, whom she also loved. Alfredo kept up the day-to-day maintenance on the huge property. When Claire's older sister visited, which was rare, she brought along her husband, the attorney. Mike only listened to the conversation between the two sisters. The husband seemed to always be exhausted. During the day, he only wanted to lie around the pool and sip vodka with ice. That was fine with Mike because he had too much work to do to entertain a man he had nothing in common with. After dinner, where the two men had been listeners, as usual, they watched movies in Mike's entertainment center. It was built like a small movie theater but was large enough to sit thirty people, if they were packed in right. After the movie had gone on for about ten minutes, Mike slipped out without saying a word. He would go and join Alfredo Palomares on the back porch of the casita. Sofia was always with Claire or nearby to get her anything she needed. Mike enjoyed listening to Alfredo's stories of growing up in a small village a short distance from the city of Chihuahua, in old Mejico. They would sip black coffee regardless of the weather, because neither of them indulged in alcoholic beverages. They would sit in the dark and observe the moon and stars. And the big half wolves, German shepherd dogs, Mona and Drake, sat next to them. Mike loved to listen to Alfredo talk about his younger days when Alfredo's father decided to relocate to Ciudad Juarez and then to South El Paso. Alfredo still recalled many of the rough characters his siblings and he encountered in Juarez. But when they moved to South El Paso, they encountered even rougher ones, and not the easiest vatos to get along with there. Finally, Alfredo's father, tired of city life, moved the family to Socorro, New Mexico, not far from Las Flores. His father landed a job at the Socorro College of Mines as a groundskeeper. They hired him because he had run a huge rancho outside Chihuahua City. Alfredo, in his early teens, took advantage of Socorro's almost depopulated ambience. And although a dull place to live, it was a great one to concentrate on studies and to learn English. Socorro reminded Alfredo of his village in Chihuahua, with the same weather and wide-open spaces to wander in. He eventually adjusted after going through some of the rebelliousness many teenagers experience. He even took some classes at the college after high school and learned about native habitats and agronomy in desert environments. He didn't graduate because when his father passed, he was offered his father's job as groundskeeper for the college. He accepted because he was already married to Sofia and had two babies to support.

Alfredo Palomares worked for the College of Mines for some thirty years without complaining. He retired a relatively young man and after doing what retirees do—play golf, travel, and work around the house—he fell ill. Alfredo was afflicted with the menace of modern man: boredom. A relative who worked for Mike Cotton told him Iron Mike needed a competent property manager to manage his hacienda in Las Flores. Alfredo put together a résumé and drove to Las Flores to see about a job he didn't need but wanted, nevertheless. Mike left Alfredo's résumé on top of his desk unopened and invited him on a walk. The two men walked on the property beyond the rock wall. Mike listened as Alfredo educated him on the changes needed and how he would do them to make the huge property conducive to walking, jogging, and walking the dogs. The first thing was to configure all the trails to meet in a central location, instead of going every whichway. Then he would utilize large branches from local trees no longer useful, arch them, and shape them to create shady areas or rest areas, all natural, without the use of brick or concrete. He would remove all plants and shrubs that were not native and needed more water and replace them with native plants. Besides, many more ideas convinced Mike to hire Alfredo on the spot and offer him the casita to live in. Alfredo had only one condition, and that was that his wife, Sofia, also be hired or be allowed to live with him in the casita. Claire liked Sofia right away, and the Palomares became almost close family to the Cottons. Alfredo and Sofia rented their home in Socorro and moved to Las Flores within a couple of weeks of being hired by Mike Cotton.

Mike Cotton couldn't help but smile when he thought of Alfredo and Sofia Palomares. Alfredo had transformed the property beyond the wall from an endless maze of trails with a mixture of nonnative plants and shrubs growing amuck, to an organized nature-like park venue. It was safer for Claire to walk or jog on the clear-cut trails and keep an eye on the big dogs, Mona and Drake. As Mike approached the old building where the Baptists held services, on the Westside of town, his smile disappeared. Now he had to wear another hat. Now he was Iron Mike to the people in the congregation, and he played the part as skillfully as any actor. It was a personality he had cultivated on his own, with help from no one. And he wasn't proud of it, not on any given day, but it was his all the same. Most people in the congregation were sheep in his eyes, from the pastor on down. They wanted to cling to him. They were needy and in some cases desperate, and he couldn't handle that with a light touch, that sort of people. He was himself and liked to talk to Alfredo Palomares and Juan Vela, his foreman; with others, it was more than difficult. He was more like a strict father than a real brother to Billy Bob. He justified his treatment of Billy Bob, because in his eyes, Billy Bob acted like a child, and he needed a father figure to guide him. He showed off in his Caddy. He wore expensive clothes and picked up sluts here and there. Mike didn't get it. Was it him or the people around him who had to accept what was real and what was not?

Mike Cotton was seen by his coreligionists as a pillar of righteousness. And not known to all, Mike Cotton perceived things a little bit differently than the average person. His steel-blue eyes, he believed, saw beyond the congregation and their simple needs. He maintained his distinguished vision grasped a separate reality in a distant dimension not reachable by the conscious pretentions of his fellow believers. Mike Cotton was a practical man in most basic considerations, but in his own estimation, his moral values were not satisfied by the boundaries of religion. He was a practicing Baptist, but not at heart. He believed in the Christ and all that the Christ represented. He even respected the others who needed Jesus more than he did. It was because of these same people in the congregation that he committed his services to the cause. He wanted to be around those people, and not necessarily close, to appraise the pulse of society. Even though, in his opinion, their view was limited in perspective. He learned about people, where their strengths or weaknesses came from, and how much force was attached to those two opposites. And to the weak, he stressed more discipline to fight the vicious, frivolous habits that decayed their souls and thrust them closer to Abaddon, the angel of the bottomless pit. And he warned the strong of their arrogance of believing they were better than others because of material possessions and superior employment. And this was where Mike Cotton let his teeth show and stressed the point of clean Christian living. He did it with such force and enthusiasm that he almost believed it himself.

Mike Cotton arrived a little late, as was his habit. He sat in the back benches of the musty, crowded building so as not to attract attention and observe his people better. Mike Cotton was a tower of a man, and he dressed in a bargain-basement suit and shoes. He was not present to make a fashion statement of any kind. He was here because he believed with all the strength in his heart and soul that Jesus wanted him to make money, lots of money. He didn't share this personal belief with others because they might want to follow his example. They would pray to Jesus for that purpose only and make a mockery of Jesus and of him.

After service, which Mike thought was too long, he walked among the people. He shook hands with the brothers and sisters because he wasn't the hugging type. He hugged only his wife when he had to. Mike felt hugging was an intimate gesture that could lead to adultery or worse. He strongly believed that the message given by a hug revealed some kind of key to open a door that otherwise should never be opened. He didn't like for his wife to hug. She had a mind of her own though, and it would have been a major disappointment for the men who lined up in droves to give Claire the movie star a hug. And even a handshake, for the less aggressive.

Mike Cotton's appeal for biblical readings was not necessarily a farce. He believed and even practiced most of the commandments. He also believed they were too soft for his liking. An eye for an eye, the old

Hammurabi law, was more to his taste. Revenge for his mother's murder was always on his mind and ate at him like a rat chewing on a dead horse. And he intended to get his revenge, even if it cost him his life.

Mike Cotton was outside and listened to a couple of tall, skinny, young men in their late teens. The young men asked Mike for employment with his construction company. Mike promised them he would look into it and almost laughed when he thought of how they would melt like white butter in the hot summer sun. And then he would have to take them to the emergency room or call an ambulance. Either one, a waste of valuable time and paperwork he had to fill out. He recalled when he started out in construction along with his brother, Billy Bob. They were just out of high school when his father, Earl, secured for them a job with a small outfit to see how long they would last. The boss owed Earl a favor and took them on. He promised to work them like the regular crew. They're big boys, the boss told Earl, but big don't cut no ice in the hot sun, digging trenches. The Mexican workers made fun of them and gave them a week, two at the most. But Mike was determined to make it and learn the business. It was a struggle because he had to carry Billy Bob. Mike was stronger than a horse and didn't wear any gloves, so the seasoned workers wouldn't make fun of him. Billy Bob wore a huge straw hat and work gloves and slipped into the trenches of the foundations when they were being filled with cement. But they stuck it out and worked like dogs for little pay. After a couple of months, the workers saw that Mike wasn't a quitter and could work as well or better than most. He was a quick learner and moved from trench digger to other jobs that required more skill. Mike and Billy Bob would eat bean burritos and tacos with the Mexican workers around the makeshift grill instead of baloney sandwiches on white bread by themselves. They drank water instead of sugary sodas as the other workers did, and because they knew street Spanish, they could banter around with the others. Mike was more on the quiet side, but Billy Bob was the life of the party. He would take off on Fridays after work and go boozing with the guys while Mike checked out books from the library on home building and read them until late at night. He would make friends with the plumbers, electricians, and architects, and he asked them millions of questions. He was made foreman in a little over a year because he worked so hard that everyone else had to work harder to keep up, and the boss liked that. He never had any problems with anyone except one time when a pendejo called him an ass kisser. He put the boy on his ass with one blow, and he expected the rest of the crew to jump on him, but no one did. Apparently, the crew didn't like that boy because he was a slacker. They gave Mike high fives and more respect.

About a year and a half later, Mike Cotton, young and eager, decided to open Cotton Construction Company. He felt he had learned enough about building homes, and that's what he wanted to do. He loved it when the last touches were put on a house and he had a hand on making it happen. He enjoyed seeing the smiles on the family that was going to move into that house and call it a home. Mike promised Billy Bob that after they started making some money, he, Billy Bob was going to go to college. Billy Bob loved the idea. Mike had an advantage over other builders because he owned a lot of vacant land that his father had purchased throughout the years when land was cheaper. That was one less expense for him to worry about, and he could offer the homes to prospective buyers at a small discount. It seemed so long ago, Mike thought, as he saw the two young boys playing grab ass.

Meanwhile, the Pastor Monroe, a tall gangly man, bald as a honeydew melon and about the same color, with big ears, waited for Mike to finish talking to the boys. Pastor Monroe was never comfortable around Mike Cotton. He still called him Mr. Cotton and Mike only when Claire was present. Pastor Monroe recognized the fact that Mike Cotton was his bread-and-butter man. And he tried hard not jeopardize the manna from heaven that kept him and his wife in comfort.

Mr. Cotton…Mike, ah…the meeting is about to start.

Well, then let's get to it, Mike said without even looking at the man. He walked fast, as he always did, with a long stride on powerful legs. The Pastor Monroe fell behind. He almost stumbled as he walked on the ugly rubber-soled shoes the clergy favor. He was disappointed because he thought Mike was going to walk with him and chat a little, then enter together. Mike Cotton was unpredictable, and the Pastor Monroe didn't have it in him to ask him why he was so rude. So he just let him go and followed, as he always did.

Mike Cotton entered the old meeting building behind the church and went straight to the lectern. The long room was crowded, but as soon as he entered, everyone stopped talking. All eyes were on him as he went directly to the first item on the agenda. Mike didn't wait for the Pastor Monroe to open the meeting with a prayer as he usually did. Mike Cotton was in a hurry because he had an important announcement to make. OK, he said. First thing, the bus. Apparently, it broke down again. Is Wilbur Jenkins still driving the bus? Let him step up here and tell us what's gone wrong with that old thing.

Wilbur Jenkins stepped up to the lectern next to Mike Cotton. Wilbur Jenkins was an Afro American who lived with others of his race in an area north of downtown Las Flores. Wilbur Jenkins had little patches of gray hair on his otherwise bald head. He had on thick eyeglasses and was retired from Sears after working many years as a tire setter. Mike Cotton liked Wilbur Jenkins because he made sense when he talked. He was the new bus driver, and he seemed the best qualified for the job.

Mike Cotton gave Wilbur a sturdy handshake, and the smaller man showed his grip. Tell us, Wilbur, what is wrong with the bus? asked Mike, as friendly as he could, without sounding disrespectful.

I'll tell you, Mike, Wilbur answered, not intimidated by Mike or anyone else. The thing is old, and the transmission is about to fall out. The tires are worn, and it burns oil like there's no tomorrow.

What will it cost to fix the thing, Wilbur?

An arm and a leg. It will cost more than the old heap is worth.

And what do you suggest, Wilbur?

Junk it. Simple as that.

I like that attitude, Mike said. Thank you, Wilbur. You can sit now. As Wilbur returned to his chair, he was given a robust applause; even Mike Cotton joined in. The Baptists were very polite people, and they seemed to like Wilbur Jenkins.

All right, Mike Cotton called out and raised his hands to settle the folks. This is what we are going to do. We are going to buy a new bus. No more secondhand piece of retired junk from the school district. We are going to own a tour bus like you see on the highway—a real bus. Our Christian ministry deserves decent transportation whenever they go on the road to spread the gospel. And, folks, you are probably asking who is going to pay for this luxury? Well, not to worry. Whatever our reserve cannot cover, I will make up the difference. The audience broke into loud clapping and repeatedly said, Thank you, Jesus.

Mike Cotton liked what he saw and heard. He enjoyed the wonderful admiration that the people expressed. Whether it was real or meant from the heart was difficult to judge. Was it because he was rich and young, compassionate, and generous with his funds? He would never know. Anyway, to him it wasn't even worth the time to bother with it. To him it was a sign of nobler events to present themselves in bigger arenas. Mike Cotton felt a thrill, close to what he felt when his dear mother took him as a boy for a strawberry milkshake in downtown Albuquerque. He had no intention to utilize this thrill, this joy, and to restrain his demons, as other weak and cowardly men tended to do. No, none of that. Mike Cotton was going to make the best of the situation and place a chain of steel around his propensity for revenge until the time came to strike. He wasn't ready to attack yet. But the black vulture of revenge circled close. He believed a little distraction would contain, somewhat, the vulture that breathed down his neck until a perfect plan was prepared.

Shall we get on with the next item on the agenda, please? Mike asked. He said it in a voice with a body language that was opposite of his usual Man of Iron persona. It was a voice that softened his blade, but the weapon was still handy, in case he needed to use it. He wanted to appear to the audience, his people, as a born-again man who had the common good of the people at heart. All people. Not only the few whose interests were only money and power. Mike Cotton wanted most of all to prove to himself and others he could modify his personality and become a sincere and reasonable man. After all, wasn't that what Jesus was all about? he asked himself. But he knew so well his detractors would call him many things and far from nice. He would have to live with criticism, and perhaps his skin would become thicker. He would have to adjust to the whiplash and proceed with the game.

Let's continue with the second item on the agenda, Mike repeated. Rare for him when addressing the folks. I apologize because my wife, Claire, is in Santa Fe visiting the children, and she presides over the Committee on Hispanic Outreach. But not to worry—the very capable Ms. Eva Alvarez, Claire's assistant, will read the report. Please step up, señorita Alvarez.

Eva Alvarez was one of the few Chicanas from the Eastside barrio who had accepted Christ with the Baptists. She had had a negative experience with the Catholics that she never talked about with anyone. She became a Baptist and made an all-out effort to recruit Catholics into the Baptist camp.

I can never fill Claire's shoes, Eva Alvarez said in a soft and shy voice. She was cute but not pretty and young enough to hold up her nose at most in the congregation. Eva waited for the room to quiet down as they had for Mike Cotton. She felt her report was as important as or even more significant than the bus issue, or any other issue. Her assignment, if successful, could mean the survival of the Baptist Church in Las Flores, or maybe even in the state. Without the younger, fruitful Latinos coming in and establishing themselves with the Baptists, the decline of the church was imminent. Most of the females in the congregation were beyond their childbearing years.

My report, Mr. Cotton, brothers and sisters, continued Eva Alvarez, when the folks had settled down. She said it in a louder and more vigorous voice. And she could claim it and call it hers because she had researched and written it while Claire Cotton was missing in action. We have brought into the hands of God many lost souls. Their spirits have awakened and have embraced the true brotherhood of Jesus Christ. When you see them in the Hall or outside, encourage them and tell them how your lives have changed for the better, under, under this holy roof. And she raised her petite fingers above her head for emphasis. Alleluia, Jesus saves, came the cry from the crowd. It brought a smile to the tight lips of Eva Alvarez. As you all know, and all of you know this, she repeated. She utilized her evangelical skills that she had established in the streets when she converted people who lacked something or other in their empty lives. As with any enterprise, and I call it that because when they enter, the prize is grand. Eva almost laughed at her ad-lib. Now she had to stop it and get down to business. She already had her little fun, and these folks were too easy. She could rang the tang around them if she wanted to.

As you all know, she said, a little more businesslike, fishing for souls does not come without a little expenditure. If you want to be successful, that is. I need my own budget expanded to compete with the tenacious forces who can unleash a greater army. I need modern advertising and better training for my fishers of men. I need better transportation to cover a larger expanse of territory, and I want the main Sunday service to be in Spanish and English.

Many of the people in attendance almost choked when Eva Alvarez had the audacity to mention Spanish in the Sunday morning service. This conversation was never held in public session. This conversation was held behind closed doors, and Mike Cotton was never invited. Pastor Roscoe Monroe, with a not-too-happy look on his horse face, took a step toward Eve to demand she change the subject. But Mike Cotton gave him a look that almost melted the rubber soles of his ugly shoes. The pastor returned to his place behind Mike Cotton and listened in silence.

That concludes my report, clarified Eva Alvarez, setting herself up for questions.

Mike Cotton jumped in and said, Excuse me, Eva. Let me thank you and congratulate you on your more than excellent report. Before you take any questions, Eva, let me say a few words. And he turned to face the people. I like and will support every item that Eva requested in her report, he said. And loud enough for everyone to hear. Financially as well as in spirit. Your committee, Ms. Alvarez—and Mike Cotton turned to face Eva—will impact the future of the congregation. The success of your committee depends on us. If we do not support your campaign, we are not the people we claim we are. I don't believe you will have many questions now, Eva. If I was not in the truth and you summoned me to the side of Jesus, I would come in on my knees.

Eva Alvarez turned her face away from Mike Cotton and blushed crimson. She had never seen or heard Mike Cotton talk like this or act in this way, so human and yet so strange. She was embarrassed instead of flattered. The man was on her side, and she should be grateful because everybody was aware Mike Cotton was the moneyman and financed the projects dear to his heart.

Mike Cotton was confounded with the words that flowed out of his mouth when he addressed Eva Alvarez. He never talked to anyone like that; that was the language reserved only for his mother. He now comprehended that his transformation was addressing his personality, and the announcement he was going to make would make the integration difficult to reverse.

I have an announcement to make, Mike Cotton cried. He was eager and glowed as Eva Alvarez almost ran back to her chair. Beads of perspiration beaded his brick-red forehead, and it even wasn't that warm inside the old building. I have an announcement to make, and many of you might find it distasteful. Others will embrace it because they comprehend the necessity of my actions. I am going to run for mayor of Las Flores in the coming election.

The people froze, especially the ones who comprehended what Mike Cotton intended to do. They stared with unblinking eyes and attempted to reconcile what they heard to their reason. The political arena to them was a sewer, where only the worst toiled and boiled in indecency. After they had digested the fact and the shock diminished, they were confident that Mike Cotton, the Man of Steel, would never succumb to the depravity of politics. If he ran for political office and was successful, it was to benefit the congregation and not himself.

Yes, my people. I am seeking office as mayor because we need better representation from the folks in city hall. If I win, with your support of course, and I will win, I will vote to loosen the ropes on the zoning laws and build our new Ebenezer Zion Church on a larger scale. The people broke into a loud applause and Jesus saves echoed throughout the crowded room. Some even held on to a sly smile because they recognized that religion and politics could mix, when the marriage was not too toxic.

And another thing, my friends: I intend to support Candy Telles when he runs against Rafa for city councilman for the Eastside. And I will also help elect a city councilman for the East Mesa and one for the North Valley as well—Christian men with all our interests at heart, and with your support, I'm sure. My intentions are to challenge the status quo and give the opportunity to the good people of Las Flores to invest in an honest and fruitful political process, if that animal exists.

Mike Cotton adjourned the meeting. And after the usual congratulations and words of support, he walked a short distance to a smaller building, where another meeting with the elders and Pastor Roscoe Monroe took place. Mike Cotton was still in the difficult stage of not wanting what he said to be true. His privacy would be a thing of the past, and his public life would be an open book for anybody to poke their nose into. But he also recognized the fact that he would have another type of privacy, one that only the political connected and wealthy could afford. Anyway, it was too late. The machine was in motion and if stopped now, he would lose all credibility, and his word was gold, he believed. Mike Cotton was on the fast train now, and the train made no stops for cowards to jump off. Besides, his mind was already busy making plans on how to utilize the new bus to take voters to the polls and when to ask Eva Alvarez to be his campaign manager.

Mike Cotton placed his heavy arm on Pastor Monroe's skinny shoulders. He said in a calm, quiet voice but with menacing eyes, Pastor, next time, do not attempt to censor Eva Alvarez on any topic. Let her say what she writes in her report and present it to the people. The Spanish issue, as you know, cannot be implemented until the congregation reaches ten percent or more of Spanish speakers. For her to reach ten percent or more, her recruitment efforts must be very successful. If she can accomplish her goal, we win. If she fails, you win.

Pastor Monroe felt the oppressive weight of Mike Cotton's arm on his frail shoulders, and he listened to the advice. He could not afford to fall out of favor with the moneyman because Mike Cotton could take the whole of the congregation to the new church he was building on property he himself had donated and find a younger pastor—perhaps a bilingual pastor, at that. Pastor Monroe grasped the reality of starting over at his age, in a state with a high percentage of Catholic families and an established church. Oh, he could take his chances and allow the church to find him a position. With his luck, he would end up in the deep South. In the backcountry and among ignorant and bigoted people who kissed deadly snakes as a form of demonstrating faith. Instead, he played second fiddle to Mike Cotton in running the Christian Ministries and the operation of any important church functions. He had seen the new house being built for the pastor behind the new church and yearned to live in a modern house with all the amenities a good pastor deserved. He wasn't going to jeopardize his new church, along with his modern abode, over a misunderstanding with Mike Cotton. And all he dared to say, and he said it, was, I stand corrected, sir.

CHAPTER 18

Mike Montes finished up grilling a filet mignon on the outside grill of his Chula Vista Estates condo in the East Mesa area of Las Flores. Alexis Cordova Riley, his girlfriend, prepared a salad in the large kitchen of the thirty-four-hundred-square-foot condo. Mike Montes couldn't stand the odor of meat—or any fried food, for that matter—cooking inside his condo. He wasn't much of a meat eater. One small steak cut in half with the salad was enough for him and Alexis, who didn't consume much red meat either. Tonight he didn't want to eat too much because he was expecting some action later on and didn't want to get all bloated and release some tear gas.

Hey, babe. How's it going? he asked Alexis when he walked in from the sizable balcony with the steak on a platter and closed the glass door behind him.

I believe it's almost ready, Alexis answered, a smile on her beautiful mouth and love in her clear eyes.

This meat is also ready. Mike planted a kiss on her soft feminine lips. He cut the steak in half. Then he cut a tiny piece of the meat, picked it up with a fork, blew on it, and placed it in his mouth. Very good, he said, and he gave Alexis a piece to taste also. How about some more wine, Alexis? I also have some bourbon and a decent scotch. I can make you a mixer, if you like.

Wine is fine, Alexis responded. She added tomatoes and cucumbers to the salad. What kind of salad dressing do you want with your salad, Mike?

I'll have what you're having because you usually pick the healthier kind. I always pick the French dressing, which is tasty but has a lot of fat.

Oh, come on, Mike. You can splurge tonight. Besides, you eat very healthy for a single man with a hectic schedule.

I won't have that status for long. And he smiled at her.

Let's eat here in the kitchen, Mike, OK? We don't want to take everything to the dining room, do we? Alexis didn't want to respond to the single-status comment because they still had to discuss career changes— her career changes.

Yeah. You're right. Let's eat here, Mike said. Alexis dished the salad into two plates and placed several bottles of different salad dressing in the middle of the island where they sat on barstools. Oh, before I forget, Mike said. He walked over to the fridge and brought out a container full of piñon nuts that he scattered on top of his salad. Help yourself, unless you believe you're denying the squirrels their food. Alexis looked at Mike but didn't say a word. She wouldn't take the bait, not tonight anyway. Mike could take it any whichway. They ate and talked little and enjoyed the food more. They both knew the real conversation would come after with the cognac and coffee.

And for dessert, we have rice pudding, Mike announced. He brought out a glass bowl filled with rice pudding from the fridge. It's kind of dry, but for store-bought, it's OK. He put a couple of scoops on a small plate for Alexis and some for himself.

After dinner, they both did the dishes, because Mike didn't like to see dirty dishes in the sink. His housekeeper would not return for a couple of days. She did the condos on a rotating basis, and he got a couple of days per week, which was all he needed. They brought their coffee and cognac to the living room and placed the cups and glasses on a good-size oak coffee table in front of the couch. Mike turned on the extra-large, gas fireplace located on the north wall. He didn't like wood burning fireplaces because of the mess and all the hassle of feeding the fire and keeping firewood handy all the time. He returned to the soft couch and sat close to Alexis but not too close. No need to. They had a grown-up, mature relationship. The couch faced west to a floor-to-ceiling window that took up almost the whole wall. The condo was on the fourth floor, the whole of the fourth floor. And through the window they captured the last light of the setting sun. The sunset was orange with moving clouds of gold mixed with crimson and deep purples. There was another floor-to-ceiling window facing east on the opposite side of the room. Through that window, Mike could appreciate the sunrise with all its own magnificence. They sat and watched in silence. They never said a word during this glorious moment until the last light dimmed and the heavens rejoiced with the brilliant stars of the night.

Big Sur, Mike said after the sun had completely disappeared in the western horizon.

I was thinking the same thing, Alexis concluded. She handed Mike his cup of coffee.

Remember when we stayed in that cabin we rented up there? And we watched the sun that evening when it vanished into the deep ocean? It was so dark. It was pitch-black on top of that bluff, and I held you tight, and I never wanted to let you go. Alexis, my beautiful Alexis. And he kissed her on the mouth.

Alexis Cordova Riley couldn't help but smile, and she kept her beaming eyes on Mike, the love of her life.

Yes, I will never forget that night, she almost whispered, full of emotional bliss. Remember that wake-up call in Convict Lake when, around three a.m., that little mouse was going through our stuff in the cabin? You took a broom and chased him outside, and then we noticed the bright, clear sky with millions and millions of stars. We didn't know if we were in California or Santa Fe.

Yes, Mike agreed. And he got closer to Alexis and kissed her beautiful hands. Those wonderful memories are etched in my heart and soul, Alexis. And you along with them. Then he said, as he held her hands and looked into her eyes, I fell in love with a gentle dove on whose wings I flew to heaven.

And Alexis, in the same mood, responded, I call her name in my sleep and sometimes even weep, for that happiness so divine, that makes my life so sweet. And they both laughed and kissed each other and laughed again. And at that exact moment, the Mexican composer Jose Pablo Moncayo's "Huapango" by the Royal Philharmonic filled the entire living room from the oak floors to the vaulted ceiling. Mike had wired his condo with electronic receptors and had speakers hidden in different areas. His favorite music came on at the precise moment the sun receded. He had a different version programmed for every evening of the month, and it included classical, rock, jazz, Latin jazz, and his favorite Spanish romantic music.

I love "Huapango," Mike. And Alexis hung on to his neck with both arms and kissed him passionately on the lips. At that moment, Mike's private phone rang. It was a number given only to a few people to call if something hot was happening. By now the news of Mike Cotton entering the race for mayor had run around Las Flores like a wildfire through a jungle of dry tumbleweed. The blaze and smoke had excited many people for many reasons. Mike didn't want to answer the persistent phone, but since he'd forgotten to put it on answering mode, he decided to answer it.

Yeah, Mike said into the receiver. Yeah. Oh really, is that right? OK. OK. Thanks for calling. He hung up the phone and pushed some buttons. I'm sorry, Alexis. I had to get that.

Everything OK? asked Alexis with a concerned look on her face.

Oh sure, it's nothing. Only that Rafa Candelaria has decided to run for mayor of Las Flores, and that makes the game a little more interesting.

I thought that other man was running, Alexis said. She was disappointed that it was only a political call interrupting the perfect ambience.

Mike Cotton is running. And Mike pretended not to show interest. When Rafa got the news that Mike Cotton was running for mayor, he threw in his hat. He doesn't like Mike Cotton that much and will go out of his way to make Mike's life a little more, shall we say, unhappy.

But you said this man Mike Cotton has a lot of money and somewhat of a political base.

He does, Mike continued. And he took a sip of his cognac. He owns Cotton Construction. He has support from the Baptist Church. That isn't much of a base, but he leans to the right with a religious fervor.

This town is and has been a home for democrats and is Catholic orientated. Does this Mike fellow stand a chance, or is he just running because he has nothing else to do with his time and money? asked Alexis. She noticed the charge Mike got from the conversation.

Catholic. Yes, especially in the Eastside barrio, but in a tight race, it can go either way. Mike Cotton has always been liked and respected by many folks in Las Flores, as was his late father, Earl. His base is small and conservative now. If he is successful in the primaries, and I believe that is his goal, then he can be more inclusive in the general election. He will have to be, if he is serious about being elected mayor.

But does Rafa have a chance, or does he want to run against Cotton because no one else will?

No. Rafa has the Machine in place. He wants it as bad as Mike does, maybe even more. But remember, Rafa has a lot of baggage in his closet. And the latest slumlord allegations didn't win him any brownie points, even though he did a good job of cleaning it up. There's a lot of apathy with many folks, especially in the Eastside. He will need to carry the Eastside with respectable numbers. For many in the Eastside, the struggle for survival is more important than whose running for mayor or councilperson.

Sad but true, Alexis said. She sipped her cognac and made a face. But who is going to take Rafa's place as councilman for the Eastside? she asked. She placed her glass on the table.

Well, that's what makes the game more interesting and fun to watch, don't you think? Candy Telles, a moderate Republican with little means, will run for Rafa's seat on the city council—among others, of course. And Mike Cotton will probably support him. Rafa, I'm sure, anticipated that move. Now he can play his own man in the race, and if successful on both, he can end up with a majority of votes on the city council and frustrate Mike Cotton on any plans he has for the city.

And what about this Candy fellow? Candy—what kind of name is that for someone who is serious about running for office?

His name is Candido Telles, known as Candy to many and Canary to some. Let me tell you a little about Mr. Telles, Alexis. He is called Candy because he had this habit of distributing candy to potential voters on Election Day. And he is known as Canary to others who accused him of ratting out his bro in a small-time cocaine bust. Candy was always short on cash but big on ambition. He ran for any office that caught his eye. He would never break the law. They say he promised his dying mother that. When the vultures of the dollar world were biting on his toes, he turned to the least offensive crime, in his eyes, and the riskiest, to anybody who knew better. That is, to sell drugs. Candy made a deal with a low-level street hustler who promised he could settle his debt with one or two good hits. Candy invested the little cash he had left because he found himself in a tight situation and didn't want to slave away at a real job; that just wasn't him. And Candy took the chance, as some do. And not to brag about it to his friends or act the part, none of that for Candy. He knew how to hustle and take care of himself in the process. At least that was his opinion of himself. A man of action…you know the type, Alexis. He made two successful hits, and the money was good. On the third one, he was busted and ratted on his partner on a plea that got him off clean and his record sealed. That happens when you know people inside and outside of city hall.

Wow, a real slime bucket, huh? conceded Alexis. What did he do after that fiasco?

Candy would never call it that, continued Mike. And he smiled. As soon as he was out on the street, they say he had it in his mind to run for office and the names of the people who were going to fund him. Never mind that he had just been released from jail or that a poor slob was going to waste a huge percentage of his life locked up like an animal. Of course, he never mentioned this criminal adventure to anyone. He had erased it from his mind as if it never happened. And when they pressed him on it, he talked about his constitutional rights and all that nonsense. And now he will run for the city council to represent the Eastside again, and again he will fail to win a substantial number of votes and will be ignored until next time.

But doesn't he need some money to enter the race? I mean…

If he rides on Mike Cotton's coattails, he'll have more than enough, I would say. But the main reason Candy won't win in the Eastside is because he won't buy kegs of beer for potential voters, like Rafa does. You see, Alexis, his religious convictions do not allow him to include alcohol, the devil's poison, to attract voters—a real hypocrite. And Rafa's men will use any method to secure votes. Many of the men and some of the women are used to the perks Rafa provides them with. That's the way it is, and that's the way it's always been—small-town politics. You know how that goes.

Why don't you run for mayor, Mike? Alexis asked. She knew Mike's position on that question. She asked him anyway, just to see if the latest political activity had given him any second thoughts. Who would dare vote against you? You're the best-looking man for the job, and for certain you would lock in all the female votes. Whata you say, you handsome man? And they both cracked up as Alexis tickled Mike on the belly, and Mike struggled to grab her hands.

Tell me more, my little chickadee. I like it, conceded Mike. He laughed and kissed her on the neck.

Really, Mike, proposed Alexis. She stopped tickling him and inched away. Why don't you run for mayor? You'll have more experience by election time, and people like you and know you.

Mike walked over to his teakwood, hand-carved bar and poured himself and Alexis another cognac. He added some seltzer water to Alexis's glass. He returned with the drinks and placed them on the long oak coffee table and sat on the couch next to Alexis.

Thanks, Alexis said.

The reason I won't run for mayor is quite simple. I don't have the killer instinct or whatever it takes to make the kind of decisions that at times hurt people and help others who need less of it. Las Flores is growing, Alexis, and changes are coming. The state senators are sending a lot of pork to New Mexico, and Las Flores is getting some of it. Wealthy folks from the east and north want to live here and are willing to pay top dollar for homes. The East Mesa and North Valley areas will soon elect their own city council people, and if the mayor keeps the vote in the city council, that gives him or her a piece of the action. I'd rather build homes and stay out of the battles that are sure to come.

So why would this man, Mike Cotton, invest so much time and money, if he's a home builder like you, and not even win? Alexis asked. She took a sip of her drink, and this time she liked it.

But if he does win, Alexis, responded Mike. He felt the cognac go down smooth and easy as he took a sip. If he does win and helps elect other council members that see the world as he does, he can make a profound change in the way we manage the affairs of the city. And he will push economic development as his main theme, which is a catchphrase for what?

Eminent domain, concluded Alexis, as Mike had known she would.

You got it, my clever fräulein. Eminent domain is probably his objective. And his main objective at that, as far as I can see.

And he wants your property, among others, to do what he wants on it, as long as it promotes some kind of economic development. I see. A cunning man, this Mike Cotton. You think he can accomplish his goals though, if he wins? A big if, in my way of looking at this.

Not with one vote, not even with two. If he can come up with three and spreads the gains around, he might be able to do it. And the first piece of property he'll go after is the property I just purchased from Vivien Madrid. Land expropriation has been a fair practice since the Spanish and Mexican settlers and other Europeans came to the Americas and ripped off the indigenous people, as you well know, my love. But at least now some of us know the law and can put up a fight through the courts.

Mike and Alexis were silent as they observed through the large window the lights of Las Flores down below. They flickered like fireflies in the clear night. They could see beyond the river to the North Valley, where the lights of the new homes were scattered among the low hills and burned like distant candles in the vast darkness of the silent night.

Let's enjoy the fire in the fireplace, Mike finally said, and forget about politics for now. They moved to another soft, comfortable sofa that faced the north wall, where a large fireplace had been built with dark, green marble. They took their drinks with them, and before he sat on the sofa, Mike threw some mesquite chips in the fire. This is better than those messy logs, Mike said to Alexis, who already had her shoes off and her long legs curled under her. She covered them with a light wool blanket and waited for Mike to sit next to her and get comfy.

The gas fire, with the mesquite chips, looked and smelled like the real thing. As Alexis and Mike gazed at the dancing flames, with all the lights out and the music low, they reflected on matters pleasant and not so pleasant. Mike thought of love and the influence it could have on his life. The two P's of life, he called them: pain and pleasure. He reasoned that he needed love in his life to be happy and fulfilled. But at the same time, he knew the pain it caused and how it could disrupt a life well planned. His biggest fear was that he might love Alexis more than Alexis loved him, and then he would become a love slave. Mike had learned that slice of wisdom from Hector El Viejo years ago. A love slave, in Mike's eyes, was a pathetic, tearful man, torn with desire for a woman who used him at will. He loved Alexis and wanted her by his side. He wanted her to be his wife, a woman to share the most intimate secrets of his life and much more. But could he adjust to one woman only? That was another concern that kept him up at night. He had done a good job since he had returned to Las Flores. He had kept his desire under control when Alexis was in Santa Fe, as difficult as it was. He had done it, and not because there was a shortage of women and girls. Many of the girls he had gone to school with were now divorced and looking for action. The younger set in their early twenties and younger were even more aggressive and better looking. He was introduced to many beautiful, young professionals and invited to many parties from Albuquerque to El Paso. He declined the invitations and never bothered with the phone numbers left on his office phone; he knew what would happen if Alexis found out he was playing around. But times like tonight, it was all worth it. No more hiding around and making up excuses of going here and there. No more phone calls in the middle of the night from a sobbing woman who insisted on seeing him. Life was good this way, he conceded. He took a sip of cognac and inched closer to Alexis.

Alexis also contemplated her life. She watched the fire and felt more than content that she had a man she loved and who loved her. A man who satisfied her every need in every way. Her perspective on love was altogether unlike Mike's. That is usually the case when a man and a woman declare strong feelings for each other. The distance in miles between them had tested that love, she believed. She had seen Mike mature. And even though he had always been sensible, now there was much more insight that betrayed his years. If he turned out like his father, Francisco, a gentle man and loyal husband with a big heart, that would certainly make her the happiest woman on Earth. And she had no doubt about that. The only question on her mind was her career. She loved her job and didn't want to give it up. They would have to have a serious discussion on the topic so there wouldn't be any misunderstandings later on. For now, her love for Mike was deep and sincere, and she wouldn't have it any other way.

You know, Mike, Alexis said. She moved her head from Mike's shoulder before the flames put her in a hypnotic stage. I really like your condo. I mean, you have a whole floor. It's larger than a lot of houses, and the views—wow. You can't beat it. You have the Turquoise Mountains to the east and the sunset and city lights to the west. You have your own private workout room and the biggest kitchen I have ever seen. A pool on the roof, a private three-car garage, a housekeeper that cleans three times a week, and it's yours. What more can you ask for, my handsome musketeer?

A beautiful woman such as you to share it with me on a full-time basis, Mike answered. He was never short for words, and he gently touched her on the cheek. But now I feel bad. Maybe I should give it all up and join a monastery. And he almost laughed.

Don't be silly, Mike. I don't want you to—

I know. I know. I'm only teasing. Please forgive me. If you don't, I'll really become a monk. No, I won't. You know that. I like it too, Alexis. When my company built these condos, I had this one built specifically for my parents, but they refused to move out of the barrio. My mother has the church next door, and my father will never leave the old house. What can I tell you? But the custom home I had built for us on Dos Cerros was the home I always wanted. It was a Southwest-style, five-bedroom, five-thousand-square-foot house on five acres, with low-maintenance, native landscaping and a rock wall. That was what I called a home. I loved the round edges and circular contours of the house, Alexis. I don't like square houses for me. I build them for other people, but they remind me of a shoebox. The master bedroom had a large Kiva fireplace and a sitting area with views of the mountains and valley. You saw it, Alexis.

Did your parents like it, Mike? Alexis asked. She knew the answer to her question.

My dad was drawn more to the glass water wall I had installed in the living room. He was fascinated by the technology and tried to figure out how it functioned. My mom…when she peeked into the master bedroom, she wouldn't enter. She commented on how the bed alone was large enough to sleep a dozen homeless people. I couldn't say if they were impressed or even if they liked it. To them, I guess, it was just a large house with no soul. And Mike smiled. That's my parents for you.

It was a big house, Mike; you have to admit.

I know, Alexis, but that's what I always wanted. In this country, you have to outdo your parents in everything. You've got to have a better-paying job and, of course, a larger house, or you're considered a failure. When I was in college in California, a professor invited the class to his home in Encino to go over some class stuff. I don't know to this day if he had an interest in our education or just wanted to show off his pad. But it was a beautiful house, and I decided then and there that one day I was going to live in a pad just as grand or even grander. You always lived in a nice home, Alexis, so you might not relate to my story.

Wait a minute, Mike, jumped in Alexis. She was hurt at the insinuation that she was in some way insensitive to his way of thinking. The home that my parents lived in when I met you, Mike, was not the home I grew up in. The home I grew up in was in a modest neighborhood in Oakland, not in the hills. My parents purchased that house when I was a freshman in college. It was more for my mother's ego than anything else, I always believed. The backyard was large, yes. I grant you that. But not even close to an acre of land, like I saw here. The first time I really noticed a clean acre of land was outside of Santa Fe. I was astonished at the amount of property an acre held. Here you build with the best quality of material on five or ten acres, like it's a normal-size lot. And a detached casita? Please, Mike. Why bother and call it a casita when those casitas can house a family of five easy?

I know, Alexis. It's a disgrace—shame on me. I sold it, as you know, but not because I wanted to. Those wealthy people from back east wanted it so bad, and they were willing to pay what I asked for it. And half a million over the one-point-two-million asking price was something I could not turn away from. Listen, my love, the woman of my dreams: I have already selected another five-acre track of property in the same area. But this time you will be included in all the planning of our new home. Tomorrow we will drive up there to see if you approve of the location. OK, honey bunny?

You're unstoppable tonight, Mike. And they both laughed out loud. It must be wonderful to be a man, Alexis continued. She didn't want to sound like she disliked being a woman or was pushing for a wedding date.

Mike studied Alexis's golden radiance in the light of the fire. He was a little surprised with her statement. He said, and tried not to be funny, Besides the fact we can release water standing up?

Seriously, Mike. Take the case of an educated woman—let's take me, for example. It is expected of me to date and marry a man with the same or even more education or an uneducated wealthy man. And time is always against a woman, as you know. In your case, you can date and marry your housekeeper, if you wish, and your mother would be more than happy with the decision. And your friends would probably say, you got a hot one, Mike. In my case, if I dated or married, let's say the pizza guy, my mother would have a baby and call it a desperate act, as well as most of my friends. It's so unfair, Mike—for a woman, that is. Don't you agree?

Mike observed Alexis as the flames from the fireplace turned her hair to copper. Her face and neck had bronzed since she'd moved to Santa Fe. It gave her a golden-brown complexion like the autumn leaves that fell from the trees. Her long shapely legs were beauty and perfection to Mike. Mike was a leg man in his time. Her lovely legs had also taken on the golden-brown color. The beautiful Alexis, he granted, was not only blessed with an outer attractiveness. She also retained a deep inner generosity and intellect. And that made her even more desirable to him. He was always amazed, and of course delighted, by the mixture of the dark Irish blood of her father and the fiery blond Spanish blood of her mother, but never like tonight. He wanted her, big time. Alexis wanted conversation, and Mike wasn't as impulsive as he was in his younger days, when he wouldn't wait or couldn't wait, as he put it.

I get it, Alexis, Mike finally said. He kissed her gorgeous hands. I believe it's a matter of economic status, class, and even cultural hubris. An educated woman, and she doesn't have to be white, with an elevated profession usually dates or marries, in that sphere. That's what the parents expect, that's what friends expect, and most important, that's what society expects. That also goes for a man, Alexis. A man will not marry too far below him for obvious economic reasons. Some men will do it, and that's a given, and more often than women. You're right about that. In my case, my parents are not in the professional, elitist class. They take a more humane approach. A more romantic approach, if you may, especially when it comes to marriage. Perhaps not practical, in the eyes of others. My parents value everyone and every act for what is felt in the heart. But don't believe that all working-class parents think that way. The less they have, the more they want. And if they have kids in those higher professions and sacrificed to get them there, of course they desire for them to date or marry their equals. You see, Alexis, it's a complicated conundrum. But really, Alexis, what do I know?

Alexis kept her eyes on Mike. She loved his thick, black hair. It gleamed with the light of the fire. And she loved his manly, handsome face and his flashing white teeth when he talked and made his case. She missed his beard and mustache. They gave him a darker and an even more masculine look. The man was perfect in her eyes. From his deep hairy chest to his muscular, wiry, and hairy legs. He was all man and more, as she saw him. But she was a little disappointed in Mike's position when it came to her view on the unfairness of educated women. She had to let it rest because Mike would cite the real gut-wrenching ordeal of poor women's rights. And it was in that arena that she worked hard every day in an attempt to make things better for disadvantaged women. And yet, here she was debating the concerns of the privileged. Mike was an attorney, as was she, and the debate could go on all night. She knew Mike was usually diplomatic. However, he could turn as vicious as an attack dog and smile at the same time. She had seen him do it. She was sure he wouldn't go there with her, but why push it on a debate they fundamentally agreed on?

Mike watched the fire intensely and saw all kinds of images dancing in the yellow and blue flames. He was sure Alexis was disappointed in his resolution to her query. He refused to get into a deep discussion on the plight of women. It could escalate into a sad and complicated theme. And tonight was the wrong night for that. On this very night, he had to decide if he was going to give Alexis the engagement ring he had purchased in the jewelry mart in downtown Los Angeles before he'd left the state. It was a three-carat princess-cut diamond set in platinum. He'd gotten an excellent price from a friend of a friend who claimed he was going out of business. This friend of a friend guaranteed that the 4Cs—carat, cut, color, and clarity—were of the highest quality. And so was the price, Mike thought. What were diamonds anyway? he always asked diamond aficionados. Weren't they just high-pressured carbon, cut, polished, and marketed by diamond cartels to extract as much profit as possible? He was sure diamond prices would hit bottom when other diamond-producing countries flooded the market. But he wasn't sure when that would happen or if it would ever happen. So Mike settled for a diamond ring, though he would have preferred a ruby. A ruby in pure form was almost as hard as a diamond. It could reach, in some cases, a ten in hardness, as much as a valuable diamond. And in his opinion, the ruby was a way more beautiful stone. But he wasn't so sure if a ruby ring was appropriate to give your baby as an engagement ring. Everyone he knew had given a diamond ring for the occasion. He would follow tradition—why not? He decided tonight was the night. He couldn't keep Alexis waiting much longer. Well, he could, but he didn't care to. There was no point in that, he reasoned. Mike walked to the bar with the empty glasses as if going to get them fresh drinks. He placed the glasses on the bar, and from behind the bar, he pulled out a little black velvet box, plain as could be, for the valuable item it carried.

Mike walked back to the sofa where Alexis contemplated the fire. He sat next to her with his heart thumping and tears in his eyes. He handed her the small box and said in a whisper, Marry me, Alexis, please.

Alexis took the box from Mike and looked at him and then the box. She blinked several times and opened the tiny box. The light coming off the fire in the fireplace caught the diamond head-on, and a sparkling flash of brilliant light illuminated the box, and Alexis almost dropped it. She was so excited by Mike's words and stunning ring she couldn't say a word. She hugged him. She held on to the box and wouldn't let go. Yes. Yes, she finally said. And the tears ran down her face. Yes, Mike. Yes. I'll marry you—of course I'll marry you. You really want me, Mike, do you?

Of course I do, Alexis. I love you. I'll always love you. And at that moment, Mozart's "Elvira Madigan" filled the room with sweet music.

Oh, Mike. The ring, the music, the fire, the stars and moon—what a perfect setting. I love you too. I have always loved you, from the very first day, believe it or not.

Try it on, Alexis, Mike said. I went by the sizes of the other friendship rings I have given you. Alexis, still shaking with happiness, allowed Mike to slip the ring on her finger.

Perfect fit, cried out Alexis. And she kissed Mike on the mouth for several minutes. It's such a beautiful ring. I hope you didn't spend a lot of money on it. Did you think I was hinting about a ring in my conversation about women, Mike? Please tell me.

No. Never, Alexis. I've had the ring for a while. I was just waiting for the perfect time, and you can't beat tonight, right?

When Mike and Alexis retired to the master bedroom and the fire in the fireplace glowed, Alexis was still admiring her ring with a huge smile on her lovely face. Mike was taking a shower. He scrubbed himself clean, as he always did before having sex and sometimes right after. He would usually invite Alexis to join him in his Jacuzzi tub, but it was getting too late for that. He got out of the shower. He dried, flossed, brushed his teeth, and sprinkled on some cologne. He was more than glad that Alexis didn't have that heavy odor downstairs that could turn him off pronto when he visited downtown. Alexis was very attentive when it came to her body and usually took care of business when it was time to make some hoops. And for that, Mike was more than grateful.

Alexis waited patiently for Mike after getting herself ready. She knew Mike's ritual and admired him for always wanting to come to bed clean. But since Mike wasn't a beefy man, he wasn't blessed with that beefy man's odor. He could definitely get away with showering less, even though she appreciated a clean, good-smelling man in bed; every woman did. Mike went a little above and beyond the call of duty, but that was her opinion only. She was too shy to ask other women for feedback on the subject. Then she noticed the painting on the front wall to the left of the door. She had not seen it before, she was certain. Mike must have recently put it up, she thought. He was very picky about the art he displayed on his walls.

Mike entered the bedroom from the bathroom wearing a black silk robe with a red dragon stitched on the back and nothing underneath. He was ready for action. He got under the sheets and noticed Alexis as she studied the painting Shonofa had given him the day before.

You like it, sweetheart?

It's…it's amazing, Alexis answered. She could not take her eyes away from the piece. The colors are something else. They seem to change and even move as the flames from the fireplace change color. Did you buy it in Las Flores, Mike?

It was a gift, Alexis. I got it only yesterday.

Does it have a name?

The Eagles Peak. That's what she called it.

Who called it?

Shonofa, an old friend of mine. Mike told her about Shonofa but left out a lot of the story for another time. He didn't want to go into Shonofa's prophecies and the Flying Man, Santiago. She works a short distance from Taos, he continued. Your father would really get into her work.

Oh yeah! He will enjoy her work—of that I'm sure. You have her card?

Yes, I do. Remind me tomorrow.

Mike turned off the night-light and removed his robe.

Mike, can you put on some of the Spanish romantic music we love so much? Please, baby love. Marco Antonio Solís and Rocío Dúrcal would be a wonderful start.

For you, my kitten, anything. Just ask.

Alexis had grown up listening to different types of music. But her mother always insisted she listen to Spanish music, and she did. She learned to love the romantic love songs from the Spanish-speaking countries. Mike also listened to that music, now more than ever. He appreciated the fact that he didn't have to translate the lyrics. That might have been cool at fifteen when you tried to impress a white girl in the back seat of the car. At thirty, it was a full-time job with nothing to win that was not already won.

Before Mike pushed the button for the music, he turned to Alexis and said, with a full smile on his lips and love in his heart, Cuando beso tus labios de seda, en la noche, con mucha ternura.

And Alexis, also lost in love, answered, tender and true, Nos a cerca muy cerca al cielo, olvidando toda la amargura, and they both giggled and went at each other like hungry children.

CHAPTER 19

The morning after Mike Montes and Alexis's blissful night, Max and Jerry were in the CI Center. They conversed about old movies. They played their show-me-what-you-know game. It was about ten in the morning, and they were alone in Max's office, enjoying their morning coffee with pan dulce. Cape Fear, said Max to Jerry, who was dunking his pan dulce in his coffee mug. The original one, not the one with De Niro.

Cape Fear, repeated Jerry. I loved that movie. Robert Mitchum acted in it. He was the bad guy, and it was directed by J. Lee Thompson in 1962.

Not bad, Jerry. Hit me.

The Petrified Forest, Jerry said. And he stuffed the soaked pan in his mouth.

Oh, you going deep, brother, Max responded, taking a sip of coffee. Let me think, he said, and he scratched the thick beard around his chin. You talking 1930s? OK. I think I have it. The Petrified Forest was a gangster flick with Bette Davis and a young Humphrey Bogart. The director was Archie Mayo, and it was released in 1936 or 1937.

Not bad, Max. It was 1937, but you still get the cigar. Your turn.

The Defiant Ones, Max said without hesitation and a smile on his bearded face.

Jerry got a serious look on his face as he recalled something he wanted to forget. He snapped out of it just as fast and said, Another excellent movie, Max. Tony Curtis and Sidney Poitier starred in it. And it was released in 1958 and directed by Stanley Kramer. Curtis took a big risk making that movie with Poitier. That was a fucked-up time for blacks.

Still is, as is for us, Max said. It made Curtis a bigger star, and it didn't hurt Poitier any either.

Here's one for you, Max, Jerry jumped in before Max started on a serious talk on civil rights. He didn't mind, but not this early in the day. Shane, he said. Tell me.

Oh yeah! cried out Max. He was grateful for Jerry's perception. Shane An old-time favorite with pretty boy Alan Ladd and bad boy Jack Palance. Directed by George Stevens in 1953.

Then they both cried out in a dramatic voice. Shane…don't leave…please…Shane…don't go! And they busted out laughing when Ruth walked in with the young man they were going to interview for the job of organizer in Chiva Town. Ruth gave them a look, then remembered what William had told her about her two boys, and she broke into a smile herself.

Having fun, guys? Ruth asked without a hint of sarcasm in her sweet smile.

Always, Max answered. And whom do we have here?

This is Armando Vallesteros. The young man from Chiva Town we are to interview this morning, Ruth answered, all smiles, obviously pleased with the young man's professional appearance.

Hey, come on in, man. You a little early.

Is it OK? the young man responded. He seemed a little shy. He had not expected such an informal group of people to interview him for what he saw as an important job. I can wait outside.

No. No need for that. It's OK, Armando; sit, Ruth insisted. Armando, this is Max Luna, the director of CI, and this is Jerry Rivera, who's in charge of extracurricular activities. And you already met my husband, William, and me. And at that moment, William walked into the office. He pulled his shirt up to his neck, attempting to hide all the red and purple marks on his lower neck.

This is all our staff, Max said. So tell us a little about yourself, Armando.

Sure, Armando replied. And he handed Max a neatly typed résumé. Max said thanks and placed on it top of his desk, not bothering to read it. They waited in silence with their eyes on Armando. He wore a coat and tie and seemed a little uncomfortable. Ruth was still all smiles. She was so relieved that Tiny Tim had not sent a Sniper in Sniper uniform, talking trash.

Ruth, who sat next to Armando, finally said to him, It's OK, Armando. You can start, if you're ready.

Oh. And Armando reddened. You want me to talk. I mean to talk about myself. I thought you were…you were going to read my résumé and ask me questions.

No, Armando. Ruth smiled. She was doing her best not to upset Armando more than necessary. She wanted Max to like him for the job, as she already did. Just tell us a little about yourself. You know, just general stuff.

Oh, OK. Armando half smiled for the first time and seemed to relax. My name is Armando Vallesteros, and I was born and raised in Chiva Town. I have an associate of arts degree, and at present, I'm working on my BA. My major is in political science, with a minor in music. I'm learning how to play the piano and score music. Not very much to tell, I'm afraid. But ask any questions you like.

You're related to Tiny Tim, I presume? asked Max. He saw that Armando wasn't going to volunteer any information unless asked.

Tiny Tim is my uncle, and as you know, he is the leader of the Chiva Town Snipers. He believes in you, Max, and your plans for Chiva Town, as I do. And no, I have never been a Sniper—maybe in spirit but in spirit only. Sure, I did some lightweight stuff…breaking into pads, fighting, smoking dope, stealing a car here and there, but I was always the lookout. I was never busted, thank God, and have no criminal record. I say light stuff because some of the bros were doing heavy stuff like homicides and armed robbery and, of course, doing hard time. My uncle finally told me to settle down and hit the books. He never permitted me to wear the colors and act the fool. He wanted me to get an education and do my best to help the people of Chiva Town.

Hey, like the godfather, Jerry said. He hadn't meant to be funny.

Max almost laughed out loud, but William and Ruth gave him the look.

That's good. I like it, Armando said. He looked straight at Jerry. He wasn't intimidated by the big tattooed fellow. He had grown up around guys like Jerry.

What happened to Bobby? asked William in a serious and almost unhappy voice.

Armando turned from Jerry to William, who sat next to Ruth on his left, and said, It was sad what happened to Bobby, and I take some of the blame. Bobby was a great organizer and a decent guy. I should have been more persistent when I warned him about that girl. His program was getting off the ground with the tutoring and organization of games, assisting the parents, and getting more people to the meetings. I helped him as much as time permitted, and we became friends. We shared our ideas and strategies on how to help the children, as well as the adults. But this girl was always flirting with Bobby. She was always after him. And when Bobby finally told her he was not interested, she lost her temper and ran to my cousin Neto with a lie, and that was that.

What does it mean when they put the guns on you? asked Ruth, still upset for losing Bobby.

When that girl went crying to Neto and told him that Bobby wanted to date her, which was a lie, Neto lost his cool and ordered the guns. You see, that girl is Sniper property. And Neto has first call. If he likes her, he'll keep her. If he doesn't, he'll pass her on to one of his lieutenants. About ten Snipers came as the sun went down, fully armed, and cleared the center of children and adults. The Snipers formed a straight line in front of Bobby and pointed their guns at him, and this was at close range. They demanded he leave that night and not return. The next time they warned him the guns would be loaded, and they would not be responsible for any unforeseen accidents.

Where was your uncle all this time? asked Max. He attempted to remain cool. He recognized that Armando had nothing to do with what happened to Bobby. He still felt bad. If anybody had to share the blame for Bobby being put at risk and humiliated, it was him. He'd sent Bobby to Chiva Town in the first place. After all, it wasn't a secret that Chiva Town was known for its dislike of strangers.

My uncle, answered Armando. He did not take the questions personally or get defensive. My uncle was staying in his rancho, a short distance from Valencia. That's where he breeds. And he was going to say cocks. He instead said fighting roosters. He did not want to offend Ruth. Neto is second in command of the Snipers. And when my uncle is away, Neto runs the Snipers. The next day, when I found out what happened to Bobby, I drove to Valencia to plead with my uncle to call off the guns and have Bobby return to the center. But when I was a couple of miles from the rancho, I turned the car around and drove back to Chiva. I realized that whatever my uncle said or did, Bobby would never return to Chiva. And I can't blame him one bit. I lost a true friend, and the folks and kids lost a true champion. Many of the kids returned to the wall, and business as usual was again a fact of life in Chiva Town.

Do you think Bobby was set up so you could take his place? asked William. He pulled on his shirt to keep his red and purple marks covered.

No. I don't believe so, replied Armando. He was calm as ever and not even offended by William's insinuation. My uncle was out of the loop, and Neto is not that clever. I never thought of replacing Bobby. His shoes were too big to fill, and I was busy with my class load. One day out of the blue, my uncle Tiny walked me over to the empty center. He told me he wanted me to continue where Bobby had left off. I tried to explain to my uncle that it wasn't that easy. That I lacked training and without support from CI, I couldn't do much. He told me not worry. To come and see you, Max, and everything would work out.

And here you are, Armando, Max said. He wanted to generate some life into the interview before they all started weeping. Tell me, why do you want the job, and what will be your take on it? Say, apart from the ideas Bobby shared with you?

Armando rubbed his chin, where he had shaved the peach fuzz that very morning. He admired Max's full growth. Bobby had some excellent ideas, and it would be presumptuous of me not to give him credit for what he did implement. The tutoring and recreation for the students were undeniably his strongest points. And I could probably get them running again without too much difficulty. The area where I would also focus more of my attention and introduce more programs would be in the adult arena. For example, I would open adult classes in nutrition, literacy, and health information for the elderly. And educate the community in ways, legal ways, to tear down the wall.

Like the Berlin Wall? jumped in Jerry. He caught all the others by surprise because he had just been listening since his last comment.

Yes. You could use that comparison, if you dare, responded Armando. He began to like Jerry for his unexpected but honest observations.

That can be accomplished soon, Max added. How do you get along with the councilman from Chiva Town? Because that's the job you should be thinking about.

Armando Vallesteros was struck with an idea that he had paid little or no attention to. Of course, he realized, that's where all the real changes came from, political or otherwise. Max knew all along that this was only the first step for a future run at councilman from Chiva Town. He had never connected the two because the councilman from Chiva did nothing and was never around except on Election Day. So this was where this was going. He had to admit, these cats were clever.

I have to be honest, Max, Armando confessed. I don't see much of the man. And now that I recall, Bobby challenged me once to confront the man and get him more involved in the community center. And to push him to get more support from the city council.

Does he even live in Chiva? Ruth asked. She was still troubled over Bobby's departure.

That's a good question, Ruth. Armando felt stupid for not connecting the dots—and him telling these folks he was a political science major. He should have said his major was in basket weaving instead. There was a problem before, Armando continued in a calm voice. He was accused of living outside of Chiva. Remember? It was in the papers, but somehow he got the city council to give him an extension. He claimed he was doing major repairs to his home in Chiva.

That was part of it, William added. Rafa sneaked in a law way before Mike Montes was mayor. That statute gave any city councilman an option to live six months out of the year outside his district until all repairs to his main residence were completed. Of course, there was a clause in fine print—isn't there always one?—and the clause stipulated that there could be another extension up to six months or longer, if the primary residence was not completed to the satisfaction of the member.

I see. Armando was embarrassed; these folks seemed to know more about Chiva Town than he did, and they didn't even live there. One can't help but notice that his house is not finished. They call it the brick-a-day house because it seems like they put in a brick a day. And yet I'm more than sure that most of the folks in Chiva, myself included, are not aware of the game the man is playing.

OK, Armando. Max changed the subject as not to make Armando feel worse. Do you have any questions about the job? Ruth and William will oversee your training. You will work on your own once in the field, unless you request assistance. We have our staff meetings once a week, and they are mandatory.

When can I start? asked Armando. He was relieved that he had the job.

You can start tomorrow if you like. Go with Ruth and fill out the paperwork; she will help you with the details. Oh, and Armando, you don't have to wear a coat and tie…unless you care to, of course.

Armando was shaking hands all around. He was very happy to be part of CI. He turned to Max and said, I like wearing a tie, Max. I'm from Chiva, and I like to show people that not all Chiva residents wear Sniper colors.

As Ruth and William stepped out of Max's office with Armando, Max stopped them and said, Remember, Ruth and William, Rafa is coming over this morning to smoke the peace pipe. I want you two to talk to him and decide if the improvements on his rentals are enough to satisfy the codes and the people who live there.

He's probably coming with hat in hand, added Ruth. She smiled and walked out with Armando.

Listen, William, Max said. He played the dick with you. Maybe Jerry can take him out back and give him a booty slasher—on the house, of course. And all three laughed out loud. Jerry smashed his fist into his big open hand and said, Hell yeah. Anytime.

No. You guys, you can't hurt Rafa. The vote for funds is coming up, and we need him to be present and in good health to cast his vote…in our favor, that is. Booty slasher—ouch. He looked at Jerry and walked out of the office laughing.

Max and Jerry remained in the office. They were still laughing when Sgt. Carlos Miranda of the Las Flores Police Department walked in. He sat in a chair as if he were the next appointment on Max's agenda.

Hey, Carlos. Come right in. Make yourself at home, why don't cha? Max said, still smiling.

Don't mind if I do, Max. I've been on my feet for hours. Carlos Miranda was a big man with a bullet head, close-cropped hair, and thick lenses on the eyeglasses that rested on his beefy, sunburned face. Hey, Jerry. And Carlos looked at Jerry. You staying out of trouble, brother?

You know I wouldn't be here enjoying my cup of coffee if I wasn't, remarked Jerry. With your brother-in-law, warthog-face Ulises, stalking me, I got no choice, Carlos.

Ha ha. You a funny man, Jerry.

So what brings you to this neck of the woods? asked Max. Don't tell me you're also running for office.

No, Max. I wanted to ask you about my Nina Victoria. I stopped by the house a couple of times. The doors and windows always seem to be locked. You know she's my godmother, right, Max? She and your late father baptized me before they were married. I found out she was in town, and I wanted to see her and say hello.

Max had forgotten that his mother and father had baptized Carlos and that his mother and father once had been close with Carlos's parents. Carlos was two or more years older than Max, and they had never been real friends. Max never had taken a liking to Carlos, and Carlos had joined the marines at a young age. After serving some ten years, he'd joined the Las Flores Police Force—a logical choice for him.

She refuses to see people, Max said. He hated to have to explain to people that his mother just wanted to be left alone. She's not in the best of health, Carlos, and wants some time out away from people. What can I tell you?

No, I understand, Max. I'll respect her privacy. I didn't know. But tell her I said hi, and I would love to see her. When she feels better, of course.

Max thought Carlos was getting ready to leave. He sat back in his chair and said, looking straight at Max, all business now, By the way, Max, this tall, skinny-looking cowboy came into the station and claimed you busted his jaw. His mouth looked pretty busted, and his nose seemed a little swollen and crooked. He said he wouldn't press charges if you paid the hospital bill. What's the story on that, Max?

Max scratched his beard with his right hand, half smiled, and said, This cowboy mention any witnesses, Carlos? You know, someone that can back up his allegation.

No. He said he was alone in an alley downtown, and you busted him on the jaw for no reason and left him bleeding in the gutter.

And how did he know it was me? Did he say? Did I leave him a calling card or what?

I have no idea, Max. Maybe he recognized your car—not many cars like yours in town. It was difficult to understand the fool; his mouth wasn't working at its normal speed.

How much is the hospital bill, Carlos? asked Max, annoyed Carlos would even mention such a trifling account of an event that, for all purposes, did not even register in his mind anymore. Did he show you some kind of hospital paperwork, a release form—something?

No, Max, nothing. He just said he wanted two or three hundred dollars in cash to pay the bill, or he would press charges for assault and battery. He knew that much.

Carlos, Max said, I have no idea who the man is, much less what he's talking about. But if he returns, and I doubt it, tell him I'll send him twenty-five dollars with Jerry. If he provides you with an address, that is. More of a charitable contribution than anything else, Carlos…the cowboy seems like he's hurting, in more ways than one.

Carlos looked at Max and then at Jerry. He expected them to bust out laughing, but since they hadn't, he said, OK. I'll give him your message. Nice seeing you, Jerry, and keep up the good work. Then he lifted his heavy frame from the chair and walked toward the door of the office. And Max, be so kind as to give my regards to my nina Victoria. He knew in his gut that these two hoodlums were up to no good, but he had no reliable evidence to make a case against them.

Say, Carlos, have your boys made any progress on the investigation of the firebombing of the widow's house? Any leads? Max asked as he followed Carlos out of the office.

Carlos turned his bullet head and looked at Max. His large, thick eyeglasses had a greenish tint on them that screened his beady eyes. They stared at Max with an intense determination to make him eat his words. Your boys was a dig—everyone knew the investigating lieutenants were a pair of dickheads. Their investigating skills were utilized in securing free coffee and doughnuts at the local doughnut shops more than anything else. The investigation has been taken over by the bomb squad, Carlos said dryly.

He walked to the door and exited the building. He was in a little bit of a huff.

What bomb squad? Max cried out.

So what do you think of our buddy Carlos? Max asked Jerry as he sat behind his desk again.

Besides him gaining a ton of weight? responded Jerry, laughing.

No, man. Carlos has come a long way: an ex-marine made sergeant at a young age with the LFPD and chief of police soon. And with a wife and kids…the man is on the move, Jerry. You can't call him Carlitos anymore; who would dare? Don't cha think?

I think he's still a fat slob, as he was when we were in the fourth grade and pulled down his pants, and the girls saw the dry shit on his culo. He wasn't wearing any chonies, remember? He was older than us, but he still cried like a baby. The girls were laughing at his tiny throttle. Jerry said this in jest, but to him it wasn't funny. He had a dislike for cops that never went away.

No, he was bawling 'cause you gave him a kick in the ass, remember?

No, man, I never gave him a kick in his flabby ass. It was the girls laughing at him that brought the tears, and I believe Big Bertha was the instigator.

He was a good sport, Jerry. He never tried to get even or pull some shit on us.

I wonder why, Jerry said. He was in a good mood again.

At that moment, Rafa Candelaria and his campaign manager walked into the office without hesitation. Rafa wore an expensive suit, tie, and shoes to match, as usual. Good morning, my dear friends, he said. And how are you all on this wonderful morning? His campaign manager just smiled. He knew better than to upstage Rafa.

Morning, Rafa. Have a seat, answered Max. He was a little less enthusiastic than Rafa. He ignored the campaign manager just the same.

Jerry just nodded and said nothing.

I hear you have big plans, Rafa. And you intend to share it with us. That so?

William and Ruth walked in holding hands and whispering tender words to each other as if they were on their second honeymoon. They separated when they took a chair and waited for Rafa to apologize or say what he'd come to say.

Here they are, Rafa said. The beautiful couple. It must be wonderful to be young and in love.

It is, Rafa, William responded. He looked straight at Rafa. His shirt was buttoned to the top button and covered his lower neck. Tell us what you want, he said, pretending he didn't know.

Oh, William, William, my dear friend, Rafa almost purred. Then he changed to the third person. Rafa only brings an olive branch. Rafa comes to apologize for the misunderstanding we had the last time we met. Rafa righted the wrong that was done to the people and set things right.

Cut the bull, Rafa, Max interjected.

Rafa turned his head and stared at Max. He quickly recognized that Max wasn't Mike Cotton or the Sloth. He smiled and directed his attention to William. Seriously, William and Ruth, I fixed up the rental. I fired my property manager and hired one more competent. And all my rentals are being evaluated. And if they need repairs, dicho y hecho, they get fixed. I just think we should be on speaking terms, that's all. We have important elections coming up, and we should work together.

What about you trying to revoke the lease on our building, Rafa? Ruth asked. She was a little skeptical of Rafa's posturing.

What about you sending those photos to the paper and smearing my name all over town? he wanted to ask. But instead he said, Oh, that was my attorney, Ruth. He was getting ahead of himself. You know how they think.

You did clean up that rental, Rafa, and treated the family with respect, added William. And you are working on the others? We've seen some progress; let's see it continue. And so, tell us: How can we assist you in your run for mayor?

Rafa's grin was all over his face. He knew the bullshit was behind them, and he had the monkeys on his side. His dark-brown face and black hair glistened with tiny beads of perspiration, and it wasn't even that hot. His campaign manager, a short man with long arms and small hands and feet, was a lot more nervous. He sat too close to Jerry in the small office. He had come in confident. He had even been a little indifferent when Rafa had told him they were going to CI to demand the CI staff work with him on his run for mayor. But then the man saw Max with long hair and a thick black beard, and a straggly beard at that. And then he saw the tattooed brute, Jerry. He appeared like a volcano ready to explode. It got him worried and fast. He was used to Rafa having his way and outtalking anyone he came in contact with. These cats were from a different litter and seemed to care little who Rafa was or how much money he had. He kept his mouth shut and let Rafa do all the talking. Even the young woman seemed tough as nails, and she wasn't going to let Rafa have his way.

I want from you guys a little favor—that's all. And Rafa flashed his dentist-whitened teeth. When you have your meetings, your evening meetings, here at the center, and I know you pack a good crowd, I want my people to pass out flyers. Political flyers, not only of me running for mayor, but also of the candidate we choose to run for city council. The person who will represent the Eastside. That's all. Ain't much, is it?

Ruth and William jumped in together, as Max knew they would. William allowed Ruth to go first out of the love and respect he had for her.

Rafa! Ruth exclaimed. She almost laughed because the request was so ridiculous. We cannot, and I repeat, cannot have any kind of political rally at the center, and you know why. We are a nonprofit, and we abide by the laws and bylaws that prevent that kind of activity. Do you want us to lose our funding? Is that it?

No. No. Ruth, please, Rafa begged in desperation. He did not want to rehash the early misunderstanding that had just been settled. I thought my people could stand at the door, and as the guests left, my people could hand out flyers. No speeches, nothing like that. Please, guys. And Rafa looked from Ruth to Max and from Max to Jerry and William. We have to work together to defeat Mike Cotton. You all know what will happen if Mike Cotton wins the election and Candy wins the seat in the Eastside. They are both right-wing conservatives with a religious bent. We cannot afford that. Las Flores will change.

Max responded before William started in on Rafa and dragged the meeting on for hours. Listen, Rafa, no one knows what will happen if Mike Cotton wins. Don't get us wrong. We're one hundred percent behind you all the way, one hundred percent. But here at the center… no can do, Rafa. But I'll tell you what, my friend. Just to show you how serious we are on your behalf, you can have your people pass out the flyers across the street from the center. But not anywhere on center property. Is that to your satisfaction?

Rafa half smiled. He believed Max was giving him the green light to cross the street to the center and, at the discretion of his people, hand out flyers and solicit the citizens for a favorable vote. And a plea for funds—and all on the sly. And if they were caught, they would have to answer to Max or Jerry. I can live with that, Max, Rafa stated before William or Ruth could mount an opposition. And I want to thank you all for helping and appreciate the fact that you comprehend how vital it is for me to win this election.

Yeah. Yeah. Rafa, William interrupted, save your victory speech for a more receptive audience. And by the way, an important vote is coming up on funding, and we need the funds. You get the votes we need.

Oh, you got it, my man. Rafa beamed. You got my vote, and when I'm mayor, your funds will increase. That's a promise. I know you guys are busy, so I'll leave you to do your work.

The campaign manager was relieved that the meeting was over. He raised his small hand to shake with somebody, with anybody. He was ignored. He followed Rafa out, not sure if they had accomplished what they came seeking.

Why did you give them that much, Max? Ruth asked, pleased but a little disappointed at what Rafa got away with.

Look at it this way, Ruth. Max scratched his beard. Rafa's gonna have his people in here before the meeting, during the meeting, and after the meeting. We might catch some, but we won't catch them all. That's the way politicians work. This way we set down some rules. If they break them, it's on them. We're covered as far as that goes. You're witnesses to what was agreed upon. We have his vote on the funding with no bad feelings. And like you said, if he's cleaned up his act on the rentals, then we must do what we can to help elect him mayor; there's no alternative.

Amen, William said. And they all left the office except Max.

Max placed his large left hand on his beard and rubbed his chin with his fingers. His thoughts were on Vanessa Renderos. He still loved her, he believed. How much he wasn't sure. But he wasn't sure of a lot of things lately. Anyway, he concluded, Vanessa deserved better. Her little boy deserved better. And he felt he had so little to give. Or was it his freedom he didn't want to compromise? That was laughable, he thought, with his mother and all.

Then there was his mother to consider, his dear mother who was dependent on him night and day. And now there was a new concern. Always something, he thought. His new distraction was the anonymous phone call early in the morning warning him of a contract put out with his name on it. A professional hit man was on his way to Las Flores that same day to kill him and anyone who attempted to stop him. At first Max had believed it was a crank call, and he was going to hang up. The voice sounded desperate, almost begging for him to listen and take action before it was too late. Max decided to pay attention to the details because the voice was that of a nervous man, who might hang up without warning. After the man hung up, and the phone was silent, Max began to worry about a crazy killer coming to take his life.

Max decided to invite Jerry to help him out. Jerry was the force he needed if things got out of hand. He was debating about William. William had the balls of an elephant and no worries there. But Ruth could be a problem. He needed both of them to make sure his plan to stop the assassin worked. Max stood up. He was pissed at the inconvenience and the danger of having to go out and do a job no one wanted to do. He would ask William anyway, and allow him to decide what he wanted to do. He had to go find the boys before they wondered and explain the plan to them in detail. He was sure William would join them, as he had before. It was almost 1:00 p.m., and the suitor was coming between 2:00 p.m. and 3:00 p.m. That was what the voice had repeated several times over the phone. He had to get the boys moving and gather the items they were going to need to make it a successful operation. He couldn't promise any rewards. Maybe he should take it to Carlos Miranda, he considered. The cops, including Carlos, would probably laugh at him and then write the report. No, he had to take care of this problem on his own. There was no other way.

Max looked at his watch as he exited his office on the way to hunt for Jerry and William in the huge building. Jerry was not difficult to find. He was either with Clair de Lune, secluded in her office, or in the weight area, improving his muscles. He didn't like to send Jerry to do many house calls on his own. Not that Jerry was a loose cannon; he wasn't. But his appearance sometimes startled an unsuspecting homeowner who might see Jerry as an intruder or worse. William was more difficult to locate; he never stayed in the office for long periods of time. He was out in the field most of the day, doing what he loved to do. Max began to worry William had left the building, until he spotted him using the phone in the office he shared with Ruth. Max was relieved because now he wouldn't have to drive all over Las Flores looking for him and wasting valuable time. Max liked the little fucker—William seemed to have an affinity for violent getaways, even though his everyday demeanor did not suggest that of him. But most people, Max concluded, had a fantasy that they wished to make real. Even if it lasted for only a few treasurable minutes.

CHAPTER 20

*M*ax, Jerry, and William were sitting in Max's office with the door shut and a Do Not Disturb sign hanging on the doorknob.

Fuck. I still can't believe it, Jerry said. He was upset about the contract put out on Max, a brother in more ways than one. The balls of those motherfuckers, whoever the fuck they are.

Max. Jerry, interrupted William. That's why we have to show those motherfuckers we are not going to lie down and be fucked in the ass at will.

We get it, William, Max said. He was a little touchy because of the operation at hand. Did you get what we need, and is it all on the truck, loaded and ready to go?

Yes, Captain, commented Jerry. He was going to salute but didn't want to take it too far. As you ordered, sir.

All we need is the driver, William put in before Jerry got too silly and made Max lose his patience. Who is gonna drive?

You drive, Max shot back. You the man, William. You got the best eyes and best ears working for you. You can't miss. You're our driver, and that's it.

Come on, Max, William almost begged. I wanted to be on the ground floor, just in case I was needed behind the counter.

Max ignored him and asked, You both know why it is best to take one truck, right?

I thought it would be faster with two trucks, William answered. He knew Max wouldn't change his mind on the driver unless Jerry had an accident in the next couple of hours. And there was a fat chance of that. I understood you wanted speed, Max, and an extra truck would speed the distance between assignments.

An extra truck would draw more attention than we want, Jerry said. He didn't get why William, a man with a practical mind and solid logic most of the time, could not see the difference. Think like a criminal, William. You are driving on an isolated road, and then out of the blue you see two trucks with able-bodied men behind the wheel… you get the picture.

No. I get it. I certainly get it, William admitted. He was a little defensive because he wanted to contribute something to the plan— something he believed would work and not fuck anything up. Max had worked out the plan, and few could do it like Max, he had to admit.

Everything has to run precise in order for it to work, Max insisted. Every second counts because we don't know how cunning an animal we're dealing with.

If he comes, he'll go down, Max. I guarantee you he'll go down, never to get up again. That is my promise to you, Max, Jerry declared. Then he bit his lower lip in an attempt to control his anger.

If he comes? Max echoed. We'll never know if we stay in the office looking at the clock. Let's do it.

The three men almost ran out of the CI building like anxious volunteers joining a fire brigade. They piled into the CI tuck. William drove with Jerry in the middle and Max riding shotgun.

Max was angry and frustrated that he had to get his best friends involved in a mission that could be a false alarm or a real situation where they could get hurt or even killed. He felt like turning back and calling the whole thing off and letting the police handle it. Or better yet, doing nothing and waiting to see what materialized. If it was a crank, and he wished it would be, nothing would be lost—just a ride in the truck to the country. But if it wasn't, hell, anything could happen, and he was sure of that. The hired gun was supposed to be a pro, a sociopath who killed people for a living and not some junkie on the nod. William, Max believed, didn't appreciate the fact that there was no second or third chance on the killer because one of them would go down to stay. Max knew he needed

Jerry with him on the ground. Jerry had more expertise than William with issues and methods of survival. Max decided, scared as he was to go ahead and make the drive, to see if the phone call was for real or someone having a good time at his expense.

William was as happy as a baby seal in a bucket of fish. And even though Max was in stress mode, William drove with purpose and anticipation—and not recklessly—to an event that could not even happen. The planning and the give-and-take with Max and Jerry added to the excitement of doing something out of the ordinary. Not that his life was boring, never that. But to participate with his best friends and colleagues in a direct action of this kind was the type of activity he only fantasized about. It energized him to the point of almost having an orgasm. And this time he was included in all the planning at the inception—not like before, where he was asked to come in at the last minute, ready or not. William was thrilled he had gotten to know Max and then Jerry. His life had an altogether different perspective that was difficult to defend, if ever asked to unravel it. To Max and Jerry, this gig was probably not even a big deal, William speculated. But to him, it was big, the biggest. William still recalled Max and Jerry as teenagers. Their reputation as ass-kickers was already established, while he, only a couple of years younger, had held Ruth's hand and always been on the sidelines. He had admired them from a distance. He'd wanted to go up to them and ask them to be his friends, but he'd lacked the courage. He'd feared being embarrassed in front of his peers, so he'd said nothing. But now, now he was one of the boys. He respected Max and was confident that, with Max as their leader, they could take down the scumbag assassin and put him in an early grave. And even though he had had a few disagreements with Jerry, Jerry was the powerful engine that moved the train. And without Jerry's propensity to risk everything, including his freedom, to accomplish what Max set out to do, their triumphs would be diminished in most cases. But as much as he wanted to, he couldn't have any debate on that now. He was focused on driving; he had to get them there and execute an act few had the balls to do. William was looking forward to the mad dog falling into their trap. The mad dog would probably ride in dreaming of an easy payday, William imagined. But he would end up in hell. Hey, he almost said it out loud. If successful, he could put it on his brag sheet. And he wanted to bust up laughing but considered it a little insensitive. So he didn't.

Jerry, on the other hand, hated to ride in the middle. He just wasn't comfortable and could never explain why. It was one of those things that he couldn't get adjusted to. He was worried about Max. Max was getting too worked up over the contract, which he had every right to be. In Jerry's opinion, if you were going to take steps to prevent an approaching disaster, you had to be on your toes every breathing second. You had to be alert to the changing dynamics of the incoming storm or pay the piper. And that was something none of them could afford to do. The only one who was almost smiling was William. That little fuck pin, Jerry concluded. William really didn't comprehend what they were up against. And if he did get it, he romanticized about it. And that was even worse. Jerry hadn't said a word. Words at this point, even if the words were sincere, would only complicate an already complicated task. And he absolutely believed that. He just wanted William to keep his thoughts to himself and contain his nervous energy, as Max and he were struggling to do.

William drove south on Santa Fe Street from the CI Center. It was a warm and clear day, unusual for November, he thought. The traffic was light, but it was still a little early for most people to be heading home from work. William looked in the rearview mirror. He noticed some grayish clouds over the Turquoise Mountains to the northeast. He wanted to comment on the weather. He respected Max and Jerry too much to start a conversation about the weather, of all things. He was sure they were memorizing every aspect of the plan, as he should be doing. One little screwup, and it would cost them dearly. William understood that he was only the driver. And maybe his part wasn't that vital. He still had to be on top of the game at all times and be prepared for any unexpected circumstances that could affect Max and Jerry's play and change the direction of their action. And if there was an actual contract killer coming in with the intent to kill Max, there was little room for any last-minute changes. That was what he had to control: when the hit man entered the trap. Once the animal was in the trap, he had to lock it up and not allow anyone else in, or Max and Jerry would be compromised in their attempt to contain and neutralize the beast. William was aware of the risk and danger involved, even though at times, he believed that Jerry lacked the confidence in him to perform the task at hand. William's heart started beating faster as he passed by the old house of Sammy Q's granny on Martinez Street. From Martinez, William drove to Mesquite Street and turned east to reach Highway 26. On Mesquite Street, the three men turned to glance at the cemetery, a short distance south of Mesquite Street. Then they quickly stared straight ahead. They were as silent as the residents of the cemetery.

The road was empty of traffic, and that was what Max expected and needed. It was old Highway 26 that ran south to north until it connected with the Old Albuquerque Road. Highway 26 had been utilized way before Highway 25 was completed for folks to travel north and south. Once Highway 25 was completed, it shot off Highway 10, and the trip north to Albuquerque and Santa Fe or south to El Paso was much faster. That practically rendered Highway 26 obsolete. It was crumbling and slow to accommodate the growing traffic moving north and south. Highway 26 snaked close to Las Flores as it connected with the Old Albuquerque Road on its way north. The old road was a straight shot through the desert until it was about a half mile from Las Flores, where it curved like an uppercase S. There were also some dried cottonwood trees on both sides of the curve—not close but close enough to cause a distraction for any driver who wasn't familiar with the area. The assassin, Max was warned, was coming in on a motorcycle. Max was certain the killer was from out of state and had never been on Highway 26 before. If the fool didn't slow down, and Max counted on it, the killer would enter the stomach of the S at almost full speed. The entrance to the S was short. Coming in from the south, it could be taken smooth and easy, but then it curved east and rapidly northwest. With the tall dried trees on both sides of the S, most drivers would focus on the trees because of going so long without seeing any. And if they didn't slow down some, the vehicle could end up in dry washes all along both sides of the S. And that was where Max planned to stage his little theater of the absurd.

William continued to drive. He never had cared much for old Highway 26. The asphalt was deteriorating and, in many places, difficult to find. The road was seldom used, except by smugglers of human cargo and other illicit goods that unsophisticated peddlers delivered north. Some believed the chances of being caught were less on the fading road. William, as well as everyone else, knew the cops never bothered with the road. And not even the state police made their rounds. Now he was worried the killer might change his plans. He could come in on Highway 25 and establish himself in Las Flores. That would give the assassin more time to take Max out. William had approached Max on several occasions with this thought, but Max insisted the killer would use Highway 26. Max was sure the killer would come into Las Flores, have a look around, and attempt the hit. And if he was successful, he'd leave on the same road. William knew his hands were tied, and there was nothing he could do but stick to Max's plan and see what came of it.

The three men checked their watches. It was a little before 2:30 p.m., and there was a slight breeze coming in from the southeast that would turn colder by sunset. The breeze would be on the killer's back and push him a little faster down the winding curve, Max calculated. Maybe not much, but every bit helped. William entered the S slowly and stopped where it curved northwest. Max opened the door of the truck. He jumped out and grabbed a long rope from the bed of the truck. He ran to the opposite side of the road with the rope in his arms. William drove Jerry a short distance farther up the curve, not far from the entrance to the S if one drove in from the north.

Don't forget your radio, Jerry, William said. Jerry also jumped out of the truck. Jerry grabbed the radio as he put on his fingerless gloves. He shoved the radio into his pocket and took off to the side of the road without saying a word. William turned the truck around and drove south down the S. He passed Max and kept going a short distance beyond the entrance of the S. He made a U-turn and drove off the road as much as he could. He parked the truck facing the entrance to the S. He hunched down on the seat to make it seem like the truck was abandoned but not so low as to miss any approaching vehicles. He held his radio close to him and waited, his heart beating like crazy.

Max continued to search for a metal fence post cemented in the ground that had been left behind when a chain-link fence was removed some years back. He glanced at his watch and said, Shit. He kicked at the brush desperately but saw nothing of the metal post. He looked at the trees, but most of them were too far away for him to use. Finally, he stepped on the rusted metal pole and removed some of the dry weeds that had covered it for years. The metal pole was around twelve inches above the ground. It was almost invisible with the dirt and dry weeds that had accumulated around and over it. Max cleaned around the pole as best he could. He did not want to expose it too much. He tied one end of the rope firmly around the pole and pulled on it several times to make sure it would stay in place. He ran with the other end of the rope across the road. He laid the rope on the road and pulled on it to make sure it was secure. He believed the biker would be too intoxicated to notice the rope on the road. He hid behind the trunk of a dead tree. He glanced at his watch, and it read a quarter to three. He couldn't stop shaking. He held the rope with his left hand and jabbed his right fist into his chest hard but not hard enough to lose consciousness. He repeated the jab a couple of times and then grabbed the rope with both hands. He was worried. He wasn't sure he could lift the rope high enough to blow the son of a bitch off his bike. He wanted to test it, but he was afraid the rope would come off the metal pole. And he didn't have time to run back across the road and tie it up again. If the killer drove in while he was chasing over the rope, it would come down to hand-to-hand combat. And that was something he wanted to avoid at all cost. Max couldn't stop shaking. His adrenaline pumped through his veins unabated. Come on, motherfucker, he kept repeating to himself.

As soon as William took off, Jerry ran across the road to secure a large, dried-up tree trunk. It was about six feet in length and weighed at least a hundred pounds. The plan was that, when the call came, he'd pull the dry log across the road to block any vehicles heading south, from entering the S.. Then he'd run down to assist Max with the killer. Jerry held on to the radio as if it were a religious icon. He hated the wireless radios because they brought back certain memories he was trying to forget. But for now, he depended on the small toy for the call to come in and for him to run down the curved road and help Max. He couldn't see a thing from where he was. And he depended on William and the radio to get him down there fast. If Max couldn't bring down the killer with the rope trick, he was going to need help to subdue the man. If the killer didn't go down quick, and he had a gun, they were fucked. But Max was assured that the mark would come in unarmed and secure his weapons in Las Flores. That way, if he was stopped by the cops, he would be clean. Jerry was uneasy. He was concerned that he couldn't get down there in time to help Max out. Jerry rolled his pant leg up and removed a metal pipe he had inserted in his sock and held with a thick rubber band around his calf. The metal pipe was about sixteen inches long and taped on one end for a solid grip. Jerry held the metal pipe in his right hand and the little radio in his left. He brought the pipe crashing down full force on the half-rotted tree trunk. He repeated the same blow several times, then breathed a sigh of relief.

William crouched low in the seat of the truck. He had one hand on the steering wheel. He couldn't stay still. He had his eyes on the road. The waiting was driving him crazy. He studied the little black handheld radio. Shit, he thought. These are kids' toys. They had them at the center for the kids to play with. They worked though. And if they didn't, William would have to use the truck to crash into the motorcycle from behind. That wasn't in the plan, but hell, he thought. He had to do something to save Max, if Max needed saving. Then William heard the roar of the big bike, and he said, Goddamn. The boy on the bike was a big redneck with a Viking helmet on his greasy head, horns and all. He was riding in on a chopped-up Harley. William placed the toy radio close to his mouth, calm as he could be. He clicked the button and almost whispered, Thar she blows, brother.

Max heard the roar of the motorcycle in the far distance. He had to wait for William's call to be sure he wasn't decapitating an innocent rider who happened to come along at the wrong time. He's in, barked Max to Jerry over the radio. Max slipped the phone in his pocket. He grabbed the rope with both hands and was ready to pull with all his might when the biker was close enough.

The rider on the motorcycle didn't even notice the truck parked alongside the road. As soon as he passed, the truck was used to block the road and prevent anyone else from entering the S from the North. The Harley entered the S at full speed, then set off east. It slowed a bit while the rider gawked at the dry trees on both sides of the curve, then surged northwest, with the wind on his back. Max pulled on the rope with both hands. He couldn't get it high enough to reach the rider's neck. The rope cut into the chopper's handlebars, and the front wheel shot upward and flipped the chopper over backward. The chopper crashed on top of the rider and then skidded rapidly off the road into a dry wash and erupted into flames. When the rider flipped over with the motorcycle, his Viking helmet flew off to the opposite direction. The rider was a bloody mess on the crumbling asphalt.

When Jerry got the call from Max, he pulled the dry tree trunk as fast as he could across the road to prevent anyone driving into the S, as they headed south. Then Jerry ran as fast as or faster than he had ever run before, down to the stomach of the S where Max was with the killer. The killer was on his back with his long legs twisted to his side. From his shoulders to his ribs, nothing could be seen but bloody, exposed tissue, plastered with pieces of brittle asphalt, as if he'd been breaded and was ready for the oven. The assassin attempted to raise his injured head and try to make sense of what he'd hit or what had hit him. Out of his functioning eye, he saw Jerry. Jerry ran at full speed with the metal pipe in his right hand. He was screaming like a man on fire.

In a split second, Jerry crashed the pipe down on the biker's head with such force that the skull almost split in half, like a ripe melon. The second blow from Jerry to the villain's head scattered brains, blood, and other goodies housed in that sacred temple. Jerry smacked the metal pipe into the injured man's head again so hard that the head was almost jerked off the body. Jerry held the metal pipe in both hands. He spread his legs wide apart and came down with the metal pipe on the head and shoulders of the stranger, as if chopping wood. Bits of bone, blood, and flesh flew off the unlucky fellow's head and shoulders like sparks in a welding shop. And all this time Jerry kept screaming at the injured man, You do not fuck with my brother, Max. You hear me, motherfucker?

When Max saw Jerry taking care of business, he pulled out his radio and said, William, get your ass down here. Then he ran across the road to undo the rope. He pulled on the rope, but the rope didn't budge. He pulled again harder and said, Shit. He turned and saw William driving slowly to the scene of the slaughter and glanced at his watch. He frantically kicked at the pole and pulled at the rope, but no go. He searched in his pocket for his knife but couldn't find it. He grabbed the rope with both hands and used all his strength and weight to pull on the rope until the rope broke loose and Max landed on his ass. He recovered. He coiled the rope and ran back to the truck.

William drove up to where Jerry was still delivering blows to a corpse. He parked close to Jerry, but not too close, and said, Hey, Jerry, can I help you?

Max ran up to the truck, pitched the rope into the bed of the truck, and told Jerry to stop because he was nailing a dead man. Then Max grabbed a five-gallon can of gasoline from the bed of the truck and splashed the gas over the dead man's torn body. Jerry stopped pummeling the carcass and ran up the road to move the dead tree trunk out of the way.

William, you follow Jerry, but slowly, Max snapped at William.

Look at that beautiful bike burn, William said. He was almost saddened at the loss.

Your ass is going to burn worse when I put my boot in it if you don't move! Max yelled.

OK. Jesus. I missed all the action, William grumbled. He drove slowly after Jerry who was running, jumping, and shouting with the bloody metal pipe in his gloved hand.

Max threw the empty gas can in the bed of the truck as William pulled away. He took a lighter from his front pocket and flicked it. There was no flame, only a weak spark. He tried again, fast and angry, but nothing. Max, his thumb on the little rollers, speed-dialed the rollers until a flame shot up. He glanced at his watch while he put the flame near a piece of clothing, and the flame engulfed the bloodied body. Maybe this will be a lesson to others, he said to the burning body. Then he ran after the truck, jumped into the bed of the truck, and hit the top of the cab. That gave William the order to roll out. Max looked at his right hand and, for the first time, felt the pain. When he'd held the rope against the trunk of the tree for leverage and the motorcycle had hit the rope with great force, the thrust had smashed his right hand against the tree's trunk. And for a moment he'd thought his right hand was broken, but he'd held on. Jerry was right, he thought. We should have brought guns to finish off the motherfucker in a barrage of bullets, old-west-style. But if we missed and the killer got away, then what?

Max finally sat down in the bed of the truck. He didn't want to see Jerry and William laughing in the front cab. He didn't want to see Jerry, still holding the metal pipe in his hand as if showing off a trophy he had won in a sports event. Then it hit Max like a jolt of electricity: What if they had killed the wrong man? That kept racing through his mind. No. No. He said out loud, It was the right fucker. It had to be. Then he put both hands on his face and said, Fuck it. William headed north on Highway 26 until it turned into Old Albuquerque Road. They would return to Las Flores by making a left on Esperanza and going west. They would catch a side street off Esperanza and enter the CI Center garage through the rear entrance. They would clean up and pretend nothing had happened.

CHAPTER 21

*J*erry felt the loneliness seep into his soul like a dark cloud saturated with unhappy sentiments and tormenting omens as soon as he arrived home. He closed the front door to escape the stench of dog shit that oozed from the trash cans that sat in front of his neighbor's yard. Jerry could always tell when people kept dogs inside the house. Their trash cans put out an outrageous odor, second only to cat shit. He walked into the unfinished kitchen. He had his hands in his pockets. He just stared. The sight made him nauseous. He was a foreigner to this house and to this kitchen—a stranger to the configuration and the ins and outs of a domestic kitchen. The worst part was that he had to face it alone. All alone with no one else to listen to his complaints and his concerns about this and that. Jerry thought about William going home to his tight-ass Ruth. And even Max. When he returned home, his mother was there waiting for him. And even though Victoria was not in the best of health, Max enjoyed her being home with him. It was better than being alone—a lot better, Jerry imagined. Mike Cotton had them all beat. And that shit face didn't deserve Claire. Jerry wanted to shout it out to the ghosts who inhabited the old house. Of course he was jealous; any man who still got hard would be jealous—and if not jealous, he would give it some serious consideration. It bothered him more when he thought of Mike Cotton thrusting his hammer into little Claire's tight, sweet-tasting cunt. He knew firsthand how tight it was. He'd had a little trouble opening her treasure chest, but once he found the key, it was pure gold.

Jerry finally decided to sit in a chair next to the kitchen table Max had helped him rescue from a yard sale for a small price. The table was not in its prime, but what the hell. It worked. Jerry was depressed. He was angry and felt other feelings he had not yet characterized. The house was a dump, and there was no getting around it. It was an old, abandoned house and had hosted squatters as the most loyal residents throughout the years. Jerry observed the kitchen sink next to a window. The sink had seen better days and probably had been, at one time, the pride of the kitchen. Now it was nicked, rusted around the faucets, and the stains refused to budge. The grout around the sink and tile countertop had crumbled ages ago. Jerry had cleaned out the stubborn pieces of grout from the countertop, and now there were empty ridges around the tile. The floor, after Jerry scraped off the stubborn, ragged linoleum piece by piece, revealed some solid wood. After it was cleaned, waxed, and polished, it made do. Jerry, with little trouble, also secured a functioning stove and fridge. The Eastside was a bargain basement for used furniture and kitchen items. The bathroom was still a mess, but the water was running. The toilet, a most difficult contraption to replace, was in and worked most of the time. His bedroom had a mattress on the floor and clean sheets. And that was better than what he'd had in prison. So maybe he shouldn't complain. But what the hell, he reasoned. Even Max's house was a mansion, compared to his own pad. And he didn't want to think of Claire's real mansion—the kind he only knew existed in movies, for movie stars and people with a shitload of bread.

Jerry studied the kitchen again from floor to ceiling. Was he disappointed because Victoria Luna had returned and claimed her territory? That was the same question that had troubled him before. He loved Victoria like a second mother and wanted to kick himself in the ass for even thinking like that. Sure, he was taken by surprise. Her presence created a dilemma for him because he had to relocate to a less-suitable abode. And that meant his old house. But he wasn't resentful, and he had struggled to convince himself of that. It was just the fact that the old house distressed him because of the many unforgettable memories of his mother and the asshole she had selected as a mate.

Jerry turned to his left to see his mother's bedroom door. It was shut at all times. Her bedroom had been left untouched. Some nights, half-awake and half-asleep, he saw a dim light crisscross the empty house. Her spirit seemed to welcome him home. It was sad, he reflected. His mother couldn't be there in the flesh to hold him in her arms, as she had when he was young and the world, to him, was of a gentler nature. His mother, Jerry reminisced, was soft, generous, and good-natured. And she believed that all people were good and kind. She would hold him tight and whisper tender words in his ear. Then she'd kiss his face again and again until he begged her to stop. They would laugh and laugh until the fears and anxieties that torment young people melted away into nothing. But then a monster entered their lives. The bad dreams were released, and they eventually turned into nightmares.

Jerry knew deep down that he was still grieving for his mother. The prison shrink had informed him on several occasions that grief affected people in different ways. That some people grieved for the loss of a loved one for weeks, while for others it took years for the pain and sadness to subside. Jerry refused to talk to the shrink after a couple of sessions. He believed he could deal with the death of his mother on his own. He was ignorant to the fact that grief was like a black vulture. And it ate away at his flesh while he was still breathing. The losses of appetite and sleep were nothing new to Jerry. The anxiety and depression that afflicted his soul were more difficult to comprehend. They hit him unexpectedly at any time, day or night, drowning him in a deep swamp, where suicide was the only option left to him. The anger he was able to manage. He could beat an inmate senseless and pay the consequences. But the guilt that he was the cause of his mother's death strangled him and left him in an emotional vortex. It left him melancholy, frustrated, and searching for answers to the same questions he had asked a million times before. The tears that had filled buckets when he was in the hole were now few. The anger was more or less under control, but the pain was not. He had been a fool, a damn fool, to believe that once he was out of prison and lived with Max, the nightmare was somehow going to disappear. And his grief and guilt were going be a part of his past, left behind in prison, like a discarded suitcase. He had never been so wrong.

Jerry took his chewing gum out of his mouth with his big fingers. He stretched his arm out to a small Mason jar filled with sugar on top of the kitchen table and rolled the gum in the sugar. He kept rolling the gum in the jar. He watched the granulated sugar attach to the gum, like metal slivers to a magnet. He needed the gum sugared to the max. He was going to work on it for a while longer. Old habits die hard, he thought. He put the sugared gum back in his mouth. He rested one leg on top of the kitchen table. He chewed his gum and contemplated the old, unfinished house. He waited for Big Bertha. She was going to visit later and give him some cooking lessons, she claimed. But for an hour or so, he would be alone with his thoughts. He had already forgotten the massacre on Highway 26 earlier that day. To him, it was already history, and there was no point in wasting energy thinking about it. What really concerned him more than anything else was Claire Cotton.

Claire baby, I love you! Jerry cried out in a half-serious, half-clowning manner. Claire was still an enigma to Jerry most of the time. A riddle that dominated his thoughts with more frequency. He didn't like it. But he was helpless to do anything about it, as much as he wanted to. It happened too fast and too easy, he thought. He had heard stories about women who were needy and sought men to fuck without any scruples or conditions. But that was only in movies and novels and prison bullshit, he believed. He wasn't blind to the fact that Claire was a wealthy, attractive woman who was connected to the spit and polish of that comfortable class. Claire gave him everything—all the sex he could handle and money, if he asked for it. And she even claimed to love him. But what she couldn't give him, and what he wanted most of all, was peace of mind. He had nothing to offer her, not a thing, besides sex. And sex, he knew so well, was something that a charmer like Claire could get in more desirable places than Las Flores. How could she ever introduce him in society, if it ever came to that, and as what? It was possible to remove the tattoos with surgery. He was aware of that, but the rest of him, with all his baggage and dark moods…no, that was impossible. He wouldn't even bring her to this dump, his own house. Oh, he was pretty sure Claire would welcome the chance to visit. And more to experience the sociological divide than a love nest. Jerry was just speculating. He couldn't tell what was in Claire's heart, and that was his major concern.

Jerry's mood began to change, as he thought more of his mamacita, Claire Cotton. The sun was down, and he didn't want to bother with the light. He sat in the dark like a father waiting for his teenage son who had taken the family car without permission. Jerry wanted to think about Claire and only Claire, the devil woman he happened to be in love with, or so he believed. This was a good time for him to peel off the mask and confront himself with Claire, the woman, along with the myth. He liked to recall the first time he visited her at the plantation. They made sure hubby and the housekeepers would be out of town for the weekend, and that wasn't unusual. Claire met him outside the main gate. She introduced him slowly to the big German shepherds, Drake and Mona. The dogs from hell. Both dogs had sniffed Jerry in the front and back. They apparently liked what they smelled, because they became friendly. Mona held back a little and stayed closer to Claire, as if Claire were in danger of being violated. After Claire introduced Jerry to the dogs, she led him to the kitchen of the huge house. Her thinking was that the dogs had to be fed, and if he fed them, the dogs would love him forever. And he could access the property when he pleased, without any ruckus, which made sense.

The kitchen, the first room in the mansion Jerry entered, was something out of a decadent novel, in its extravagant luxury. After he fed the dogs and washed his hands, Claire led him by the hand up the stairs to her bedroom. Apparently, for reasons that were not obvious to Jerry, Mike Cotton slept in his own bedroom. Claire showed no interest in giving him a tour of the house. That was done by people who allowed the house to overshadow them in every aspect. And that was Jerry's assumption. Jerry had glanced quickly at the expensive furniture. At the sculptures and art hanging on the walls. He was impressed by Claire's good taste in putting the house in top order. They finally reached Claire's bedroom, and Jerry was relieved. He had seen enough of what seemed to him acres of furniture and other household items that could cram many homes in the Eastside, including his own. Claire closed the door behind them when they entered her bedroom. She changed into something black and silky. She smiled and kept saying, Wait, sweetheart. Just wait one more minute. Then Claire put on a reddish wig from several she had on top of the bed. It was made out of human hair, Jerry was sure. In an instant, Claire transformed into a young Lucia Mendez. She walked with a lot of class to a small stage set up in a corner of the large bedroom. She leaped up onto the stage with skillful, athletic ability.

Once on the stage, Claire made a bow. She pulled out a cordless mic from somewhere. She pushed some buttons on a sophisticated sound system that was also on the stage and sang, "Amor Imposible"—"Impossible Love"—along with Lucia Mendez, the Mexican diva. Claire put on a show for Jerry. She became Lucia Mendez in her younger days. She poured her heart and soul into the song, a torch song about an impossible love. The protagonist was going to let her lover go to be with the other woman. She did not want to hurt her. The other woman had been there for him when he needed her. She only wanted him to make love to her for the last time. She would leave at dawn forever. She was going to surrender her greatest love to show compassion. The song could bring tears and release other stronger emotions, more so if the heart had felt the sting of an impossible love. And Claire seemed to agonize deep down as she sang the lyrics in Spanish and performed like a woman who was really giving up her lover. Jerry was certain he had seen tears rolling down Claire's cheeks, and her face was flushed.

Jerry was moved by Claire's production. He recalled his mother had played that song when his father left them. She had played it late at night when she believed Jerry was sleeping. She played the song over and over so many times that he wanted to go into her bedroom and put his arms around her. He hadn't out of respect for her space. He knew she needed to be alone to deal with the pain. And now years later, Claire sang the same song to him. And he couldn't understand why or if the song was even directed at him. The song was so touching and real that Jerry's eyes and emotions never left Claire for a second. Jerry realized that Claire resembled Lucia Mendez much more than she resembled Vivien Leigh. When he had seen Lucia Mendez on the cover of his mother's LPs as a teenager, his imagination had been inflamed and his hand relentless. And now he had Lucia Mendez in Claire, and he recognized that this was as close as he was ever going to get to the diva. He picked Claire up in his arms. He put her on the bed and made love to her all night, like a man possessed.

In the early morning of the following day, after he had ravished Claire for several hours, she made Jerry some toast with a glass of orange juice. Claire went back to bed, and Jerry fed the dogs on his way out. And this was what troubled his mind. Why didn't she ask him to stay and spend the day together, like normal people did? She was so hot for him during the night and early morning. And then she went cold and didn't say a thing except, Feed the dogs on your way out. And that was the perplexing part about his situation with Claire. He couldn't set up any parameters. He couldn't do shit but wait for her to contact him. Jerry felt at times like one of the big dogs, always hungry and depending on Claire to throw him a bone. But what the hell—he had to admit that he should count his blessings. He had scored with a rich and beautiful woman. He was sucking the finest ass in Las Flores. And that was the dream and inspiration of a vast number of vatos, in or out of prison. Jerry smiled again. He never came to any reasonable conclusions about Claire. He decided to take a shower, trusting there would be enough hot water to do him justice. He would put on a different hat and wait for Big Bertha. And Claire Cotton would continue to tickle his balls, as always.

Jerry sat in his half-finished living room on an old couch that Max had given him. He had his right leg crossed over his left. He looked straight at the front door like a man who waited for the big cigar that never came. The couch was old, but it was still in good shape. It had not acquired that particular odor that old couches have the reputation for. He sat and waited for Big Bertha. He was a lot more relaxed after his shower but not excited about her coming over. Big Bertha helped him alleviate the loneliness that tortured his soul without mercy. A loneliness so dark and deep that at times it made prison seem like a picnic. Big Bertha was a carnal distraction that filled the empty hours of the night when he couldn't be with Claire or Max. He felt guilty and wanted to tell Big Bertha the truth. But what was the point? he asked himself many times. Claire could stop her infatuation anytime, but Big Bertha was solid, and he could depend on her for the long run. He wasn't sure how long the long run was going to be. He needed someone to hold his hand and his dick. Someone to make him feel he was alive and not the walking dead, as some cons seemed to be. To come out of prison with no marketable skills or a support group, as many had, was a challenge. And with no one to love or to love you, it was like walking on quicksand with heavy boots on. Jerry decided to stay with Big Bertha, as long as she put up with him and his dark moods. She was good in bed and not a bad cook. But what did he know about decent cooking? Compared to prison chow, everything was good, including what she made for him.

Jerry glanced at his watch again. Time crawled. It was still six thirty, and Big Bertha was due at seven. The sun was down, and the evening was cold and getting colder by the hour. He turned on a small lamp that rested on a wooden crate next to the couch where he kept his books. He didn't want big Bertha to drive off if she saw the house dark, thinking he was off with Max. It wasn't often that Big Bertha got an evening off from her job at the Bandera Azul Bar. And Jerry liked to take advantage of the early evening. That was the time that dragged for him. Big Bertha usually visited after the bar closed. And by that time, he had already escaped in sleep, and the dream world had encapsulated him in a cocoon of devilish nightmares or sexual dreams of unconventional delight. In sleep, he could elude his harsh reality and travel in worlds of ever-changing landscapes, with boundaries and encounters only his imagination could conceive. Sleep and soul travel saved his ass in prison from going mad. And now, on some nights, Jerry depended on them to keep him from losing it on the outside, where he definitely needed to be. He knew for certain that prison for him was death. Death of the spirit, of the mind, and eventually left only a corpse, rotting in its own filth.

As Jerry waited for Big Bertha, he attempted to clear his mind. He wanted to control his thinking. He wanted to eliminate all the useless crap that never amounted to anything but worry and stress. He wanted to end all the clatter and all the noise. Or at least minimize all the bullshit that led to unrealistic grasping at straws. He wished only for the pure thoughts of love and death to dominate his thinking and nothing else, at least until Big Bertha arrived. Love because it represented his mother, in all that was good and virtuous. And death because…because death was inevitable and the end. A river of no return. Silent death, a dark pathway where all his problems would end. And all his fears and worries would dissipate like the morning fog. And his mind—his mind at last empty and free. His flesh left behind to rot and be consumed by maggots, useless as all the material possessions that cluttered his life. Death was the captain of the ship that sailed regardless of the season. And all the luggage was left behind. Jerry could see himself on that ship. The first on board, if need be. Except he was afraid. Yes. He was afraid of his thoughts about death, and he looked around at the silent shadows in the dimly lit house. He jumped off the couch and ran to the front door. He thought he heard a noise coming from his mother's bedroom. He was shaking like a young boy who believed there were skeletons in the closet. But it was only Big Bertha with a smile on her thick, red lips and bags in her arms. She was knocking on the screen door.

Big Bertha attempted to open the screen door after calling out for Jerry several times. Jerry opened the door for her and helped her with the bags, immensely happy it was her.

I brought you your laundry, sweetheart, Big Bertha said. She smiled as she always did. She placed the bag of laundry on top of the couch. She looked at Jerry and said, Why, Jerry, you look as if you seen a ghost. Do I look that bad? She broke out laughing.

No, babe, of course not, Jerry replied. He was embarrassed and a little defensive; tough guys don't believe in ghosts.

I'm only teasing, Jerry. Big Bertha beamed. It's OK. Look. I brought you your laundry, all clean and folded. And in the bag you are holding are the beans and rice for the week. I made you black beans this time. They are very healthy for you. You can put them in the fridge for now. Oh, and I also brought you a half a pecan pie. The kids ate half before I reminded them that the pie was for you, for us. You know, for the bean taste.

Babe, you didn't have to go to all that trouble, Jerry said. He relaxed. He loved all the fuss and attention he got from Big Bertha.

Hey, c'mon, Jerry. You'd do the same for me—no trouble at all, honest. I enjoy doing it.

After Jerry and Big Bertha had exhausted the many different positions in the art of making love, they lay naked next to each other on the mattress. They stared in silence at the stained ceiling. Big Bertha put her mouth on pause. Her brain kept speeding on at one hundred miles per second, as it always had. She waited for Jerry to say something. Jerry remained quiet. She spoke up because she had to encourage her man to perk him up and do the right thing.

You can do it, Jerry, Big Bertha insisted. You can fix the house up, then flip it. You got everything going for you, sweetheart. You got the title and not the bank. The house is free and clear—no mortgage. C'mon, babe; you can sell it. You can invest the cash in a nicer home and move up. Maybe to the Westside. Nothing wrong with that.

I'll never move to the fucking Westside, Jerry replied. He was a little pissed off because he was caught off guard. You claim the Westside is nicer because white people live there.

Oh, Jerry. And Big Bertha placed her hands over her mouth. You poor dear, forgive me. I completely forgot you…you were gone for some time. The Westside has gone brown…significantly.

You mean white flight, right? Jerry asked with obvious satisfaction on his dark face.

No, Jerry, honey, Big Bertha said as if pleading with a third grader to cut the shit. The whites are older now, Jerry. And cannot, in a million years, make babies like we can, and that's a fact. When many, and not all, of the white folks get older, they check into homes for the elderly. Their kids, if they have any—in most cases but not all; I have to be fair—they are not in the habit of taking care of their old folks, like some of us do. And that's regardless of the burden put on the family. Most of us, although there are cases, will not abandon our old people like yesterday's shoes. Besides, the Westside is not Chernobyl. It's a nice place with a little more turf to extend your wings. Anyway. I'll help you, Jerry, as much as I can, Big Bertha continued, a smile on her full lips. You got it, babe. I'm all yours and all I have. Little as it is.

Jerry studied Big Bertha in the dim light of the bedroom. He didn't want to say something stupid or insensitive to Big Bertha. She only offered to help him, but he couldn't help it.

So what's in it for you, babe? Jerry finally asked. I mean this place is gonna take a lot of physical labor, along with a healthy dose of cash. And that's only to take her up to code. Sales are a step a little higher, but you know that.

Please don't get defensive, Jerry baby, Big Bertha pleaded. It's because I love you. But if love is not enough for you, then maybe you can add my name to the deed. And that would depend on how much I contribute to the rehabilitation of the old house. I'm only teasing, Big Boy. Don't imagine anything else, please. I just want to help you, Jerry, simple as that. I don't like to see you all down, thinking crazy about your future. And no, babe, I don't expect you to marry me. Although that would be nice, she wanted to add. Instead she said, I've been down that rathole, and believe me, Jerry, it's not all kisses and sunshine.

No. No, babe. It's nothing like that. Jerry attempted to correct his aggressive behavior and act a little more civilized. It's just that, that the task at hand is huge. I live it and breathe it. I know. It's a hell of a lot. But thanks, Bertha. That…that really means a, you know…means a whole lot to me. It does, I promise. And the silence engulfed them again. Jerry was speechless. And that was not common for him. There was nothing else he wanted to say. It was awkward, and so it was best to shut it.

Big Bertha followed Jerry's lead. The conversation wasn't coming out the way she'd hoped it would. Jerry was sometimes difficult to talk to. Big Bertha had noticed recently that Jerry's intensity in bed had come down a notch or two. She referred to the enthusiasm that pushed the last button that made the volcano explode. And not just any orgasm but the orgasm that blew her top off. The orgasm that confirmed she was with a real man, who knew how to treat a woman in bed. But lately, Big Bertha reflected, Jerry was not taking her there or giving her the opportunity to arrive with a smile before she allowed the Big Boy to take a vacation. Big Bertha knew men. And not many, but some. And most, if not all, according to her calculations, were weak, cowardly, and full-blooded liars. And she would bet money on it. All except Jerry, she concluded. Jerry was confident and was not weak physically. His psychological processing needed a little help, especially in the compassion arena. His dark moods, along with his temper, were a handful, if not managed in a delicate manner, as she was able to do. And that was an ongoing challenge. Except tonight. Tonight Big Bertha felt in her heart that Jerry wanted to confess something that was eating on him. She felt Jerry wanted to uncap the well and set the black demons free. She felt Jerry was ready to cleanse his soul and tell her about men fucking men behind prison walls. And if it involved him, the better, she confessed. She also felt it was the right time to ask him. Like most people, she was curious about men in prison. And she had to admit, there was a little turn-on. Especially when vivid details were included. She would have to ask him gently and structure it with delicate words. She did not want to put him off.

And for sure she'd offer something intimate from her own life. That was to gain the Big Boy's confidence. That was never a problem for her.

Jerry, sweetheart, purred Big Bertha. She broke the silence. Can I talk to you about something very sad that happened in my life?

Jerry was impassive, as many men get after sex. Especially if the sex is losing its luster. He responded after a few minutes. He attempted to demonstrate he was still in the game. Anything you want to tell me, babe, you know it'll stay with me. So c'mon, Bertha baby, lay it on me. I'm all ears. And Jerry turned to face her.

This ain't easy, Jerry, Big Bertha stated. She was almost in tears. You have to promise me that you will also confide in me after? OK. It's sad and painful. Here it goes; bear with me. I might get too emotional. When I was around nine or ten years old, my parents would step out to go dancing on Friday and Saturday nights. Us kids would stay home with our grandfather on our mother's side. One night, when the younger kids were sleeping, my grandfather entered my bedroom and sat next to me on my bed. He had a book in his hands. He claimed he was going to show me a little of what life was about and said not to be alarmed by what he was about to show me. Every page he turned in the book had a filthy image of penises and disgusting pictures of the human anatomy. But the worst part, Jerry…Big Bertha paused for effect. The worst was when my grandfather grabbed me from the back of the neck with his left hand and penetrated me with his right thumb.

Big Bertha fell silent as tears filled her eyes and trickled down her cheeks. She was hurt. She couldn't or wouldn't recall if the incident with her grandfather really had happened or she'd made it up. So many fingers and thumbs up her pussy by that age that it was difficult for her to say. But her tears were real because, to this day, she felt violated.

Jerry was not sure what to say. What can I really say? he asked himself several times. Sorry wasn't going to cut it at this late date. So he said, Wanna a beer, babe, or some water? Then he asked, to stay involved, Where was your grandma all this time?

Oh, my grandmother had passed some years before, Big Bertha answered. She was surprised at the question.

Did he hurt you? Jerry asked. He acted like a defense attorney questioning a rape victim but striving to be as delicate as he could. Did you bleed?

Oh, Jerry. Please, that's a myth. And Big Bertha rolled her large almond-shaped eyes. You know little girls bust their hymen at an early age with physical activity.

No. Honest, babe. I didn't know; forgive me.

There's nothing to forgive, Jerry; I believe you. But you have to understand, Jerry, I couldn't tell anyone about it. It would have caused a scandal. Can you imagine the whipping I would have gotten? The man was considered a saint. And you can't accuse a saint of touching his grandkids in that kind of kinky way. And I did the only thing I could do. I kept my mouth shut and the pain to myself. I had no other choice. And my worst fear wasn't the adults in the family, Jerry. They would cover it up and mandate a gag order for the duration. No. It was the kids. You know how cruel children can be, especially the randy boys. Can you imagine the twisted minds and the sick thinking of my male cousins and their weirdo friends? That's what I dreaded. Shit like, hey, Bertha, did you give the old man a blow job? Or, hey, Bertha, how did you like frenching Granddaddy? Did he take out his false teeth, or did you take them out with your tongue? Crap like that, Jerry, you know? I could have never gone back to school, Jerry. Those fuckers be in my face forever. Forget that. I stayed shut like a clam, to this day. I'm opening up to you because you're my special babe, and I trust you. And you can trust me too. You know I love you, Jerry. And she gently rubbed his muscular biceps and neck with her hands, especially around the scorpion tattoos. She kissed his pecs and face with her soft lips. She barely touched his skin and then gave him a little lick with her moist tongue after the kiss. But that's enough about me, Big Daddy, Big Bertha almost whispered. It's your turn, OK. You promised, remember? You can tell me anything, love, anything. I'll take it to my grave, if you ask it. Talk to me, baby. Trust me. It's OK. Take your time.

Jerry vaguely remembered that he had promised anything. It didn't matter though; he also had stories to tell. OK, babe, he finally said. But you have to consider that my experience was not, shall we say, as severe or outrageous as yours. Yours is a classic beyond critics, while mine is a rough draft, collecting dust on the shelf, if I may put it that way.

No. Please don't say that, baby doll. You know you don't believe it. And Big Bertha moved a little away from Jerry, but her hand continued stroking his powerful legs. Her eyes were alive, and her mouth held a slight smile. She anticipated being enlightened by a man who had seen it all. And she was sure, almost sure, the man had participated, willingly or unwillingly, in the hot pursuit of savage passion. Big Bertha couldn't understand why this compulsion meant so much to her. Maybe, she contemplated, it was a crucial, primitive need in her to explore the human dimension of the caged beast, as he groped in the dark for flesh. Slimy and sweaty bodies who performed sexual acrobats behind locked doors. Brutal and violent degrading sex, among proud macho jerk-offs. Some who had wounded girlfriends, wives, mothers, aunts, and other females in their insatiable quest. To be what, men? Ha. What a joke; give me a break, Big Bertha said to herself. She wanted to laugh out loud but changed her mind.

Jerry was thinking about Big Bertha. He was impressed and at the same time puzzled. The babe had some knowledge on how to get information from a person. She was smooth and a promoter of good will. When it came to sex, she had skillful hands, and her erotic techniques could be considered professional. She was sensitive and creative, and her purring was catlike. And even romantic, if one was inclined. She could do wonders with her mouth. Her soft, full lips and white teeth appeared healthy and robust. And she was not afraid to probe in the infinite and heavenly zones of pleasure. She was quite a woman, Jerry had to admit. And her acting wasn't shoddy either. Her presentation was animated but not overdone. She had natural rhythm and not robotic pelvic crunching or bleeding-back nail scratching. She was nothing like that. She was just a hot body who rocked his cradle, with plenty of quality. And yet…why wasn't he convinced that she was for real? And why am I so cynical? he kept asking himself, more and more every day. He was always on guard. He might be out of the joint, but the joint was still taking some of his time. Jerry knew it was deep and entrenched in his psyche. He wanted to let it go and run with the little pigeon until he couldn't run anymore and dropped like a whipped dog, whining for mercy. Maybe that was his fear: performing subpar. But why go there? This was not the time, he concluded. He needed every booster he could muster.

Jerry finally said to Big Bertha, OK, I'll share something deep as you have, and he cleared his throat. He looked at her. He hesitated, and then he said in a serious tone. I'll tell you, but it cannot be repeated. I must insist. You cannot tell anyone—ever.

My lips are sealed, angel love. Please go on. Yes, baby, talk to me. Don't be shy, she cooed, almost holding her breath. She didn't want to seem anxious. She knew she was close to something new and dark. This could be better than broom-closet fucking, she thought.

Jerry started telling his story in a deliberate and composed manner. It happened when I was at State, he said. And he scratched his chin. I remember the evening as if it was yesterday. I stayed outside in the yard to pick up the balls and bats that were left out and bring them back inside. I was alone. Not many people liked to bring back in the equipment so eagerly taken out. The moon was out, and it looked huge. It looked like a big yellow hardboiled egg. I kept looking at the moon and saying, Damn, that baby is sure out tonight. I was holding a basketball and other stuff in my arms, but my eyes were on the moon. Take me with you, baby, I kept saying. Take me with you. Then I saw this bluish light to my right, in the middle of the basketball court. I took my eyes off the moon and began checking out the weird blue light. It wasn't blinding, and I wasn't scared. As a matter of fact, I dropped the things I was holding and walked toward the light, instead of away from it. There was no noise, nothing but silence and blue light. As I came closer to the light, I noticed creature-like beings standing in front of the blue light. They seemed to summon me to come to them. I wasn't scared. I didn't think about the guards or calling for help or nothing. I just walked right up to the sphere of light, and I never felt any heat or fire. It was comfortable. I was in the sphere before I knew it, and the beings were in there with me. They weren't hostile or threatening. I couldn't say they were friendly either. The sphere was a space vehicle of some kind. At first, I thought it was the guards attempting to pull off a joke on me. I quickly realized they were too stupid to pull off anything like this. This was clever; this was high-IQ shit.

Jerry paused and pulled the sheet over his nakedness. He felt the privacy of his manhood suddenly becoming a priority. He studied Big Bertha and decided to continue with the story. He was certain that it wasn't what Big Bertha had expected to hear.

The inside of the vehicle was nice, Jerry continued. It was real cozy. It had padded chairs and a huge instrument panel that covered half the ship. The other half housed soft comfortable sitting areas with sofa-type furniture. But the creatures didn't sit in them. I sat on a chair right away because I needed a break to get my thoughts together, especially when I saw the earth below and the ship accelerating at a speed beyond any I had experienced before. But you know, Bertha, I still didn't panic. I wasn't scared. It was like I was going home or maybe someplace that felt like home. And then I stared at a big screen that projected the scene as if looking out a window of a fast-moving train or bus. I saw millions and millions of bright lights. They were stars, I guess. And then I realized that they were the souls of all the people that had died on Earth throughout the history of the planet. I mean all people, children, old men and women, not so old—you know what I'm saying, right? And this was the energy that kept…that kept the planet going. This was the life source of the planet. As soon as someone died, their soul traveled up to space and regenerated light, replenished it. And then it streamed back into a newborn infant. And that, Bertha, is why we sometimes feel that we know a certain person. But it's because that person has a particle of that life force that was here on Earth before. Get it, Bertha? Does it make any sense? You think I'm nuts? Tell me, and I'll stop. That was what was going through my mind and more.

No. No, Big Bertha insisted. Go on. But did the critters touch you? Did they…you know, want to experience your…candle? Talking of light, as it is.

No. I'm not sure, Jerry responded, a little put out but not surprised with the question. The critters, he continued. They brought out this contraption that resembled an X-ray device but not as cumbersome. They placed it in front of me but not too close. They turned on some lights on the device, and they could see through my body and examine every aspect, from the large to the small. But if my memory serves me right, they never physically touched me. I felt OK, Bertha. I wasn't thirsty or hungry. I wasn't tired or angry. To be honest, I felt great. But after a while, I did feel sleepy, and I crashed. I was awakened by a couple of fucking guards kicking on me. We were on the roof of the administration building, and the guards were pushing me around. They wanted to know how the fuck I had managed to get on the very top of the three-story building. I told them the truth: that I had no idea. I wanted to tell them that I was abducted by ET. But they'd probably just push me off the edge of the building, not wanting to deal with another psychiatric problem. So yeah, Bertha, the fuckers accused me of attempting to escape and put me in the hole for two months.

Was that all? Big Bertha asked. She was not sure how to ask. I mean…wasn't there any sex or any—

Jerry cut her off a little strong. Whatcha mean, is that all? Isn't that enough? I was in another world and in another dimension, in a time warp, and you asking is that all. No. He continued. He was still a little excited. There was no fucking—at least earth fucking, as we know it. Maybe the creatures had their own way of getting off; I was not aware of their method. I'm sorry to disappoint you, Bertha.

No. No. Please don't take it like that, Jerry baby. It's that, ah…I just care about them critters hurting you—that's all. Please believe me, OK.

As far as I know, they didn't hurt me, Jerry said. He calmed down. He wanted to see how his story had gone over with Big Bertha, who he had wanted to fuck since they were in the fourth grade.

Big Bertha moved to the end of the mattress and lit a cigarette. She kept her eyes on Jerry. She blew the smoke away from Jerry. She wasn't in the mood for a lecture on the evils of secondhand smoke. She was convinced the Big Boy was clever and could put together a good story.

Jerry was going to tell Big Bertha to put out the nasty thing. He figured it was what she expected. He didn't say a word and just let her smoke.

Big Bertha took a few more hits and drowned the half-smoked cigarette in an empty beer can. She knew what Jerry was thinking. The sheet still covered his privates and half of his muscular torso. Jerry's head was resting on a couple of pillows. His eyes were on her, as if she had materialized into one of the critters he claimed to have seen in the spaceship. Big Bertha was still naked. She moved next to Jerry and placed her hand on his arm. They said nothing. The only sound heard was that of a lone cricket and the tap-tap of a leaky faucet. It was getting a little nippy. Big Bertha didn't want to cover her body with anything, not yet. She relished staying naked next to a man; a hunk of a man like Jerry was her preference. Many times she had to settle for less but not tonight. Tonight was her night.

After what seemed like hours of silence, Big Bertha said, somewhat emotionally, but not to the point of throwing a fit, Jerry, sweetheart, aren't we the ugliest people ever? You and me.

Jerry looked at Big Bertha as if she had been given permission to express herself in the nuthouse. He was going to say, Speak for yourself, bitch. He said instead, We are the ugliest people in the whole world or close to it, baby. And if they started a contest to select the ugliest people, we would take first prize. Yes, we would and no doubt about it.

No, Jerry, Big Bertha asserted. She was not annoyed, but she was in a discerning mood that could go any which way. I don't mean ugly to win a contest. I mean ugly to pretend what we're not.

And what we are not are only characters in what we are supposed to be. We play the part to get by, Jerry said. Ugly is a presence felt by many people, as you know, angel cake. But its dominance has created a huge industry in beauty products. Everyone has a yearning to be someone else. And that someone else has to be more financially secure, and good looks are a must. And many times, with loads of cash, you can get away with ugly—

Jerry. Jerry. Please, interrupted Big Bertha. Don't get all philosophical on me. I have to think twice when you go all pinto on me. And then when I ask you to explain, you make a face.

Jerry sensed the humor in Big Bertha's words. She knew he didn't like to get upset, and he hadn't with her. And if he did get upset with her, there was no one to beat on, except Big Bertha. And Jerry didn't punch out women—that wasn't his thing. He'd rather make love to them. He needed to get Big Bertha off his back for now. It was too early to dismiss her like a babysitter and send her home. He had to rely on diplomacy; Big Bertha provided him with substantial assistance, and he didn't want to provoke her by suggesting he had an early day tomorrow. Or over a conversation that hadn't even made any sense. Big Bertha, Jerry believed, was taking advantage of her contribution that kept him in clean clothes and food in the fridge, besides other extras that made his life a little more comfortable. But it was normal, and this also Jerry believed, for humans to feel exulted when helping someone in need. In many cases, they begin to feel superior to that person, even if they are not. And their ideology had to be respected at all times. The battle of wills was on a seesaw. Big Bertha was set firmly on the ground, and Jerry was left hanging. His legs were not even close to solid terrain.

I'm sorry, honey, Jerry affirmed. He didn't know any other way to proceed. I think we should change the subject. We should drink another beer, listen to some music, and just relax. Whatcha you think, babe?

I'm all for it, Jerry, Big Bertha replied. She held back a smile. She said to herself, Don't fuck with me, Big Boy, or I'll cut the goodies—all of them. The beer and the music sound good. Then she placed her arm around Jerry's neck, in an uncomfortable position for Jerry, and said, her mouth close to his face, What sounds better, Jerry, is you on top of me, making your power plays.

Oh crap, thought Jerry. She wants more action. And he was about to zone out to his own universe, where no questions were asked. Now he was going to be forced to be creative. If he refused or made up a lame excuse, she could claim he didn't love her, and that conversation never ended in a draw.

CHAPTER 22

*T*he following day, Max Luna drove alone. It was around 2:30 in the p.m., and he was on Highway 26. He headed north. He left Las Flores behind like a mirage sculpted in the desert with wax and vanishing slowly under the hot sun. He was driving out to the Hideout, a nightclub built in the middle of nowhere. It was about seven miles north of Las Flores. It was far enough to escape city jurisdiction and close enough to conduct business in a nonintrusive location. The owners were numerous and changing all the time, as not to attract attention. The building was a huge monstrosity built with gray brick. And it stood alone in that desert environment, like an abandoned battleship in a sea of sand. There was a large sign on the roof with large letters that lit at night with neon lights, and they spelled out The Hideout in bright colors. And that was the only advertisement; nothing else existed to remind anybody that the Hideout was indeed open for business.

On his arrival, Max parked the truck in the large parking lot located in the back of the building. It was suitable for the more discreet visitor. He almost chuckled when he recalled that it was here, in this same parking lot, where an off-duty cop had busted Canary tailgating a young chick. But of course, he wasn't arrested. Canary had connections in city hall. The cop gave Canary a slap on the back and reminded him that the chick was underage. The Hideout was a place Max never had any reason to visit. It was too far out of the way, and the drinks were expensive. The Hideout, for all general purposes, had become an exclusive club patronized by people who had money to spend. And where men could bring their mistresses, girlfriends, and men friends, and women could do the same. And no one would consider it anything other than what it was. Max had only stopped by once or twice since he had returned to Las Flores. The only reason he was here on this early afternoon was because Billy Bob Cotton had insisted they meet here. And Billy Bob had sounded desperate over the phone. He pleaded that no other place would do. Besides, Billy Bob sounded like the voice on the phone who had called him early that morning. The same voice who had warned Max about the contract killer a couple of days before.

Max parked the truck next to Billy Bob's Caddy. He was surprised to see several parked cars in the lot, this early in the day. He entered through a back door that led to the tunnellike room known as the Cave. The Cave was darkness, by any definition. The lights were strictly regulated and kept to a minimum. And those were only to assist the waiter in finding your table and pushing the drinks. Max entered the Cave. He couldn't see a thing, even after he took off his shades. He just stood there and waited for his eyes to adjust. Then out from the darkness and almost in a whisper, his name was called. Max turned to the voice. He walked cautiously to where Billy Bob Cotton sat in a black leather booth. He motioned for Max to join him. Max slid into the leather-crusted booth large enough to sit a party of ten.

Sit, Max, Billy Bob said. I ordered you a whiskey; I hope you don't mind. We don't want the waiter to interrupt, and he will. Billy Bob expressed himself in a nervous tone, as when asking a hot call girl for the price of a good fuck and lacking the funds to cover it.

Whiskey's fine, responded Max. He wondered what the fuck he was doing here, drinking a whiskey with Billy Bob Cotton, a man he had maybe spoken to once in his life. What can I do for you, Mr. Cotton? Max asked after he took a hit from his glass of whiskey.

Please, Max. Call me Billy Bob, Billy Bob insisted. He didn't know Max but knew of him.

OK. Billy Bob. Tell me why we're here.

Billy Bob downed his whiskey with one gulp. He wiped his mouth with the back of his hand and attempted a smile. I...I was the one who warned you over the phone about the contract put out on you, he finally uttered.

There was the silence of an empty church in the dark, cavernous room. It seemed like they were the only ones in the room, but Max wasn't sure. He was unfamiliar with the configuration of the enormous room. Max waited. He was apprehensive but composed. He waited for Billy Bob to give him more information about the contract killer and the reason he was singled out.

It's a long and complicated story, Max. Billy Bob finally broke the silence. And I am ashamed to have anything to do with it. Here it is, all in its gory detail. It might be difficult for some people to buy. And I'm not doing it out of spite or jealousy, as some may speculate. I'm doing it to save my assets and the assets of my sister-in-law and her two children. You see, Max. And Billy Bob continued. He was fortified by the whiskey. My brother, Mike Cotton, proprietor of Cotton Construction, is involved in a sinister plot to distribute hard drugs out of Las Flores. And, and he believes you are one of the few who can actually stop him. He wants you out of the way and will pay big money to get it done.

Billy Bob, Max interrupted. He was more confused than alarmed. I have no idea what you're going on about. Why don't you slow down and start at the beginning, all right?

I apologize, Max, Billy Bob stated. He inched closer to Max. I jumped too far ahead of the sad and disgusting story. Let me back up a little. OK. You might not know this, Max. My late father, Earl, sold what was then the beginning of the Las Flores Airport to the city of Las Flores. All six hundred and fifty acres and for a very reasonable price. And he only asked that fifty acres remain in a family trust. And that my brother, Mike, be the main beneficiary. My father, before his demise, Max, asked Mike to pave a runway and construct some hangars on the property. Mike was already taking lessons for his pilot's license, and he planned to purchase a small plane or two. When my father realized how expensive it would be to develop the entire parcel from a small airport to a significant one, he had second thoughts. He approached the city council with the plan for a city airport and the sale of cheap land to build it on. And all he asked in return was the fifty acres and unlimited free family usage when completed. Oh, and one more thing, Max: Earl also wanted the airport to be named after him, but only if the citizens of Las Flores approved. And there is still contention between my brother and the city council over that.

Skip the politics, Billy Bob, Max almost cried out. He did not want to bother with the whole bloody war between Mike Cotton and the city council. Get to the point. I don't know about you, but I'm on the clock.

I took the day off. Billy Bob shrugged, and he took another hit of whiskey.

Max couldn't say if it was indifference or distrust that Billy Bob felt working for his brother, Mike Cotton. Or just an I-don't-give-a-fuck attitude. Don't rub it in, Max said. He refused to have a discussion on the subject. And how do you know all this shit about your brother? Max asked. When you claim to be distant from all the shit your brother is mixed in.

I bugged his phone, Billy Bob responded without hesitation. His eyes glowed in the dim light. He stared at Max with the intensity of a mongoose ready to jump on a deadly cobra. I had to put the bug in the phone of the work trailer parked at the construction site, Billy Bob bragged. A smugness manifested all over his flushed, fat face. I was going to put the bug in his office phone at his house, but Mike is a power freak. When you visit his house, he must know exactly where you are and what you're doing. If you wander off to another part of the huge house, Mike will find you and ask you quick and to the point if you're lost or just exploring the premises. I could never get close to his office. I had to settle for the work trailer. But as it turned out, it was on the trailer phone where most of the planning about buying and selling drugs was talked about— and other things, such as hiring assassins.

Why are you telling me all this? Max asked. He wanted the conversation to end. He was worried about his mother and the drive back to Las Flores in a truck low on gas.

Billy Bob pulled a bottle of Irish whiskey from under the table. He filled his glass and offered Max a hit. Max placed his hand over his glass. Billy Bob had sneaked in the bottle, as he always did. He paid for one drink and used the same glass. He asked only for ice when the waiter approached. He placed the half-empty bottle back under the table. He downed half the glass with one gulp. And after he took in some air, he said, I want to save your life, Max. I want to keep you from harm; my brother wants you out of the way. He believes you will disrupt his operation. As I mentioned before, he believes you are one of the few who can stop him. He wants you dead. And if not dead, incapacitated. The sooner, the better.

There was a restrained silence in the dark cavern. The two men, different in so many ways of observing the world, eventually had to agree or attempt to settle on a solution to remedy the menace that threatened them. They stared at each other like barn owls searching the night for the elusive mouse. The only sound was made by Billy Bob sloshing the melting ice in his whiskey glass. That was the only sound that reminded them that they belonged in the world of men and not in the shadowy existence of a world without light, where darkness ruled supreme. And Billy Bob needed Max in the light, at least for now. He understood that he had thrown a ton of bricks on top of Max. And there was still a ton of granite coming on top of that. The weight might be too much for the young man to take. Before Billy Bob spoke of things no one wanted to hear, Max, exasperated, broke the silence.

Why does your brother want to fuck with me? Max almost shouted. I have never negotiated any business with your fucked-up brother, never. How can I stop his dirty operation? I'm not a cop, and I don't command a fucking army. And what can I do to hamper his corrupt transactions? And why didn't you call the cops on your fucked-up brother? You had all the relevant info for a big bust and maybe even to save me from all this bullshit. I just don't get it, Billy Bob, Max concluded. He was dejected but helpless to do anything about the situation. The only thing he could do at this point was place his hand around his empty glass and squeeze and pretend it was Mike Cotton's neck.

I know. I know. Billy Bob pleaded with Max before Max ran out the door in a huff, and he had the opportunity to break the bad news to him. You can't imagine how many times I held the phone in my hands. I was ready to make that call, Max. And take the cops to the hangars where he hides the dope. Then I thought about my sister-in-law, Claire, and her two children. You see, Max, the cops here aren't the brightest, as you well know; they eventually would have called in the DEA. And even at the risk of splitting the company assets and all other possessions of value, leaving Claire and the children destitute. Listen, Max, please. And Billy Bob wanted to hold Max's hand. He wasn't sure if that was the right thing to do with Max. My brother is an evil man. And he has done a lot of evil to get his way, but this time he has gone a bit too far. He has contracted another lowlife. Another professional assassin, and this time from the East Coast, to kill you and anyone who gets in his way.

Max slammed his right hand on the table so hard that his empty glass tumbled over and rolled to the carpeted floor. Goddamn, fucking shit, he cried out. And this time he was unable to control his temper. And when is this motherfucking sicario coming into town?

Bad news, Max, Billy Bob said. He sucked on some ice. He was afraid Max might blame him and turn the meeting into a violent confrontation. Billy Bob didn't know Max personally, but he knew of his unpredictable temper and the brutality he used to deal with the opposition. Billy Bob spit the ice back into his glass. He didn't want to take any chances of the conversation ending in a complete misunderstanding and him not accomplishing what he came here to accomplish. The sicario checked in last night, Billy Bob continued. He utilized Max's Spanish noun for assassin. He is staying at the Palace, that seedy motel on Alameda Street in the Westside.

And when were you going to tell me, Billy Bob, next fucking week? Max screamed at Billy Bob. He sprang from the table. He wanted to grab Billy Bob by the throat and throttle the bastard. He calmed down instead and sat as before. He did not want to go off on Billy Bob. There might be more vital information coming, and it would not be communicated well if Billy Bob's teeth and blood were decorating the table.

Billy Bob had arrived at the same conclusion. He stretched his fat neck and attempted to calculate the distance to the front bar, in case he needed assistance from that quarter. And even though Billy Bob had dealt successfully with erratic behavior from his brother, this was Max Luna, a man not known for his gentle nature.

No, Max. Please listen, Billy Bob pleaded. He attempted to talk his way out because his fists had always failed to rescue him from any compromising situation. The sicario, and Billy Bob used the Spanish word again. He liked the sound of most words in Spanish. This one fascinated him, except the meaning. I was going to tell you today, Max. I promise. If you refused to meet with me here, I was going to tell you over the phone. Please, Max, believe me. The sicario will need two or three days to study the town and lay out his plan of action. He's not going to rush the operation and risk fucking up, like the last clown did. And I'm sorry that I have to be the one to break the bad news, Max; there ain't no one else.

You did good, Billy Bob, Max said. His heartbeat regained its regular tempo. Anything else you want to add to this dangerous charade? Tell me now and not later. Max needed to know. He was already conceiving a plan of attack for the faceless intruder. Max jumped to his feet. Before he exited the dark cave, he said, If anyone close to me is harmed by this motherfucker, Billy Bob, blood will flow in Las Flores. And your brother, Mike Cotton, will be the first to bleed.

That's all I ask for, Billy Bob whispered to himself. He raised his hand to shake with Max, but Max was already out the door.

Max sped away from the Hideout like a hit-and-run driver after a fatal accident. He headed North back to Las Flores on Highway 26. He was concerned about Jerry, Ruth, William, and his mother in Las Flores. He was worried, not knowing what was going on in Las Flores, and anxious about a contract killer on the prowl. Seven miles around Las Flores was nothing, Max reflected. On this isolated desert road, it was an eternity. He kept looking at his watch and speedometer. He slowed the old truck to seventy-five from ninety-five. He knew that if he hit a hole or a tire blew, the truck could flip over. And then he'd find himself in deep shit. Besides, the truck was low on gas, and he had to make it to Las Flores. Once in town he could hitch a ride to the center. If the truck ran out of gas between the Hideout and Las Flores…good luck—he'd be fucked.

Max continued to drive on Highway 26 as fast as he dared. The dry, brown desert landscape was a monotonous blur and shot by like an out-of-whack newsreel from the fifties. It wasn't an ugly landscape by any means, if one appreciated the desert scene. But now was not the time for him to indulge in nature's spectacle. His mind was occupied with matters of survival, and the time was ticking away. It was already 3:30 p.m., and his anger returned. He had to involve his two friends in a dangerous mission again. He wasn't as worried about Jerry as he was about William. If something happened to William, Ruth would never forgive him, and he couldn't live with that. Besides, he knew he was even more vulnerable because of his mother. His mother refused to stay with anyone else and was always alone in the house. And for the first time, Max doubted the wisdom of returning to Las Flores to live. And he wanted to scream and scream loud, but he wasn't sure at whom or at what.

Max calmed down some. He realized that screaming wouldn't get him jack. He thought of calling in the cops. He knew if the assassin was arrested, he would be out on bail in twenty-four hours. He would insist he was only a tourist on his way north. He could ask Tiny Tim for a couple of his shooters, but the Snipers could muck everything up and even shoot the wrong person. Besides, the Snipers were not allowed in the Westside after midnight. That was an unwritten law, and it kept the cops out of Chiva Town unless there was an emergency. Fuck it! Max yelled. It has to be me and my boys! And he pushed the truck to its limits racing home. His present was already compromised and his future sold to the highest bidder.

When Max was meeting with Billy Bob Cotton at the Hideout, Jerry Rivera was alone at the center. He was paid a surprise visit by Mike Cotton. Jerry was hitting the heavy bag with serious power and with a focus that put all his effort and thoughts behind the deadly punches. Every punch directed at the bag was a futile attempt to dissipate the frustration that still ate at him from the night he'd spent with Big Bertha. It was a feeling he couldn't understand. A feeling of deep despair that he couldn't shake until he punched the bag with a fury that knew no bounds. The brutal attack with both hands on the bag would drop most men to the dust. Jerry couldn't put an image or an action behind the rage to give him some motive for his outburst of tearing up the leather bag with his fists. He was at this point of mental chaos when he heard a loud hello that echoed throughout the vast building. Jerry said, Fuck. He wasn't finished exorcising the demons that were encroaching at will in his private domain. Besides, he was in no mood to deal with a parent or any other shit to do with center business.

Jerry finally turned his tensed, sweating, muscular body to face the intruder. His tank top was soaked and his gloved hands hot and bruised from the relentless pounding of the bag. Mike Cotton faced him. He looked like a man who waited to enter the confessional after years of abstaining. Jerry knew who he was without ever having seen him before. This is it, he thought. Big Mike Cotton had come to claim what was his, in the eyes of God and the law. The fucker couldn't have come at a more opportune time, and Jerry almost smiled. Mike Cotton, in Jerry's eyes, was big and solid. He was almost as big as Max but older. If the son of a bitch mentioned Claire, Jerry was going to bloody him. He was going to give him a booty slasher and kick his ass out into the alley, like he did that other asshole not that long ago.

Mike Cotton was speechless. The last time he had lain eyes on Jerry, he'd resembled a starving wolf. A young wolf locked up behind barbwire and concrete, his liberty taken away by men who preferred tyranny over freedom. Mike Cotton was stunned by how Jerry had matured into a man of steel, muscular and savage looking. Jerry reminded Mike Cotton of when he was Jerry's age. He also had been a bodybuilder, although never as cut.

Jerry? Jerry Rivera? Mike Cotton inquired, his voice in a high pitch.

Who's asking? Jerry responded. He already knew the answer.

Allow me to introduce myself. I am Mike Cotton, the director of Christian Charities, the organization that was instrumental in securing your release from incarceration. We provided your late mother, may she rest in peace, the transportation, room, and board, to make her visits to Santa Fe a little more stress-free. I'm not bragging, Jerry. That is only one function of our charity. We help people, people in need. We just don't preach about it, as others do. I do apologize for not being able to get you here for your mother's funeral. You were in the hole at the time, and the warden insisted on no exceptions.

I will be forever grateful, Jerry responded. And if you are the director of the charity, as you claim you are, then accept my wholehearted thanks. But I'm more than sure that you're not here to get my thanks in person, Jerry added. He was still calm and collected.

His rage had lessened by a few degrees.

No. No, Jerry! Mike Cotton exclaimed. He was already on the defensive and not even close to the reason for the unannounced visit. No, Jerry, Mike Cotton repeated. I came with something else in mind. Be assured of that. I introduced myself as the director of Christian Charities and told you what Christian Charities did for you to see me on your side, Jerry. I'm here on your behalf. I'm here to offer you a full-time position that will provide you with a comfortable living and a secure future.

Thank you, Mr. Cotton, for your consideration. I don't do construction, Jerry replied. He was already bored and pissed with Mike Cotton for intruding and preventing him doing his cooldown routine.

Please, Jerry, call me Mike. And Mike Cotton attempted a smile. The position is not in construction, Mike Cotton continued. He was disappointed that Jerry refused to work for him, even now. You know, Jerry, I had a job waiting for you in my company. You chose to work here at the center with your friend, Max Luna. That was the main stipulation of your parole—that you had suitable employment at the ready once out.

And included in that stipulation was that if several job offers existed, it was my option to select the one that suited my interests. And my interests were here at the center and still are.

Of course, Jerry; I meant no disrespect. That was your choice, and I value your selection of employment. We at Christian Charities were also influential in securing the release of John Slaughter. He joined my company, Cotton Construction, upon his release from State.

Yes. I'm aware that Mr. John Slaughter was employed by you. Until he decided to crawl, once again, on the dragon's back.

Well, that's true, uttered Mike Cotton. He turned red and hated it. We let him go. We had to, for his own good as well as ours. But listen, Jerry, I'm not here to discuss the weaknesses of John Slaughter or to offer you a job in my company. I'm here to ask for your help. Yes, that's right, Jerry; I need your help. But before I go on, is there someplace a little more private where we can discuss this? And Mike Cotton turned his big head to the right and left. He wanted a more secluded place to talk.

It can't get more private than this, Jerry answered. He tried not to smile. He wasn't going to invite the stranger into Max's office. Jerry needed space to maneuver in case the shit face started any funny business. We are the only ones here, Jerry said. If someone enters the building, we can see them from here. Jerry kept his gloves on.

How about my wife's office? No. On second thought, forget it, Jerry. She won't appreciate it, if she ever finds out.

I'm telling you, Mr. Mike; this is the best place. And you best get on with it. The children and the college volunteers will show up in an hour or less.

You're right, Jerry, Mike Cotton said. He looked around to make sure they were alone. I am going to build a private prison for hardcore offenders with my own money. It will be built outside Las Flores, near Snake Town and Santa Maria. I'm negotiating to purchase five hundred acres in that location. And Snake Town and Santa Maria are included in the parcel. It's a perfect area for a prison because it's close to Las Flores but not too close.

OK, Jerry said. He was not moved by the news. You're going to build a prison. Why do I have to know about it?

No. Listen, Jerry. Mike Cotton licked his lips. I want you to run the prison, as warden or as head of security—your choice.

Jerry couldn't make up his mind whether to laugh or get back to thrashing the heavy bag. Not able to contain himself, he asked. What makes you so sure I have the know-how to run a prison? Or would care to take on that kind of responsibility?

You would be perfect for the job, Jerry, in all honesty. You…You… Mike Cotton said, hesitating. He wanted to say, Because you're a pinto, after all, but he didn't. Mike Cotton didn't want to upset the young gladiator at the early stages of the conversation. So instead he said, You are blessed with the intelligence and the drive to accomplish anything you set your mind on. And besides, you have the experience to deal with incarcerated men, Jerry. And that's a great advantage for the position I'm offering you.

And why would you consider me for this prestigious position? What's the catch? Do you want me to kill somebody, is that it?

No. No. It's nothing like that. Mike Cotton responded, and he turned red again. The boy is clever or fishing, he thought. Remember I mentioned I needed your help? And Mike Cotton inched closer to Jerry. He was almost whispering.

What kind of help would you need from me, Mr. Mike? And Jerry stepped back away from Mike Cotton. Mike Cotton's breath was pretty potent. I told you. I don't do construction, Jerry added. He hoped Mike Cotton wouldn't inch close again.

Let me start from the beginning, Jerry. That way there won't be any misunderstandings later, all right? It started when my mother, may she live with the angels in heaven, was murdered in the high mesa. An Okie by the name of Wayne Cruthers was arrested for the murder. He was convicted on a first-degree manslaughter charge, on a plea. He might get out anytime soon. What I need from you, Jerry, and please don't cut me off until I finish, OK? This man, Cruthers, is in the pen in Santa Fe. He is doing time as we speak. He is locked up in cell block two, my sources assure me. I'm sure you know where it is, Jerry…no offense. I will find out exactly where the snake is housed before you go in. Cruthers has to die, Jerry, and I will claim responsibility for his death. I will avenge the death of my mother. And Mike Cotton's face changed color and, it seemed to Jerry, even texture. He had the fire of a born-again Christian who had just had a serious conversation with Jesus Christ. You will be my instrument, Jerry, Mike Cotton continued. He was going to say brother Jerry, but Mike Cotton wasn't sure how close Jerry was to Jesus. You will go and slay the serpent, and Satan will provide him with permanent quarters in hell. Then Mike Cotton raised his eyes and arms to the ceiling and stared at space without saying a word.

And how am I to accomplish this feat? Jerry interrupted. He was concerned with the transformation of Mike Cotton from a bland businessman to a fanatic with a religious side. Jerry realized the man was serious, in a crazy way.

Mike Cotton snapped out of his trance. He was worried that he had lost Jerry. The murder of his mother still provoked in him deep feelings of despair. I apologize, Jerry, Mike Cotton said, himself again. It was my mother, Jerry. And she cries from heaven for me to avenge her death. And I must do it. No, I correct myself, Jerry. You will do it for me. You will enter the building where that serpent sleeps. The pilot lights for the gas heaters will be off. All you have to do is release the deadly gas and then leave. Sometime in the early morning, a criminal in the den of thieves will light up a cigarette. The guards have reported this to me. And before they smell the deadly gas, the explosion and fire will turn Wayne Cruthers into ashes.

And you think it's that easy? To walk into a state prison and blow up anything or anyone, Mr. Mike? Jerry asked. He was not sure why he was still involved in the conversation with the madman.

No, Jerry, of course not. The plan is all worked out. And the right people paid and all. You will walk in through the back door. You know the door that's on the far northwest side of the pen? Then you will find your way to the cellblock of that cockroach. The grills will be open, and the guards on the graveyard shift are few in number. And they know enough to leave the target area. It will be well after midnight in the middle of the week, and the cons will be sleeping like babies. You just release the gas as I instructed you. The pilot lights will be turned off. And the first con who lights up early in the morning will spark the explosion. The damage will be contained to that complex, and the fire will be put out soon after. And then, Jerry, and then I will build the private prison close to Las Flores. A private institution to house criminals of the worst kind. The state and even the feds will pay top dollar to house that level of lawbreakers. You can run the new prison, Jerry, if you like. Or head security—that is up to you. But you'll be perfect for either job. And of that, I'm more than sure.

As sure as you are of torching the state prison and getting away with it? Jerry asked. He was losing his patience but stayed calm. And by the way, what made you so goddamned certain I was willing to go along with your insane plan? You think I was going to settle for a fucking job based on a pipe dream? You ain't gonna build nothing, mister. You'll end up locked up in that same prison you want to destroy if you keep fucking around with such dangerous ideas. And what if I was stupid enough to go along and somehow pull off your ridiculous plan? What about the innocent men that would burn to death in that inferno after the explosion?

What about them, Jerry? Forgive me for not being sympathetic, Mike Cotton responded. And he twisted his mouth in disdain. The men you refer to as innocent are nothing but toilet scum. They are criminals of the worst kind. They are not Boy Scouts applauded for their good deeds, as you well know. Society will not mourn them, and the taxpayers will be more than pleased.

Jerry closed his gloved right fist. Time to put this motherfucker away, he thought. You best leave, mister. The children will be here any minute, and they are an inquisitive bunch, he said. He was still as calm as ever.

Oh! All right, Jerry. No, I mean. And Mike Cotton began to backpedal toward the door. He had sensed he had overstayed his welcome. I didn't expect an answer today, Jerry. I realize it can be a tough choice. No. Hey, take all the time you need.

Jerry wanted to laugh out loud. He wasn't sure if the businessman was being clever or just showing his ignorance. Either way, Mike Cotton had to leave—and leave pronto—before Jerry violated his parole by sending the big man to the hospital on a stretcher. And then Carlos Miranda would haul his ass off to jail. He'll make a hell of a mayor, Jerry said to no one in particular, as Mike Cotton almost ran out of the building to his truck. He wanted to avoid his wife, Claire, and having to explain to her why he was at the center.

CHAPTER 23

Max, Jerry, and William sat in Max's office with the door shut. Max had just shared what Billy Bob Cotton had dropped on him at the Hideout not more than an hour before. Naturally, the three musketeers were in a dark mood. A mood as dark as Mike Cotton's heart. And Jerry didn't even start the conversation he had with Mike Cotton. It made more sense to him now. He was going to wait and tell Max later. Max was under a lot of strain, as it was. The conversation at hand demanded their undivided attention, without any unnecessary distractions.

As far as we know, the sicario probably checked in last night, Max said. He's staying at the Palace Motel on the Westside. It's not in the swanky part of town, but it's still the Westside. And any loud commotion will bring out the best of Las Flores PD, flying in with weapons at the ready—

I know the Palace, William interrupted. He was all excited, like he was bragging about getting his first blow job in the back seat of his dad's car at the drive-in theater. Julio is the name of the vato who runs the Palace. Remember Jenny Melon? She cleans the rooms and shacks up with Julio after work. Julio has a bedroom behind the main office. After midnight, they go to bed and sleep tight. I know because I used to sneak into the office. I grabbed a key to a room and used the room for a couple of hours. When I returned the key, I could hear Julio and Jenny Melon snoring the night away. And probably after a good fuck. Jenny still has a good-looking ass on her.

OK, William. We get the picture, Max said. He didn't want William to narrate Jenny Melon's personal and social life. Where does your friend Julio keep the keys to the rooms?

William wanted to laugh at Max mentioning Julio as a friend. They needed some humor to carry the day, bad as it was.

As you walk into the office, Max—and the door won't be locked, of that I'm sure—the key box will be hanging on the wall to your left behind the counter, like in a million other sleazy motels around the country. The keys of the occupied rooms are kept in the top drawer of the desk behind the counter.

I'll go and grab the key to the room, Max said. And I'll meet you guys back outside the room. Your buddy Julio might recognize you, William, and that could be a problem. And I know Jenny Melon is on your caseload. I hope you didn't fuck her. That would be unethical.

This is not exactly the right time or place to discuss ethics, Max. And no, I didn't fuck her. I'm still on my honeymoon—

Your story about tonight straight with Ruth, William? Max interrupted. He realized he was wrong to put William on the spot. We may be out late and stay out. Max wanted to say, he knew the danger he was putting his friends through again.

Ruth was OK with William's night out with the boys because all they usually did was drink some beers, shoot hoops, and talk. Ruth also took advantage of that time to meet with friends and family, mostly family. She could expect William late on any of those given nights without worrying too much. Max was on the phone on the hour to check on his mother, Victoria, those nights. They weren't that numerous, but at times they were necessary to release energy that needed releasing.

It was after midnight when Max parked the truck in the vacant lot William had pointed out. The lot was in the back of the Palace Motel, and a six-foot-high chain-link fence fronted the hotel property in the back and sides. A small section of the fence was missing. It was large enough for anyone to access the property. Thick shrubs, as tall as the fence on the motel side, also had a path cut through them. The three men, after making sure they had everything they needed, walked through the path in the shrubs as quietly as the circumstances permitted. They knew the room number where the sicario was staying. They had come to take care of business. They wanted to believe it was the last time. Killing was not a thrill to them, not anymore. It had become more telling on their personalities than they had ever expected. Max wanted little noise, and less noise it had to be. And that made the job more on the difficult side.

A couple of yards from room 126, where the killer was staying, Max gestured to Jerry and William with his hand. He was going for the key to the room and wanted them to stay put until he returned. Jerry, with the metal pipe in his right hand and a nylon rope six feet in length in his left, felt uneasy. He held the pipe next to his right leg. He felt it was too visible. He shifted to his left side, away from the door of room 126. Then he felt the rope could be seen, even though the light from the light pole a short distance away wasn't that bright. He stood behind William, who gave him a look and inched closer to the door of room 126.

Max felt the cold chill of the early November morning on his nose as he made his way to the motel office. A cold wind blew in from the north. He always felt the cold on his nose and then the rest of his body. He attempted to detect the odor of smoke from the metal drum barrels used by the young and homeless to stay warm or bullshit the time away. Then he recalled that in the Westside, that was a good enough reason to call the police. The citizens believed that people who stayed up all hours of the night feeding a fire outdoors were up to no good. On the Eastside, no one gave a fuck, and some neighbors even joined the fun. When the wood burned out, the folks burned old tires. The brothers did not care about the noxious fumes—as long as it burned, it was OK.

As Max approached the door to the motel's office, he wanted to believe William that access to the room key was easy, a piece of cake. But nothing was ever easy, he believed—maybe to others, but never to him. Max didn't see any blaring lights advertising the existence of the motel. That usually meant to Max that the motel was doing well with the steady clientele of pleasure seekers and needed little help from the occasional visitor who somehow decided to park it in Las Flores. It worked out better for Max this way. He didn't need all that light. Max wasn't a praying man, but he prayed William was right about the key's location. He'd hate to wake up Julio and his squeeze, Jenny Melon. That could get messy. He wasn't in the mood to carry on a discussion of any kind with anyone. He could imagine William, hard as steel. He would sneak into the motel office and grab a key to a room while Ruth waited outside for him, wet and ready with anticipation. William and Ruth never ceased to amaze him, and that was why he liked them so much.

They were good people. And he could trust them, along with Jerry.

Max opened the unlocked front door of the motel office very gently. He expected a bell to announce his presence. There were no bells or chimes. Nothing but a lighted office and empty of any human smell. Max turned to his left on entering the office and noticed the box of keys hanging on the wall behind the counter, just as William had described it. He walked around the counter and opened the top desk drawer for the room key. Slow night, he thought. There were only two keys in the drawer: one for room 126, and the other didn't matter. Max took the key for room 126 from the drawer and looked around the office to see if there were any witnesses. Satisfied there were none, he walked out of the office as quietly as he had entered.

Jerry and William waited patiently outside room 126. William inched closer to the door. He turned the doorknob slowly. The door opened. He was surprised, and his heart beat rapidly. William gestured to Jerry with his left hand to follow him inside the room. He carefully opened the door wide enough to gain entrance and tiptoed into the room.

Fuck, Jerry whispered. Max is not going to like this. He had no choice but to follow William into the musty room.

Jerry and William entered room 126. They were scared of even breathing too loud and waking the beast within. They closed the door behind them as quietly as possible. It was not completely dark inside the room. The curtains on the window facing the parking lot were slightly cracked in the middle. A dim light entered the room, and the darkness was ruptured by the sliver of light, which created a thin vertical line across the middle of the bed. It revealed in the gloomy, shadowy light a naked, luminous creature in the shape of a sleeping man. The man slept on his back. His feet faced the door, and he was clean-shaven from his chin to the nape of his burly neck. His large, disproportionate gut swelled out even more, it seemed, in the shadowy light. The big-gutted man was bone white and smooth skinned. Jerry figured the freak was over six feet tall and close to three hundred pounds, if not more, and not all muscle. Thank God, thought Jerry. It would probably be hard enough to bring down the hippo as it was. More muscle would only complicate things more. Jerry noticed the night-stand next to the headboard, and in the murky light, he recognized the cornucopia of legal and illegal drugs and evidence of using.

Jerry had gone to the left and William to the right side of the bed upon entering the room. Jerry decided not to wait any longer for Max. The water buffalo was medicated. And now was the time to jump him and not take the chance he would reach for a gun and hurt somebody. Jerry placed the metal pipe on the floor next to him. He slowly laced the loop of the nylon rope through the big, stinking left foot of the brute, all the way to his ankle. He was going to slip the rope around the opposite foot and bind his feet in case the killer attempted to stand up. If he did, he would tumble to the floor like a heap of rubble. The rope going over the foot must have tickled the sicario. The roaring, opened mouth twisted into a grotesque smile. He attempted to turn over on his side, to the right side of the bed. Jerry panicked and tried to tie the loose end of the rope to the foot of the bed before the sicario figured out what was going on.

William was on the right side of the bed and couldn't believe his eyes. The size of the naked man was beyond anything he had ever seen. His gut was like a mountain of white Jell-O. He was hairless as a salamander and probably as slimy. The thought raced through William's mind. He pulled out a six-inch fishing knife he used to gut large river fish. The plan was to jab the vato in the eyes and blind him, so the killer couldn't see where the blows were coming from. The mountain of jiggling Jell-O attempted to turn to William's side, and William almost shit himself.

Jerry, Jerry, he whimpered. His eyes opened wide, and fear whipped his mind. He held the fish knife in his right hand, but he couldn't decide what to do with it.

Jerry secured the loose end of the rope as best as he could to the foot of the bed. He knew the assassin would feel the pull of the rope around his left ankle and wake up in a nasty mood. As the killer made the attempt to turn onto his side, the rope held his leg, and the demonic grin on the assassin's grotesque mouth turned to a howling sneer. The bloodshot animal eyes struggled to focus on William. His chemical-fueled brain couldn't register any danger. And the confusion gave Jerry the extra seconds he needed to pick up the metal pipe with his right hand and crash it hard on the upper left ear of the brute when he turned his clean-shaven head to face William. The assassin screeched out loud in pain, like a coyote caught in a metal bear trap. The ape turned to face Jerry and at the same time attempted to get up. His left leg refused to budge, even when he pulled with all his might. The nylon rope dug deeper into his ankle. He kept squealing and pulling to free his leg, and that gave Jerry the precious time to wrap both hands around the metal pipe. He held it like a baseball bat. He was ready to knock a fast ball out of the park. When the confused butterball looked up, he flailed his arms at Jerry. It was a feeble attempt to protect himself. He struggled to see who was trying to scramble his brains. Jerry came in full force with the metal pipe and caught the shrieking, foul-smelling jackal right on the forehead. Jerry felt the impact through his gloved hand up to his wrists. But the tub of lard still didn't go down to stay.

William found his courage. Now that Jerry was involved, he jumped on the bed with the sharp knife in his hand, like a Navy Seal. He aimed for the eyes. The killer shifted his head, and the knife sank deep into his left ear. William slashed down with the knife. He did major damage to the inner ear. Blood gushed out like water from a ruptured water hydrant and then oozed down the damaged ear like a reluctant waterfall. The blood trickled down the fat body of the assassin and all over the bed. The assassin screamed louder and grabbed for William. He was blinded by the blood and blows from Jerry's metal pipe. He managed to grab William by the right ankle and pulled. William fell back, and his head hit the floor. His legs and lower back remained on the blood-soaked bed. The knife flew out of his hand toward the floor, next to the wall. He screamed at Jerry to free him from the fucking, bleeding beast. Jerry jumped on top of the bed and hit the killer across the nose. And another splatter of blood erupted from where the nose used to function. The killer still didn't go down. The killer held William tight with his right hand. He attempted to pull him up the bed. He used his left hand to fend off Jerry and the metal pipe. He was blinded with his own blood in both eyes and roped to the bed, like a hog being slaughtered for Christmas tamales.

As Max left the motel office with the key in his hand, he was glad it had been so easy to take. Then he heard the sound of a dying animal coming from room 126. Fuck, he said. So much for the noise factor. He ran full speed to the room. He pushed the door open and entered. Max saw in the murky light a scene painted by a mad artist who had used human blood to illustrate the carnage and mayhem humans can inflict on one another. There was blood all over the bed and walls of the room. Jerry was bloodied like an amateur butcher on his first day on the job. He was on top of the bed. He was bashing a shapeless object covered in blood with the metal pipe. William was on his back. He was screaming at Jerry to get the motherfucker off him. The bloodied, wounded assassin held William by the ankle and was jerking him up toward him. Max, seeing no other way out, pulled a .357 Magnum revolver loaded with hollow-point bullets from his back pocket. He jumped on the bed and placed his knees on top of the killer's legs. He told Jerry to step aside. He held the gun with both hands. He inched up to the unrecognizable face and pumped a bullet through the big head. Blood, brains, bone, and other matter that the skull holds intact tore out the back of the head and plastered the headboard of the bed and the wall behind the bed.

Let's go—go, Max persisted. He jumped off the bloody bed and attempted to regroup his men. Jerry tried to take the rope off the dead man's ankle. Leave it, Jerry! Let's get out of here; c'mon—move it. William, you're free now; move out. William tried to stand up and fell on his ass. His face was contorted with pain, and his ankle was not able to support his weight. Jerry ran over. He handed Max the metal pipe smeared with blood and picked up William in his arms, as one does a child, and raced out of the room to the truck. My knife, William managed to shout at Max. Jerry dashed through the parking lot, and William hung on for fear of Jerry falling on the cold, dirty lot and plummeting on top of him. Shit, Max said out loud. Then he saw the knife on the floor, bloodied to the hilt. He picked it up and ran after his two friends. They all made it to the truck without incident. Jerry helped William into the truck, then got in. He closed the door without making a sound. Max jumped in behind the steering wheel. He placed the bloody pipe, knife, and pistol under the seat.

Max, Jerry, and William drove in silence in the early, chilly November morning. Each was lost in his own scary thoughts. Max drove slow, but not too slow. He drove north on Main Street, toward downtown. They were still on the Westside of town. The sun was behind the Turquoise Mountains.

The weak rays were escaping the mountains' hold, providing the sleeping sky with a tinge of muted pink and gold. The early desert light appeared in slanted segments, and every segment seemed to emit a distinctive light that created a panorama of color. They were not as deeply colored as a sunset. It was a softer light that made it difficult for the early riser to jump out of bed. Max drove in that magical dawn light and felt like driving forever and ever and leaving the melodrama of his life behind. But he knew that realistically it was impossible. The sky was getting a brighter gold, and the whitish pink was taking on a purplish red, almost crimson. The mountain could no longer refuse the mighty sun its entrance with its explosion of blazing light, a huge ball of fire rising from the east that proclaimed its dominance over all living things. The daylight was approaching, and it was clear to Max that exposure was more likely.

Max broke the silence that smothered the three brothers like an uninvited visitor. He asked William about his ankle. William responded. He was embarrassed by the fact that he hadn't fought hard enough to break the hold the son of a bitch had on his ankle. And worse, William deliberated, was that he'd lost the knife. It had slipped through his hand like a wet noodle. And in times of war, that was considered a sin. Jerry didn't say anything. He was alarmed the assassin hadn't stayed down with all the blows to the head he'd delivered to the faceless monster. Jerry began to consider the idea he was losing his power. And that somehow his power had abandoned him, without warning. He couldn't stop thinking about it. And wanted to know—but not really—if Max and William had noticed. He had seen it happen before, in prison. A pinto lost his power and then his balls. And that was it; he was easy prey for the predators.

OK, guys, Max said. This is what we must do if a copper stops us. If it's one cop, and he demands answers about the blood and wants us on the curb, I might have to shoot him. I mean shoot him dead, and let's keep our fingers crossed the fellow will not be from the Eastside, or worse, someone we know. But we cannot allow any witnesses to ID us later in a trial, in case it gets that far.

Can't we just say we were deer hunting? William said. He considered the ramifications of killing a cop.

Yeah, added Jerry. We can say we brought down a giant moose, gutted it, and left the meat for the vultures and coyotes.

No, William, Max attempted to clarify, without sarcasm. We are not equipped for hunting—not game, anyway. A copper will see that right away and sit us on the curb. And maybe he will cuff us while he searches the truck. If it's more than one cop, I'll make a run for it. And after I lose them in the Eastside, I'll drop you two off. I'll switch trucks, come back, and pick you guys up. Stay in one place, if at all possible. Jerry, you'll look after William—you know, his ankle and all.

That goes without saying, Max, Jerry replied. He was in a better mood. I'll take care of the little brother. He showed a lot of balls slashing at the tub of lard, in that fucking dump of a room of the world-famous Palace Motel.

Hey! Hey! Max agreed. Look at that. And he almost shouted, We're out of the fucking Westside and in downtown. Max relaxed as he drove in more familiar turf. The traffic picked up as the early city workers reported to work. Max and his comrades blended in with the other men, mostly Latinos who worked on the crews that collected the trash and other jobs that required physical labor, dependability, and early rising. Many of the men also drove pickups of every make and model, some with their elbow out the window, holding a cup of coffee in one hand, allowing the chilly morning air to wake them up for the long day ahead.

Max breathed easier, as did Jerry and William. From Main Street Max made a right on Church Street and proceeded east. He passed the railroad tracks and left the busy downtown early traffic behind. Max drove east on Church until he reached Calle de los Angeles. On Calle de los Angeles, he made a right and drove south. Then he cut a left onto Santa Teresa Street and drove east. Santa Teresa would take them straight to the center.

Max and his crew finally arrived at the center. They were weary as hell. And every car on the road appeared to be the cops coming after them. Every car seemed suspicious. The necessity to kill a cop had increased the exhaustion that had crept into their blood with the action of the last few hours. At the center, they felt safe and relieved. They recaptured some of the lost adrenaline and went about their business in a methodical way. Max told Jerry to clean up the truck while he helped William into the center. It was still early, too early for any visitors to drop in, but Max still worried that Ruth might surprise them. And to provide Ruth with a reasonable pretext for bloody clothing could be a challenge.

Max helped William to the men's room. William removed all his bloody clothes, except for his underwear. He scrubbed himself down with a washcloth with water from the sink. When William was putting on some clean clothes from his locker, Max stripped and took a cold shower. Jerry came in and collected the pile of soiled, bloody clothes. He took them outside and dumped them in the fire he had started in a metal drum. He then took off all his own clothes, including his socks and shoes, and also deposited them in the metal drum. Then he ran naked back into the center. He held his privates with one hand and shouted, A cold motherfucking morning, you all. Jerry showered and put on some clean clothes. He joined Max and William in Max's office. William was soaking his ankle in a plastic bucket of warm water with salt.

Did you burn everything that needed burning? Max asked Jerry as he poured more salt into the bucket.

Yeah. Good thing we covered the truck seat and floor mats with burlap, Jerry replied. The truck is clean, and the knife, metal pipe, and gun are in their proper place. How is William doing?

I'm good, Jerry. I just have a little swelling around the ankle and some pain—

OK, Max interrupted, it's almost five thirty. When we drop you off, William, you tell Ruth I landed on your ankle as we went up for a rebound. And you have to be convincing—Ruth is no dummy.

Max and Jerry drove William home and helped him inside the house. That way Ruth wouldn't think of them as cold for dropping him off injured at an ungodly hour of the morning and leaving him outdoors to fend for himself like a homeless dog. Ruth was capable of that kind of thinking when it came to William. She was as sweet as a jelly doughnut, but she could turn sour quick if provoked. When William was inside his home, on the way to the bedroom to wake Ruth up, Max and Jerry hurried out of the house like two mice going on a cheese run. Max then drove Jerry home. Jerry was no hassle. He could drop him off right outside his pad or a block away and force him to walk the rest of the way. Except he would never do that to his best friend.

See you later, Jerry. Sleep late or take the day off if you need it, Max suggested when Jerry got out of the truck in front of his house. Max was worried about his mother, Victoria. He felt guilty he hadn't called her from the center. He hadn't called her because if she was in deep pain, she would want him home right away. She would be anxious over his absence and would want him home to make certain he was not in harm's way. But Max had things to take care of at the center before leaving. And this is where the guilt came into play. He couldn't decide if he preferred to be with Jerry and William, instead of at his mother's bedside, attending to her every need. This sort of thinking kept him up nights and was the catalyst for the melancholia that resulted from such negative thinking. Max loved his mother, but did he love her enough? He constantly wondered about this. Her absence in his most tender years had bred a resentment in him. A resentment Max believed he had buried deep in a compartment of his mind that was never to be opened again. He had forgiven her, and he loved her like a mother he had grown up with. The results of that newborn love, as he called it, gave him a profound satisfaction of accomplishing the impossible. The bond he formed with his mother was like the fusing of two elements with opposite compositions. He was confident that since his mother had returned from exile, they had established an emotional connection that only a mother and a son can have.

And this grave topic was what surged through Max's mind like an unrelenting deluge as he drove home. At times such as these, now and again the demons seemed to crawl out of that suppressed compartment, only to remind him of the past and his days of despair. Max fought them, but he questioned if the effort was enough to justify the hours he kept away from her. He always wanted to be at her side to comfort her in her hour of need, as any son would honor his mother. He at times found excuses—legitimate or not, they were still excuses—to stay away. And this behavior tormented him with a heavy dose of turmoil about his real feelings, feelings that acted like a sharp blade and made his soul bleed. It was worse when he saw her in pajamas with her bony knees held tight in her skeleton arms, in pain and many times soiled. He was convinced that he would do anything she asked of him—anything.

Max drove a little faster. He was anxious to get home and take care of his mother as he always did. Victoria's pain seemed to be less in the early morning and got worse as the day dragged on. The stomach cancer was eating her alive, and Max didn't know how long she could cope with the pain. She complained little, but Max was aware that the excruciating pain was killing her appetite and inflicting a devastating blow on her will to live. He felt useless, and his conscience was always on overdrive as he saw her waste away. The doctors were clueless on how to proceed besides giving her stronger medication, but the deadly disease was persistent.

CHAPTER 24

Mike Montes, the mayor of Las Flores, was in the courthouse office of Rafa Candelaria. Mike, or Mayor Mike, as he was called by some, had been negotiating with Rafa for at least a couple of hours. There were complaints of too many chickens and goats residing in the Eastside barrio. Rafa Candelaria and his pal were two city councilmen, one with too much time on his hands and Rafa, who represented the Eastside. Rafa had engaged Mike Montes, who defended the goats and chickens. Rafa, in his expensive suit and shoes, demanded zero tolerance. He wanted the full city council, with the mayor's approval, to commission Animal Control, backed by city police, to round up all the goats and chickens and quarantine them in a city corral. Rafa insisted that the Eastside was getting a bad reputation that kept new businesses and developers from investing money there. He claimed that many of his constituents kept no animals besides dogs and cats. Rafa was no longer in the mood to provide another extension for the few who continued to ignore the law, which had been in the books for more than ten years. This time the animals had to go, and another six-month extension was out of the question.

Mike Montes countered that the citizens in the Eastside who still kept goats and chickens were the older citizens of Las Flores. The same people who in the past had provided meat and eggs to people whose financial situations forbid them the convenience of the supermarket. Mike attempted to convince Rafa that the keeping of goats and chickens was a cultural tradition and not necessarily a necessity. The people, he added, saw the critters as pets and not with hunger in their stomachs, as in the past. Mike also wanted to open Rafa's eyes and help him understand that young children enjoyed the contact with the animals when they fed them. That chicks, hatched and transforming into fuzzy walking critters, touched children's hearts enough to keep their innocence much longer than children who missed out on this natural phenomenon. That a child who held a gentle baby goat for the first time and looked at those large brown eyes could become more sensitive and accept humans more eagerly. And Mike cited other scientific research that had proved that children with pets grew up to be better parents and less hostile toward the environment.

Hogwash, Rafa responded. He was frustrated. The mayor would not favor his position and vote on his side. Those studies, as you know, Mike, were conducted on a small sample of people. And they probably didn't even see or hold live critters. They saw them only on monitors and in color photos. So those studies are not valid and prove nothing.

What about the children who hurt, torture, and kill animals? Mike asked. There is strong evidence that some of them become serial killers as adults.

Oh please, Mike. Most, if not all, of the population of Las Flores has kicked a dog or a cat at least once—maybe more. And that does not, by a long shot, turn them into serial killers. The other councilman smiled, and it was a smug smile at that. He loved to see Rafa duke it out with Mayor Mike. The pit bull against the German shepherd. He had promised Rafa his vote, and Rafa had promised him trucks full of concrete to complete a for-pay parking structure he was building in the downtown area.

Look, Mike, Rafa continued. He was losing his patience. Another six months will drag on and then six more. It has been the case several times. We need to get rid of all those smelly critters as they did in the Westside years ago. And they both glanced at the councilman from the Westside, who hadn't uttered a word.

You cannot compare the Eastside to the Westside, Rafa. What if we ask Max Luna, the director of Community Impact, and his staff to conduct a study? Not a psychological scientific study, because they don't have the expertise. No, it would consist of a report on the number of animals that are housed in the barrio and the impact it might have on the owners, especially the elderly and the young. Dogs and cats would be excluded, of course.

And how long would this so-called study take? Rafa asked, astounded by Mike's laughable scheme.

I know what you're thinking, Rafa, but it's not a crazy idea. Think about it.

I have already. And how much time would this study involve?

Give it six months. A six-month extension, and if the study is not completed in six months, Rafa, I promise you and your witness here. I promise you that I will bring the ordinance to the full city council for a vote, and I will vote on your side. The only item I will not support is the city police riding along with Animal Control to enforce the ordinance. The LFPD, as we both know, has more important duties to perform, like—let's say—fighting crime.

OK, Mike. You've got six months. And we'll see if we can hold you to your word.

Deal, Mike said. And they all touched skin.

Mike left the angry Rafa and his pal in Rafa's office, probably betting that Max Luna would never go along with the insane idea of a mini census to find out how many goats and chickens lived in the barrio and the impact it would have on the owners if they were removed. Mike recalled that his mom still had a couple of old chickens. In six months, the chickens might die; he wasn't sure though. If the chickens were still alive, he was sure he could talk Rafa into another six-month extension. Max Luna and his staff were a clever lot, and Mike was positive they would not only embrace his plan but utilize it to come up with a strategy to get something out of Rafa.

Mike Montes drove back to his office in his 1948 Tucker Tropedo, maroon in color. It had aircraft-style doors for aerodynamics and the ease of entry. It had the non-shatter pop-out windshield, a novelty in its time, and the padded dash and doors. He owned one of the only forty-seven that survived of the fifty-one automobiles made. The Tucker also had a rear-mounted helicopter engine. And folks still insisted it resembled an old Studebaker. Mike paid them no mind. Ignorance is bliss, he thought. He drove east on Esperanza Street. He had wanted a Tucker automobile ever since he saw one in a Pebble Beach, California, car show. He knew it was the best automobile built during that time, but for various reasons, it never made the big time.

Mike reached Caballo Blanco Road and made a left, going north to his office in the east Mesa. He recalled how he came to own the Tucker. He was successful in the bid to build a 10,000-square-foot mansion with seven bedrooms, five bathrooms, and an Olympic-size indoor pool on forty acres of land on the Calle de Las Estrellas development in the east Mesa. He met all the specifications and stayed on budget for his multimillionaire Middle-Eastern client. Mike got along well with the man, and they had interesting conversations about many subjects but never about politics. When the wealthy client secured his collection of valuable automobiles in the mansion's extensive garage, he allowed Mike to check them out. Mike kept his eyes on the 1948 Tucker Tropedo. He couldn't keep his eyes and hands off the rare and expensive car, accepting that it could never be his. The wealthy man noticed that Mike studied the car as if it were an attractive naked woman. He eventually offered Mike the Tucker for a reasonable price—a price that Mike could not turn down, and that was the intention of the wealthy man.

When Mike arrived at his office, he remembered that his mother, Alma, and his cousin Christopher were coming to visit. Christopher, a cousin on his mother's side, was a Catholic priest, a vocation his mother had begged Mike to pursue on more than one occasion. Alma and Father Benjamin would corral him and talk to him for hours about being a man of God. His father, Francisco, never said a word about it and was never present during those conversations among his mother, the priest, and him. Mike always had seen his cousin as a normal boy growing up. They used to play rough, and Christopher could give as well as take. Christopher had grown up in Silver City, but they had played during visits. They were close until Christopher was in high school, when he had turned serious. Mike could no longer talk about girls because Christopher would tune him out and not say a word. When Christopher entered a seminary after high school, Mike realized he had lost a good friend.

Mike observed his cousin when he entered the office. Christopher was a little taller than Mike and had the light skin and eyes of his mother,

Alma's, people. A young and good-looking priest, Mike thought. What a combination; someone is going to score. And he bit his tongue.

Sit. Sit. Excuse my manners, Mike eventually said and moved a couple of chairs closer to his desk. Mike didn't feel comfortable sitting behind his desk, dominating the power spot, but he was getting used to it. After giving his mother a hug and shaking hands with Christopher, Mike sat in his chair.

A Jesuit in my office, Mike stated. And he looked straight at Christopher. Ignatius of Loyola would be so proud, Christopher. You have come a long way. I always admired the Jesuits. The Jesuits, in my opinion, were more organized and planned communities more efficiently than the other religious orders. And since they were highly educated, they tended to be more tolerant toward the natives, which possibly led to higher conversion rates. That was what it was all about, in the end, right?

Sure, Mike, Christopher said, trying hard not to lose his patience. He wasn't here to be schooled on a subject he was familiar with. You don't have to go there, Mike. I am aware of the good work the Jesuits do and did—and not only in the new world but also in Asia.

And I guess you are also aware that the Jesuits, the Soldiers of God, also kept slaves in this country. Howard University was—

Boys. Boys, Alma, Mike's mother interrupted. Miguel, my darling boy. We are here because Father Christopher, your cousin, needs two hundred acres of land. He is not here to discuss your term paper on the Jesuits.

Mike was taken off guard by his astute mother. He was a little disappointed. He wanted to debate the cura. That was his favorite thing to do, cura or not.

Miguel, my beloved son, Alma continued, Father Christopher needs the property to build a school, K through twelfth grade. The plan includes a dance theater and gymnasium, among other things. And the school will be coed.

I see, Mike said. He scratched under his chin with his thumb. It was a habit he couldn't break. So this visit wasn't to say hello? And he addressed Christopher. You lobbied my mother, your aunt, to advance your cause?

No, Mike. And Christopher almost jumped out of his chair. My aunt Alma was the one who suggested I accompany her to your office and ask you for the property. I had no idea that you owned the land in the vicinity where our school is to be built until my aunt advised me of the fact.

Oh! I see, Mike responded. And it was only recently that you became aware of my ownership of the property in question. And how long have you planned this religious school? If it needs Vatican approval, it means that the planning stages had to be submitted to lower-echelon bureaucracies, long before they reached the Vatican.

It's a process, Mike. It's like any other large organization. We have been approved by the Vatican budget committee, and half the funds are allocated. We are waiting for matching funds.

Are poor children from the barrio who can't afford tuition to be admitted? Or is the school going to be for only the elite, the well off? Particularly the religious of mind who believe that a Catholic education of their children is superior to any other. That practice only separates society and creates tension among the people—

Please, Miguel, the love of my life, don't be so dramatic, Alma interrupted in a calm voice. You know very well there is and always has been a sliding scale for tuition. If the economic resources of a family are suspect, they are admitted, and the fewer resources they have, the more benefits they receive. And please, don't use poor as a word for intimidation, Miguel. I have experienced poverty on a certain level. I don't need to read books to find out about it.

Aunt Alma. Please allow me to clarify to Mike the intent and beauty of the school we want to build and open. You asked about the people in need, Mike. Naturally we have plans for children whose parents lack the funds to pay the costs and still yearn for their children to be educated in a Catholic school. They will be allowed to participate in the complete program; tuition and uniforms will be provided at no cost to the families. The beauty of our program, Mike, is that boys and girls will join in all activities together. The teachers will be the most qualified we can recruit, and included will be priests, nuns, and lay teachers.

I don't want to sound negative, Christopher, Mike interjected before Christopher wrote a novel. To get teachers, lay teachers, to sacrifice the little money that they make to teach in a private setting…I don't know. Catholic schools, as you know, Christopher, do not have the reputation for paying teachers decent wages.

You also have to understand, Mike, that we are talking about people who have a great faith in Jesus Christ. That is what inspires them to work and teach in the Catholic system. It's not the extra dollars they can get somewhere else. It's the dedication to God and the willingness to be in his grace. To do his work and worship him in an institution with peace and joy. A workplace where there is no need to hide because they feel closer to God. No restrictive laws where God is kept out of the classroom and the lives of the students. They are people such as your future wife, Alexis—and congratulations on your coming wedding—who can make more money employed by a huge corporation than Catholic Charities can afford to pay.

Christopher paused and then continued, See, Mike, some people give, but they don't necessarily change. The giving is what softens the heart. And your perception of life is restructured. You become a man with a mission and with the tendency to never stop giving. Giving has allowed you the tranquility to observe and become more determined to seek out God. If you donate the property to the church, you will feel the overwhelming fulfillment in time. And believe me: it will change your life. And no one has to know but you.

I'm flattered, Christopher, Mike replied, before Christopher took out the baptismal water. You mean if I donate my property to the church, two hundred acres, that in the process I will be transformed to a life of bliss and concentrate more on finding God? And I will have in me the capacity to retain this feeling because I give and give some more? Isn't this the classic technique used to train the mind to do your bidding? It is done by the government, and it's highly affective. The church, all religions, have done it much longer and with a higher rate of success. It worked on you, Christopher, and that's fine, but don't expect it to work on everyone.

It's all about faith, Miguel, my dear boy, Alma interrupted again. You always had a little thing about faith. I'm so happy that you will marry Alexis, a woman with a solid religious background. But let's get to the subject at hand, Miguel. Are you or are you not going to donate the two hundred acres or more to the church? Father Christopher needs to know.

Marriage, Christopher jumped in before Mike had an opportunity to respond to Alma. Marriage, and even though I personally have not experienced the institution firsthand, I believe with all my heart and soul that it is the epic center of a divine utopia. You can say that it is the self-preservation of humanity, in all forms. Marriage between a man and a woman, as God wants it, is the most rapid and least painful solution to equality between the sexes.

Mike realized he was being challenged on two fronts. He had to respect his mother and not go off on her, and Christopher might be the priest officiating for his wedding vows. He wanted to tell the priest what he had seen in many failed marriages among his friends and relatives. He couldn't say much because it would for certain get back to Alexis, and then he would have to clarify his position about marriage to her. Mike took the safest route and said, I give plenty to charity, Christopher, including to the Catholic Church.

We will continue that conversation at another time, Mike. Christopher almost smiled. He knew he had silenced the great debater, and the presence of Alma had a lot to do with it. Now we have to get down to business. You know why I'm here. I need your answer today, Mike. Tomorrow at the latest. You can write it off as a loss. You comprehend the tax codes as well as anyone, I would guess.

I have larger losses, Christopher, and this is not the place to discuss them. What I do want to discuss is the future school policy of admitting transgender, gay, and children with disabilities. You haven't mentioned any of those children. Tell me you are not going to discourage the parents from enrolling their children by telling them that the public schools have more money and programs to facilitate the conditions of their children.

Well, it's true, Mike. And that's a known fact. We do not hire a school psychologist, and we hire few counselors. When there is a need, and the parents' consent to have the child tested for a learning disorder, the school nurse calls in a public-school educational psychologist—

In my opinion, my dear boy, it is best that you donate the land to the church, Alma interrupted again because she believed the boys were enjoying themselves too much, slinging hash. I say that, Miguel, because there is a group who might take your property by designating it as a Native American burial site. And you know what that means, Miguel. You are certainly no fool. At least the church has deep pockets and will lawyer up to hold on to the property as long as it takes.

It's a con, Mother, Mike said, not surprised that his mother, Alma, had done her homework. It's run by a con artist by the name of Juan Buenostro, also known as Carlos Red Bird. They pulled that fraud in southern Utah last year. Red Bird and his friends planted sacred funerary objects and human bones from Native Americans pilfered from a museum in Phoenix, Arizona. Redbird filed the documents needed with the Department of the Interior and almost got away with the scheme. The museum recognized the bones and the other objects when they were displayed on the front page of a small-town newspaper. The museum demanded DNA testing and then cross-referenced the results with their own samples. Redbird wasn't charged with the theft and planting of the bones. He claimed the bones and sacred objects belonged to a known lineal descendant of the man he was helping to recover them and make sure his ancestors' land was respected.

Carlos Redbird walked a free man and keeps pulling the same scam. But not to worry, Mother—I hired an archeologist, and he reassured me that the only bones he could find on the property were wild animal bones. Besides, the land is not even close to federal land or tribal land unless Redbird wants to claim Santa Maria as tribal land. And good luck with that, I say.

I am so proud of you, Miguel, my darling son. You have done your lesson well and deserve an A plus and nothing less. I mean it with all my heart. You are careful and wise, and that is an important step to maturity. And pray tell, Miguel, why has this property taken your interest? You have others, many others.

I'm glad you asked, Mother. This property means so much to me because I'm going to build a mall on it. The location is perfect. The property is close to Las Flores and the many homes being built in the area. We have conducted a property analysis survey, and the projections favor the site at a pretty good rate. The population will support another mall if the environment is classic and the stores are high quality. Now you see, Mother and Christopher, it's not that I wish to be a scrooge. It's just that the mall has been in my dreams for a long time. I now have the financial means to make it happen. I will own close to eighty percent, and the rest will be shared by investors.

Well, in that case, Miguel, we will not put a dent in your dream. Give my regards to Alexis, and we will expect you for dinner on Sunday. And if you need to cancel for whatever reason, call me as soon as possible, so I won't have to cook.

Yes, of course, Mother. And Mike hugged her like he meant it and gave her a peck on the cheek. Where are you going now? he asked. He felt bad but not that kind of bad.

We are going to visit another donor who might have it in his heart to be more generous. No offense meant, my sweet boy.

None taken, Mother. I can't believe you are going to solicit Mike Cotton. As far as I know, Mike Cotton doesn't own any large property that close to Las Flores.

Not now, my devoted son. But there are rumors that he has his eyes on a prize, if he is elected mayor.

Mike couldn't help it and laughed out loud. The chances of Mike Cotton being elected mayor of Las Flores are worse than Rafa Candelaria being canonized by the pope, he said between giggles. And any scheme he might employ to somehow appropriate the property in question will be utterly defeated in and out of court.

It doesn't hurt to approach the man and show him the plans for the school, Alma replied. She knew that Mike was bothered, and his laughter could not mask it, not from her. And even though he is a full-fledged Baptist, he might have a sliver of decency still in him. And besides, strange things occur when it comes to land rights.

Mike touched skin with Christopher and politely walked them out of his office.

When Christopher and Alma were out the door, Christopher turned and said to Mike, God works in mysterious ways, Mike.

CHAPTER 25

*M*ax and Jerry were talking in Max's car while Jerry drove. They were parked about half a mile from Mike Cotton's residence. It was an exclusive area of million-dollar-plus homes in the Dos Cerros Estates. It was around nine thirty at night. The night was cold, and the moon and stars were hidden away by a layer of thick clouds. The foothills, or Dos Cerros, were not visible in the darkness. To the northeast, a short distance away, the Turquoise Mountains were also swallowed by the night. The large, expensive homes were not close together. Each house was built on five to ten acres and in some cases more. They were enclosed by rock walls up to six feet high, and that gave the homes complete privacy and isolation. The elite of Las Flores and many wealthy folks from the cold belt called these minimansions home.

See, Max, Jerry said. The security patrols are run by younger dudes during the night shift. Some bring their girlfriends along. They park and make out, smoke weed, or drink, and sometimes for hours. They know that to break into one of these pads at night, it has to be a pretty well-organized unit. Professionals, at least. Security is pretty tight inside the walls. They are well equipped with alarms and cameras, besides dogs. They have seen me and the car before, and they probably think I'm a handyman doing some kind of work for Mike Cotton. I'm sure they have seen the car parked outside the gate on several occasions and have never bothered to stop and investigate. And sometimes I'm there late at night and early morning.

Lucky you. Max smiled at Jerry. You believe we can just walk into the residence as if invited to sip a drink with the Cottons?

I know we can, Max. And that's the easy part. The big dogs know me, and I have the key to the gate. And Jerry showed Max the key. Oh, and another thing, Max. The expensive camera system is not working yet. The techs couldn't locate a vital part to switch the cameras from nighttime to day and take pictures as far away as half a mile. The cameras are German-made, and they had to order the part from Germany. The man in charge promised Mike Cotton that it would take only a few days. It has already been more than a week and still no working cameras.

That's good news for us, Jerry. I still can't believe Mike Cotton would go so long without a security camera system to watch over his mansion.

It's pure ego, Max. That son of a bitch is too cocky. He believes and believes with all his might that no one has the balls to fuck with him and his possessions.

And that's where the motherfucker is wrong, Jerry. He's like all the rest of the assholes who walk that line. They believe that their money will buy anything they desire. They refuse to accept the fact that money, a powerful asset, cannot guarantee your life. And we are going to prove that maxim tonight.

Are you sure you don't want me to handle it, Max? Jerry asked in a kind of sad tone.

Thanks, Jerry. I mean it. I know you can do the job as well or better than I can. But this is personal. The asshole paid two professionals to put me down. He didn't consider or didn't give a shit about other people getting hurt or killed. I have to do this, Jerry. Tonight might be our only chance. When the security cameras are functioning and the alarm system is on, it's going to take some technical skill to dismantle them.

No. I hear you, Max. If that hog set a killer after me, man, I would go bonkers. And I'd shoot to kill, no questions asked.

You can handle Claire, right, Jerry? I mean, I don't want her to get hysterical and attempt to be a martyr and get shot for her troubles. We cannot afford any witnesses who can point us out in a lineup.

Claire won't get excited or scared, Max. She might attempt to talk us out of it in a calm way, for the children's sake. And that would be the extent of it. Once I make it clear to her that her foolish husband is putting her and the children in danger, she will be glad to see him go.

I trust you with that, Jerry. You know her better than I do. I'll drop you off a short distance from the gate so you can handle the dogs. I'll wait for about ten minutes and then meet you at the gate. No longer than ten minutes, Jerry.

Jerry got out of the car and walked rapidly to the smaller gate between the main gate and an empty guard shack. He whistled low, and the giant dogs came running at a trot. They raced toward Jerry like overfed ponies on the open range. Jerry unlocked the gate and caressed Mona and Drake as if they were his lost children. Drake wanted to bark. He was so happy and jumped all over Jerry. Jerry struggled to calm him down. Drake knew that Jerry was good for a meal, a full meal, because it didn't cost him a thing. The huge dog could smell meat on Jerry, cooked meat with gravy.

Jerry led the hungry dogs to the garage as quietly as he could manage it. He placed his hands on the dogs' necks and walked in the middle, leading them to the garage's side door. He murmured in a low voice to his friends in a language they knew and loved. Jerry opened the garage side door and walked inside with Mona and Drake and closed the door behind them. He pulled out a doggie bag of leftover meat and potatoes. They were the leftovers of the steak dinner Max and he had enjoyed earlier that evening. He knew the leftovers were going to come in handy, knowing the appetite the dogs had. He opened the bag and dropped what was left of a T-bone steak on the floor, along with the skin of a baked potato saturated with butter. Drake attacked it without hesitation. Jerry walked away a short distance and dropped the other steak and potato for Mona. He crumpled the bag and stuffed it in his back pocket. Mona studied the meat and sniffed it. She then looked up at Jerry as if to ask his consent to eat it. Her manners were impeccable. She was a graceful lady, and Jerry could see a little of Claire in her. Jerry finally said, Come on, Mona, baby. Go for it. It's all yours, girl. He wanted Mona occupied so he could get away and out of the garage and leave the dogs inside. Mona, after noticing that Drake was making quick work of his bones, decided to taste the meat before Drake came sniffing.

Jerry took small steps toward the garage door. He didn't want the big dogs to follow him outside. They might not take to Max and could raise a ruckus. There was no time to introduce the dogs to Max. Max didn't have any cooked meat on him, and Mona could be difficult.

Max waited anxiously at the gate for Jerry. The whole area was well lit. He had parked the car right next to the empty guard shack as indicated by Jerry. This was the exact place where the security patrol had seen the car on numerous occasions.

Jerry approached, taking huge steps and attempting to stay in the shadows. He whispered to Max to follow him. They raced to the kitchen door almost on tiptoes. Jerry opened the kitchen door and walked in as if expected for tea and biscuits. He placed his fingers on his lips once out of the kitchen and gestured to Max to follow him upstairs. When they reached the top of the landing, Jerry pointed to Mike Cotton's bedroom door and whispered to Max to wait. Jerry went straight to Claire's bedroom door, opened it, and walked in.

Claire Cotton was listening to Vivaldi's The Four Seasons (Spring). She was sitting on the bed arranging her CDs when Jerry bolted in. Claire was shocked when she saw Jerry dressed all in black and wearing black leather gloves in her bedroom. She didn't recall inviting him to visit. She jumped off the bed and almost ran to him. She was fully dressed, and fear raged through her mind. She refused to believe that Jerry had lost it. She took a deep breath to calm herself but didn't say a word. She knew Jerry was no fool, and if he barged in like that, there had to be a reason.

Jerry placed his gloved index finger to his lips and whispered, Where's your hubby?

Claire, still anxious and frightened, whispered back, He's in the tub. Wednesday is bath night. I told you.

Jerry walked back to the door, opened it, and whispered to Max, who was waiting in the hall. Bathroom, tub. Then he returned to Claire's bedroom, shut the door, and locked it.

Jerry, what are you doing here? Claire asked in a voice full of anxiety. She was worried that her husband might walk in any minute. Tonight is not a good time. Mike is home. You, you never…

It's OK, sweetheart. And Jerry attempted to calm her down. Max is with your hubby. Don't worry about him interrupting our conversation.

Claire calmed down some. She knew the time had come to choose sides. The day of reckoning was here. She was sure Jerry would protect her in case things got out of hand. Max was capable of anything. She heard talk about Max at the center from people in the community and from the older kids. He didn't say much to her, but she was aware that he kept a close eye on her.

Jerry. Jerry, please, baby. Why are you here and with Max? She knew, but she wanted to hear it from Jerry.

It's OK, angel. We're here to protect you from danger. Your hubby and his transactions are endangering not only you but also the children. There is no other way, Claire. You will be financially ruined and maybe even jailed—who knows—if your hubby continues his reckless ways. Trust me; it's for the best.

Claire came closer to Jerry and placed her hand on his muscular arm. She felt the warm leather of the black jacket and squeezed, ever so gently. Will you spare him for the sake of the children? she asked with tears in her eyes.

If he cared for you and the children, my love, he would have spared you from his disastrous actions. Max will not change his mind; it's too late. He will not harm you, Claire, I promise. But you have to leave now, right away. You have to drive to Santa Fe this minute. Take a few belongings and all your expensive jewelry and cash. We have to make it look like a home-invasion robbery.

Did you harm the dogs, Jerry?

No. Never. Take the dogs with you. And be sure to take both of them.

But I only take Mona, Jerry.

No. Listen, you have to take Drake. The police will want to know why Drake didn't bark or act crazy. You explain to the cops if they ask you that you want your kids to spend more time with the dogs so that the memory will always be fresh.

Claire grabbed a bag and put stuff in it. She knew the time for debate was over. Her most expensive jewelry was in a safe-deposit box in a bank in Santa Fe. They would be too outrageous for the functions in Las Flores. She placed the minor pieces in the bag anyway, along with some clothes and her CDs.

Hurry, Jerry insisted. You have to hit the road pronto.

Claire, bag in hand, approached Jerry for a kiss and hug.

Jerry moved away. He hated to, but he knew what might happen if their lips met. No, Claire. We better not. We'll get carried away and end up in bed. Later, perhaps. I love you and will always love you, no matter what happens.

Claire walked to the door, disappointed. She turned before she walked out of the room and said, in a low voice, I love you, Jerry.

Max pulled a .357 magnum Python revolver from his back pocket with his right hand and a silencer with his left hand from his jacket pocket. He screwed the silencer on the barrel of the magnum as soon as Jerry gave him the word on the whereabouts of Mike Cotton. Max opened the bedroom door very slowly and deliberately. He walked inside Mike Cotton's bedroom with the gun pointed to the floor. Mike Cotton was not in the bedroom, but he smelled cigar smoke coming from the bathroom. He made his way to the bathroom and approached the open door. The large bathroom was lit with candles of various sizes and shapes. Max could see Mike Cotton submerged in the extra-large tub, full of soapy water up to his chin. He had an expensive Montecristo Cuban cigar in his right hand above the water and a girly magazine, also above the water, in his left.

Max walked into the bathroom and pointed the huge gun with the silencer at Mike Cotton.

Mike Cotton finally noticed Max. What the fuck? he said in an angry voice.

Well, well. What do we have here? And Max inched closer to Mike Cotton. A believer and a pious man, smoking and checking out the naked babes in a smutty magazine.

How did you get in here? Mike Cotton shouted, but not too loud. He was outraged and still in disbelief that anyone could just walk in on him, and in his own house at that. I don't have any cash on hand, if that's what you're looking for.

You know it ain't, motherfucker. Did you believe that the killers you sent after me completed the job successfully? If you wanted me out of the way so bad, why didn't you come after me yourself? Drown that piece of shit before I put a bullet in your hand. And keep both hands out of the water behind your head.

Mike Cotton plunged the cigar into the water. He also let go of the magazine and placed his hands behind his head.

You better not harm my wife, Claire. You better not, Mike Cotton stammered, angry as hell but helpless to do anything about it.

Or you'll do what? Max almost laughed. You'll do shit, you fucking coward, and you know it. Don't worry about your gorgeous wife. She's in good hands. She's with Jerry. You know Jerry, right? You offered him a job in a fantasy prison you were going to build with the money you were going to make selling drugs. One word from me, and Jerry will forget his manners and let his dark side take over. And you sure as hell don't wanna see that. Tell me where you stashed the drugs, and maybe I'll just cripple you, and your children can push you around in a wheelchair for the rest of your miserable life.

Drugs! What drugs? Mike Cotton exclaimed in an exasperated and desperate voice. I don't know anything about drugs. I'm a Christian man and father of two children. Leave now, and I will say nothing to the police about your wild-goose chase.

You are not in any position to make demands. Not while I have this loaded baby pointed at your big head. I'm not gonna ask you again. Tell me where the drugs are and your connections in Las

Flores, and I'll spare your life.

Mike Cotton relaxed a little. He now believed that Max didn't want to kill him outright. That Max was all talk, hiding behind the huge gun. That Max came to his house to cut a deal and extort him for drugs or profit from the sale of drugs. He was sure that Max was like all the rest and wanted to enrich himself from someone else's work. He made up his mind to splash soapy water in Max's eyes and then jump out of the tub and wrestle the gun away from him. He would then beat Max unconscious with the gun and shoot Jerry Rivera dead. And naturally, Mike Cotton didn't give any serious consideration to the fact that he was in a tub filled with soapy water on his back with both hands behind his head. And that a slippery-slide ejection out of the tub like Superman to jump on Max was almost impossible to accomplish.

Max kept his eyes on Mike Cotton. The man was a fool, and he might try something stupid. He held the magnum low in his right hand, his elbow pressed to his rib cage, and pointed at Mike Cotton. Max was half sitting on a stool less than six feet away from Mike Cotton. He cocked the magnum as Mike Cotton brought his hands forward in a futile attempt to make it out of the slippery tub. His feet couldn't find any traction, and he almost tumbled underwater when the hollow point bullet hit him between the eyes as his head was submerging. The bullet caught him low, almost on the bridge of the nose. The skull cracked open in the back with the impact. Blood, pieces of brain, and small bones scattered out of the damaged skull like blood from a severed main artery, and Mike Cotton descended into hell. The bloody stew was mostly contained in the water and on the back and sides of the large tub. The same comfy tub where Mike Cotton had luxuriously soaked for hours, smoking his expensive cigar, checking out the images of nude babes in the slutty magazine, and stroking his meat.

When Max pulled the trigger, he jumped back, knocking the stool over. He didn't want to get splashed with blood, but he almost tripped with the stool, and that was not cool. He didn't want to leave any evidence for the detectives who were going to investigate the assassination of Mike Cotton. The city police detectives acted like a BBC production of fictional sleuths. But when it came to solving crimes, a major item in their job description, they were less than successful. Max saw the body of Mike Cotton in the tub. The soapy water was mixed with floating carnage, and it resembled a tub of warm soup for hungry cannibals.

Max turned and headed to the door. He closed the bathroom door behind him and never bothered to look back, even for something he might have dropped. He went straight to Claire's bedroom, opened the door, and let himself in as if he were home. Jerry was ransacking the room and enjoying it. When he saw Max, he stopped and controlled a smile. He knew this was serious business.

The fucker dead? Jerry asked, not really wanting to know.

The motherfucker ain't gonna say grace at the table for many years to come. Max was in the twilight zone. He had enjoyed the killing too much, and that didn't go right with his way of thinking. He comprehended that it was his obligation to erase scum like Mike Cotton, but the thrill was feeling more like an act of decency and not what it really was. The conclusion confused Max. Taking a life, any life, was a difficult thing to do, and he knew that. But to him, it came easy, and that was what worried him the most.

You OK, Max? Jerry had to ask. You look a little unsettled. Did Mike Cotton put up a struggle for his life, or did he go the saintly way?

Sorry, Jerry. My head is spinning. I didn't want to see Claire here, in this room. I didn't want to have to kill her, Jerry. But you know I would have to do it and maybe, you know, enjoy it. And that's what's creepy, Jerry. Don't worry. I'm not going nuts—not yet anyway. I can still handle it, Jerry. I'm worried that a day will come when I won't be able to.

It's OK, Max. Jerry expressed himself in a friendly manner, not paranoid, like a person speaking to a deranged man. You got too much brain power, brother. Those powerful brain cells will put up a fight and deter the demons from entering and creating chaos, at least for most of the time. We better get to Mike Cotton's bedroom and mix things up a bit. We have to make this gig look like a home invasion gone fucked-up. And Claire hit the road about ten or twenty minutes ago. I told her to take the dogs and forget about pleading for her husband's life, a silly errand that could cause her much pain. I don't want you to believe that I hid her someplace in the house, Max.

Men have done much more than that for women they loved, Max responded. His spinning head was somewhat slowing down.

But that's only in the movies, Jerry said. He was happy that Max was becoming more lucid.

Of course—where else? And they both walked into Mike Cotton's bedroom.

Mike Cotton's bedroom was sparse compared to Claire's. He slept in an old army bed with a thin mattress and no sheets. An olive-green army-issued wool blanket covered the mattress, along with a pillow flat as a corn tortilla that was no longer white but yellow. There was a large wooden crucifix with the body of a bleeding Christ nailed to the wall behind the bed. The spacious room was empty of furniture except for a small table next to the metal bed. The wooden table, an expensive item once, held a small lamp and an open Bible, giving the impression that someone actually utilized the bed.

This motherfucker lived like a monk when it came to sleep time, Jerry commented to Max as he turned the bed over and kicked the table, sending the Bible flying to a corner of the room.

If he only had the faith of a real monk, he would probably still be alive, Max said, and he opened the door to the walk-in closet and walked in. The closet was almost empty. Only a few cheap suits hung in one corner, and shoes, work clothes, and work boots occupied the rest. A large metal safe was on the floor in the middle of the closet. The door was ajar, and the safe was empty, except for little brown spiders that made it their home.

Jerry walked into the closet and kicked the door to the safe wide open. He turned to Max and said, Nothing there. Let's get the fuck out of here. We've done what we came to do.

Are you sure the caretakers won't surprise us? Max asked Jerry on their way out of Mike Cotton's bedroom. He was worried he might have to kill again, and that was something he didn't look forward to, he tried to convince himself.

No. They hit the sack early, Jerry explained to Max as they rushed out of the house. They have to get up at the crack of dawn to prepare Mike Cotton's coffee and biscuits. They won't hear a thing. The casita is a distance from the main house.

OK, then. Let's get on. Max and Jerry left the kitchen door open as they made a run to the car. They were going to torch the house after the deed was done but decided not to. They figured someone might spot them when the building blazed, and that was a big chance to take.

CHAPTER 26

*T*he day after Mike Cotton's demise, around noon, Max and Jerry were in Max's office. They were reading the morning paper. Mike Cotton's picture and some details of his gruesome murder were plastered all over the front page. Max read out loud from the paper: Mr. Mike Cotton, longtime citizen of Las Flores and proprietor of Cotton Construction, was found brutally murdered in his residence early this morning. The Las Flores Police Department attributed the brutal murder to a home invasion. Mrs. Clairisa Cotton, wife of Mr. Mike Cotton, was in Santa Fe, visiting her children during the tragic assault. Mrs. Cotton was still in shock and had no comment at this time. She has secluded herself with her children somewhere in the Santa Fe area and will not be available to detectives until the end of the week. The property managers claim not to have heard any unusual noise coming from the main residence, and the family's dogs were with Mrs. Cotton at the time of the crime. The police detectives will not release any more information due to the ongoing investigation. The Las Flores Police Department encourages anyone to call them if they witnessed any unusual activity in or around Mr. Cotton's residence the night of the murder.

Wow! Jerry exclaimed. They did in Mike Cotton. What kind of a world are we living in?

Max put the paper aside and said, Not to mention the kind of people populating it.

Hey, Max, Jerry said, how do you think Mike Cotton got connected to a drug cartel? I mean, he claimed to be a model citizen and a Christian. A family man and all that.

Who knows? Max replied, a concerned look on his face. The only person who might have had that type of connection was Juan Vela, his foreman. Juan lives in Juarez, and maybe he introduced Mike Cotton to people there. I can't prove it though. I guess we'll never know. Listen, Jerry,

Max continued. He seemed worried and sad. Not to change the subject, but my mother is in the hospital. She's pretty bad off. And she wants me to bring her home. I'm leaving right now, and I want to ask you if you don't mind coming along. I know it's an emotional compromise, and if you say no, it's a legitimate response. I will respect any decision you make and keep the honor of calling you my true brother.

Jerry's eyes suddenly opened wide, as if an electrical wire had pierced his heart. Max, Jerry responded, in a voice full of undeniable emotion. I'm with you, Max, and will be until our soldiering has led us to our grave. Lead the way, brother, and the orders are yours to command.

Max was relieved and thankful to Jerry for being a true friend, even though the unexpected could pop up its ugly face. We will leave Armando in charge, because William and Ruth are on vacation, Max said as he gathered his things and exited the office.

Max and Jerry drove in the old CI truck to the hospital, going west on Santa Teresa Street. Victoria was hospitalized in the old hospital on the Westside of town. The hospital administrators claimed that the new hospital in the East Mesa lacked the needed facilities to accommodate Victoria. The hospital didn't matter to Victoria. She couldn't care less about how many beds the hospital had or how new it was. To her, any bed, anywhere, would be the same. Her pain screamed louder than any inconvenience. The medication was losing its effect, and the pain, driven by the cancer, was rampant.

Victoria wanted her son, Max, to come and take her home and out of the public view. She wanted to die with some dignity. The same dignity she had when she was full of life. Victoria had known for some time that the end was close. She refused to admit it in the beginning. She saw and felt the vulturish cancer devour her, soul and spirit, and there was not a thing in the world she could do to save herself. She made peace with death and promised not to struggle. She wanted to go home and talk to her son, Max, for the last time. She wanted to talk to Max in the privacy of their own home, not in a crowded hospital, within earshot of strangers.

Victoria realized that she was adding a lot of weight to Max's life. She also knew that Max was on the verge of drowning with the weight he already carried. She was selfish in more ways than one. But the excruciating pain numbed every moral conviction that she'd once considered sacred. She asked Max to take her home without authorization from any medical professional. She was too ill to inquire and get upset over procedures or jargon that involved patients being kept medicated to prolong their stay and claim higher insurance benefits. She was desperate, and her behavior might seem odd to some and erratic to others. But she was still conscious and sound of mind. Her decisions seemed clear to her, and the concerns of others were beyond her ability to care.

Max and Jerry continued the drive on Santa Teresa, going west. It was a little afternoon, and the clear autumn sky was a brilliant blue. The shrubs and trees had submitted to nature. Their leaves turned brown or were gone altogether and would not return until spring. Santa Teresa would take them all the way to the Westside. The street passed right in front of the hospital. The traffic was not bad, but it was gaining momentum as they approached downtown. Max was driving slowly and cautiously. Today was not a good day to be stopped by a cop. Today was a day for big decisions, decisions that could alter fate.

Max turned to Jerry and said, What I don't get, Jerry, is that the fucking doctors insist that Victoria stay in the hospital and suffer in pain. They naively believe that they can hold off the cancer and buy her up to ten more months, at the most. They underestimate the staying power of the disease. A killer that has been around for years and continues to evolve as people's life habits change. I just hope that voters approve the Die with Dignity Law. If only to save people all kinds of grief.

I hear you, Max, Jerry replied. He really felt bad for Max, and he didn't know what to say to make him feel better. He finally said, You know, Max, some of those doctors are using the system to make a buck. Sure, others do it, but doctors are held to a higher moral standard; that's what we're made to believe anyway. I suppose greed poisons their perception and turns the heart into stone. I'm sure it's not all of them, but the ones who do it blow it for the rest.

I get your point, Jerry. And then Max said, Look, there's the hospital. And he drove into the hospital parking lot off Santa Teresa. He parked the truck, and they walked to the front door of the three-story building. Once in the building, they took the stairs to the second floor and straight to Victoria's room. Max entered the room, pushed the plastic curtain aside, and went straight to Victoria's bed. Jerry stationed himself outside, right next to the door, to get a better look at who was coming or going.

Victoria attempted a smile when she saw Max. She raised her thin, bony arms to welcome her savior. Tears rolled down from her bloodshot eyes, and all she could say was, You came, Max. Max, you're really here.

Max was careful when he hugged Victoria. She was connected to a heart monitor and had long plastic tubing coming from an IV in one arm. It's OK, Mom, Max said. I'm gonna get you home. You're positive you want to go home now?

Yes, please, Max. The pain. I can't take it anymore. And Victoria sobbed.

Max carefully removed all the attachments from her hands and arms. He picked her up in his arms like an infant and walked out of the room. Jerry led the way through the hospital hallway. A male nurse on his way to check on Victoria couldn't believe his eyes.

Hey, you! the nurse almost shouted at Max. You can't just take a patient out of the hospital in your arms like that. She needs a wheelchair and a doctor's release. The nurse walked straight over to confront Max. He ignored Jerry, who was walking in front of Max and Victoria. Jerry shoved the nurse with both hands, and the nurse flew off the floor and landed on his back on top of a metal supply cart. The metal cart flipped to one side, and the nurse crashed to the floor. Then the metal cart fell on top of him. Max kept on walking with Victoria in his arms and Jerry opening doors until they reached the parking lot. Jerry opened the passenger-side door of the truck. Max handed Victoria to Jerry while he climbed in.

Jerry. Jerry. Thank you, Jerry. Thank you, Victoria whispered but kept her eyes closed. She was nauseous, and there was no color in her face.

Victoria, if you don't want to stay in the hospital, you don't have to, Jerry replied. And nobody is going to stop us from taking you home. Jerry tried hard not to choke up.

When Max was situated on the passenger side of the truck, Jerry placed Victoria in his arms as gently as he could. Jerry closed the door of the truck and ran to the driver's side. He jumped in and started the truck.

Let's go home, Jerry. Max rested Victoria's head on his chest and covered her eyes with a headscarf to protect her from the sunlight.

Jerry drove Max and Victoria east on Santa Teresa, and no one spoke a word. Jerry attempted to avoid all the potholes and bumps in the road that he could. He continued east on Santa Teresa until he reached Santa Fe Street. On Santa Fe, he cut right and drove south, all the way to Mariposa Street. When he reached Mariposa, he turned left, going east for a couple of blocks, and arrived at Max's house.

When Victoria was in her bedroom resting, Max said to Jerry, You better leave, Jerry. I'm more than sure that, by now, the cops are on their way. I would hate for you to get in any more trouble than you are already.

Jerry stood up from the couch, looked straight at Max, and said, I'm not going anywhere, Max, unless you physically kick me out of the house. You know as well as I do that, by now, my PO has dotted the last i for my arrest warrant.

A police car parked at the end of the long driveway on the street in front of the house. The two officers were communicating information with others, via a car phone.

Max and Jerry moved away from the living room window that faced the street. The window wasn't large, but it was large enough that people inside could be observed.

Max entered his room and returned with a .357 magnum revolver but not the one utilized to subdue Mike Cotton. He kept away from the window but stood close enough to see the comings and goings of the coppers.

This is the best time for you to leave, Jerry. When the cops come too close to the front door, I'm gonna shoot. I'm gonna shoot just to keep them away for a while. If they want to play western sheriff and keep coming, that's shoot-to-kill tactics. Go out the back door, and jump the fence in the backyard before the cops block all the exits.

I told you, Max—I ain't going nowhere. So get me a weapon, and I'll be your partner in crime. As I am in everything else.

Max handed the magnum to Jerry and took out a 9mm pistol he had stashed in the back pocket of his jeans.

The two cops, on orders from the front desk, walked toward the front door of the house. They were rookies, and the hesitation in their stride proved it. One was more aggressive than his partner and wanted to rush up to the door, gun in hand, and demand an ID from every individual in the house above the age of twelve.

When the cops reached halfway to the front step of the porch, Max opened the front door and let go a couple of rounds from the 9mm pistol. The shots were fired at the sky and far from the heads of the police officers. One ran like a frightened jackrabbit, and his hat flew off his head and hit the dirt. The other one, the one who wanted to be the hero, crawled on his hands and knees, as if running away from heavy machine-gun fire.

Max entered Victoria's bedroom and shut the door behind him. Victoria's eyes were shut, but she was in deep thought, and even that added to the unbearable pain felt in every atom of her body. Her mind was busy with a dialogue that questioned some decisions she had made that influenced her life. Her marriage came to mind and would not let her be. She was aware that marriage was to raise children and be loyal to your husband. But she was also aware that there was another side to life, besides being married and producing children. The death of her husband was painful, and leaving Max had been difficult, but that gave her the freedom to explore that other side. She was positive that her spirit would have never rested until she had tasted that world of independence—to go anywhere she could afford to go, anytime she wanted, and with anyone she chose. She rewarded herself with what she wanted in life, without having to justify any of it to anyone. Most of her life, she had made decisions important to her, and she was always in control, except now. On one of the most important decisions to be made, her hands were tied; she languished in a tumultuous sea of pain.

Victoria did not want to open her eyes. She was aware that Max was in the room with her. She couldn't get it out of her head that Max had been born to take her pain away. It beat on her brain continually like a drum in perpetual motion. She gave birth to Max and suffered the pain of love for him. To her, Max had to be brave and release her from the pain that was killing her. She knew the cancer was death, tenacious and undermining the modern medical profession and all its acclaimed technology. She also knew that death was taking too long to claim victory, and she was running out of patience.

Max sat on the bed and held Victoria's emaciated hand. He wanted to plead with her to give the doctors more time. But seeing her in a destabilizing stage of pain and suffering, he changed his mind. Her beautiful face was now sallow, her eyes were sunken, and the skin around them was dark and dry. Her thick hair was matted and turning gray at an alarming rate. Her teeth were still white and seemed healthy in comparison to the rest of her declining body. Max held a glass of water to her parched lips and fought the tears he refused to shed. Tears might hint to Victoria that he had reservations about his mission and was searching for alternatives. He didn't want to add to her worry and grief, even though it tore him to pieces when he thought about the dreadful task ahead.

Victoria finally opened her sad eyes and looked at Max. She attempted a weak smile. Her lips were cracked, dry, and were crusting white. Max, I want to talk to you, she whispered, and every word was a stab with a hot iron in the center of her being. Forgive me, please. Please forgive me. I always wanted you to be free and not a slave to the emotional grasp of your mother, of me. I held back my love, so you would be independent with the freedom to soar through life and separate yourself from entanglements. Never to cave in to emotional entrapment and escape the pain and sorrow that eventually come. A mother can be a heavy load and drown a son in her despair. It was difficult to do what I did, Max, and God has punished me for it. The results turned out the same or worse. You are entangled in my life, and I came to depend on you. Please, Max, forgive me. And Victoria shed tears that came from the most compassionate section of her heart.

Max's words were wedged in his throat, and he couldn't express himself in a manner that would mollify his mother. He was eventually able to say, There is nothing to forgive, Mother. I was like you in many ways, until it was too late. I'll send in Jerry. He'll want to say goodbye.

When Max stepped out of Victoria's bedroom, he saw through the living room window that the area was crawling with cops. Jerry was sitting on the floor behind the couch, holding on to the .357 magnum revolver.

Max sat next to Jerry and said, Best go and say your farewell to Victoria. She doesn't have much time left.

Jerry handed Max the magnum and stayed low as he approached Victoria's bedroom. He entered and closed the door behind him. He got close to the bed, and Victoria could barely open her eyes.

Grimacing in pain, faintly audible, she whispered, Jerry, my second son. I will always be grateful for the love and loyalty you shared with Max. You two boys have given me strength and courage when I had nothing but false hope. Take care of Max, Jerry, and in return, he will look out for you. And please forgive me for being so weak, please. Tears filled her eyes. She couldn't put any more words together. The pain was making her vertiginous, and then would come the vomit. Please, Jerry, tell Max that I need to see him. And she closed her eyes.

Jerry kissed her on the forehead and exited the room to call Max. Max entered Victoria's bedroom, a room he would enter for the last time.

Victoria, without opening her eyes, said, Please, Max, now. I can't take it anymore.

Max picked up the extra pillow next to Victoria on the bed and, without saying a word, placed it gently over her face. He laid his heavy hand on top of the pillow and kept it there until Victoria stopped breathing. He replaced the pillow next to Victoria and pulled the blanket up to her chin.

Max's hands began to tremble, and he felt a deep sadness he'd never felt before. He wanted to undo what he had just done. But then he saw his mother, Victoria, at peace and with a slight smile on her mouth as if she were sleeping and dreaming of better times. Max wanted to lie next to his mother on the bed and pray or do something. But the harsh reality reminded him that life was still a battle for him and Jerry, and he had to deal with the gathering storm he had unleashed with his actions.

One look at Max, and Jerry knew that Victoria was not among the living. He wanted to offer his condolences, but he decided it was best to say nothing. The huge dilemma they faced was not going away, and the crowd outside the house was thick with men in blue.

Jerry, there is still time for you to leave and save yourself. You can slip out the back door and jump the fence in the backyard, Max said, and his eyes were on the floor. The image of his mother was still fresh in his mind.

Max, I ain't going nowhere. Besides, there is no way out. The coppers have us sealed in. There is a barricade behind the back fence crawling with men armed to the teeth. I will not go back to prison for allowing Victoria to die with some dignity.

You will not go alone, Jerry. We'll go together or not go at all.

Jerry studied Max for a few minutes without saying a word. He decided to tell Max the real story behind the scorpion tattoos on his neck. And perhaps, he thought, Max would change his mind about going to prison.

Max, please listen, Jerry insisted, like a man running out of time. Let me tell you the truth, the real reason I cannot be returned to prison. The scorpion tattoos on my neck were inked there without my permission. You see, Max, the Black Scorpions, a prison gang, wanted me in their stable, to serve as their stable boy. And untouchable by the rest of the prison population. The problem was that the Red Scorpions, another vicious prison gang, also wanted me in their lodge, to be the lodge keeper. And instead of an all-out war over a Chuke, the two gangs let the scorpions decide. They held me down naked on a filthy mattress and placed the two scorpions on my belly. I tell you, Max. And Jerry wanted to shed tears, thinking of the hurtful misfortune that had almost led to his suicide. I tell you, Max, I fought the motherfuckers, but they were too many and too strong.

The Black Scorpions, Jerry continued after a pause, they smuggle in black scorpions from Durango, Mexico. They are large, nasty critters, while the Red Scorpions bring in reddish-brown scorpions from Arizona. The two scorpions danced the Dance of Death, even though they were both male. I can still feel them on my belly, Max. They didn't sting me, but I felt the stinger on my flesh, when they missed their opponent. The gangsters must have injected them with something because the critters were in a killer mood. The black scorpion was victorious, and I became the property of a sadistic gang. Before I knew it, they had a gangster on either side of my neck with needle and ink. And you know the rest, Max. I don't have to spell it out. It's beyond emasculation, and dehumanizing, and you never get it out of your system. You feel like shit and vomit smells, and being with women can present a problem. I did manage to kill the motherfucker who had his stinky arm around my throat while the scorpions were dancing on my belly.

Jerry turned his eyes away from Max. He was embarrassed, but he had to tell Max what happened. I got him alone in the showers, and I broke his neck. Then I placed my foot on his nose and mouth until he stopped breathing. I emptied a fifty-gallon drum used for wet towels and I shoved the corpse in the drum and refilled it with the wet towels. The Black Scorpions were disciplined when it came to missing members. They waited to see if the body was in the morgue and not kidnapped by the guards before they made plans for revenge. I was going to be cut loose the following day, and I had to keep the Black Scorpions and the guards guessing until I was released. By the time the body was found, I would be at Fat Henry's enjoying a burger.

I don't want to make it out as funny, Max. And Jerry looked straight at Max. It was crazy shit, and that's the reason I can't go back. I'll be dead before the lights are turned out.

Max stared at the floor, not wanting to look at Jerry. He felt more guilt now because of what Jerry had gone through in prison. The brutalities he'd had to endure, by men who had known nothing else, and that he'd managed to survive elevated Jerry to a true warrior. What could he say to Jerry at this point? Words, Max concluded, could not fill the vacuum in his wounded heart. Only an honorable act would save Jerry and him from repeating the mistakes of the past.

Jerry. And Max lifted his head to address Jerry. I don't want to go to prison. And I'm not going. You don't have to go, either, Jerry. But if you follow my path, there will be no changing your mind, because it will be too late.

You lead, Max. And I'll follow—no questions asked. Max and Jerry ran down the hall that led to the garage. They entered the two-car garage and jumped into a CI truck. Max was behind the wheel and Jerry on the passenger side. They had their weapons in their hands and were ready to take on the world. Max started the truck. He put it in first gear and pressed on the gas pedal with his right foot. He released the clutch, and the truck crashed through the old wooden garage door. Before the truck was less than fifty feet out of the garage, with pieces of wood tearing off the front bumper and hood, a hail of bullets rained on the truck from the front and sides.

Hold your fire! Hold your fire! Carlos Miranda shouted as loudly as his lungs permitted.

CHAPTER 27

The men in charge of the city police department had elected Carlos Miranda as head honcho of the risky hostage operation. If there was a fuck-up, and in some hostage-negotiation cases, especially with armed men, it could be potentially explosive, Carlos Miranda would be saddled with the damage. A career-ending kind of damage for career-minded police officers. Carlos was a good choice. Not only was he a boy from Las Flores, but he seemed to handle the natives with a softer but firm touch. The administrators presumed as much. Carlos, even though he was only a sergeant and in charge, didn't care much for speculation. He was going to try like hell to save Max and Jerry from being massacred. Besides, he was glad that he didn't have to take orders from shit hogs who were ready to call in the National Guard. They wanted to storm the house, like in the movies, regardless of collateral damage. They refused to consider the temperament of Max and Jerry and the harm that could come to Victoria, the victim they claimed they wanted to rescue. Carlos was for negotiating for a peaceful surrender, but if Max and Jerry came out of the house with serious firepower, his hands were tied.

Carlos attempted numerous times to reach out to Max and pleaded with him to surrender. He promised that Jerry and he would get a fair trial by a jury of their peers. If they would release Victoria to the doctors at hand, no harm would come to them. When Carlos got closer to the front door, Max opened the door slightly, pointed his gun at Carlos, and yelled at him to get back to his dogs. Carlos even brought Vanessa Renderos, Max's girlfriend, to plead with Max to surrender. She used a megaphone and, in tears, begged Max to allow Victoria to be seen by the doctors and save himself and Jerry. She wanted to walk up to the house and check on Victoria, but Carlos decided that it was too dangerous. Carlos allowed other relatives to talk to Max using the megaphone, close to the police barricade, but Max didn't respond. Carlos wanted to get William and Ruth involved, but they were out of town.

Carlos had to deal not only with gun-crazy cops from the sheriff's department and the state police but also with the citizens of Las Flores. Numerous people knew Max and Jerry and had been helped at the CI Center. The news was out, even though Carlos had kept the TV cameras and reporters as far away from the scene as he possibly could. Carlos, with help from his men, kept most of the gathering crowd away from Mariposa Street. But the people kept a vigil on Santa Fe Street that ran north and south, not far from Max's house. Carlos found out that people were bunching up on Caballo Blanco Road, which also ran north and south and crossed Mariposa, several blocks from Max's house. The people wanted to see firsthand what was going on and how the cops would handle the situation. They did not believe that Max would harm Victoria or that Jerry would stand by and do nothing.

The local sheriff, a stunted, bowlegged excuse of a man, was on the phone to the governor's office. He wanted to talk the governor into putting him in charge of the dangerous hostage situation. He had already been turned down by the city council, with Mayor Mike Montes casting the unfavorable vote. Carlos was aware of what the sheriff was attempting to do. Carlos was running out of time and options, and Max was still as stubborn as ever. Carlos was getting pressured from the community, the bowlegged sheriff, the state police, and the doctors who wanted to see Victoria. Then he got a call that Tiny Tim, the leader of Chiva Town Snipers, was leading around fifty Snipers toward the scene.

The chief of the state police, as tall as Carlos but not as bulky, kept insisting that Carlos allow his hostage-negotiating team to monitor the situation. He followed Carlos around like a lapdog, assuring Carlos that his hostage negotiators had experience in dealing with the problem, having saved dozens of lives. Carlos continued to ignore him because he knew that once the hostage team was deployed, and the paperwork filled out, Max and Jerry would be charged with abducting Victoria from the hospital. If he could persuade Max and Jerry to give up and allow Victoria to be seen by the doctors, he could charge them with resisting arrest and gun violations. To Carlos, Max could be a lot of things, but he wasn't stupid. If Victoria, who was gravely ill, wanted to come home to die, Max would bring her home, but never against her will. Victoria wasn't a hostage, but he couldn't convince any of the fools around him to think straight. And now Tiny Tim, with his fucking army on the march, was advancing to add gasoline to the fire.

Tiny Tim, the leader of the Chiva Town Snipers, all three hundred pounds of him, in his six-foot-five-inch frame, was leading the Snipers. Tiny Tim had handpicked fifty of his most disciplined men to go along. He left crazy Neto, his nephew, behind in Chiva Town. He didn't trust Neto to behave too close to the volatile situation. Tiny Tim led the Snipers, single file, south on Santa Fe Street, toward Max's house. The Snipers all wore their brown baseball caps and dark shades. They all had on Levi jackets with the sleeves cut off. On the back of the jackets and on the front of the baseball caps was their emblem of a snake curled around a long rifle. On top of the snake and rifle were the large stitched letters, CTS. Some were in army fatigues, others in jeans, and all were unarmed. That was the only way Tiny Tim and his men could march out of Chiva Town and attempt to save Max. Carlos had warned him that any armed Sniper would be arrested on sight, and Carlos was not a man to fuck with. Tiny Tim agreed to the terms, knowing that there would be too much firepower for his Snipers to do any good with weapons. But he had to see Max and maybe save his life. Max had always been true to the Snipers, and his grandparents had always been generous to the needy families of Chiva Town. He hated to see Max go under the bullet and not achieve what he was put on this earth for: to help the most unfortunate.

The Snipers were ordered to stop and not to take another step by thirty or forty armed men in official uniform. They were stopped as Tiny Tim crossed Calle Catolica, which ran east and west. Tiny Tim raised his hands high and expected his men to do the same. He clearly understood that any type of confrontation would lead to a mass execution of his men and him. And the city would cheer his demise and then attend mass, with no serious moral consequences. The sergeant in charge of the operation instructed Tiny Tim that he and his men had been prohibited from getting any closer to the hostage situation. My orders, the sergeant continued, were to stop you before you reached Calle Catolica. It's nothing personal, Tiny. It's just that these men are ready and willing to kill. I don't want you and your men to be the victims of a misunderstanding.

As the sergeant continued talking with Tiny Tim, a hurricane of gunfire came from Max's house. Tiny Tim bent a knee, bowed his head, closed his eyes, and crossed himself out of respect for Max and Jerry. He realized it was over for those two warriors. He was sad and, at the same time angry that it was Max and Jerry, lives full of potential, and not him, being shot by the coppers. But that was his destiny, and it seemed that Lady Luck, a mysterious personality, had taken a liking to him and spared him the honor. Now he would probably die the death of an old fat man on a crusty mattress, the echoing nightmare of his youth.

Carlos Miranda had his back turned to the garage as he discussed options and strategies with other officers. When Max and Jerry crashed through the garage door, Carlos heard the splintering of wood. When he turned and faced the oncoming truck with pieces of wood on the hood and windshield, it was too late. Bullets of various calibers zoomed in at the truck from the front and sides. It was like a blizzard of hail, unstoppable and relentless. Carlos shouted with all his might for the bullets to stop, but it was futile. Some people, Carlos inferred, loved to shoot live ammo at people, especially if the other couldn't return the fire. The truck was stopped by the waves of deadly bullets, its motion neutralized, and Max and Jerry were shredded by the endless barrage of ripping metal.

The blitz of bullets finally ceased, and Carlos ran to the bullet-damaged truck unarmed. He opened the passenger door of the truck, and Jerry's body spilled out like a carcass mauled by hungry wolves. Bullets, glass, and wood had mangled his face and head beyond repair. His lifeless body tumbled to the dirt, almost on top of Carlos's boots. Carlos saw what was left of Max, and he shuddered. Max's head had been torn off his body. A portion of the head, with the face obliterated, was attached to what was left of his right shoulder. It was a bloody muddle of metal, crushed skull, and steering-wheel fragments all mingled into one. His lower neck and upper chest resembled a crushed plastic water bottle, oozing blood, pieces of bone, and other substances beyond description.

Carlos shouted at his men to secure the crime scene and to keep everyone away until further orders. He ran to the house and walked in to find Victoria's bedroom. He opened the door, and right away he knew

Victoria was in heaven, without having to take her pulse. He covered her face with the blanket and crossed himself. He whispered, Rest in peace, and then he ran out the door to deal with the circus that would not go away.

The day before Max and Jerry took Victoria home to die, Ruth and William were cruising up and down in the town of Española, called the Lowrider Capital of the World, about a half an hour's drive north of Santa Fe. They had always wanted to cruise the Boulevard, a tradition that had become Española's trademark. They'd never had the right wheels to join the cruising lowriders who showed off their custom cars and trucks. When they told Max that they were going to take a week off and stay in a B&B in Taos, he offered the loan of his custom 1950 Mercury. At first, they had refused, not wanting the responsibility, but Max insisted, telling them that the car was not being driven enough. Ruth and William were also going to celebrate Ruth's first pregnancy, and Max convinced them that they deserved a real celebration and a ride in a hot car.

Ruth and William selected the bed and breakfast they had frequented on other occasions. It was in a secluded, wooded area, a short distance outside of Taos. A stream of clear mountain water ran near the property, and a lovely meadow with golden wildflowers still possessed some colors. A lover's paradise, William had stated. Mature juniper trees and piñon pines encircled the B&B and a perfect view of the mountains, crested with majestic pine trees, could be seen from their bedroom window. After cruising in Española and admiring the custom cars, they drove north to Taos. Before checking in at the B&B, they stopped at the Taos Pueblo to see the Native American dancing and drumming. It was always a favorite event to watch on their visits to Taos.

Ruth and William were in a good mood after enjoying the dancing and drumming. They had a good dinner at a Mexican restaurant, picked up a bottle of wine, and cautiously drove the lowered car to the B&B, listening to music on the car radio and conversing. William turned to Ruth and said, Ruth, my love. Tomorrow we can go to Rancho de Taos and visit the San Francisco de Asís Mission. Don't you think?

Oh yeah, sweetheart, Ruth replied, enthusiastic as ever. I never get tired of seeing the life-size painting of Christ in The Shadow of the Cross as Jesus stands on the shore of the Sea of Galilee. Can you imagine it was painted in 1896?

We must see it again, William jumped in, not wanting to interrupt Ruth but helpless to stop himself. I love it when the lights are turned off, and the profile of Jesus seems three-dimensional, like a real man. Oh! And the white clouds in the blue sky and the green water seem to glow around him, as if they were under the light of the moon.

Yes, William, and over his left shoulder, I could see the shadow of a cross. I decided to stop smoking pot after that. They both laughed and laughed and poked each other gently on the arm.

And not only that, Ruth, I saw the bow of a small fishing boat on the shore. And that blew my mind. I believed that I was the only one who could see it—beside you, that is.

Hey, William. Ruth almost jumped out of her seat. Remember when Max and Vanessa came along with us?

How can I forget? William smiled. It was the week after Christmas and instead of skiing in Taos, we decided to take the ride up to Red River, not even an hour away.

Max surprised me, Ruth said. He is an excellent skier. And Vanessa, wow, she is good. Ruth closed her eyes to bring back the time.

Come on, babe. You're a hell of a skier, and you know it. Max learned to ski in Big Bear, California. Big Bear is a beautiful mountainous ski resort a couple of hours from Los Angles. I visited Big Bear with my parents on our last trip to California. I was twelve or thirteen at the time. One day we will vacation there together. I promise you, sweetheart.

That'll be nice. Listen, William, I'm sorry about your spill; that's why I didn't want to mention Red River.

No, hey, it's fine. I mentioned Red River, not you, silly. I still get some pain in my left shoulder. That's where I landed. But I'm sure if you massage it in the hot tub, it will relieve the tension. If you don't mind, that is.

Oh no, my precious darling, not at all. For you, the world. A massage you will get, wherever you need it. I promise. Hey, look, William, we're already here. Let's go check in and get the hot tub nice and hot.

In the morning, in what worked out as a sleepless night filled with desire, carnality, and bliss, William couldn't stop talking about it. His images were vivid but not vulgar or distasteful. His love for Ruth was a love he had never been able to imagine. And he felt so passionate with love from Ruth, and its essence was so simple. Joy, just joy.

We're gonna be parents. And Ruth jumped into William's arms, taking him by surprise, because he'd thought she was listening. I know you're gonna be a good daddy, William. I just know it. But I have doubts about myself. I want to be a great mother, William, but I freak out at the thought.

Ruth, Ruth, my love, listen to me. And William hugged her close to him. You are going to be a fabulous mother. It is in your nature, and nature has blessed you with kindness and generosity, among other beautiful gifts. No one else in the world can claim to be a better mother than you will be.

Ruth wrapped her arms around William and squeezed tight, and the tears ran down her smooth cheeks. William backed her up to the bed gently, kissing her scrumptious neck. They indulged in a morning after, with the intensity of a young couple in splendid love. The kind of sex that people who sleep in late get to enjoy. The early birds are rushed for work and miss out on the perfect time. Ruth and William cuddled in bed, observing the majestic mountains to the north, the famous Sangre de Cristo Mountains at their bloody best. Their private thoughts were on the future and the changes involved in raising children. It was around eleven or close to twelve in the late morning, and William was thinking about going on a run. Ruth excused herself and walked to the bathroom to take a shower and get the day started. William decided to flip channels and check out the morning news, even though he had promised Ruth to limit TV time.

William jumped out of bed and got closer to the TV. The breaking news was about Las Flores. William was still in his boxer shorts and couldn't believe what he was seeing and hearing. It was Max's house, and even though the reporters couldn't get any closer, the cameras picked up an army of cops surrounding the house. William felt the blood rush to his head, and he screamed at Ruth to come quickly. The reporter was repeating that two armed men held a woman abducted from the hospital inside the house and would not allow the police or the doctors to see the hostage or get close to the house.

Ruth came out of the bathroom running, still wet, with a towel wrapped around her. She had never heard William scream out her name with such anguish. Are you OK, William? And then she saw what William was so agitated about.

William pointed to the TV. He dropped the control, and trembling with anger, he said, We have to go back to Las Flores, Ruth. I have to help Max, and I'm positive that Jerry is with him. I have to go, Ruth. The fucking cops are going to kill him. I know it. I know it. He grabbed his suitcase and started throwing stuff into it, not realizing he was still in his underwear. You can stay, Ruth, but I have to go, right now. Before he finished his sentence, with his back to the TV, he heard a thunderous barrage of gunfire. The cameras stopped filming, and the TV station went to a commercial.

William threw himself on the bed and cried and cried, like he had never cried before. The sobs came from deep in his heart, and he couldn't stop. He punched at the pillow with all his strength. He knew that Max and probably Jerry had been gunned down, killed in cold blood, and there was nothing he could do about it. I got to go help them, he repeated, again and again, but he made no effort to get up and dress. He knew it was over for Max and Jerry, but it was difficult for him to accept it.

Ruth turned off the TV and sat on the bed next to William. She was also in shock but had to control it to help William. She placed her hand on his shoulder and wept. She finally wiped her tears with the towel and said to William, I know you are hurting, my love, as am I. But there is nothing we can do to help Max and Jerry.

I have to go to Las Flores, William kept repeating. I have to go now.

Listen, William. Ruth was as gentle with her words as she was with her hand massaging his shoulders. Max had a plan, William. You know he always planned everything. Think about it. Why do you think he wanted us to take a week off and drive out here? He even offered us his car. He wanted to protect you, William. And spare me from the life of a widow with a young child. That was Max—you always assured me of his love for us. We need you, William, now more than ever. Don't you see? I do not want to live my life without you. If you go, even now, God knows what will happen to you. You cannot save Max or Jerry, and if you try, things will end up bad. I know they will, William. Think about our baby and the future of our baby. Max is gone, and so is Jerry. If Victoria asked Max to bring her home from the hospital, Max was going to bring her home to die, and Jerry was going along. And you, William, you know you would have been involved in some way if you had been there. Please, my love, stay with me, and we will go later today, if you wish. Ruth broke into uncontrolled sobbing, and her whole body trembled with a deep sorrow as she placed her hands on her face.

William removed his face from the pillow and raised his head to look at Ruth. He felt bad for making Ruth go through this hell. He got out of bed and hugged Ruth tight with both arms, and they cried together. They held each other and let the tears and emotion flow, with no end in sight. They had lost two great friends, and they were inconsolable. There were not sufficient words in the dictionary to express their feelings. The black clouds in their hearts prevented the sunlight from penetrating, even for a few seconds. They felt like two people tumbling into the abyss, a bottomless pit of misery, and the angels with broken wings were unable to save them.

CHAPTER 28

*M*any citizens of the Eastside were outraged at the killing of Max and Jerry. They packed the city council meetings and shouted insults at the council members and police commissioners. Some irate citizens had to be escorted out and threatened with jail time for their disruptive behavior. Carlos Miranda was blamed for the tragedy. Many wanted him fired, and others wanted him arrested for murder. The police commissioners attempted to defend Carlos, but the facts were not easy to defend. The local bowlegged sheriff testified that the city council had refused to put him in charge of the explosive confrontation. And even though he respected Carlos, everyone knew that he was only a sergeant and lacked the experience needed to lead a dangerous operation against armed men holding a hostage. The chief of police also testified that Carlos had refused to allow his hostage-negotiating team to get involved and possibly avert the sad misfortune that ensued.

The police commissioners were certain that Carlos Miranda was cooked. Behind closed doors, they advised him to retire and keep his pension and other city benefits that he was sure to forfeit if fired. Carlos at first defended his actions and refuted any wrongdoing. Even though he had people who advocated for him, they were few in number and stayed out of public view. Carlos eventually came to the sad conclusion that he had no alternative but to retire—especially after he was informed that Max's relatives had hired an attorney and were filing a wrongful-death suit against the city. And the lawsuit could implicate him, if the police commission's report on the use and abuse of deadly force did not exonerate him.

Carlos was troubled by the fact that his law-enforcement days were numbered. He would have to relocate to another town or city, and his family was his main concern. He could always seek employment as a cop in a large city, where police indiscretions were not frowned upon by the hiring department heads.

William and Ruth Moreno returned to Las Flores the following day. They left Armando Vallesteros and the college volunteers to run the CI Center. William stayed home and slept all day. In the evening he would get out of bed and clean the house to stay busy. He held Pluma in his arms for hours. Close to midnight, he would go in the garage and cry. He would cover his mouth to muffle the sound, so Ruth wouldn't hear him. He would cry and then hit the heavy bag he had hung up in the garage. He would tear into the bag with explosive anger until he was exhausted. Then he would go outdoors and jog around the block for a couple of hours. He didn't want to see or talk to anyone. This late at night or early morning, no one was about, and that's the way he liked it. At dawn he went back inside the house and sat with Pluma on the couch. The grieving over Max's and Jerry's deaths was killing him inside, and he didn't know what to do about it. His appetite was gone, and sleep was difficult. That was the reason he stayed up all night thinking and thinking. He was losing weight, and his conversations with Ruth were few and far between.

William felt bad for Ruth, but he felt helpless to do anything about it. He unplugged the TV, his music box, the phone, and anything that connected him to the outside world. He missed Max and Jerry, and he couldn't make himself stop thinking about them. His mind raced with different scenarios of how he could have made a difference in the outcome of their demise. And how he could have saved them at the end from being butchered. And today they would all three be shooting hoops and joking around, instead of him feeling like he deserved to die. Then he would burst into tears and bawl like a child missing his mother. When the sunlight entered through the kitchen window, he placed Pluma on the floor and washed his hands. He went to the kitchen and prepared coffee, oatmeal, and toast for Ruth, with sliced apples and pears on the side. That was the least he could do for her at this point.

Ruth woke up early. She knew William had been up all night and her breakfast would be on the kitchen table. She was sad and hurt, but she knew William, and it was best to give him the time and space he needed. She also missed Max and Jerry. And the pain in her heart never ceased, but she missed William more, much more. William was alive, and she was positive that their love had survived. But the silence and distance between them, day and night, was heartbreaking for her, a feeling unlike any other. She sat on her chair alone in the kitchen, nibbling at her food, staring out the window and thinking of better times. She was aware William was in the tub, taking a hot bath. And when she left the house, William would go to bed and sleep or attempt to sleep all day.

After breakfast, Ruth would leave the house without saying goodbye. She knew William would be in the tub or in bed with his eyes closed and would only nod something, and that was it. Ruth stayed busy as much as possible. She went to the administrative offices of the school district to make certain the district had sent out grief counselors to the schools to talk to the CI students or any other students who requested grief counseling. She visited the CI Center on occasion to make sure that Armando was providing space for the grief counselors. She spent most of the day with her parents. Her parents were aware of the situation and left William out of the conversation. They knew that Ruth was a sensitive and intelligent woman, and she knew what she was doing. They supported her as much as possible in every aspect of her grieving and never for a moment doubted that William still loved her and the unborn child.

By the end of the second week, Ruth and William had broken the silence and were conversing a little bit more. They were sitting on the living room sofa when Ruth came up with the idea to name the center the Max Luna and Jerry Rivera Community Impact Center. William loved the idea, and his eyes sparkled for the first time in days. Ruth assured him that the community would approve, and if they didn't, she would fight them tooth and nail. William smiled, chuckled a little, and held her hand for the first time in two weeks. Ruth fought back the tears, and she smiled. She didn't want to cry anymore. She wanted to laugh and be hugged and kissed again and again by William, as he always had before. At that precise moment, Ruth's cell phone rang. She'd forgotten to turn it off like the other phones. She was going to click message when she saw that it was Mike Montes, the mayor of Las Flores.

Mike Montes arrived at 11:00 a.m., exactly at the appointed time, at Ruth and William's residence. It was a Friday morning, and William didn't want to meet with Mike Montes, or anyone else, for that matter. He was feeling a lot better and was planning to return to work at the center on the coming Monday. He wanted Saturday and Sunday to be stress-free; he would avoid visitors and relax. But Ruth told him that Mike Montes was coming to see them not as the mayor but as an attorney, to discuss Max's will. William accepted the visit and promised Ruth to be on his best behavior, knowing that Mike Montes was a no-nonsense kind of guy.

After Mike expressed his condolences, he, Ruth, and William sat around the kitchen table. Mike opened his briefcase and placed the documents on the table. I was approached by Max, he said, and he paused to glance at William and Ruth. It was a couple of months ago, after a council meeting, when we were alone. He asked me if I could recommend an attorney to write up his will. I was surprised that someone so young would be interested in a will—a will for him, no less. I didn't want to appear nosy and ask him for too many details. But I did informed him that I could write up the will, if he didn't mind. He said fine and took my card.

Ruth placed a glass of water next to Mike and a glass for William. Mike thanked Ruth, took a sip, and noticed Pluma on William's lap.

A month or two passed, Mike continued, and Max called for an appointment and mentioned that his mother, Victoria, was in town to stay. Apparently, she was ill with cancer, and the disease was spreading at an alarming rate. He expressed, as best as he could, that she would die soon and that he might leave town. And since he didn't get along with his relatives and had no children of his own, he wished to leave all Victoria's assets that would come to him, along with his own, to you, Ruth and William Moreno, in the circumstance that something should happen to him.

What? William almost shouted. He looked at Ruth, and Ruth looked at William. Uncertainty and disbelief appeared on their bewildered faces.

Mike Montes cleared his throat. He wanted to give Ruth and William more time to digest the news, but his time was money. He wanted to scratch the cat's neck, but he hesitated. Mike Montes loved cats; he was a cat man. He resumed. Max left you the net worth of Victoria Luna's insurance policy and the profits from the sale of her condo in Chicago. All that, of course, was bequeathed to Max, and he in turn left it to you two. The insurance policy and condo money will amount to over half a million dollars, maybe more if the real estate market remains robust. The money is to be placed in a college fund for your children until they attend college full-time or reach the age of twenty and five. You two were named as beneficiaries and will monitor the funds until your children reach the age specified in the will.

Mike paused to give Ruth and William a chance to catch their breath. But then he remembered his appointments for the day and continued. And that is not all. Max also left you his personal assets of the house, the two cars, and thirty thousand dollars from his savings account. The house—and only if you agree—he wanted it to be utilized as a day-care center for the children of the Eastside. The insurance money should be in this account in a month or two. The condo money, as soon as the sale is in escrow. I have already contacted the insurance company and made the necessary arrangements. And Mike handed Ruth a bankbook with the logo of a local bank on the cover. Fortunately, Victoria had an excellent insurance plan. All hospital and doctor bills have been paid in full. And that includes pharmacy invoices.

Ruth and William signed the documents, and Mike gave them a copy.

Oh, and one more thing. Mike took another sip of water and gave Pluma another look. Max wanted Victoria cremated and himself, if there was ever a need. He requested in his will to ask you if you would scatter Victoria's ashes, as well as his, in the river next to the big tree. I assume you two know what big tree he was referring to. The ashes will be ready next week, and I left word that you would stop by and pick up the urns.

There was another moment of silence. Ruth and William were speechless. They looked at each other and wanted to cry but held in the tears, at least until Mike left.

Finally, Ruth asked, Has anyone claimed Jerry's body?

No one, Mike stated, a little uncomfortable. I took it upon myself to have Jerry's body cremated, along with Max and Victoria. I took care of all the paperwork and paid for the cremation. I wanted to ask you, as a favor, if you could also pick up Jerry's urn and scatter the ashes along the river, with Max's and Victoria's.

Yes, of course, William responded. And what about Jerry's house?

That property will go into probate. Jerry did not leave a will, and so far no relatives have shown up to claim it. The back taxes will be paid, and any outstanding loans held by the bank. Then it will be put on the market by the city assessor's office and sold to the highest bidder to recover any loss.

Mike Montes glanced at his watch and said, If you do not have any more questions or concerns, I will leave you two alone. I realize you have a lot to discuss. If you encounter any problems with the insurance money, or any other concerns, feel free to call me. You have my number. I bid you goodbye.

After thanking Mike and walking him to his car, Ruth and William retreated to the bedroom and reclined on the bed. They stared at the wall at a large print. It was a print of Amor Eterno by Simon Silva in a polished black wood frame. The artist portrayed a family embracing. A husband and wife with a child in their arms and another older sibling with her arms wrapped around the father. They didn't say anything about Max's will, but the art piece caused them to think about a family with children. And they were still digesting all the facts and decisions they had to make concerning Max's generous gesture.

Eventually, William turned to Ruth and said, in a calm voice. I'm sorry, Ruth, my love. I know I put you through a lot. Please forgive me. I wasn't myself. I was falling apart, Ruth. And instead of coming to you for help, I avoided you. I was running, Ruth, and not knowing where—just running and hiding to escape myself. Please forgive me. And he held her hand and kissed it.

There is nothing to forgive, sweetheart. Ruth held back the tears. I knew you needed time and space. I knew you would come back to me. I knew it. I was sure our love would endure, William. And it has. And she kissed him gently on the mouth.

William smiled and asked, Have you seen Nelson Sola? And if you have, how is he?

Nelson took it bad, William. He was close to Jerry, as were the other kids. But Nelson, you know. I drove Nelson and his parents to Albuquerque so that Nelson could see a child psychologist. He refused to attend school and was having nightmares. His parents still take him once or twice a week, and he is coping a lot better.

I need to have more patience with Nelson, Ruth. And I will. I promise. I also have to go and apologize to my parents and brothers and sisters for ignoring them all this time.

Your father is fine, William. Your mother, at first, insisted on coming over to see you. She was worried and wanted to be with you. But your father convinced her to wait until you were ready for company, and she reluctantly agreed. My parents were also concerned, but I talked to them and spent a lot of time with them.

Did you get a chance to see Vanessa? I know that Max was not seeing her, but I believe they were still friends.

Vanessa was devastated. She believed she could have saved Max. She told me that if Carlos hadn't prevented her from going to the house and talking to Max and Jerry, they would both be alive today. I feel so bad for her. Hey, maybe we can ask her to be a partner in the day-care center we're going to open at Max's house. You are in favor of respecting Max's wishes about a day-care center, right, William? And Ruth had a worried look on her lovely face.

William looked away from Ruth for a minute, but then turned to face her with a huge grin on his unshaven face and said, You bet, Ruth. We are going to run the best day-care center in the city. And our children will always have plenty of playmates.

Ruth smiled back and said, How many children are we talking about, William? I mean who will be ours.

Oh, at least six or seven. We have to keep up with our parents. William hugged and kissed Ruth on the mouth and face numerous times before she could respond.

When Ruth and William Moreno were meeting with Mike Montes, discussing Max's will, Billy Bob Cotton and Claire Cotton were also meeting. They met in the parking lot of a bar, a few miles on the outskirts of Albuquerque. Claire didn't want to be seen with Porky. She didn't want any sick rumors to circulate and hurt her chances of landing a second husband with sufficient financial assets to maintain the standard of living she and her children had become accustomed to.

Billy Bob walked fast, glancing to his right and left as he approached the black Mercedes s500 with tinted windows. His heart was thumping as he opened the door and got in.

Claire was all in black, including a black hat, and dark shades covered her beautiful eyes. She turned to face Billy Bob and said, Your task now is to sell my house and all the toys in it to the highest bidder. And inform me of the precise value of Cotton Construction and other businesses owned by Cotton Inc. I will allow my attorney to carve out what is legally mine and the children's. I don't expect it today or even tomorrow. I know that you need time to meet with your attorney, if you haven't already done so, and attempt to hide the essentials. But I warn you, don't try any tricks. They won't work and will only stain your reputation even more when you have to stand in front of a judge. You have the account information and the bank where I want my money deposited. Is that clear, Porky? Or do I have to repeat myself?

Crystal, Billy Bob replied. He wanted to move on to another topic. What about my brother?

What about him?

Did you ever love him?

Your brother was unfixable. Let me put it that way.

What about that boy, Jerry? I bet you fell for him.

Claire rapidly removed her shades with her right hand, and livid with rage, she almost shouted, What the hell do you know about love, Porky? Your definition of love is spending the night in a sleazy motel with a two-bit slut and driving away the next morning. Jerry was special—I never realized how special until now. So don't you ever, ever in my presence, mention his name again.

Billy Bob was wounded. Lacerated with the kind of hurt that only a woman can inflict when it involves love—that wild emotion of the heart. I loved my brother, Claire. And Billy Bob almost choked up. I never wanted him killed like that.

Wait a minute. Claire made a face as if she had tasted something nasty, found only in sewers. You set Mike up. You double-crossed him, you slimy, filthy hog. You paid and arranged for the contract killers to come to Las Flores. And then sold Max Luna a sack of shit. You told Max that it was Mike who wanted him killed. You persuaded Max to believe that it was Mike who was buying and selling drugs out of Las Flores. And that you were only an innocent bystander, trying to make things right, and avoid a disaster for me and the children. You were sure that Max and Jerry would kill Mike for paying professional assassins to execute Max. You knew of Max's personal vendetta against drugs in the Eastside and exploited that to get him interested in Mike and his stupid scheme. You knew I was close to Jerry, and if he and Max were caught for the murder of Mike, you could turn on me and claim that I was in collusion with Max and Jerry. And that we double-crossed Mike, killing him to keep all the drug profits. And that would send us to prison and leave you free to live the life. How can you call yourself human?

And Claire was turning red with anger. Oh! she continued, and she pointed her finger at Porky. That's why you convinced Mike that you would be in charge of installing the security cameras at the house. How much did you pay them to delay the project? You fat fuck.

Billy Bob placed his fingers on his dry lips. He needed a drink and bad. I don't know what you're talking about, Claire, he finally said in his defense. You're probably gonna accuse me of Max's and Jerry's demise at the hands of the police.

You're not that clever, Porky. That was a sad coincidence that no one could predict. But now I see the complete picture. You played with Mike and his obsession with that stupid private prison he insisted on building. You talked him into believing that buying and selling drugs would get him more money and faster. He took all the risks, while you acted the part of the dense little brother, as you have done all your sorry life. Goddamn, you fat slob. You even convinced me that you cared about the welfare of my children.

I still don't know what you're talking about, Claire. Billy Bob attempted a weak smile. And you can't prove any of the things you're saying. I saved you, us, from financial and legal ruin by going to Max Luna and exposing my brother, your crazy husband, as an insane drug dealer.

Get out of my car! Claire screamed and threw the trendy sunglasses at Porky. Do not call me or attempt to see me again. My attorney will deal with you from now on. The sight of you makes me want to puke.

Billy Bob closed the door of the black Mercedes as gently as he could and walked away to his Caddy. He refused to argue with Claire. She would continue to berate him with a slurry of hateful words and accusations. What a beautiful and deadly female scorpion Claire is, thought Billy Bob as he drove south to Las Flores, and she drove north to Santa Fe. She eliminated her male and carried her babies on her back. But he was still in love with her—and would probably always be, he had to admit. He cheered up at the thought as he listened to Gato Barbieri's "Lluvia Azul." Tomorrow he had an important meeting with Juan Vela at the construction site. Yes! he shouted at the music.

THE END

About the Author

Writer and therapist Sal Mirabal has dedicated his life help at-risk youth. He studied at California State University, the University of Southern California, and Loyola Marymount. He received his master's degrees in education, counseling, and educational psychology.

Mirabal has lived in Los Angeles most of his adult life. He is the author of Sotol, The Dance of the Scorpions, El Cerro de la Mancha Azul, in Spanish, and Tomorrow's Goodbye, all fictional novels. He incorporates Chicano culture into his novels. His fiction earned an honorable mention at the Writer's Day Festival at Mt. San Antonio College.